## Praise for #1 bestselling author Lee Child and his Reacher series

"Lee Child [is] the current poster-boy of American crime fiction." —*Los Angeles Times*

"Jack Reacher is a tough guy's tough guy."
—*Santa Monica Mirror*

"Like his hero Jack Reacher, Lee Child seems to make no wrong steps." —Associated Press

"Jack Reacher is one of the best thriller characters at work today." —*Newsweek*

"Reacher is Marlowe's literary descendant, and a 21st-century knight—only tougher."
—Minneapolis *Star-Tribune*

"Child has long been one of the best contemporary thriller writers." —The Daily Beast

"That this Reacher is so effortlessly larger than life is evidence of how intense the overall series has become." —Janet Maslin, *The New York Times*

"No one kicks butt as entertainingly as Reacher."
—*Kirkus Reviews*

## Praise for A WANTED MAN

"If there were such a thing as a writer-magician, Lee Child would be the face above the cloak."
—Associated Press

"The indomitable Reacher burns up the pages of every book in Child's series." —*USA Today*

"Child's prose is muscular and fast-paced."
—*Entertainment Weekly*

"A solid addition to the canon . . . Each of his books is meticulously plotted and magically propulsive."
—*The Boston Globe*

"Feverishly thrilling . . . the pure giddy rush we get reading undiluted Reacher, straight from Child's fertile imagination. . . . With Child, you can always count on furious action—and a damned good time."
—*The Miami Herald*

"Seductive writing and irresistible plot twists keep Child's books from feeling like they were written on autopilot, and the latest is subtle and nuanced. Another constant appeal is Reacher's moral code."
—*Newsweek*

"A page-turning caper filled with well-timed surprises." —*The Wall Street Journal*

"The sangfroid is what makes the big impression. . . . Quick action and solid detective work elevate the second part of this book until it segues into one of the best of the series's climactic assaults: the expected, wildly over-the-top moment when Reacher must single-handedly penetrate some kind of huge, geometrically interesting, top-secret high-security fortress." —Janet Maslin, *The New York Times*

## THE AFFAIR

"The novel fans have been waiting for." —*USA Today*

"As usual, plenty of eggs get broken in spectacular style on the way to making a Reacher omelet. Child's mastery of high-octane plotting remains remarkable, as does his ability to inject what, in other hands, might have been cartoon characters with all the sinews that power human beings." —*Booklist* (starred review)

"He is the best in the business and this only solidifies that truth." —*RT Book Reviews*

"Exciting and suspenseful, with deceit and cover-ups, violence, and sex, this is another great entry in Child's compelling series. Reacher's many fans can only hope there will be many more. Highly recommended for anyone who likes intelligent, well-written, tense thrillers." —*Library Journal* (starred review)

## WORTH DYING FOR

"At times here, he channels Hemingway, which makes a certain sense, since Reacher is nothing if not a chiseled Hemingway hero without the self-pity. He still channels the tough-guy prose as well as anybody alive. . . . This series is as good as pop fiction gets."
—*The Miami Herald*

"A master craftsman of action thrillers. More than just compulsively readable, Mr. Child's work shows a perfectly-fashioned understanding of his protagonist, dogged and moralistic. Reacher may get old sometime, but he's sure not showing any signs of it."
—*The Wall Street Journal*

"Don't pick up the latest Jack Reacher novel if you don't have some time on your hands, because *Worth Dying For* is difficult to put down. . . . Child manages to get an amazing amount of suspense into the novel."
—Associated Press

## 61 HOURS

"Child's writing is superb. Not only is this thriller believable, but the descriptions of the blizzard will make readers want to hug their furnaces. Fast paced and exciting, this is highly recommended for thriller fans."
—*Library Journal* (starred review)

"Child keeps his foot hard on the throttle. . . . As always, Child delivers enough juicy details about the landscape, the characters, and Reacher's idiosyncrasies to give the story texture and lower our pulse rates, if only momentarily. . . . This is Child in top form, but isn't he always?" —*Booklist* (starred review)

"Jack Reacher is much more like the heir to the Op and Marlowe than Spenser ever was. . . . Reacher is as appealingly misanthropic as ever." —*Esquire*

## GONE TOMORROW

"Hold on tight. This is No. 13 in Lee Child's action-packed series starring ex–military cop/pit bull Jack Reacher, and it may be the best. . . . This novel will give you whiplash as you rabidly turn pages, packed with layers of intrigue, murder, deceit and mystery."
—*USA Today*

"Thriller fans like books that start on the first page. This newest page-turner from Lee Child starts with the first sentence. . . . Child really is that good at heroic suspense writing." —*The Philadelphia Inquirer*

"Child is famous for his can't-catch-your-breath openings, and *Gone Tomorrow* features one of his most provocative . . . Edgy, nerve-wracking and thoroughly engrossing, *Gone Tomorrow* is so insanely fast-paced that it's simply over too soon." —*The Miami Herald*

## NOTHING TO LOSE

"Electrifying . . . utterly addictive . . . dazzles. Not for nothing has the cover art of his recent books depicted a bull's-eye." —*The New York Times*

"Explosive and nearly impossible to put down."
—*People,* "Sizzling Summer Reads"

"Child's hard-boiled meal ticket shows no signs of drying up anytime soon. Thank goodness."
—*Entertainment Weekly* (A-)

## BAD LUCK AND TROUBLE

"Electrifying . . . A top-tier Reacher book."
—Janet Maslin, *The New York Times*

"As always, the action is intense, the pace unrelenting, and the violence unforgiving. Child remains the reigning master at combining breakneck yet brilliantly constructed plotting with characters who continually surprise us with their depth."
—*Booklist* (starred review)

"Perhaps there are action-lit writers more recognizable than Child, but the bet is that none of them will turn in a tighter-plotted, richer-peopled, faster-paced page-turner this year."
—*Kirkus Reviews* (starred review)

## THE HARD WAY

"The best thriller writer of the moment."
—*The New York Times*

"Jack Reacher, the tough-minded hero of a series of best-selling noir thrillers, has all the elements that have made this genre so popular among men for decades. He travels the country dispensing his own form of justice, often violently and without remorse. . . . Reacher is doing something surprising: winning the hearts of many women readers."
—*The Wall Street Journal*

## ONE SHOT

"Ranks in the first tier . . . Before it's all, vividly, over, one feels confident that Reacher—smart, rootless, and brave—will not only get his man but make him suffer." —*The New Yorker*

## By Lee Child

# Lee Child

*Dell* New York

# A Wanted Man

A JACK REACHER NOVEL

*A Wanted Man* is a work of fiction. Names, characters, places,
and incidents either are the product of the author's imagination
or are used fictitiously. Any resemblance to actual persons,
living or dead, events, or locales is entirely coincidental.

2013 Dell Mass Market Export Edition

Copyright © 2012 by Lee Child
Excerpt from *Never Go Back* copyright © 2013 by Lee Child
"Deep Down" copyright © 2012 by Lee Child

Published in the United States by Dell, an imprint of
The Random House Publishing Group,
a division of Random House, Inc., New York.

Title page art from an original photograph by
Benjamin Earwicker

DELL is a registered trademark of Random House, Inc., and
the colophon is a trademark of Random House, Inc.

Originally published in hardcover in the United States by
Delacorte Press, an imprint of The Random House Publishing
Group, a division of Random House, Inc., in 2012.

ISBN: 978-0-553-84095-7
eBook ISBN: 978-0-440-33936-6

Cover design: Carlos Beltrán
Cover photograph: Ryan McGinnis/Flickr/Getty Images

Printed in the United States of America

www.bantamdell.com

2 4 6 8 9 7 5 3 1

Dell mass market export edition: May 2013

*For Jane, standing by the major oak*

# A WANTED MAN

# Chapter 1

The eyewitness said he didn't actually see it happen. But how else could it have gone down? Not long after midnight a man in a green winter coat had gone into a small concrete bunker through its only door. Two men in black suits had followed him in. There had been a short pause. The two men in the black suits had come out again.

The man in the green winter coat had not come out again.

The two men in the black suits had walked thirty brisk feet and climbed into a bright red car. Fire-engine red, the eyewitness called it. Vivid red. Fairly new. A regular four-door sedan, the eyewitness thought. Or maybe a five-door. Or a three-door. But definitely not a two-door coupe. A Toyota, the eyewitness thought. Or maybe a Honda. Or a Hyundai. Maybe a Kia.

But whichever, the two men in the black suits had driven away in it.

There was still no sign of the man in the green winter coat.

Then blood had pooled out from under the concrete bunker's door.

The eyewitness had called 911.

The county sheriff had shown up and gotten the story. He was good at hustling folk along while looking patient. It was one of his many talents. Eventually the eyewitness had finished up. Then the county sheriff had thought for a long moment. He was in a part of the nation where in every direction there were hundreds of square miles of emptiness just over the dark horizon. Where roads were long lonely ribbons.

He was in roadblock country.

So he had called the highway patrol, and then he had ordered up the helicopter from the state capital. He had put out an urgent APB on a bright red import carrying two men in black suits.


**Jack Reacher rode** for ninety miles and ninety minutes with a woman in a dirty gray van, and then he saw bright vapor lights up ahead at the highway cloverleaf, with big green signs pointing west and east. The woman slowed the van, and stopped, and Reacher got out and thanked her and waved her away. She used the first ramp, west toward Denver and Salt Lake City, and he walked under the bridge and set up on the eastbound ramp, one foot on the shoulder and one in the traffic lane, and he stuck out his thumb and smiled and tried to look friendly.

Which was not easy. Reacher was a big man, six

feet five inches tall, heavily built, and that night as always he looked a little ragged and unkempt. Lonely drivers wanted pleasant and unthreatening company, and Reacher knew from long experience that visually he was no one's first choice of companion. Too intimidating. And right then he was further handicapped by a freshly broken nose. He had patched the injury with a length of silver duct tape, which he knew must make him look even more grotesque. He knew the tape must be shining and glittering in the yellow light. But he felt the tape was helping him medically, so he decided to keep it in place for the first hour. If he didn't get a ride inside sixty minutes, he would consider peeling it off.

He didn't get a ride inside sixty minutes. Traffic was light. Nebraska, at night, in the wintertime. The cloverleaf he was at was the only significant interchange for miles around, but even so whole minutes passed with no action at all. Up on the bridge the through traffic was fairly steady, but few people seemed keen to join it. In the first hour only forty vehicles showed up to turn east. Cars, trucks, SUVs, different makes, different models, different colors. Thirty of them blew past without even slowing. Ten drivers checked him out and then looked away and accelerated onward.

Not unusual. Hitchhiking had been getting harder for years.

Time to shorten the odds.

He turned away and used a splintered thumbnail to pick at the edge of the duct tape on his face. He got half an inch of it loose and gripped that makeshift tab between the pad of his thumb and his forefinger. Two schools of thought. One went for the fast rip. The other advocated a slow peel. An illusory choice, Reacher thought. The pain was the same either way. So he split the difference and opted for a fast peel. No big deal on his cheek. A different story across his nose. Cuts reopened, the swelling lifted and moved, the fracture itself clicked and ground.

No big deal on the other cheek.

He rolled the bloodied tape into a cylinder and stuck it in his pocket. He spat on his fingers and wiped his face. He heard a helicopter a thousand feet overhead and saw a high-power searchlight beam stabbing down through the darkness, resting here, resting there, moving on. He turned back and put one foot in the traffic lane again and stuck out his thumb. The helicopter hung around for a spell and then lost interest and hammered away west until its noise died back to nothing. Traffic heading cross-country on the bridge stayed sparse but steady. Feeder traffic heading north and south on the county road got thinner. But almost all of it turned one way or the other on the highway. Almost none of it continued straight. Reacher remained optimistic.

The night was cold, which helped his face. Numbness dulled the ache. A pick-up truck with Kansas plates came out of the south and turned east and slowed to a roll. The driver was a rangy black guy bundled into a thick coat. Maybe his heater wasn't working. He eyeballed Reacher long and hard. He almost stopped. But he didn't. He looked away and drove on by.

Reacher had money in his pocket. If he could get to Lincoln or Omaha he could get a bus. But he couldn't get to Lincoln or Omaha. Not without a ride. He took to tucking his right hand under his left arm between cars, to stop it from freezing. He stamped his feet. His breath pooled around his head like a cloud. A highway patrol cruiser blew by with lights but no siren. Two cops inside. They didn't even glance Reacher's way. Their focus was up ahead. Some kind of an incident, maybe.

Two more cars almost stopped. One out of the south, and one out of the north, minutes apart. They both slowed, stumbled, stuttered, eyeballed, and then picked up speed and drove on by. *Getting closer,* Reacher thought. *It's coming.* Maybe the late hour was helping. People were more compassionate at midnight than midday. And night driving already felt a little out of the ordinary. Picking up a random stranger wasn't such a big leap.

He hoped.

Another driver took a good long look, but kept on going.

And another.

Reacher spat on his palms and slicked his hair into place.

He kept the smile on his face.

He remained optimistic.

And then finally, after a total of ninety-three minutes on the ramp, a car stopped for him.

# Chapter 2

The car stopped thirty feet upstream of him. It had a local plate, and was a reasonable size, and American, and dark in color. A Chevrolet, Reacher thought, probably dark blue, or gray, or black. It was hard to tell, in the vapor light. Dark metallics were always anonymous at night.

There were three people in the car. Two men in the front, and a woman in the back. The two men were twisted around in their seats, like there was a big three-way discussion going on. Like a democracy. *Should we pick this guy up or not?* Which suggested to Reacher that the three people didn't know each other very well. Such decisions among good friends were usually instinctive. These three were business colleagues, maybe, a team of equals, thrown together for the duration, exaggeratedly respectful of each other's positions, especially the outnumbered woman's.

Reacher saw the woman nod, and he lip-read her *yes,* and the men turned back and faced front again, and the car rolled forward. It stopped again with the front passenger's window alongside Reacher's hip. The glass came down. Reacher bent at the waist and felt warmth on his face. This car's heater was working just fine. That was for damn sure.

The guy in the front passenger seat asked, "Where are you headed tonight, sir?"

Reacher had been a cop in the army for thirteen years, and then for almost as long had lived on his wits, and he had survived both phases of his life by being appropriately cautious and by staying alert. All five senses, all the time. Deciding whether or not to take an offered ride depended mostly on smell. Could he smell beer? Weed? Bourbon? But right then he could smell nothing at all. His nose had just been broken. His nasal passages were clogged with blood and swellings. Maybe his septum was permanently deviated. It felt entirely possible he would never smell anything ever again.

Touch was not an option in that situation, either. Nor was taste. He would learn nothing by groping around like a blind man, or by licking things. Which left sight and sound. He heard neutral tones from the front passenger, no marked regional accent, an educated cadence, an air of authority and executive experience. On all three of them he saw soft uncalloused hands, unmuscled frames, neat hair, no tans. Indoor people. Office folk. Not at the top of the tree, but a long way from the bottom. They each looked somewhere in their middle forties, perhaps halfway through their lives, but more than halfway through their careers. Like lieutenant colonels, maybe, in army terms. Solid achievers, but not superstars.

Each of them had on black pants and a blue denim shirt. Like uniforms. The shirts looked cheap and new, still creased from the wrapper. A team-building exercise, Reacher figured. Some kind of corporate bullshit. Fly a bunch of middle-ranking executives out from their regional offices, get them together in the wilderness, give them shirts, set them tasks. Maybe all the hoo-hah was making them feel a little bit adventurous, which was why they were picking him up. And maybe there would be candid mutual critiquing afterward, which was why they had labored through the big three-way democratic discussion. Teams needed teamwork, and teamwork needed consensus, and consensus needed to be unforced, and gender issues were always sensitive. In fact Reacher was a little surprised the woman wasn't riding in front, or driving. Although driving might have been seen as a subservient role, for the only woman in a trio. Like fetching coffee.

A minefield.

"I'm heading east," Reacher said.

"Into Iowa?" the front passenger asked.

"Through Iowa," Reacher said. "All the way to Virginia."

"Hop in," the guy said. "We'll get you some of the way there."

The woman was sitting behind the front passenger, so Reacher tracked around the trunk and got in on the driver's side. He settled on the rear bench and closed the door. The woman nodded to him a little shyly. A little cautiously, maybe. Perhaps because of his busted nose. Maybe the sight upset her.

The guy at the wheel checked his mirror and took off up the ramp.

# Chapter 3

The county sheriff's name was Victor Goodman, which most folks thought was entirely appropriate. He was a good man, and he was usually victorious in whatever he set his mind to. Not that there was a necessary connection between the two halves of his name. He won not because he was good, but because he was smart. Smart enough, certainly, to check and re-check his prior decisions before moving on. Two steps forward, one step back. That was his system. It served him well. It always had. And right then it was leading him to believe he had been hasty with his APB.

Because the crime scene in the concrete bunker was serious shit. The man in the green winter coat had been executed, basically. Assassinated, even. There had been some direct and to-the-point knife work going on. This was not a dispute or a scuffle that had gotten out of hand. This was professional stuff, straight from the major leagues. Which was rare in rural Nebraska. Practically unknown, more accurately.

So first Goodman had called the FBI in Omaha, to give them a heads-up. He was far too smart to worry about turf wars. And second he had reconsidered the two men in the red car. Fire-engine red, the eyewitness had called it. Vivid red. Which made no sense. It was way too bright for professionals to use as a getaway vehicle. Too obvious. Too memorable. So it was likely the two guys had stashed an alternative vehicle nearby, in a convenient spot. It was likely they had driven over there and switched.

And it was the work of a second to take off two suit coats. The eyewitness was unclear about their shirts. White, he thought. Basically. Or cream. Maybe striped. Or checked. Or something. No ties. Or maybe one of them was wearing a tie.

So Goodman got back on the line to the highway patrol and the airborne unit and dumbed down his APB: now he wanted any two men in any kind of vehicle.

**The guy in** the front passenger seat turned around in a fairly friendly fashion and said, "If you don't mind me asking, what happened to your face?"

Reacher said, "I walked into a door."

"Really?"

"No, not really. I tripped and fell over. Not very exciting. Just one of those things."

"When?"

"Last night."

"Does it hurt?"

"Nothing an aspirin wouldn't put right."

The guy twisted farther around and looked at the woman. Then at the driver. "Do we have an aspirin available? To help this man out?"

Reacher smiled. A team, standing ready to solve problems big or small. He said, "Don't worry about it."

The woman said, "I've got one." She ducked down and picked up her bag from the floor. She rooted around in it. The guy in the front passenger seat watched her do it, full of eager attention. He seemed excited. A goal had been set, and was about to be met. The woman came out with a packet of Bayer. She shook one pill loose.

"Give him two," the guy in the front said. "He looks like he could use them. Hell, give him three."

Which Reacher thought was a little too commanding. Might not play well in the postgame analysis. It placed the woman in a difficult situation. Maybe she needed her aspirins for herself. Maybe she had an internal condition. Maybe she would find it embarrassing to say so. Or perhaps the guy up front was into some kind of a double bluff. Maybe he was so stainless in every other way he could get away with making control look like innocent exuberance.

Reacher said, "One will do the trick, thanks."

The woman tipped the small white pill from her palm to his. The guy up front passed back a bottle of water. Unopened, and still cold from a refrigerator. Reacher swallowed the pill and split the seal on the bottle and took a good long drink.

"Thank you," he said. "I appreciate it."

He passed the bottle back. The guy in front took it and offered it to the driver. The driver shook his head, mute. He was focused on the road ahead, holding the car between seventy and eighty, just bowling along. He was close to six feet tall, Reacher figured, but narrow in the shoulders, and a little stooped. He had a thin neck, with no fuzz on it. A recent haircut, in a conservative style. No rings on his fingers. The cheap blue shirt had arms too short for him. He was wearing a watch full of small complicated dials.

The guy in the front passenger seat was shorter but wider. Not exactly fat, but hamburgers more than once a week might push him over the edge. His face was tight and pink. His hair was fairer than the driver's, cut equally recently and equally short and brushed to the side like a schoolboy's. His shirt was long in the arms, small in the waist, and loose in the shoulders. Its collar was still triangular from the packet, and the wings were resting tight against the flesh of his neck.

Up close the woman looked maybe a year or two younger than the men. Early forties, possibly, rather than mid. She had jet black hair piled up high on her head and tied in a bun. Or a chignon. Or something. Reacher didn't know the correct hairdressing term. She looked to be medium height and lean. Her shirt was clearly a smaller size than the men's, but it was still loose on her. She was pretty, in a rather severe and no-nonsense kind of a way. Pale face, large eyes, plenty of makeup. She looked tired and a little ill at ease. Possibly not entirely enchanted with the corporate bullshit. Which made her the best of the three, in Reacher's opinion.

The guy in the front passenger seat twisted around again and offered his smooth round hand. He said, "I'm Alan King, by the way."

Reacher shook his hand and said, "Jack Reacher."

"Pleased to meet you, Mr. Reacher."

"Likewise, Mr. King."

The driver said, "Don McQueen," but he didn't try to shake hands.

"What were the odds?" Reacher said. "King and McQueen."

King said, "I know, right?"

The woman offered her hand, smaller and paler and bonier than King's.

She said, "I'm Karen Delfuenso."

"I'm pleased to meet you, Karen," Reacher said, and shook. She held on a split second longer than he had expected. Then McQueen got off the gas in a hurry and they all pitched forward a little. Up ahead brake lights were flaring red. Like a solid wall.

And way far in the distance there was rapid blue and red strobing from a gaggle of cop cars.

# Chapter 4

Two steps forward, one step back. Check and re-check. Sheriff Victor Goodman was revisiting the issue of the alternate car he figured the two men had switched to. He tried to stay as current as a guy in his position could, way out there in the sticks, which wasn't easy, but a year or so before he had read a sidebar in a Homeland Security bulletin, which said that at night a dark blue color was the hardest to pick out with surveillance cameras. Coats, hats, cars, whatever, dark blue showed up as little more than a hole in the nighttime air. Hard to see, hard to define. Not that Goodman's county had any surveillance cameras. But he figured what was true for an electronic lens would be true for the human eye, too. And he figured the two men might be clued in about such stuff. They were professionals, apparently. Therefore the car they had stashed might be dark blue.

Or it might not.

So what should he do?

In the end, he did nothing. Which he figured was the wisest choice. If he was guessing wrong, then to ask the roadblocks to pay special attention to dark blue cars would be self-defeating. So he let his revised APB stand as it was: he wanted any two men in any kind of vehicle.

**At that point** the Interstate was a six-lane road, and the three eastbound lanes were jammed solid with inching vehicles. Cars, trucks, SUVs, they were all creeping forward, braking, stopping, waiting, creeping forward again. McQueen was drumming his fingers on the wheel, frustrated. King was staring ahead through the windshield, patient and resigned. Delfuenso was staring ahead too, anxious, like she was late for something.

Reacher asked in the silence, "Where are you guys headed tonight?"

"Chicago," King said.

Which Reacher was privately very pleased about. There were plenty of buses in Chicago. Plenty of morning departures. South through Illinois, east through Kentucky, and then Virginia was right there. Good news. But he didn't say so out loud. It was late at night, and he felt a sympathetic tone was called for.

He said, "That's a long way."

"Six hundred miles," King said.

"Where are you coming from?"

The car stopped, rolled forward, and stopped again.

"We were in Kansas," King said. "We were doing real well, too. No traffic. No delays. Up till now. This thing here is the first time we've stopped in more than three hours."

"That's pretty good."

"I know, right? Minimum of sixty all the way. I think this is literally the first time Don has touched the brake. Am I right, Don?"

McQueen said, "Apart from when we picked Mr. Reacher up."

"Sure," King said. "Maybe that broke the spell."

Reacher asked, "Are you on business?"

"Always."

"What kind of business?"

"We're in software."

"Really?" Reacher said, trying to be polite.

"We're not programmers," King said. "That's all pizza and skateboards. We're in corporate sales."

"You guys work hard."

"Always," King said again.

"Successful trip so far?"

"Not so bad."

"I thought you might be on some kind of a team-building thing. Like an exercise. Or a retreat."

"No, just business as usual."

"So what's with the shirts?"

King smiled.

"I know, right?" he said. "New corporate style. Casual Fridays all week long. But clearly branded. Like a sports uniform. Because that's how software is these days. Very competitive."

"Do you live here in Nebraska?"

King nodded. "Not so very far from right here, actually. There are plenty of tech firms in Omaha now. Way more than you would think. It's a good business environment."

The car rolled forward, braked, stopped, moved on again. It was McQueen's own vehicle, Reacher guessed. Not a rental. Not a pool car. Too worn, too messy. The guy must have drawn the short straw. Designated driver for this particular trip. Or maybe he was the designated driver for every trip. Maybe he was low man on the totem pole. Or maybe he just liked driving. A road warrior. A road warrior who was taking time away from his family. Because he was a family man, clearly. Because it was a family car. But only just. There was kid stuff in it, but not a lot. There was a sparkly pink hair band on the floor. Not the kind of thing an adult woman would wear, in Reacher's opinion. There was a small fur animal in a tray on the console. Most of its stuffing was compressed to flatness, and its fur was matted, as if it was regularly chewed. One daughter, Reacher figured. Somewhere between eight and twelve years old. He couldn't be more precise than that. He knew very little about children.

But the kid had a mother or a stepmother. McQueen had a wife or a girlfriend. That was clear. There was feminine stuff everywhere in the car. There was a box of tissues with flowers all over it, and a dead lipstick in the recess in the console, right next to the fur animal. There was even a crystal pendant on the key.

Reacher was pretty sure he would be smelling perfume on the upholstery, if he had been able to smell anything at all.

Reacher wondered if McQueen was missing his family. Or maybe the guy was perfectly happy. Maybe he didn't like his family. Then from behind the wheel McQueen asked, "What about you, Mr. Reacher? What line of work are you in?"

"No line at all," Reacher said.

"You mean casual labor? Whatever comes your way?"

"Not even that."

"You mean you're unemployed?"

"But purely by choice."

"Since when?"

"Since I left the army."

McQueen didn't reply to that, because he got preoccupied. Up ahead traffic was all jockeying and squeezing into the right-hand lane. Those slow-motion maneuvers were what was causing most of the delay. A wreck, Reacher figured. Maybe someone had spun out and hit the barrier and clipped a couple of other cars on the rebound. Although there were no fire trucks present. No ambulances. No tow trucks. All the flashing lights were at the same height, on car roofs. There were so many of them and they were blinking so fast that they looked continuous, like a permanent wash of red-blue glare.

The car inched onward. Start, stop, start, stop. Fifty yards ahead of the lights McQueen put his turn signal on and bullied his way into the right-hand lane.

Which gave Reacher a straight line of sight to the obstruction.

It wasn't a wreck.

It was a roadblock.

The nearest cop car was parked at an angle across
the left-hand lane, and the second was parked a little
farther on, at the same angle, across the middle lane.
Together they sat there like arrows, one, two, both
pointing toward the right-hand lane, giving drivers no
choice at all but to move over. Then there were two
cars parked in the middle lane, in line with the traffic
flow, opposite two parked in line on the shoulder, and
then came two more, angled again, positioned in such
a way as to force people through a tight and awkward
turn, all the way across the width of the road, all the
way into the left-hand lane, after which they could fan
out and accelerate away and go about their business.

A well-organized operation, Reacher thought. A
slow approach was guaranteed by the congestion, and
slow progress through the obstruction was guaranteed by the sharp left turn at the end of it. Careful and
extended scrutiny was guaranteed by the long narrow
gantlet between the two in-line cars in the middle lane
and the parallel in-line pair on the shoulder. This was
no one's first rodeo.

But what was it for? Eight cars was a big deal. And
Reacher could see shotguns out. This was no kind of
a routine check. This was not about seat belts or license tags. He asked, "Have you had the radio on?
Has something bad happened?"

"Relax," King said. "We get this from time to time.
Escaped prisoner, most likely. There are a couple of

big facilities west of here. They're always losing people. Which is crazy, right? I mean, it ain't brain surgery. It's not like their doors don't have locks."

McQueen made eye contact in the mirror and said, "It's not you, I hope."

"Not me what?" Reacher asked.

"Who just escaped from jail."

A smile in his voice.

"No," Reacher said. "It's definitely not me."

"That's good," McQueen said. "Because that would get us all in trouble."

They inched onward, in the impatient queue. Through a long glassy tunnel of windshields and rear windows Reacher could see the troopers at work. They were wearing their hats. They had shotguns held low and big Maglites held overhand. They were shining their flashlight beams into one car after another, front, back, up, down, counting heads, checking floors, sometimes checking trunks. Then, satisfied, they were waving cars away and turning to the next in line.

"Don't worry, Karen," King said, without turning his head. "You'll be home again soon."

Delfuenso didn't reply.

King glanced back at Reacher and said, "She hates being on the road," by way of explanation.

Reacher said nothing.

They crept forward. Up ahead the routine never changed. Eventually Reacher sensed a pattern. The only circumstance under which the troopers were checking trunks was when there was a male driver alone in a car. Which ruled out King's escaped prisoner theory. No reason why an escaped prisoner couldn't hide in the trunk of a car occupied by two people, or three, or four. Or five, or six, or a whole busload. Much more likely the troopers had gotten a specific tip about a lone guy hauling something large and something bad. Drugs, guns, bombs, stolen goods, whatever.

They crept forward. Now they were third in line. Both cars ahead had lone men at the wheel. Both got their trunks checked. Both got waved onward. McQueen rolled forward and stopped where a trooper told him to. One guy stepped in front of the hood and flicked his flashlight beam across the license plate. Four more stepped up, two on each side, and shone their lights in through the windows, front, back, counting. Then the guy in front stepped aside and the guy nearest McQueen waved him onward, his hand gesturing low and urgent, right in McQueen's line of vision.

McQueen eased forward and hauled on the wheel and made the tight left turn, and then the tight right turn, and then he was facing a thousand miles of free-flowing emptiness ahead of him. He breathed out and settled in his seat, and beside him King breathed out and settled in his seat, and McQueen hit the gas and the car accelerated hard and drove on east, fast, like there was no more time to waste.

A minute later and across the barrier Reacher saw a car coming on equally fast in the opposite direction. A dark Ford Crown Victoria, with flashing blue lights behind the grille. A government vehicle, clearly, rushing toward some kind of a big emergency.

# Chapter 5

The dark Crown Victoria was an FBI squad car out of the Omaha field office. The duty agent there had taken Sheriff Goodman's call and had reacted instantly. Goodman had said *professionals,* which in FBI terms meant organized crime, and organized crime was the FBI's preferred diet, because reputations were made there, and glory and promotions were earned there. So an on-call Special Agent had been dispatched immediately, a decorated twenty-year Bureau veteran, highly qualified, highly experienced, and highly regarded.

Her name was Julia Sorenson, and she was just shy of forty-seven years old, and she had been in Omaha just shy of forty-seven very happy months. Omaha was not New York or D.C., but it was not a Bureau backwater, either. It was not Siberia. Not even close. For some unknown historical reason crime followed the railroad tracks, and Nebraska had some of the planet's biggest rail yards within its state lines. So Sorenson's talents were not being wasted. She was not frustrated and she was not unfulfilled.

She dialed as she drove and called Sheriff Goodman's cell and told him she was on her way. She arranged to meet him at the crime scene, in one hour's time.

**Goodman was in** his car when he took that call. He had one deputy securing the crime scene and babysitting the eyewitness, and all the others were blocking the local roads out of the county. Which left himself as the only available mobile unit. He was out and about, looking for the bright red car.

His county was large but not geographically complicated. A century earlier someone had drawn a square on a map, and the shape had stuck. The square was transected twice, first by a two-lane road running all the way across it left to right, west to east, and again by a two-lane road running bottom to top, south to north. Those two roads met near the middle of the square and made a crossroads, around which a town of eight thousand people had grown up. Cross-county traffic east to west and west to east was light, because the Interstate fifty miles north ran parallel and took most of the load. But traffic north to south and south to north was markedly heavier, because in one direction the Interstate attracted traffic, and in the other direction it dumped it out. It had taken local businesspeople about five minutes to notice that pattern, and three miles out of town to the north they had developed a long ragged strip with gas and diesel and diners and motels and bars and convenience stores and cocktail lounges. Relaxed citizens thought of the place as merely another business district, and uptight citizens called it Sin City. It was subject to exactly the same laws, rules, and regulations as the rest of the county, but for fifty years in an unspoken way those laws and rules and regulations had been enforced with a very light touch. The result was keno and poker machines in the bars, and strippers in the cocktail lounges, and rumors of prostitution in the motels, and a river of tax revenue into the county's coffers.

Two-way traffic, just like the two-lane road.

Goodman was headed to Sin City. For no moral reason, but simply because the place was the last stop before the distant highway, and it was pocked with abandoned lots and long-dead enterprises and windowless cinder block walls. If you wanted to stash a getaway car and transfer to it unmolested, it was about the only game in town.

He cleared the crossroads and left the respectable neighborhoods behind. Next came a soybean field, and then came a quarter-mile stretch of shoulder with old fourth-hand farm machinery parked on it. All of it was for sale, but most of it had waited so long for a buyer it had rusted solid. Then came more beans, and then came Sin City's glow in the distance. There were gas stations at each end of the strip, one on the west side of the road and one on the east, both of them as big as stadium parking lots, for the eighteen-wheelers, both of them lit up bright by lights on tall poles, both of them with oil company signs hoisted high enough to see for miles. In between were the diners and the motels and the bars and the convenience stores and the cocktail lounges, all of them variously scattered on both sides of the road at random angles, some of them lit, some of them not, all of them standing alone in parking lots made of crushed stone. Some had survived fifty years, and some had been abandoned to weedy decay long ago.

Goodman started on the east side of the two-lane. He looped past a diner he patronized from time to time, driving slow and one-handed, using the other on the interior handle for the spotlight mounted on his windshield pillar, checking the parked vehicles. He drove around the back of the diner, past the trash bins, and then onward, circling a cocktail lounge, checking a motel, finding nothing. The gas station at the end of the strip had a couple of fender-bent sedans parked near its lube bays, but neither was bright red, and judging by the grime on their windshields both had been there for a good long spell.

Goodman waited for passing traffic and then nosed across the road and started again on the west side, at the north end, where the first establishment was a bar made of cinder blocks painted cream about twenty years before. No windows. Just ventilators on the roof, like mushrooms. No red cars anywhere near it. Next place in line was a cocktail lounge, fairly clean, said to be Sin City's most salubrious. Goodman turned to figure-eight around the front of it, and his pillar spotlight lagged a little, and there it was.

A bright red import, parked neatly behind the lounge.

# Chapter 6

Reacher leaned to his right a little, to see past Don McQueen's head and through the windshield to the road in front, which put his shoulder nominally in Karen Delfuenso's space. She leaned a corresponding amount to her own right, hard against her door, to preserve her distance. Reacher saw the flat spread of headlight beams, and beyond them nothing but darkness rushing at him, with a lonely pair of red tail lights far away in the distance. The speedometer was showing eighty miles an hour. Fuel was showing three-quarters full. Engine temperature was showing dead-on normal. There was a Stovebolt logo on the airbag cover, which meant the car was a Chevrolet. Total recorded miles were just over forty thousand. Not a new car, but not an old one, either. It was humming along quite happily.

Reacher settled back in his seat, and Delfuenso tracked his movement. Alan King half turned in the front and said, "My brother was in the army. Peter King. Maybe you knew him."

"It's a very big institution," Reacher said.

King smiled, a little sheepish.

"Sure," he said. "Dumb comment, I guess."

"But a common one. Everyone assumes we all knew each other. I don't know why. I mean, how many people live where you live?"

"A million and a half, maybe."

"Do you know them all?"

"I don't even know my neighbors."

"There you go. What branch was your brother in?"

"He was an artilleryman. He went to the Gulf the first time around."

"So did I."

"Then maybe you did know him."

"We were half a million strong. Everyone went."

"What was it like?"

"Didn't your brother tell you?"

"We don't talk."

"It was hot," Reacher said. "That's most of what I remember."

"What branch were you in?"

"I was a cop," Reacher said. "Military Police. Criminal Investigation Division, man and boy."

King half shrugged, half nodded, and said nothing more. He faced front again and stared out into the darkness.

On the shoulder a sign flashed by: *Welcome to Iowa.*

* * *

**Sheriff Goodman aimed** his car into the lounge's rear lot and put his headlights on bright. The parked import was not a Toyota, or a Honda, or a Hyundai, or a Kia. It was a Mazda. A Mazda 6, to be precise. A five-door hatch, but the rear profile was sleek, so it looked pretty much like a regular four-door sedan. It was a late model. It was fire-engine red. It was empty, but not yet dewed over. It hadn't been parked for long.

Next to it on both sides were plenty of empty spaces. Behind it was fifty yards of weedy gravel, and then basically nothing all the way to the Denver suburbs seven hundred miles to the west. In front of it was the lounge's rear door, which was a plain steel rectangle set in a mud-colored stucco wall.

A good spot. Not overlooked. No witnesses. Goodman pictured the two guys climbing out of the Mazda, shucking their suit coats, stepping across to their new ride, getting in, taking off.

What new ride?

No idea.

Taking off to where?

Not east or west, because they couldn't get out of the county east or west without first driving south, back to the crossroads, and no one drives a getaway vehicle back toward the scene of the crime. So they had carried on north, obviously. Because the Interstate was up in that direction, just waiting there for them beyond the dark horizon, like a big anonymous magnet.

Therefore they were long gone. Either they had gotten out of the county minutes before the local northern roadblock had been set up, or they had gotten through it undetected minutes afterward because at that point the deputies were still looking for a bright red car.

Goodman's own fault, and he knew it.

He got on his radio and told his guys to close down their local roadblocks. He told them exactly why. He told two of them to secure the area behind the cocktail lounge, and he told the rest of them to resume their general duties. He called the highway patrol's dispatcher, and got no good news. He checked his watch and calculated time and speed and distance, and he breathed in and breathed out, and he put his car in gear, and he set off back to the crime scene again, ready for his appointment with Special Agent Julia Sorenson.

His fault.

The two men were out of the state already.

It was the FBI's problem now.

# Chapter 7

Julia Sorenson found the crossroads easily enough, which was not surprising, because her GPS showed it to be the only cartographical singularity for miles around. She made the right turn, as instructed, and she drove west a hundred yards toward a pool of light, and she saw a concrete bunker with a sheriff's car and a deputy's cruiser parked right next to it.

The crime scene, exactly as described.

She understood the cars better than the bunker. The cars were Crown Vics like her own, but painted up in county colors and fitted with push bars front and rear and light bars on their roofs. The bunker was harder to explain. It was rectangular, maybe twenty feet long and fifteen feet deep and ten feet tall. It had a flat concrete roof and no windows. Its door was metal, bowed and scuffed and dented. The whole structure looked old and tired and settled. The concrete itself was worn by wind and weather, spalled and pitted, hollowed out here and there into fist-sized holes. Brown flinty stones had been exposed, some of them smooth, some of them split and shattered.

She parked behind the deputy's car and climbed out. She was a tall woman, clearly Scandinavian, handsome rather than pretty, with long ash-blonde hair, most of which color was natural. She was wearing black pants and a black jacket with a blue shirt under it. She had solid black shoes on her feet, and she had a black pear-shaped shoulder bag which carried all her stuff except her gun, which was in a holster on her left hip, and her ID wallet, which was in her pocket.

She took out the wallet and flipped it open and walked toward the sheriff. She judged him to be about twenty years older than she was. He was very solid but not tall, like three-quarters of a football player. Not bad for an old guy. He was wearing a winter jacket over his uniform shirt. No gloves, even though the night was cold. They shook hands and stood quiet for a second, facing the concrete bunker, as if wondering where to start.

"First question," Sorenson said. "What is this place?"

Goodman said, "It's an old pumping station. It brought water up from the aquifer."

"Abandoned now?"

Goodman nodded. "The water table fell. We had to dig a deeper hole. The new pump is about a mile from here."

"Is the dead guy still in there?"

Goodman nodded again. "We waited for you."

"Who has been in there so far?"

"Just me and the doctor."

"There's a lot of blood."

"Yes," Goodman said. "There is."

"Did you step in it?"

"We had to. We had to make sure the guy was dead."

"What did you touch?"

"Just his wrist and his neck, looking for a pulse."

Sorenson squatted down and opened up her pear-shaped shoulder bag. She took out plastic booties, to cover her shoes, and latex gloves, to cover her hands, and a camera. She put one foot in the sticky puddle and opened the bunker's door. One hinge squealed, and one hinge moaned. The two sounds together made a kind of banshee wail. She put the other foot in the puddle.

"There's a light inside," Goodman said.

She found the switch. It operated a caged bulb on the ceiling. Old cage, old bulb. Maybe two hundred watts. Clear glass. It gave a bright, harsh, shadowless light. She saw the stumps of two fat old pipes coming up through the floor, maybe ten feet apart. Both pipes were about a foot wide, and both of them had once been painted smooth institutional green, but they were now chipped and scaly with rust. Both of them were open at the top, and both of them terminated with wide flanges, where bolted joints had once been made. A municipal system, long disassembled. Sorenson guessed for many years groundwater had come up through one pipe and had been boosted onward through the other, horizontal and underground, to a water tower somewhere close by. But then one day the pumps had started sucking on dry rock honeycombs, and it had been time for a new hole. Irrigation, population, and indoor plumbing. Sorenson had read her briefing papers. Two and a half trillion gallons of groundwater a year, more than anywhere except Texas and California.

She moved on.

Apart from the water pipes there was old grit on the floor, and a heavy-duty electrical panel on one wall, several generations old, and a faded diagram on another wall, showing the nature and purpose of the hydraulic equipment that had once connected one green stump to the other. And that was it, in terms of permanent infrastructure.

The non-permanent infrastructure was the dead guy, and his blood. He was on his back, with his elbows and knees bent like a cartoon sketch of a man dancing an old-fashioned number. His face was covered in blood, and his midsection was covered in blood, and he was lying in a lake of blood. He was maybe forty years old, although it was hard to judge. He was wearing a green winter coat, cotton canvas padded and insulated with something, not old, but not new either. The coat was not zipped or buttoned. It was open, over a gray sweater and a cream checked shirt. Both sweater and shirt looked worn and dirty. Both sweater and shirt had been tugged out of the guy's waistband, and then they had been pulled up past his rib cage.

He had two knife wounds. The first was a lateral slash across his forehead an inch above his eyes. The second was a ragged stab wound in the right side of his midsection, about level with his navel. Most of the blood had come from the second wound. It had welled out. The guy's navel looked like a thimble full of drying paint.

Sorenson said, "How do you see it, Sheriff?"

From outside the door Goodman said, "They nicked him in the forehead to blind him. A sheet of blood came down in his eyes. That's an old knife-fighting trick. Which is why I thought of them as professionals. And from that point on it was easy. They pulled up his shirt and stuck the knife up under his ribs. And jerked it around. But not quite enough. It took him a few minutes to die."

Sorenson nodded to herself. Hence all the blood. The guy's heart had kept on pumping, valiantly but fruitlessly.

She asked, "Do you know who he is?"

"Never saw him before."

"Why did they pull up his shirt?"

"Because they're professionals. They didn't want the blade to snag."

"I agree," Sorenson said. "It must have been a long knife, don't you think? To get up into his thorax from there?"

"Eight or nine inches, maybe."

"Did the eyewitness see a knife?"

"He didn't say so. But you can ask him yourself. He's waiting in the deputy's car. Keeping warm."

Sorenson asked, "Why didn't they use a gun? A silenced .22 would be more typical, if this is a professional hit."

"Still loud, in an enclosed space."

"Pretty far from anywhere."

"Then I don't know why they didn't," Goodman said.

Sorenson used her camera and took photographs, zooming out wide for context, zooming in tight for details. She asked, "Do you mind if I disturb the body? I want to check for ID."

Goodman said, "It's your case."

"Is it?"

"The perps are out of the state by now."

"They are if they went east."

"And if they went west, it's only a matter of time. They got through the roadblocks, apparently."

Sorenson said nothing.

"They switched to another car," Goodman said.

"Or cars," Sorenson said. "They might have split up and traveled separately."

Goodman thought about the empty spaces either side of the parked Mazda. Thought about his final APB: *Any two men in any kind of vehicle.* He said, "I didn't consider that possibility. I guess I screwed up."

Sorenson didn't reassure him. She just picked her way around the blood and squatted down in the driest patch she could find. She put her left hand out behind her for balance and used her right hand on the corpse. She pressed and patted and searched. There was nothing in the shirt pocket. Nothing in the coat, inside or out. Her gloved fingers turned red with rubbery smears. She tried the pants pockets. Nothing there.

She called, "Sheriff? You're going to have to help me here."

Goodman picked his way inside, on tiptoe, using long sideways steps, like he was on a ledge a thousand feet up. Sorenson said, "Put your finger in his belt loop. Roll him over. I need to check his back pockets."

Goodman squatted opposite her, arm's length from the body, and hooked a finger in a belt loop. He turned his face away and hauled. The dead guy came up on his hip. Blood squelched and dripped, but slowly, because it was drying and mixing with the grit on the floor to make a paste. Sorenson's gloved hand darted in like a pickpocket, and she poked and prodded and patted.

Nothing there.

"No ID," she said. "So as of right now, we have ourselves an unidentified victim. Ain't life grand?"

Goodman let the guy roll back, flat on the floor.

# Chapter 8

Jack Reacher was no kind of a legal scholar, but like all working cops he had learned something about the law, mostly its practical, real-world applications, and its tricks and its dodges.

And he had learned the areas where the law was silent.

As in: there was no law that said people who pick up hitchhikers have to tell the truth.

In fact Reacher had learned that harmless fantasy seemed to be irresistible. He figured it was a large part of the reason why drivers stopped at all. He had ridden with obvious cubicle drones who claimed to be managers, and managers who claimed to be entrepreneurs, and entrepreneurs who claimed to be successful, and employees who said they owned the company, and nurses who said they were doctors, and doctors who said they were surgeons. People liked to spread their wings a little. They liked to inhabit a different life for an hour or two, testing it, tasting it, trying out their lines, basking in the glow.

No harm, no foul.

All part of the fun.

But Alan King's lies were different.

There was no element of self-aggrandizement in what he was saying. The guy wasn't making himself bigger or better or smarter or sexier. He was telling stupid, trivial, technical lies for no clear reason at all.

As in: the blue denim shirts. They were not a corporate brand. They were not crisp attractive items with embroidered logos above the pockets. They had never been worn before, or laundered. They were cheap junk from a dollar store, straight from the shelf, straight from the plastic packet. Reacher knew, because they were the kind of shirts he wore himself.

As in: King claimed they hadn't stopped in three hours, but the gas gauge was showing three-quarters full. Which implied the Chevy could run twelve hours on a single tank. Which was close to a thousand miles, at highway speeds. Which was impossible.

And: the water King had given him with Karen Delfuenso's aspirin was still cold from a refrigerator. Which would be impossible, after three hours in a car with the heater blasting.

Lies.

As in: King claimed somewhere in Nebraska as his residence, but then said there were a million and a half people living where he lived. Which was impossible. A million and a half was close to Nebraska's entire population. Omaha had about four hundred thousand people, and Lincoln had two-fifty. There were only nine U.S. cities with populations of more than a million, and eight of them were either emphatically bigger or smaller than a million and a half. Only Philadelphia was close to that number.

So were these guys really from Philly? Or did King mean a metro area? In which case Philadelphia was too big, but all kinds of other places would slide up the scale and become possibilities. Columbus would fit the bill, maybe, or Las Vegas, or Milwaukee, or San Antonio, or the Norfolk–Virginia Beach–Newport News sprawl.

But not anyplace in Nebraska.

Not even close.

And why wasn't Karen Delfuenso talking? She had said *I've got one,* about the aspirin, and she had said her name during the mutual introductions, and then she had said nothing more. Reacher himself was quite capable of silence for hours at a time, but even he had been making an effort in terms of polite conversation. Delfuenso looked like the kind of woman who would join in with such social proprieties. But she hadn't.

Why not?

*Not my problem,* Reacher thought. His problem was to get himself on a bus to Virginia, and he was closing in on that target at close to eighty miles an hour, more than a hundred feet a second. He leaned back in his seat and closed his eyes.

**Julia Sorenson hopped** around outside the bunker and peeled her plastic booties off, and then she sealed them in a bag with her gloves. Evidence, possibly, and certainly a biohazard. Then she found her phone and called out full-boat teams of FBI medical examiners and crime scene investigators.

*Her case.*

She got in the back of the deputy's car with the eyewitness. No reason to haul the poor guy out into the cold. Goodman got in the front and the deputy twisted around behind the wheel. It was a regular little conference, two and two, separated by the bullet-proof shield.

The eyewitness was a man of about fifty, whiskery, not well groomed, dressed in winter farm clothes. He ran through his story with the kind of imprecision Sorenson expected. She was well aware of the limitations of eyewitness testimony. As a Quantico trainee she had been sent to interview a doctor suspected of Medicare fraud. She had waited for her appointment in his crowded waiting room. A guy had burst in to rob the place for drugs, firing a handgun, rushing here, rushing there, rushing out. Afterward, of course, she found out the whole thing was staged. The doctor was an actor, the robber was an actor, the handgun rounds were blanks, and everyone in the waiting room was a law enforcement trainee. There was no consensus on what the robber looked like. Absolutely none at all. Short, tall, fat, thin, black, white, no one really remembered. Since that morning Sorenson had taken eyewitness testimony with a pinch of salt.

She asked, "Did you see the man in the green coat arrive?"

The guy said, "No. I saw him on the sidewalk, that's all, heading for the old pumping station, right there."

"Did you see the red car arrive?"

"No. It was already there when I looked."

"Were the two men in the black suits in it?"

"No, they were on the sidewalk too."

"Following the other man?"

The guy nodded. "About ten feet back. Maybe twenty."

"Can you describe them?"

"They were just two guys. In suits."

"Old? Young?"

"Neither. They were just guys."

"Short? Tall?"

"Average."

"Black or white?"

"White."

"Fat or thin?"

"Average."

Sorenson asked, "Any distinguishing marks?"

The guy said, "I don't know what that is."

"Anything special about their faces? Beards, scars, piercings? Tattoos? Like that."

"They were just guys."

"What about the color of their hair? Was it light or dark?"

"Their hair?" the guy said. "I don't know. It was hair-colored, I guess."

Sorenson asked, "Did you see a knife when they went in?"

"No," the guy said.

"Did you see a knife when they came out?"

"No."

"Did they have blood on them?"

"I guess one of their suit jackets looked wet in a couple of spots. But it was black, not red. Like it could have been water. On a black suit, I mean."

Sorenson said, "The streetlights are yellow."

The guy glanced out his window, as if to confirm it, and said, "Yes."

"So blood might have looked black, in the yellow light."

"I guess."

Sorenson asked, "Did the red car belong to the two men?"

The guy said, "They got in it, lady."

"But how did they look when they got in it? Like they were totally familiar with it? Or did they fumble around?"

Goodman looked a question from the front seat. Sorenson said, "The dead guy had nothing in his pockets. Including no car keys. So how did he get there? Maybe the red car was his."

Goodman said, "Then how did the two men get there? They didn't walk. It's cold, and they weren't wearing coats."

"Maybe they all came together."

The eyewitness said, "I don't know, lady. They got in the car and drove away. That's all I saw."

So Goodman let the eyewitness make his way home to bed, and then he drove Sorenson north, to let her take a look at the abandoned red car.

# Chapter 9

Reacher's eyes were closed and his nose wasn't working, so taste and touch and hearing were taking up the sensory slack. He could taste copper and iron in his mouth, where blood was leaking down the back of his throat. He could feel the rear bench's mouse-fur upholstery under his right-hand fingertips, synthetic and dense and microscopically harsh. His left hand was in his lap, and he could feel the rough cotton of his pants, thick and fibrous and still slick with the manufacturer's pre-wash treatments. He could hear the loud zing of concrete sections under the tires, and the hum of the motor, and the whine of its drive belts, and the rush of air against the windshield pillars and the door mirrors. He could hear the give and take of seat springs as he and the others floated small quarter-inches with the ride. He could hear Don McQueen breathing slow and controlled as he concentrated, and Karen Delfuenso a little anxious, and Alan King changing to a shorter, sharper rhythm. The guy was thinking about something. He was coming up to a decision. Reacher heard the scrape of cloth against a wrist. The guy was checking his watch.

Then King turned around, and Reacher opened his eyes.

King said, "I really want to get to Chicago before dawn."

*Suits me*, Reacher thought. *Plenty of morning departures from Chicago. South through Illinois, east through Kentucky, and then Virginia is right there.* He said, "That should be possible. We're going fast. It's wintertime. Dawn will be late."

King said, "Plan was Don drives the first half, and I drive the second half. Now I'm thinking we should split it into thirds. You could drive the middle third."

"Not Karen?" Reacher said.

No response from Delfuenso.

"Karen doesn't drive," King said.

"OK," Reacher said. "I'm always happy to help."

"Safer that way."

"You haven't seen my driving yet."

"It's an empty road, straight and wide."

"OK," Reacher said again.

"We'll switch next time we stop for gas."

"Which will be when?"

"Soon."

"Why?" Reacher asked. "You've been driving for three hours but the tank is still three-quarters full. At that rate we could get halfway to New York before we need gas. Maybe more."

King paused a beat. Blinked. Said, "You're an observant man, Mr. Reacher."

Reacher said, "I try to be."

"This is my car," King said. "I think you can trust me to know its quirks and its foibles. The gas gauge is faulty. There's a malfunction. All the action is in the first little bit. Then it falls off a cliff."

Reacher said nothing.

King said, "Believe me, we'll have to stop soon."

**The two deputies** securing the area behind the cocktail lounge had parked their cruisers at matching angles, pretty far from the red Mazda, as if the car was dangerous in itself. As if it was radioactive, or liable to explode. Goodman nosed his Crown Vic into the implied no-go triangle and stopped twenty feet from the target. Sorenson said, "No witnesses came forward here, I assume?"

"Today isn't my birthday," Goodman said. "It's not all my Christmases rolled into one, either."

"Is this lounge abandoned too?"

"No, but it closes at midnight. It's a respectable place."

"Compared to what?"

"The other lounges up here."

"What time would the red car have gotten here?"

"Earliest? Not before twenty past midnight. Too late for witnesses."

"I'm guessing you never worked in a bar, did you?" Sorenson asked.

"No," Goodman said. "I never did. Why?"

"Just because the customers go home at midnight,

it doesn't mean the staff does too. You can be sure some poor dumb waitress will have been here for a little while afterward. Do you know the owner?"

"Sure."

"So call him."

"Her," Goodman said. "Missy Smith. She's been here forever. She's a well-known character. She won't be pleased if I wake her up."

Sorenson said, "I won't be pleased if you don't."

So Goodman dialed his cell and stumped around near his own car while Sorenson went to take a look at the Mazda. It had North Carolina plates, and a little barcode strip on the rear window, and it looked neat and clean and fresh inside. She called in the plates and the VIN to her Omaha office, and she saw Sheriff Goodman writing on his palm with a ballpoint pen, with his phone trapped up between his ear and his shoulder. She saw him put his pen away and click off his call, and then he said to her, "Missy Smith left here at midnight exactly, with the last of the customers."

But there was no triumph in his voice. No told-you-so tone.

"And?" Sorenson asked.

"One of the waitresses stayed behind to clean up. Apparently there's a rotational system. Every night one of them gets paid until half past midnight."

"And that's her number you got on your hand?"

"Yes, it is. Her cell phone."

"This Mazda is a rental car," Sorenson said. "Out-of-state plates, barcode for the return reader, valeted twice a week."

"Nearest car rental depot would be the Omaha airport. I could call it in."

"I already did. You should call the waitress."

So Goodman put his left palm in his headlight beam and dialed his cell with his right-hand thumb.

# Chapter 10

Not far into Iowa the Interstate went down to two lanes and got long and lonely. Exits were many miles from each other. Each one was an event in its own right. Each one was preceded by three blue boards, spaced out in sequence hundreds of feet apart, detailing first gas, and then food, and then accommodations, in a style that was half information and half advertisement. Some boards were blank. Some places had food but no gas, or gas but no motel, or an inn but no diner. Reacher knew the grammar. He had traveled most of the Interstate system. Some boards would be deceptive, leading drivers fifteen or twenty miles down dark rural roads to places that would be shut when they got there. Others would be ahead of tight knots of establishments where a driver would be spoiled for choice, Exxon or Texaco or Sunoco, Subway or McDonald's or Cracker Barrel, Marriott or Red Roof or the Comfort Inn. It was all about lights in the distance. The deceptive exits would be dark, and the promising ones would have a red and yellow glow on the horizon.

They drove on, numb and silent and patient, and eventually Alan King chose a no-name turn not long after Des Moines.

He said, "This one will be fine, Don."

There was a single brand on each of the blue boards ahead of the exit, all different. Reacher recognized none of them specifically, but all of them generically. He knew the grammar. There would be a no-name gas station, and a microwave oven and an urn of stewed coffee in a dismal hut across the street, and a faded mom-and-pop motel a mile down the road. He could see the gas station lights a mile away, blue and white in the nighttime mist. A big place, probably, set up for trucks as well as cars.

Don McQueen slowed well ahead of the turn, like a jumbo jet on approach. He checked his mirror and used his signal, even though he must have known there was no one closer than a mile behind him. The asphalt on the ramp was coarse and loud. The ramp led to a two-lane county road, and then the gas station was a hundred feet away to the right, to the south, on the far shoulder, to the east. It was a big place in terms of area, but sketchy in terms of facilities. Six pumps and an air hose and an interior vacuum for regular-sized vehicles, and a separate area with truck pumps and puddles of spilled diesel. No canopy. A small pay hut, and a bathroom block standing alone and distant on the edge of the lot. No food.

But sure enough, directly across the street from the gas station was a long low ramshackle barn-shaped building, with *Food And Drink All Day All Night* hand-painted in white on the slope of its roof, in shaky letters close to six feet high. Beyond the barn was a smaller version of the blue accommodation sign, with a discreet arrow pointing onward into the darkness toward the motel. There was knee-high night mist above the roadway, with the glitter of ice crystals in it.

McQueen drove the hundred feet on the two-lane and turned in at the gas station and eased to a stop, facing the way he had come, with the flank of the car next to a pump. He shut the motor down and dropped his hands off the wheel and sat still in the sudden silence.

Alan King said, "Mr. Reacher, you go get us all coffee, and we'll fill the car."

Reacher said, "No, I'll get the gas. Seems only fair."

King smiled. "Gas, ass, or grass, right? The price of hitchhiking?"

"I'm willing to pay my way."

"And I'd let you," King said. "But I don't buy the gas. Not for a trip like this. This is company business, so we spend company money. I couldn't let you subsidize the corporation I work for."

"Then at least let me pump it. You shouldn't have to do all the work."

"You're about to drive three hundred miles. That's work enough."

"It's cold out there."

King said, "I think you want to see how much gas goes in the car. Am I right? You don't believe my gauge is busted?"

Reacher said nothing.

King said, "I believe it would be minimally courteous to trust a simple factual statement made by the guy who has offered to get you a considerable part of the way to your destination."

Reacher said nothing.

"Coffee," King said. "Two with cream and one spoonful of sugar, plus whatever Karen wants."

Delfuenso didn't speak. There was a beat of silence, and King said, "Nothing for Karen, then."

Reacher climbed out of the car and headed across the two-lane.

**Sheriff Goodman's call** went straight to voice mail. He said, "The waitress's phone is switched off."

"Of course it is," Sorenson said. "She's fast asleep. She's tired after a long evening's work. Does she have a landline?"

"The cell was the only number Missy Smith gave me."

"So call the Smith woman back and get an address. We'll have to go bang on her door."

"I can't call Missy Smith again."

"I think you can." But right then Sorenson's own cell started ringing. A plain electronic sound. No tune. No download. She answered, and listened, and said, "OK," and clicked off again.

"The Mazda was rented at the Denver airport," she said. "By a lone individual. My people say his DL and his credit card were phony."

"Why Denver?" Goodman asked. "If you wanted

to come here, wouldn't you fly into Omaha and rent a car there?"

"Denver is much bigger and much more anonymous. Their rental traffic must be twenty times Omaha's."

Her phone rang again. The same plain electronic sound. She answered and this time Goodman saw her back go straight. She was talking to a superior. Universal body language. She said, "Say that again, please?" Then she listened a little, and then she said, "Yes, sir."

And then she clicked off the call.

She said, "Now this thing just got weird."

Goodman asked, "How?"

"My guys over at your pumping station already transmitted the dead guy's fingerprints. And they already came back. And along the way they lit up some computer at the State Department."

"The State Department? They aren't your people. That's foreign affairs. You belong to the Justice Department."

"I don't belong to anyone."

"But why the State Department?"

"We don't know yet. The dead guy could be one of theirs. Or known to them."

"Like a diplomat?"

"Or someone else's diplomat."

"In Nebraska?"

"They're not chained to their desks."

"He didn't look foreign."

"He didn't look like anything. He was covered in blood."

"So what do we do?"

"Maximum effort," Sorenson said. "That's what they're asking for. Where are the two guys now?"

"Now? They could be in a million different places."

"So it's time to gamble. Before I get taken off this thing. Or supervised. One or the other is sure to happen first thing in the morning. That's what *maximum effort* means. So suppose the two guys are still on the road?"

"But which road? There are a million roads."

"Suppose they stayed on the Interstate?"

"Would they?"

"They're probably not local. They're probably running home right now, which could be a big distance."

"In which direction?"

"Either one."

"You said they might be traveling separately."

"It's a possibility, but a small one. Statistics show most paired perpetrators stick together after the commission of a serious crime. Human nature. They don't necessarily trust each other to deal with the aftermath."

"Statistics?"

"We find them to be a useful guide."

"OK, if they're still together, and if they're still on the Interstate, and if they went west, they must be about a quarter of the way back to Denver by now. And if they went east, they must be well into Iowa."

"Speed?"

"Close to eighty, probably. Most Highway Patrols don't get very excited by anything less than that. Not around here. Unless there's weather. But it's pretty clear tonight."

*Maximum effort. Gamble.* Sorenson thought hard for thirty seconds and then got back on her phone and called up two final Hail Mary roadblocks on the Interstate, both to be in place in less than one hour's time, the first in the west, a quarter of the way back to Denver plus eighty miles, and the second in the east, well into Iowa plus eighty miles. Both were to be on the lookout for two men, unspecified age, average appearance, no distinguishing marks, possible bloodstained clothing, possible possession of a bladed weapon showing signs of recent use.

# Chapter 11

Reacher came out of the food shack carrying four cups of coffee in a pressed cardboard tray. He fully expected three of them to be wasted. He fully expected the car to be gone. But it wasn't. It had moved off the pump, but it was waiting for him near the air hose and the interior vacuum, with its lights on and its engine running. Alan King was in the front passenger seat and Karen Delfuenso was behind him. Don McQueen was out of the car, standing near the driver's door, looking cold and tired. Reacher had been right about his height and build. The guy was about six feet and slender, all arms and legs.

Reacher carried the coffee across the two-lane and gave one of the cream-and-sugars to McQueen. Then he tracked around the hood and gave the other to Alan King. Then he opened Delfuenso's door and held out the third cup. He said, "Black, no sugar."

Delfuenso hesitated a second, and then she took

the cup. She said, "Thank you. That's how I like it. How on earth did you know?"

Thirteen words. Which was eight more than he had heard from her so far, ever since they had met. He thought: *Everyone knows thin women in their early forties don't use cream or sugar.* He said, "It was just a lucky guess."

"Thank you," she said again.

He stepped over to the trash barrel next to the vacuum and dumped the cardboard tray. Don McQueen opened the driver's door for him, like a little ceremony. He slid into the seat and put his coffee in the cup holder. McQueen got in behind him.

Reacher found the lever and racked the seat back for legroom. It hit McQueen in the knees. Reacher looked at Alan King and said, "Why don't you trade places with Mr. McQueen? We've got the two tallest people one behind the other here."

King said, "I always ride in front."

"Always?"

"Without exception."

So Reacher shrugged and adjusted the mirror and fastened his seat belt and got himself comfortable. Then he nudged the lever into Drive, and touched the gas, and eased out onto the two-lane, and drove the hundred feet, and took the ramp, and got back on the highway.

More proof they hadn't been driving three hours.

No one had used the restroom.

\* \* \*

**Sheriff Goodman clicked** off his cell and said, "Now Missy Smith has got her phone shut down."

Sorenson nodded. "It's late. The civilians are asleep. Do you know where she lives?"

No answer from Goodman. Wariness in his silence.

"Obviously you know where she lives," Sorenson said. "She's been here forever. She's a well-known character. We'll have to go bang on her door, before we go bang on the waitress's door."

Goodman said, "We can't go bang on Missy Smith's door. Not in the middle of the night."

Sorenson didn't answer that. She had taken a small sideways step, leftward from the red Mazda's driver's-side flank, and she was looking at an angle through the gap between the cocktail lounge and the cinder block bar. She said, "I can see the gas station from here. Across the street."

Goodman said, "So?"

"Anyone over there could see me."

"You thinking about witnesses? We'd be pretty lucky if some long-haul trucker was pumping his gas at the exact minute our guys arrived here and took off again. And was gazing in the right direction, and was paying close attention instead of scratching his butt. And anyway, how would we find him?"

"No, I'm thinking the gas station might have cameras. Maybe wide-angle. Like fisheyes. They might see over here."

Goodman said nothing.

"Does the gas station have cameras?"

"I don't know," Goodman said.

"It might," Sorenson said. "Some of those big trucks

take a hundred gallons. And times are hard right now. Drivers might be tempted to take off before paying. Oil companies wouldn't like that. They might take defensive measures."

"We should go find out."

"We will," Sorenson said. "And then we'll go bang on Missy Smith's door. Don't think we won't. The old gal can sleep a little more, but not forever."

Reacher was an adequate driver, but nothing more than that. Physically his body worked only two ways: either extremely slow or extremely fast. Most of the time he rumbled along with typical big-man languor, often appearing quiet and lazy, sometimes appearing positively comatose. Then if necessary he could explode into furious action, for as long as it took, a blur of hands and feet, and then he would lapse back into torpor. He had no middle setting, and a middle setting was what good driving needed. Action and reaction had to be prompt but controlled, alert but measured, rapid but considered, and it was hard for Reacher to identify that kind of middle ground. Typically he found himself either twitching at a danger two hundred yards ahead, or ignoring it completely, on the grounds that it might go away by itself. He had never killed or injured anyone with a car, except deliberately, but he was a realistic man and didn't kid himself: his driving was much worse than average.

But as promised the Interstate was straight and wide, back up to three lanes again by that point, and the big soft Chevrolet held its line very well. Nighttime traffic was very light and neither action nor reaction was much called for. In fact the biggest challenge was to stay awake, but Reacher was good at that. He could grind along at some basic level of consciousness more or less forever. He kept both hands on the wheel, ten and two, and he checked his mirrors regularly every twenty or so seconds, first the passenger door, then the windshield mirror, then the driver's door, then the windshield again. Behind his right shoulder Karen Delfuenso sat awake but silent, tense and anxious, and next to her Reacher could hear Don McQueen breathing slow, not quite asleep but not quite awake either. Alan King was awake in the passenger seat, looking mute and morose and a little preoccupied. His head was half turned, so he could see the road ahead and Reacher together, and the speedometer too, Reacher thought.

So Reacher drove on, at an approximately legal speed, with the crystal pendant on the key tapping him on the knee from time to time, as the car rocked and swayed.

It turned out that the gas station had four cameras, all of them monochrome, none of them color. They fed a hard disk recorder located on a shelf in the booth behind the register, right next to the cigarettes. The four separate feeds were displayed in real time on a quad-split LCD screen to the left of the cash drawer.

Three of the cameras were of no interest to Sorenson. The first and the second were mounted low down at the vehicle entrance and exit, to capture plate numbers. They were zoomed in too tight to show any background. The third camera was mounted in the ceiling of the cashier's booth itself, high up behind the guy's right shoulder, to make sure he wasn't ripping the place off. Standard practice, in a cash business. Trust but verify.

But the fourth camera was better. Marginally. It was a black glass hemisphere mounted high on a bracket halfway up the sign pole. It was dialed back to a wide angle view of the whole property. For insurance purposes, the cashier said. If two semi trucks backed up and got their trailers tangled, it was useful to know which one had moved first. If someone stole gas or diesel, it was useful to show the court a composite narrative, the plate number entering, the guy pumping, the guy driving away, the plate number leaving.

The field of view from the fourth camera was wide enough to show the county two-lane heading north and south, and the gravel patch beyond its far shoulder, in front of the cinder block bar, and the cinder block bar itself, and part of Missy Smith's cocktail lounge, and the gap between those two buildings. The way the fishbowl distortion tilted the picture made it look like the camera was peering more or less horizontally into the gap. Bright pools of light were visible on the live feed, right at the edge of the shot, from the deputies' parked vehicles.

Picture quality was not great. The nighttime world was shown in shades of gray. Lights from passing cars bled and smeared and fluoresced and lagged their sources' lateral movement.

But it was better than nothing.

*Maximum effort. Gamble.*

"OK," Sorenson said. "Show me how to rewind this thing."

# Chapter 12

The gas station night cashier was a willing kid, pretty smart, and certainly young enough to be right at home with technology. He hit a button and made the fourth camera's feed go full screen on the LCD monitor. He hit another button and brought up plus and minus signs next to the time code. He showed Sorenson which arrow on the keyboard matched which sign. He told her to hold the arrows down to make the recording jump backward or forward in fifteen-minute segments, or to tap them once to make it run backward or forward at normal speed.

Sorenson started by jumping the recording all the way back to just before midnight. Then she let it run. She and Goodman crowded shoulder to shoulder in front of the screen, and tried to make sense of what they were seeing at the edge of the shot. The picture was vague and soupy, like cheap night vision, but gray, not green. Headlights flared and burned. The cinder block bar had no cars parked outside, but Missy Smith's lounge had at least three.

There was nothing visible through the gap between the buildings.

"Does this thing have fast forward?" Sorenson asked.

"Hold down the shift key," the kid said.

Sorenson sped through the next five minutes. The time code hit thirty seconds before midnight. She tapped the arrow for normal speed and watched. Nothing happened at the cinder block bar. But customers started coming out of the cocktail lounge, vague human shapes, grays on gray, smeared by the oily motion of the digital video. They climbed into cars, lights blazed, cars reversed, cars swooped forward. Most of them went south. Last thing out through the lounge's front door was a stout shape that looked female. It climbed into what Sorenson took to be a Cadillac, and disappeared.

Two minutes past midnight.

"That was Missy Smith," Goodman said.

The neon in the windows clicked off behind her.

The edge of the screen stayed quiet for sixteen more minutes.

Then at eighteen minutes past midnight there was a moving flare of light in the gap between the lounge and the bar. Headlight beams on bright, almost certainly, projecting forward from a car approaching over rough ground, from the left of the screen, from the south, over the crushed stone behind the buildings. The beams slowed, and then paused, and then turned tight through ninety degrees, toward the patient camera, whiting out briefly as they hit the lens head-on, and then they continued their lateral sweep and came to rest out of sight behind the lounge.

"That's them," Goodman said. "Has to be."

Sorenson used two fingers and toggled between the forward and backward buttons and isolated the brief sequence where part of the car was visible in the gap. There wasn't much to see. Just the bright lights, and a blur of a three-quarter view of what must have been the car's hood behind them, and then the flash as the lights hit the camera directly, and then a blur of what must have been the car's driver's-side flank, and then nothing, as the car parked out of sight and killed its headlights.

The car had looked a light, luminous gray, which could have been red in real life.

"OK," Sorenson said. "They drove north from the crime scene, and they pulled into the back lots at the south end of the strip, and they drove all the way up behind the buildings, and they parked at the lounge's back door, and they switched vehicles. We need to know what kind of car was waiting there. So we really need to talk to that waitress."

"Too early," Goodman said. "The waitress didn't get off for another twelve minutes. They must have been long gone by then."

"You never worked in a bar, did you? We established that, right? The owner had already gone home. The cat was away, so the mice could play. The staff is paid for thirty extra minutes, but they don't necessarily work for thirty extra minutes. They get through as fast as they can and then they get the hell out of there.

She could have been leaving right at that moment. And even if she wasn't, she could have been in and out the back with trash or empty bottles."

"OK," Goodman said.

Sorenson said, "Let's see how long our window is, before they leave again."

She tapped the forward arrow and the time code started spooling onward again. She counted in her head, five seconds for them to get out of the Mazda, five seconds to unlock the new vehicle, five seconds to get in, five seconds to get settled, five seconds to start it up.

She leaned closer to the screen and studied the angled view into the gap, ready to see the new vehicle crawl left-to-right across the empty space as it prepared to loop north behind the cinder block bar on its way back to the road. Its lights would be tangential to the camera's fishbowl field of view. There would be no flare. No whiteout. There would be at least one frame where most of the vehicle's front-to-back length would be clearly captured. It might be possible to determine make and model. It might even be possible to guess at color.

Sorenson watched.

And saw nothing.

No vehicle slid north through the gap. Not in the first minute, or the second, or the third, or the fourth or the fifth. She hit fast forward and raced onward. Nothing happened. The picture stayed immobile, a tableau, a still life, absolutely no activity at all, uninterrupted for almost fifteen whole minutes, until a random pick-up truck drove by on the two-lane, heading south, and crossed with a random sedan driving north. After that brief blur of excitement the screen lapsed back to stillness.

Sorenson said, "So where the hell did they go? South? Behind the buildings, all the way back to the other end of the strip?"

Goodman said, "South makes no sense at all."

"I sincerely hope you're right," Sorenson said. She pictured in her mind her Hail Mary roadblocks on the Interstate, hundreds of miles apart, each one of them complicated and expensive and disruptive, each one of them a potential case-breaker or career-breaker, depending on results, or lack of them.

*Gamble.*

# Chapter 13

The Interstate through Iowa stayed flat and ruler straight for mile after mile. Traffic was light but consistent. Allegedly a million Americans were on the move at any one time, night and day, and clearly Iowa was getting its share of that million, but a minority share, probably proportional to its population. Reacher held the Chevy a little under eighty, just rolling along through the empty vastness, relaxed, at ease, surfing on the subdued growl of the motor and the rush of the air and the whine of the tires, sometimes overtaking, sometimes being overtaken, always counting off each mile and each minute in his head, always picturing the Greyhound depot in Chicago in his mind. He had been there before, many times, on West Harrison on the near South Side, a decent place full of heavy diesel clatter and constant departures. Or maybe he could try a train from Union Station. He had once ridden the train eighteen hours from Chicago to New York. It had been a pleasant trip. And there were bound to be routes that continued onward to D.C., which was pretty close to where he ultimately wanted to be.

He drove on, fingers and toes.

Then all over again brake lights flared red up ahead, like a solid wall, and in the distance beyond them there were flashing blue and red lights from a big bunch of cop cars. Beside him Alan King groaned in disgust and closed his eyes. Karen Delfuenso had no audible reaction. Don McQueen slumbered on. Reacher lifted off the gas and the car slowed. He got over into the right-hand lane well ahead of the jockeying. He braked hard and came to a stop behind a white Dodge pick-up truck. Its big blank tailgate loomed up like a cliff. It had a bumper sticker that read: *Don't Like My Driving? Call 1-800-BITE-ME.* Reacher looked in the mirror and saw a semi ease to a stop behind him. He could feel the beat of its idling engine. Alongside him the middle lane slowed and then jammed solid. Beyond it and a second later the left-hand lane jammed up in turn.

The Chevy's lights against the Dodge's white tailgate threw brightness backward into the car. Alan King turned his face away from it, toward his window, and tucked his chin down into his shoulder. Reacher heard Don McQueen cough and snore and move. He looked in the mirror again and saw the guy had thrown his forearm up over his eyes.

Karen Delfuenso was still wide awake and upright. Her face was drawn and pale. Her eyes were on his, in the mirror.

And she was blinking.

She was blinking rapidly, and deliberately, over and over again, and then she was jerking her head sideways, sometimes left, sometimes right, and then she was starting up with the blinking again, sometimes once, or twice, or three times, or more, once as many as nine times, and once as many as thirteen straight flutters of her eyelids.

Reacher stared in surprise.

Then the semi sounded its horn long and loud and Reacher glanced forward again to find the Dodge had moved on. He touched the gas and crept after it. Evidently the Iowa cops had arranged the obstacle the same way the Nebraska cops had. Everyone was cramming over into the right-hand lane. A mess, potentially, except that the cops had two officers out and about on foot, with red-shrouded flashlights. They were regulating the maneuvers. And some kind of Midwestern goodwill or common sense was in play. There was plenty of *after you, neighbor* stuff going on. Reacher figured the delay might amount to ten minutes. That was all. No big deal.

He glanced in the mirror.

Karen Delfuenso started blinking again.

**Sorenson replayed the** critical quarter-hour window two more times, once backward and once forward, both at high speed. As before she saw the Mazda arrive, and as before she then saw nothing at all until the random traffic blew by on the two-lane fifteen minutes later, the pick-up truck heading south and the sedan heading north.

*Gamble.*

"South still makes no sense?" she asked.

"No sense at all," Goodman said.

"Are you sure?"

"There's nothing there."

"Bet your pension?"

"And my house."

"Shirt off your back?"

"My firstborn grandchild, if you like."

"OK," Sorenson said. "They went north. And you know what? We saw them do it."

"Where?"

"Right here," Sorenson said, and she froze the picture on the random traffic, as the northbound sedan passed in front of the southbound pick-up truck. She said, "That's them, in the sedan. Has to be. It's the only vehicle going north. They spent fifteen minutes doing something else, and then they got back on the road by looping around south of the lounge, not north of it. It's the only logical explanation."

"Fifteen minutes doing what?"

"I don't know."

"Fifteen minutes is a long time to delay a getaway for no reason."

"Then obviously there was a reason."

The kid behind the register said, "I heard a car alarm at about twenty past midnight."

Sorenson stared at him.

She said, "And you didn't think to mention that before?"

"Why would I? You didn't ask me. You didn't ex-

plain yourselves. You still haven't. And I only just remembered anyway."

"Twenty past midnight?"

"About."

"Definitely a car alarm?"

"No question. Pretty loud, too. The highlight of my
night so far. Until you guys showed up."

"Where was it?"

The kid waved his hand.

"Over there," he said. "Could have been behind
Missy Smith's lounge, for sure."

"OK," Sorenson said. "Thank you."

Goodman asked her, "So what are we saying? They
spent fifteen minutes stealing a getaway car?"

"Maybe they did, and maybe they didn't. But whatever, a car alarm going off is another good reason why
the waitress might have stuck her head out the back.
She would have been worried about her own car, if
nothing else. We have to find her, right now. It's time
to go bang on some doors."

Goodman checked his watch.

"We better hurry," he said. "Those guys will be hitting the roadblocks about now. You should have put
them a hundred miles out, not eighty."

Sorenson didn't reply.

# Chapter 14

Nine minutes, Reacher thought. Not ten. He had overestimated the likely delay, but only slightly. The cops on foot had done a fine job of corralling the approaching flow, and the cops at the roadblock itself were evidently fast and efficient. Traffic was moving through at a reasonable clip. Reacher couldn't see the search procedure in detail, because of the Dodge pickup's bulk right in front of him, but clearly the protocol was nothing more than quick and dirty. He rolled on, and paused, and rolled on, and paused, with the red-blue glare ahead of him getting brighter and fiercer with every car length he traveled. Next to him Alan King seemed to have gone to sleep, still with his face turned away and his chin ducked down. Don McQueen still had his arm over his eyes. Karen Delfuenso was still awake, but she had stopped blinking.

A hundred yards to go, Reacher thought. Three hundred feet. Maybe fifteen vehicles in the queue ahead. Eight minutes. Maybe seven.

\* \* \*

**Missy Smith lived** in what is left when a family farm gets sold to an agricultural corporation. A driveway, a house, a car barn, a small square yard in front and a small square yard in back, all enclosed by a new rail fence, with ten thousand flat acres of someone else's soybeans beyond. Sheriff Goodman drove up the driveway and parked twenty feet from the house. He lit up his roof lights. The first thing people did after a nighttime knock on the door was to look out their bedroom window. Quicker to let the lights make the explanations, rather than get all tangled up in a whole lot of yelling and hollering.

Sorenson stayed in the car and let Goodman go make the inquiry. His county, his population, his job. She saw him knock, and she saw some upstairs curtains twitch, and she saw the front door open four minutes later, and she saw the old gal standing in the hallway, in a robe. Her hair was neatly brushed. Hence the four minutes.

Sorenson saw Goodman bow and scrape, and she saw him ask the question, and she saw Missy Smith answer it. She saw Goodman write something down, and she saw him read it back for confirmation, and she saw the old gal nod. She saw the front door close, and she saw the hallway light go off, and she saw Goodman trot back to the car.

"Miles from here," he said. "As luck would have it."

He turned the car around and headed back to the road.

\* \* \*

The white Dodge pick-up truck got through the roadblock with no trouble at all. Cops peered into it from every angle and checked the load bed and then waved it onward. Reacher buzzed his window down and put his elbow on the door and squinted against the bright red-blue strobes and rolled the Chevy forward. A grizzled old trooper with stripes on his arm stepped up He bent at the waist and scanned the car's interior.

Looking for something.

But not finding it.

So the guy started to straighten up again, already dismissing the Chevy, already thinking about the next car in line, but his eyes came to rest on Reacher's face, and they widened a little, as if in sympathy or wonder or appreciation, and he said, "Ouch."

"My nose?" Reacher said.

"That must have stung."

"You should see the other guy."

"Where is he now?"

"Not in your state."

"That's good to know," the trooper said. "You drive safe tonight, sir."

Reacher asked, "Who are you looking for, captain?"

"That's very kind of you, sir, but I'm only a sergeant."

"OK, who are you looking for, sergeant?"

The guy paused.

Then he smiled.

"Not you," he said. "That's for sure. Not you."

And then he moved a foot toward the rear of the

car, ready to greet the next in line, and Reacher buzzed his window up and threaded through the improvised chicane, and then he got settled in his seat and took off again, accelerating through forty, fifty, sixty, seventy miles an hour, with nothing at all in front of him except darkness and the white Dodge's tail lights already half a mile ahead.

# Chapter 15

The address Missy Smith had given to Sheriff Goodman turned out to be what is left when a family farm gets sold to a homebuilding corporation. The farmland itself had been added to some giant remote holding, but a shallow acre had been retained alongside the road and a row of four small ranch houses had been built on it. They were maybe twenty years old. In the moonlight they all looked bravely maintained and in reasonable shape. They were all identical. They all had white siding, gray roofs, front lawns, short straight driveways, and mailboxes at the curb, on stout wooden posts.

But there was one clear difference between them.

Three of the houses had cars on their driveways.

The fourth didn't.

And the fourth was the address Missy Smith had given to Sheriff Goodman.

"Not good," Sorenson said.

"No," Goodman said.

All four houses were dark, as was to be expected in the middle of the night. But somehow the house with no car looked darker than the other three. It looked quiet, and undisturbed, and empty.

Sorenson climbed out of the car. The road was nothing more than an old farm track, blacktopped over. It was badly drained. Rain and run-off from the fields had left mud in the gutters. Sorenson stepped over it and waited at the mouth of the empty driveway. Goodman stepped over the mud and joined her there. Sorenson checked the mailbox. Reflex habit. It was empty, as was to be expected for an evening worker. An evening worker picks up her mail before going to work, not after.

The mailbox was white, like all the others. It had a name on it, spelled out in small stick-on letters. The name was Delfuenso.

"What's her first name?" Sorenson asked.

Goodman said, "Karen."

Sorenson said, "Go knock on the door, just to be sure."

Goodman went.

He knocked.

No response.

He knocked again, long and loud.

No response.

Sorenson cut across the lawn to the neighbor's door. She rang the bell, once, twice, three times. She took out her ID, and held it ready. She waited. Two minutes later the door opened and she saw a guy in pajamas. He was middle-aged and gray. She asked him if he had seen his neighbor come home that night.

The guy in pajamas said no, he hadn't.

She asked him if his neighbor lived alone.

The guy said yes, she did. She was divorced.

She asked him if his neighbor owned a car.

The guy said yes, she did. A pretty decent one, too. Not more than a few years old. Bought with money from the divorce. Just saying.

She asked him if his neighbor always drove to work.

The guy said yes, she did. It was that or walk.

She asked him if his neighbor's car was usually parked on the driveway.

The guy said yes it was, all day long before work, and all night long after work. It was parked right there on top of the oily patch they could see if they stepped over and looked real close, because of how a leaky transmission was the car's only fault. The neighbor should have had it seen to long ago, on account of it being liable to seize up otherwise, but some folks plain ignore stuff like that. Just saying.

Sorenson asked him if his neighbor ever spent the night away from home.

The guy said no, she didn't. She worked at the lounge and came home every night at ten past midnight, regular as clockwork, except for when she had the clean-up overtime, when it was maybe twelve thirty-five or so. Mrs. Delfuenso was a nice woman and a good neighbor and the guy hoped nothing bad had happened to her.

Sorenson thanked him and told him he was free to go back to bed. The guy said he hoped he had been helpful. Sorenson said he had been. The guy said if she wanted to know more, she should go talk to the other neighbor. They were closer. Friends, really. They did things for each other. For instance, Mrs. Delfuenso's kid slept over there, while Mrs. Delfuenso was working.

Sorenson said, "Karen has a child?"

"A daughter," the guy said. "Ten years old. Same as the neighbor's girl. The kids sleep over there and then Mrs. Delfuenso takes over and gives them breakfast and drives them to the school bus in the morning."

# Chapter 16

Reacher had never been hypnotized, but in his opinion driving empty highways at night came close. Basal and cognitive demands were so low they could be met by the smallest sliver of the brain. The rest coasted. The front half had nothing to do, and the back half had nothing to fight. The very definition of relaxation. Time and distance seemed suspended. The Dodge's tail lights would be forever distant. Reacher felt he could drive a thousand hours and never catch them.

Normally numbers would fill the void in his head. Not that he was a particularly competent mathematician. But numbers called to him, twisting and turning and revealing their hidden facets. Perhaps he would glance down and see that he was doing 76 miles an hour, and he would see that 76 squared was 5,776, which ended in 76, where it started, which made 76 an automorphic number, one of only two below 100, the other being 25, whose square was 625, whose square was 390,625, which was interesting.

Or perhaps he would take advantage of the fact that all the cops for miles around were on roadblock duty behind him, and let his speed creep up to 81, and muse about how one divided by 81 expressed as a decimal came out as .0123456789, which then recurred literally forever, 0123456789 over and over and over again, until the end of time, longer even than it would take to catch up to the Dodge.

But that night words came to him first.

Specifically four words, spoken by Alan King: *Plus whatever Karen wants.* The coffee order. Two with cream and sugar, *Plus whatever Karen wants.* Which attacked Reacher's impression of them as a team. Team members knew each other's coffee orders by heart. They had stood on line together a hundred times, in rest areas, in airports, at Starbucks, at shabby no-name shacks. They had ordered together in diners and in restaurants. They had fetched and carried for each other.

But King had not known how Karen liked her coffee.

Therefore Karen was not a team member, or not a regular team member, or perhaps she was a new team member. A recent addition to the roster. Which might explain why she wasn't talking. Perhaps she felt unsure of her place. Perhaps she simply didn't like her new associates. Perhaps they didn't like her. Certainly Alan King had spoken impatiently and even contemptuously about her, right in her presence. Like she wasn't there. He had said, *Karen doesn't drive.* After she hadn't ordered coffee, he had said, *Nothing for Karen, then.*

They were not a trio. King and McQueen were a duo, barely tolerating an interloper.

**Sorenson met Goodman** back on Karen Delfuenso's empty oil-stained driveway, and she told him about Delfuenso's kid.

"Jesus," Goodman said. He glanced at the other neighbor's house. "And the kid is in there now?"

"Unless she sleepwalks. And she's expecting to see her mommy in the morning."

"We shouldn't tell her. Not yet. Not until we're sure."

"We're not going to tell her. Not now. But we have to talk to the neighbor. It's still possible this whole thing is nothing. Something innocent might have come up, and Karen might have left a message."

"You think?"

"No, not really. But we have to check."

So they cut across the other lawn together and Sorenson tried to weight her knock so that a sleeping adult might hear it but sleeping children wouldn't. Hard to do. Her first attempt woke nobody. Her second might have woken everybody. Certainly it brought a tired woman of about thirty to the door.

There had been no message from Karen Delfuenso.

# Chapter 17

The next words into Reacher's empty mind had been spoken by the grizzled old State Police sergeant: *Not you.* Eventually they led to numbers, first six, then three, then one. Six because they contained six letters, and three because each word had three letters, and taken together they had three vowels and three consonants. Reacher had no patience for people who claimed that *y* was a vowel.

Three, and six.

Good numbers.

A circle could be drawn through any three points not on a straight line.

Take any three consecutive numbers, the largest divisible by three, and add them up, and then add the digits of the result, again and again if necessary, until just a single number is left.

That number will be six.

But eventually the words *Not you* led past the number six, and then past the number three, and then all the way down to the number one, simply because of their content. Reacher had asked: *Who are you looking for, sergeant?* The sergeant had answered: *Not you.* Not: *Not you guys* or *not you people.*

*Not you.*

They were looking for a lone individual.

Which was consistent with what had happened at the earlier roadblock. Reacher had gotten a better view back there, and he had seen men driving alone getting extra scrutiny.

But: *Not you.*

Which meant that the cops had at least a rough description of the guy they were looking for, and that Reacher categorically wasn't that guy. Why not? There could be a million reasons. Right off the bat Reacher was tall, white, old, and heavy. And so on, and so forth. Therefore the target might be short, black, young, and skinny. And so on, and so forth.

But the sergeant had paused first, and thought, and smiled. The *Not you* had been emphatic, and a little wry. Maybe even a little rueful. As if the difference between Reacher and the description had been a total contrast. Or completely drastic. But it wasn't possible to be drastically tall, unless they were looking for a dwarf or a midget, in which case the merest glance into the car would have sufficed. It wasn't possible to be drastically white. White or black was an everyday difference. No one thought of degrees of blackness or whiteness. Not anymore. Reacher wasn't drastically old either, unless their target was a fetus. And Reacher wasn't outstandingly heavy, unless their target was practically skeletal.

*Not you.* Said right after Reacher's deliberate mistake about the guy's rank, which would have been understood as a pro-forma compliment, just one regular guy to another, probably one veteran to another. Common ground.

*Not you.* Emphatic, wry, rueful, and good natured. Just one regular guy to another, one vet to another, right back, equally. Still surfing on the earlier stuff about the busted nose. Referring back to it, in a way. A continuation of the banter. Common ground, established and repeated.

Therefore the guy they were looking for didn't have a busted nose.

But then, most people didn't have a busted nose.

Which meant the sergeant had been generalizing. As if to say: *I'm pretty sure our description would have included that nose of yours, for instance.*

Which meant they had been told their target didn't have anything especially noticeable about him. No first-glance singularities. Nothing obvious. No scars, no tattoos, no missing ears, no glass eyes, no yard-long beard, no weird haircut.

Reacher had been a cop for thirteen years, and he remembered the rote expression very well: *No distinguishing marks.*

**Sorenson and Goodman** stepped over the muddy gutter again and climbed back into Goodman's car and Sorenson said, "You should check in with your dispatcher. You should see if anyone reported a lone woman wandering about, maybe confused or disoriented. From now on our working hypothesis is that the two guys stole Delfuenso's car. And they might have hit her over the head to get it."

"They might have killed her."

"We have to hope for the best. So you should get your deputies to check the area behind the lounge, too. Very carefully. She could be unconscious in the shadows somewhere."

"By now she'd be halfway frozen to death."

"So you should do it quickly."

So Goodman got on the radio, and Sorenson got on her cell, to check in with the distant troopers in two separate states. They were both negative on a pair of men traveling together, with average appearance and no distinguishing marks, and they were negative on bloodstained clothing, and they were negative on bladed weapons. Sorenson did the math in her head. The two guys were almost certainly already through. Time and space said so. But she asked the troopers to stay in place for another hour. The two guys could have had a flat tire. Or some other kind of unexpected delay. She didn't want to have the roadblocks dismantled only for the guys to roll through the vacated space five minutes later.

Then she clicked off her call and Goodman told her his dispatcher hadn't heard a thing, and that all his deputies were searching hard, behind the Sin City lounge and all over town.

# Chapter 18

Reacher drove on, with Alan King fast asleep next to him and Don McQueen fast asleep behind him. Karen Delfuenso was still awake, still upright and tense. Reacher could feel her gaze on his face in the mirror. He glanced up and made eye contact. She was staring at him. Staring hard, as if mutely willing him to understand something.

Understand what? Then numbers came back to him, this time specifically thirteen, and two, and three, and one, and nine. Delfuenso had blinked out those numbers, in five separate sequences, between emphatic shakes of her head.

Why?

Communication of some kind?

A simple alphabetical code? The thirteenth letter of the alphabet was *M*. The second was *B*. The third was *C*. The first was *A*. The ninth was *I*.

*MBCAI.*

Not a word. Not a Roman numeral. A corporation?

An organization? An acronym, like SNAFU or FUBAR?

Reacher looked way ahead into the darkness and fixed the upcoming mile in his mind, all four dimensions, and then he met Delfuenso's eyes in the mirror again and silently mouthed the letters, all lips and teeth and tongue and exaggerated enunciation: *M, B, C, A, I?*

Delfuenso glared back at him, eyes bright, half ecstatic that he was trying, half furious that he wasn't getting it, like a thirsty woman who sees an offered drink snatched away.

She shook her head. *No.* She jerked her chin once to the left, and then once to the right. She stared hard at him, eyes wide, as if to say, *See?*

Reacher didn't see. Not immediately. Except to grasp that maybe the jerk to the left signified one thing, and the jerk to the right signified another thing. Two different categories. Perhaps the blinks preceded by the jerks to the left were letters, and the blinks preceded by the jerks to the right were numbers. Or vice versa.

M-2-C-A-1?

13-B-3-1-I?

Then Alan King stirred and woke up and moved in his seat, and Reacher saw Delfuenso turn her face away and stare out her window.

King looked at Reacher and asked, "You OK?"

Reacher nodded but said nothing.

King said, "You need another aspirin?"

Reacher shook his head, no.

King said, "Karen, give this guy another aspirin."

No answer from Delfuenso.

King said, "Karen?"

Reacher said, "I don't need another aspirin."

"You look like you do. Karen, give him a couple."

"Maybe Karen needs her aspirins for herself."

"She can share."

"Don't worry about it."

"But you look zoned out."

"I'm just concentrating on the road ahead."

"No, you look like you're thinking about something."

"I'm always thinking about something."

"Like what?"

"Right now, a challenge," Reacher said.

"What kind?"

"Can you talk coherently and at normal speed for a whole minute?"

"What?"

"You heard."

King paused.

"Yes," he said. "Of course I can."

"Can you talk coherently and at normal speed for a whole minute without using a word that contains the letter *A*?"

"That would be tougher," King said. "Impossible, probably. Lots of words contain the letter *A*."

Reacher nodded. "You just used three of them. Total of eighteen since you woke up ten seconds ago."

"So it's a stupid challenge."

"No, it's an easy challenge," Reacher said.

"How?"

"I'll tell you later," Reacher said. "Go back to sleep."

"No, tell me now."

"I'll tell you later," Reacher said again. "Think of it as something to look forward to."

So King shrugged and then stared into space for a minute, distracted, maybe a little disgruntled, maybe even a little angry, but then he turned away and closed his eyes again.

Reacher drove on, and started thinking about the twin roadblocks they had passed through. Eight cars and eight officers in each location, with flashlights and plenty of time for close scrutiny. He imagined himself a wanted man of average appearance, traveling alone, suddenly at risk and vulnerable, perhaps anticipating those roadblocks up ahead. What could such a man do to prepare?

He could disguise one or other of those fatal tells, that's what he could do.

He could alter his average appearance, with makeup or putty or wigs or fake piercings or fake tattoos or fake scars.

But that would not be easy, without skills and practice. And that would not be easy at short notice, either.

So he would have to address the other tell.

He would have to make himself no longer alone.

Which would be easy to do, even without skills or practice. Which would be easy to do even at short notice.

He could pick up a hitchhiker.

# Chapter 19

Sorenson called in Delfuenso's name and address, and less than a minute later she knew that Delfuenso's car was a four-year-old Chevrolet Impala, dark blue in color, and she knew its plate number. She passed on that information to the roadblock crews. Both said the plate number was not on their scribbled lists of cars carrying two men. Both said they would check their dashboard video to confirm. Both said that process could take some time.

So Sheriff Goodman drove Sorenson back to the cocktail lounge, where the search for a dead or unconscious woman had turned up negative results. The deputies had traced ever-widening circles from the lounge's back door and had found nothing of interest. They had checked the shadows, the abandoned doorways, the weedy fence lines, the trash bins, and all the puddles and all the potholes.

Goodman said, "She could be further afield. She could have gotten up, and wandered off, and collapsed again. That kind of thing can happen, with bangs on the head."

One of the deputies said, "Or they could have bundled her into the car and then rolled her out later. In the middle of nowhere. Safer for them that way. So she could be anywhere. She could be fifty miles away."

Sorenson said, "Say that again."

"She could be fifty miles away."

"No, the first part."

"They could have bundled her into the car."

*Her plate number was not on their scribbled lists of cars carrying two men.*

Sorenson said, "You know what? I think they did. And I think she's still in the car. I think she's a hostage. And a smokescreen. Three people. Not two. They've been getting a free pass all the way."

No one spoke.

"What was she wearing?"

No reply.

"Come on, one of you has been in this lounge on your night off. Don't pretend you haven't."

"Black pants," Goodman said.

"And?"

"A black and silver top," Goodman said. "Kind of sparkly. Not much to it. Very low cut."

"Distinctive?"

"Unless you're legally blind. We're talking about a major display here."

"Of what?"

"Well, you know."

"I don't."

"I mean, she would be practically falling out of it."

"And this is the respectable lounge? What do they wear in the others?"

"Thong underwear."

"Is that all?"

"And high heeled shoes."

Sorenson got back on her cell. Long-distance traffic, through Nebraska and Iowa, in the middle of the night, in the middle of winter. Truckers, farmers, solid bible-believing Midwestern citizens. A low cut sparkly cocktail-waitress outfit would have stood out like a beacon. Bored troopers would have spent extra time on *that* car, for sure.

But no Nebraska trooper had seen a low cut sparkly cocktail-waitress outfit.

And no Iowa trooper had seen a low cut sparkly cocktail-waitress outfit either.

**Reacher drove on,** his left hand resting on the bottom curve of the wheel, his right hand resting on the shifter, for variety, to stop his shoulders locking up and getting sore. He could feel a little vibration in the shifter. His right palm was registering a faint buzz. The linkage was transmitting some kind of internal commotion. He nudged the lever one way and the other, just fractionally, to make sure it was seated properly. He glanced down. It was squarely lined up on the D. The tiny vibration was still there. No big deal, probably. He hoped. He knew very little about cars. But army vehicles vibrated like crazy, and no one worried about it.

Next to the shifter the sequence P-R-N-D-L was lit

up with a soft glow. Park, Reverse, Neutral, Drive, and Low. Alphabetically the sixteenth letter, then the eighteenth, then the fourteenth, then the fourth, and finally the twelfth. An unlucky and cumbersome sequence, if you had to blink it out, for instance. Three of the five letters were beyond the halfway point. Better than *WOOZY* or *ROOST* or *RUSTY* or *TRUST,* but still. Blinking or tapping or flashing a light in a linear fashion was not an efficient transmission method for a twenty-six-letter alphabet. Too time consuming, and too easy for either the transmitter or the receiver to lose count. Or both of them together. Old Sam Morse had figured all that out a long time ago.

Reacher glanced down again.

*Reverse.*

Karen Delfuenso had not blinked more than thirteen times. Which meant that all her letters were in the first half of the alphabet. Which was possible, but not statistically likely.

And an amateur who didn't know Morse Code might still understand the same basic drawbacks Samuel Morse had foreseen. Especially an amateur who was for some reason tense and anxious and who had limited time for communication. Such an amateur might have improvised, and come up with a shortcut system.

Drive, and reverse.

Forward, and backward.

Maybe the jerk of head to the left meant count forward from *A,* because in the Western nations people read from left to right, and therefore the jerk of the head to the right would mean count backward from Z.

Maybe.

Possibly.

Right thirteen, left two, right three, right one, left nine.

N, B, X, Z, I.

Which didn't make a whole lot of sense. *NB* could be the standard Latin abbreviation for *nota bene,* which meant *note well,* or in other words *pay attention,* but what was *XZI?*

Gibberish, that's what.

Reacher glanced in the mirror.

Delfuenso was staring at him again, willing him to understand.

*In the mirror.*

Her image was reversed.

Maybe she had anticipated that. Maybe left was right, and right was left.

Forward thirteen, back two, forward three, forward one, back nine.

M, Y, C, A, R.

*My car.*

Reacher looked in the mirror again and mouthed, *This is your car?*

Delfuenso nodded, urgently and eagerly and desperately and happily.

# Chapter 20

Sorenson stepped back and turned and looked and said, "They went south first, and then they got back on the road and went north. Why?"

Goodman said, "That was the way they came. Maybe they didn't know they could get back on the road any other way."

"Bullshit. They glance north, they see the old bar and an acre of gravel, and they know they can get out that way."

"So maybe they went for gas at the other station."

"Why would they? There's a gas station right here, at this end of the strip, staring them right in the face. Or do you think they were worried about price comparisons?"

"Maybe they saw the cameras."

"If one has cameras, the other has cameras too. You can bet on that."

"The price is the same anyway, both ends. It always is."

"So why did they loop back south?"

Goodman said, "For some other reason, I guess."

Sorenson set off walking south, fast over the frozen gravel, past the back of a closed-up diner, past the back of a no-name bar, past the back of a broken-down motel, past the back of a lit-up and open convenience store.

She stopped.

Ahead of her was a wide gap, and then another bar, and then another cocktail lounge, and then nothing at all until the other gas station.

She said, "Let's assume they didn't want a drink or a meal. Let's assume they weren't interested in a room for the night. And if they wanted gas, they'd have used the nearer station. So why did they come back this way?"

"The convenience store," Goodman said. "They needed something."

They hustled around to its front door and went inside to bright cold fluorescent glare and the smell of old coffee and microwaved food and antiseptic floor cleaner. A bored clerk behind the register didn't even raise his head. Sorenson scanned the ceiling. There were no cameras.

The aisles were close-packed with junk food and canned food and bread and cookies and basic toiletries, and automotive requirements like quarts of oil and gallons of antifreeze and screen wash and clip-on cup holders and patent self-extinguishing ashtrays and collapsible snow shovels. There were rubber overshoes for wet conditions, and tube socks, and white underwear for a dollar an item, and cheap T-shirts, and cheap denim shirts, and canvas work shirts, and canvas work pants.

Sorenson took a close look at the clothing aisle, and then she headed straight for the register, her ID at the ready. The clerk looked up.

"Help you?" he said.

"Between about twenty past and half past midnight, who was in here?"

"Me," the guy said.

"No customers?"

"Maybe one."

"Who?"

"A tall skinny guy in a shirt and tie."

"No coat?"

"It was like he ran in from a car. No time to get cold. No one walks here. This is the middle of nowhere."

"Did you see the car?"

The clerk shook his head. "I think the guy parked around the back. He sort of came around the corner. I guess that was my impression, anyway."

Sorenson asked, "What did he buy?"

The guy straightened out a curling helix of register tape spilling out of a slot. He traced his thumbnail over pale blue ink, in an irregular pattern, stop and go, leaping backward from one time stamp to another, then pausing at an eleven-line entry.

"Six items," he said. "Plus subtotal, tax, total, tender, and change."

"He paid cash?"

"He must have, if I made change."

"You don't remember?"

"I don't pay much attention. This is not a dream job, lady."

"What did he buy?"

The guy examined the tape. "Three of something, and three of something else."

"Three of what, and three of what else? This was tonight. This is not ancient history we're talking about here. We're not asking for a prodigious feat of memory."

"Water," the guy said. "I remember that. Three bottles, from the refrigerator cabinet."

"And?"

The guy looked at the tape again.

He said, "Three other things, all the same price."

"What three other things?"

"I don't remember."

Sorenson said, "Have you been smoking tonight?"

The guy went wary.

He said, "Smoking what?"

"Maybe that's a question for Sheriff Goodman. You in shape for a search tonight?"

The guy didn't answer that. He just bounced his hand up and down, rehearsing a triumphant finger snap, waiting to remember. Trying to remember. Then finally he smiled.

"Shirts," he said. "Three denim shirts, on special. Blue. Small, medium, and large. One of each."

**Sorenson and Goodman** walked out of the store and looped around to the back lot again. Sorenson said, "Karen Delfuenso was their hostage and they planned to use her as their smokescreen, so they couldn't let her stay in the skimpy top. Too memorable. They knew there could be roadblocks. So they made her change."

"They all changed," Goodman said. "Three people, three shirts."

Sorenson nodded.

"Bloodstains," she said. "Like the eyewitness told us. At least one of their suit coats was wet."

"We screwed up," Goodman said. "Both of us. I told the roadblocks two men in black suits. Then any two men. You told them any two men. But it wasn't any two men. It was any three people, two men and a woman, all in blue denim shirts."

Sorenson said nothing. Then her phone rang, and the Iowa State Police told her they had rewound their dashboard video and located Karen Delfuenso's car. It had passed through their roadblock more than an hour ago. It had not attracted their attention because it had four people in it.

# Chapter 21

Sorenson hunched away from Goodman and switched her phone to her other hand and said, "*Four people?*"

The State Police captain in Iowa said, "It's a kind of shadowy picture, but we can see them fairly clearly. Two in the front, and two in the back. And my sergeant remembers the driver."

"Can I talk to your sergeant?"

"Can I shut down this roadblock?"

"After I talk to your sergeant."

"OK, wait one."

Sorenson heard scratchy sounds in her ear, and the filtered rattle of an idling truck engine. She turned back to Goodman and said, "We were even more wrong than we knew. There are four of them in the car." Then she heard a cell phone change hands and a rusty voice said, "Ma'am?"

She asked, "Who was in the car?"

The sergeant said, "Mostly I remember the driver."

"Male or female?"

"Male. A big guy, with a busted nose. Badly busted. I mean raw, like a very recent injury. He looked like a gorilla with its face smashed in."

"Like the result of a fight?"

"He more or less admitted it. But he said it didn't happen in Iowa."

"You talked to him?"

"Briefly. He was polite enough to me. Nothing to report, apart from the nose."

"Was he acting nervous?"

"Not really. He was quiet. And stoic. He had to be, with a nose like that. He should have been in the hospital."

"What was he wearing?"

"A winter coat."

"What about the passengers?"

"I don't really recall them very well."

"You're not on the witness stand here, sergeant. You're not under oath. Anything you can remember might help me."

"All I have is impressions. I don't want to mislead you."

"Anything at all might help."

"Well, I thought they were like Peter, Paul and Mary."

"Who?"

"Folk singers. From back in the day. Before your time, maybe. They were all dressed the same. Like a singing group. Two men and a woman."

"Blue denim shirts?"

"Exactly. Like a country music trio. I figured their

trunk would be full of steel-strung guitars. I thought maybe they were heading from last night's show to tonight's. We see that sometimes. And the woman was all made up, like she had just come off stage."

"But the driver was different?"

"I thought he was maybe a manager. Or a roadie. You know, big and rough. Just an impression, like I said."

"Anything else?"

"Don't quote me, OK?"

"I won't."

"There was an atmosphere. The woman looked mad. Or resentful, somehow. I thought maybe the shows weren't going so well, and she wanted to quit the tour, but it was two against one. Or three, if the manager guy had a stake. It was late, but she was wide awake, like she had something on her mind. That was my impression, anyway."

Sorenson said nothing.

The sergeant said, "They were the targets, right?"

Sorenson said, "The two men in the shirts, yes."

"I'm sorry."

"Not your fault."

Then the captain came back on. He said, "Ma'am, you told us to look for two fugitives, not some family psychodrama involving a car full of vaudeville players."

"Not your fault," Sorenson said again.

"Can I break down this roadblock now?"

"Yes," Sorenson said. "And I need an APB on that plate number, all points east of you."

"I have no units on the road east of me, lady. I had

to bring them all here. Face it, ma'am, whoever those guys are, they're long gone now."


**Reacher could wink,** but only with his left eye. A childhood inheritance. As a kid he had slept mostly on his left side, and on waking would keep his left eye closed against the pillow and open only his right, to peer around whatever darkened bedroom he happened to be in. And he wasn't sure Delfuenso could see his left eye. Not from the back seat, with the mirror set the way it was. And to mess with his vision was not a good idea at eighty miles an hour, anyway. So he raised his right hand off the shifter, so she could see it, and then he dropped it back.

He jabbed his thumb to the left. No mirror involved. They were both facing the same way. Left was left. He tapped his index finger three times. Then left again, one tap. Then right, nine, his pale finger fast but clear in the low light, and then left, ten, and left, one, and left, three, and finally left, eleven.

He looked in the mirror and raised his eyebrows, to supply the question mark.

*Carjack?*

Delfuenso nodded back at him, eagerly.

A definite *yes*.

Which explained a lot of things.

But not the matching outfits.

Reacher took his hand off the shifter and plucked at the shoulder of his coat, finger and thumb, and he looked quizzically in the mirror and mouthed, *Shirts?*

Delfuenso glanced left, glanced right, frustrated, as

if unable to find a quick way to explain. Then she looked hard to her left, as if checking on McQueen, and she started to unbutton her shirt. Reacher watched the road with one eye and the mirror with the other. Three buttons, four, five. Then Delfuenso pulled her shirt wide open and Reacher saw a tiny black and silver garment under it, like fancy underwear, like a bodice, laced tight against her stomach, her breasts resting high and proud on a fabric shelf made from two vestigial cups.

Reacher nodded in the mirror. He had seen similar outfits. Most men had. Every soldier had. She was a cocktail waitress, maybe a bartender. She had been coming off her shift, maybe getting into her car, maybe waiting at a light, and the two guys had pounced. They had stopped somewhere and bought her a shirt, to eliminate an APB's inevitable headline description: *a dark-haired woman wearing practically nothing.*

Delfuenso started buttoning up again. Reacher jabbed his finger in Alan King's direction and his thumb in Don McQueen's, and then he opened his hand and raised it uncertainly, questioningly, like a universal semaphore: *Why them too?*

Delfuenso opened her mouth and closed it, and then she started blinking again, a long and laborious sequence.

Forward two, forward twelve, backward twelve, backward twelve, forward four.

B, L, O, O, D, *blood.*

Backward twelve, backward thirteen.

O, N, *on.*

Backward seven, forward eight, forward five, forward nine, backward nine.

T, H, E, I, R, *their.*

*Blood on their clothes?* Reacher mouthed.

Delfuenso nodded.

Reacher drove on through the darkness, with the white Dodge's tail lights still a mile ahead, past quiet lonely exits spaced miles apart, with questions in his head spinning like plates on sticks.

# Chapter 22

Sheriff Goodman hunched deeper into his coat against the cold and turned a full circle in the convenience store's back lot. He said, "I assume they parked here. Therefore they probably changed here too. Maybe they trashed their old jackets. The knife too, possibly. We should check the trash cans."

Sorenson said, "You volunteering?"

"I have deputies with nothing better to do."

"OK," Sorenson said. "But it's probably a waste of time. A buck gets ten they pitched the jackets in Delfuenso's trunk. And they probably dropped the knife down one of the water pipes in the bunker."

"Are you going to try a third roadblock?"

"Iowa doesn't have the manpower."

"Illinois, then. If they're staying on the Interstate, they're most likely going all the way to Chicago. You could have the Illinois cops waiting for them, right on the state line."

"They have to know they're pushing their luck.

They've survived twice. They won't risk a third time. They're going to take back roads now. Or go to ground somewhere."

"So we're done with roadblocks?"

"I think there's nothing more to be gained."

"Will their thinking match yours?"

"I'm trying to make mine match theirs."

"Then that's bad news for Karen Delfuenso," Goodman said. "They don't need the smokescreen anymore. They'll dump her out in the middle of nowhere."

"They won't," Sorenson said. "She's seen their faces. They'll kill her."

**The first question** in Reacher's mind was: would they call out roadblocks in two separate states for a carjacking? And the answer was: yes, probably. Almost certainly, in fact. Because carjacking where the owner was forced to stay on board was kidnapping, and kidnapping was a big, big deal. A federal case, literally, handled by the FBI, which was the only agency capable of coordinating a multi-state response.

And the local terrain was huge and empty. Blocking the roads was about the only option for any kind of law enforcement in that part of the country.

That, and helicopters.

And Reacher had seen a helicopter, a thousand feet up, with a searchlight.

Second question: what were the odds against two sets of roadblock-worthy and helicopter-worthy and FBI-worthy fugitives being on the loose on the same winter night in the same lonely place? Answer: very long odds indeed. Very unlikely. Coincidences happened, but to be there to witness one was a coincidence in itself, and two simultaneous coincidences was one too many.

Therefore: the roadblocks had been for King and McQueen.

Two guys, not one.

Almost certainly.

Which made no sense, initially.

Because: the first roadblock in Nebraska had been looking hard at lone drivers. Which was explicable, in a way. Obviously a lone guy could disguise himself by picking up a second guy, and two guys could disguise themselves by picking up a third guy, and so on, and so on, forever. An addition method. But subtraction could work too. As in: two guys could disguise themselves by one of them hiding out of sight. And the Nebraska cops had been smart enough to anticipate that maneuver. Lone drivers had had their trunks searched, not for drugs or guns or bombs or stolen goods, but for a second guy curled up and hiding.

But: the Nebraska cops shouldn't have been looking for two people. They should have been looking for three people. The two perpetrators, plus the carjack victim, a more-or-less topless cocktail waitress.

Which introduced an incongruity.

As in: King and McQueen clearly believed the APB would be for those three people. Themselves, and Delfuenso. Because they had given Delfuenso a shirt. To alter her appearance. The disguise method. And then they had gone the extra mile. They had given a hitchhiker a ride. Reacher himself, a fourth person. The addition method.

Four people, not three. A smokescreen. A deception, starting with the bland shirts, and continuing even to the extent of getting Reacher himself into the driver's seat for the second roadblock. A smokescreen, a deception, and more than anything else a diversion. The busted nose. Any cop would have been distracted by it.

And there had been no democratic discussion at the cloverleaf, right back at the beginning. That particular conversation had been of a different kind entirely. King and McQueen had twisted around in their seats and told Delfuenso they would hurt her bad if she betrayed them. They had spelled it out: *Keep your mouth shut.* Then they had pressed her: *Are we clear on that? Do you understand?* Reacher had seen her nod, yes, quiet and scared and timid, just before he got in the car.

And the aspirin episode had not been about concern for a stranger's health. By that point Alan King had already decided he wanted Reacher driving later. And he had not monitored Delfuenso's search through her bag out of innocent eagerness or excitement. He had been making sure she didn't find some way of signaling for help.

Reality.

Reacher was no one's first choice of nighttime companion.

King and McQueen had offered the ride for one reason only.

They were defending themselves against a three-person APB.

But the actual APB had been for two people.

Why?

Only one possible answer: the FBI had known there were two guys on the run, but they hadn't known the two guys had jacked a car and taken a hostage.

In which case: did the FBI know now?

And therefore: the roadblocks had not been for the carjacking. Not in and of itself. Not if the FBI didn't even *know* about the carjacking.

The roadblocks had been for the primary crime.

Which must therefore have been pretty bad.

*Blood on their clothes.*

Reacher drove on, eighty miles an hour through the Iowa darkness, breathing slow and steady.

**Goodman and Sorenson** walked back to the red Mazda. Sorenson's FBI crime scene team had moved up from the pumping station and were all over it. They had already found blood and fingerprints, and hairs and fibers. The two men had taken no forensic precautions. That was clear.

Sorenson said, "They were very disorganized."

Goodman said, "Most criminals are."

"But these guys are not like most criminals in any other way. This was not a mugging or a robbery gone wrong. They wore suits. The State Department is involved. But they were completely unprepared. They didn't plan. They're improvising all the way. They even had to hijack their getaway vehicle, for God's sake. Why?"

"Maybe they didn't plan because they didn't know they needed to plan."

"You come all the way to Nebraska to kill a guy, you know you need to plan."

"Maybe they didn't come to kill the guy. Or not yet, anyway. Maybe something got out of hand all of a sudden. Most homicides are spontaneous."

"I agree," Sorenson said. "But nothing else about this case feels spontaneous."

Goodman sent a deputy to check the dumpsters behind the convenience store. Then the head crime scene technician backed butt-first out of the Mazda and walked over to Sorenson with two photographs in his hand. The first was a color Polaroid of the dead guy's face, cleaned up, eyes opened, blood wiped away, arranged to look as close to a live guy as a dead guy can get. He had dark eyes, shaped like almonds, tipped up a little at the outside corners. He had a small circular mole low down on his right cheek, south and west of his mouth. On a woman it would have been called a beauty spot. On a man it just looked like a mole.

The second photograph was a monochrome blowup of the same face. From a video still. From a surveillance camera, almost certainly. It was of poor quality, very grainy, smeared a little by movement and a cheap CCD camera and fluorescent light and a low-bit digital recording. But the eyes were clearly recognizable. And the mole was there, in the same place, perfectly positioned, as unique as a barcode or a fingerprint, and as definitive as a DNA sample.

"From where?" Sorenson asked.

"The rental counter at the Denver airport," the technician said. "The victim rented the Mazda himself, just after nine o'clock this morning. Now yesterday morning, technically. The mileage on the car indicates he drove straight here with no significant detours."

"That's a long way."

"A little over seven hundred miles. Ten or eleven hours, probably. One stop for gas. The tank is low now."

"Did he drive all that way alone?"

"I don't know," the technician said. "I wasn't there."

A cautious guy, old school, data driven, and possibly a little bad tempered. Night duty, in the winter, in the middle of nowhere.

Sorenson asked, "What's your best guess?"

"I'm a scientist," the guy said. "I don't guess."

"Then speculate."

The guy made a face.

"There's no trace evidence in the back of the car," he said. "But both front seats show signs of occupation. So he might have had a single passenger from Denver. Or he might have driven in alone, in which case the passenger seat trace would come from the two perpetrators using the car to get from the crime scene to this location."

"Yes or no?"

"I would say he probably drove in alone. There's

more trace on the driver's seat than the passenger's seat."

"Like the difference between a seven-hundred-mile drive and a three-mile drive?"

"I can't specify a ratio. It doesn't happen that way. Most trace gets rubbed in over the first minute or two."

"Yes or no? Real world?"

"Probably yes. The driver's seat shows heavy use, the passenger's seat doesn't."

"So how did the two guys get here? Wearing suits and no winter coats?"

"Ma'am, I have no idea," the technician said, and walked back to the car.

"I have no idea either," Goodman said. "My guys have seen no abandoned cars. That was one of the things I told them to look for."

Sorenson said, "Obviously they didn't abandon a car. If they had their own car, they wouldn't have had to hijack a cocktail waitress. And we need to know where the fourth guy came from, too. And we need to figure out where he was while his pals were busy in the bunker."

"He sounds distinctive."

Sorenson nodded. "A gorilla with its face smashed in. Anyone should remember a guy like that."

Then her phone rang, and she answered it, and Goodman saw her back go straight and her face change. She listened for thirty seconds, and she said, "OK," and then she said it again, and then she said, "No, I'll make sure it happens," and then she clicked off.

A straight back, but she had said *OK*, not *Yes, sir.*

Not a superior from her FBI field office, therefore, or from D.C.

Goodman asked, "Who was that?"

Sorenson said, "That was a duty officer in a room in Langley, Virginia."

"Langley?"

Sorenson nodded.

She said, "Now the CIA has got its nose in this thing too. I'm supposed to provide progress reports all through the night."

# Chapter 23

It was technically challenging to take out a guy in the front passenger seat while driving at eighty miles an hour. It required simultaneous movement and stillness. The driver's foot had to stay steady on the pedal, which meant his legs had to stay still. His torso had to stay still. Above all, his left shoulder had to stay still. Only his right arm could move, which would dictate a backhand scythe to the passenger's head.

But it would be a relatively weak blow. It would be easy enough to fake a lazy cross-body scratch of the left shoulder, and then launch the right fist through a long half circle, like a backward right hook, but the top edge of the Chevy's dash roll was fairly high, and the bottom edge of its mirror was fairly low, so the swing would have to be carefully aimed through the available gap, and then it would have to be kicked upward for the last part of its travel.

And Reacher's arms were long, which meant he

would have to keep his elbow tucked in to stop his knuckles fouling against the windshield glass. Which would dictate an upward kick *and* a snap of the elbow in the final inches, which together would be very hard to calibrate in order to avoid an action-and-reaction jerk to the left shoulder. And any movement of the left shoulder would be a very bad idea at that point. A minor slalom at eighty miles an hour on a straight wide road would be easily recoverable in theory, but there was no point in announcing hostile intent and then spending the next five seconds with both hands on the wheel fighting a skid. That would give the initiative straight back to the passenger, no question about it.

So all in all it would be better to settle for a light tap, not a heavy blow, which meant the exact choice of target would be important, which meant the larynx would come top of the list. An open hand held horizontally, like a karate chop, and a light smack in the throat. That would get the job done. Disabling, but not fatal. Except that Alan King was asleep, with his face turned away and his chin tucked down to his chest. His throat was concealed. He would have to be woken up first. Maybe a poke in the shoulder. He would straighten up, he would face forward, he would blink and yawn and stare.

Easy enough. Poke, scratch, swing, *pop*. Technically challenging, but entirely possible. Alan King could be handled.

But Don McQueen couldn't. Science had never found a way to take out a guy sitting directly behind a driver. Not while that driver was doing eighty miles an hour. No way. Just not feasible. No kind of four-dimensional planning could achieve it.

Reacher drove on, at eighty miles an hour. He checked the mirror. No traffic behind him. McQueen was asleep. He checked again a minute later. Delfuenso was staring at him. He learned the road a mile ahead and looked back in the mirror. He nodded, as if to say: *Go ahead. Begin transmission.*

She began.

Forward nine.

I.

Forward eight, forward one, back five, forward five.

H, A, V, E, *have.*

Forward one.

A.

Forward three, forward eight, forward nine, forward twelve, forward four.

C, H, I, L, D, *child.*

*I have a child.*

Reacher nodded, and lifted the small stuffed animal out of the center console, as if to say: *I understand.* The toy's fur was stiff with dried saliva. Its shape was distorted by the clamp of a tiny jaw. He put it back. Delfuenso's eyes filled with tears and she turned her head away.

Reacher leaned over and poked Alan King in the shoulder.

King stirred, and woke up, and straightened, and faced forward, and blinked and yawned and stared.

He said, "What?"

Reacher said, "The gas gauge is through the first little bit. I need you to tell me when to stop."

**The deputy came** back from the convenience store and told Goodman there were no bloody coats or knives in the trash cans. Sorenson called the head technician back from the Mazda again and said, "I need to know about the victim."

"Can't help you there," the guy said. "There was no ID and the autopsy won't be until tomorrow."

"I need your impressions."

"I'm a scientist. I was out sick the day they taught Clairvoyance 101."

"You could make some educated guesses."

"What's the hurry?"

"I'm getting hassle through two separate back channels."

"Who?"

"First the State Department, and now the CIA."

"They're not separate. The State Department is the political wing of the CIA."

"And we're the FBI, and we're the good guys here, and we can't afford to look slow or incompetent. Or unimaginative. So I'd like some impressions from you. Or informed opinion, or whatever else they taught you to call it in Cover Your Ass 101."

"What kind of informed opinion?"

"Age?"

"Forty-something, possibly," the guy said.

"Nationality?"

"He was American, probably," the guy said.

"Because?"

"His dental work looks American. His clothing is mostly American."

"Mostly?"

"I think his shirt is foreign. But his underwear is American. And most people stick to underwear from their country of origin."

"Do they?"

"As a general rule. It's a comfort issue, literally and metaphorically. And an intimacy issue. It's a big step, putting on foreign underwear. Like betrayal, or emigration."

"That's science?"

"Psychology is a science."

"Where is the shirt from?"

"Hard to say. There's no label in it."

"But it looks foreign?"

"Well, basically all cotton clothing is foreign now. Almost all of it comes from somewhere in Asia. But quality and cut and color and pattern all tend to be market-specific."

"Which market?"

"The fabric is thin, the color is cream rather than white, the collar points are long and narrow, the design of the checks is purely graphic rather than imitative of a traditional weave. I would say the shirt was bought in Pakistan, or possibly the Middle East."

# Chapter 24

Alan King jacked himself upright and craned to his left. He took a good long look at the fuel gauge. He said, "I think we'll be OK for a spell more. Let me know when it hits the three-quarter mark."

"Won't be long," Reacher said. "It seems to be going down awful fast."

"That's because you're driving awful fast."

"No faster than Mr. McQueen was."

"Then maybe the fault has corrected itself. Maybe it was only intermittent."

"We don't want to run out of gas. Not out here. It's pretty lonely. Can't count on getting help. The cops are all back at that roadblock."

"Give it another thirty minutes," King said. "Then perhaps we'll start to think about it."

"OK," Reacher said.

"Tell me about that thing with the letter A."

"Later."

"No, now."

"I said later. What part of that is hard to understand?"

"You don't like to be pushed around, do you, Mr. Reacher?"

"I don't know. I've never been pushed around. If it ever happens, you'll be the first to find out whether I like it or not."

King turned his head away and gazed forward into the darkness for a full minute more, completely silent, and then he slid down in his seat and tucked his chin back down and closed his eyes again. Reacher checked the mirror. McQueen was still out cold. Delfuenso was still awake.

And she was blinking again.

Backward seven, forward eight, forward five, backward two.

T-H-E-Y, *they*.

Forward eight, forward one, backward five, forward five.

H-A-V-E, *have*.

Forward seven, backward six, backward thirteen, backward eight.

G-U-N-S, *guns*.

*They have guns.*

Reacher nodded in the mirror, and drove on.

The scene behind the cocktail lounge stayed quiet for five more minutes. The lab guys took a long sequence of close-up photographs inside the Mazda, using strobes. The car's misty glass lit up from within with irregular flashes, like a thunderstorm viewed from a great distance, or a battle on the other side of a hill. Goodman's deputies searched the ground and found nothing of significance. Sorenson interrogated federal and state databases by phone, looking for large men with recent facial injuries. She came up empty.

Then came the sounds of a whispering V-8 engine and tires on crushed stone, and the dip and bounce of headlight beams in the mist, and a dark sedan nosed its way north toward them. It was a navy blue Crown Vic, identical to Sorenson's own, same specification, same needle antennas on the back deck, but with Missouri plates. It came to a stop at a respectful distance and two men got out. They were wearing dark suits. They stood in the lee of their open doors and struggled into heavy down parkas. Then they closed their doors and moved closer, scanning the scene as they walked, noticing and dismissing the county deputies, noticing and dismissing Sheriff Goodman, noticing and dismissing the crime scene technicians, before settling their attention on Sorenson. They stopped six feet from her and pulled IDs from their pockets.

The same IDs as hers.

FBI.

The agent on the right said, "We're from Counterterrorism, central region, out of Kansas City."

Sorenson said, "I didn't call you."

"Your field office's duty log triggered an automatic alert."

"Why?"

"Because the crime scene location is sensitive."

"Is it? It's an abandoned pumping station."

"No, it's an open and uncapped well head with direct vertical access to the largest groundwater reserves in the United States."

"It's a dry hole."

The agent nodded. "But only because the water table fell below the bottom of the bore. Dry or not, if you poured something down that pipe, it would find its way into the aquifer. That's inevitable. Gravity alone would make sure of it. Like dripping ink on a sponge."

"Poured what?"

"There's a number of things we wouldn't want to go down there."

"But it would be a drop in a bucket. Literally. A very tiny drop and a very big bucket. I mean, there's a lot down there. They use two and a half trillion gallons every year. And even one of those big road tankers is, what, five thousand gallons? That's nothing in comparison."

The guy nodded again. "But terrorism is an asymmetrical business. As a matter of fact, you're right. Five thousand gallons of poisonous chemicals or viruses or germs or whatever wouldn't do much harm. Not scientifically. But can you see a way of convincing people of that? There'd be mass panic. There'd be a mass stampede out of here. Total chaos throughout a large part of the nation. And that's exactly what terrorists like. Plus we'd have severe disruption to agriculture, for years. And there are military installations here."

"Are you serious? That's chemical and biological warfare."

"We're completely serious."

"So why hasn't that pipe been capped?"

"There are ten thousand holes like that one. We're working as fast as we can."

Sorenson said, "This is a homicide. I don't see a terrorist angle."

"Really? Did you get a call from State? About the victim?"

"Yes."

"And CIA?"

"Yes."

"So there's some kind of overseas issue here. Don't you think?"

Sorenson heard her technician's voice in her head: *I would say the shirt was bought in Pakistan, or possibly the Middle East.*

She said, "So are you taking over from me?"

The agent on the right shook his head and said, "No, it's still your case. But we're going to be looking over your shoulder. Night and day. Just until we're sure. Nothing personal. We hope you don't mind."

Reacher heard McQueen wake up behind him. He looked in the mirror and saw the guy staring out his window, at the empty traffic lanes alongside him. Then he saw him look the other way, beyond Delfuenso, at the shoulder of the road.

They passed an exit sign. They passed three blue boards, one of them blank. Gas and accommodations, but no food. There were no lights on the horizon. No welcoming glow. A deceptive exit, in Reacher's opinion. Fifteen or twenty miles of dark rural roads, and then places that would be shut when they finally got there.

"Take this one," McQueen said.

"What?" Reacher said.

"Exit here."

"You sure? Looks pretty dead."

"Just do it."

Reacher glanced sideways at Alan King. McQueen saw him do it. McQueen said, "Don't look at him. He's not in charge here. I am. And I'm telling you to take this exit."

# Chapter 25

The two counterterrorism agents from Kansas City did not look over Sorenson's shoulder. Not literally. They just stood with her, sometimes one on either side, sometimes in a tight collegial triangle. They introduced themselves as Robert Dawson and Andrew Mitchell, equal rank, both of them with more than fifteen years in. Dawson was a little taller than Mitchell, and Mitchell was a little heavier than Dawson, but otherwise they were very similar. Fair-haired, pink-faced, early forties, dressed in navy blue suits under their parkas, with white shirts and blue ties. Neither one of them seemed particularly tired or stressed, which Sorenson found impressive, given the nighttime hour and the pressures of their assignment.

But equally neither one of them had much to offer in terms of procedural suggestions. By that point the investigation was essentially stalled, and Sorenson was well aware of it. The perpetrators were somewhere east of Des Moines, and the hostage was already dead or close to it, and therefore a little ten-year-old girl was already a motherless child, or close to it.

Further progress would depend on luck and forensics, and resolution would be painstakingly slow and uncertain.

Not one for the show reel.

Front and center on no one's résumé.

Sorenson said, "We should alert Chicago, I guess."

Dawson said, "Or Milwaukee, or Madison, or Indianapolis, or Cincinnati, or Louisville."

Mitchell said, "Or Interpol. Or NASA, maybe. By now they could be anywhere in the known universe."

"I'm wide open to ideas, Agent Mitchell."

"Nothing personal," Dawson said.

Then the same sights and sounds happened all over again: the whisper of a V-8 engine, and the crunch of tires over crushed stone, and the flicker of headlight beams in the mist, and another plain sedan nosed its way north toward them. It was another Ford Crown Victoria, another government car, but not quite identical to Sorenson's own, or Dawson and Mitchell's own. It was built to the same specification, but it had different needle antennas on the trunk lid, and it was light in color, not dark, and it had official U.S. plates.

It came to a stop thirty feet away and the driver got out. He was wearing chino pants and a sweater and a coat. He moved closer, scanning the scene as he walked, ignoring the deputies, ignoring Goodman, ignoring the crime scene technicians, aiming straight for Sorenson and Dawson and Mitchell. Up close he looked like the kind of guy who would be more comfortable in a gray three-piece suit, but who had gotten a panic call in the middle of the night and grabbed the nearest things to hand, like a banker woken by his elderly dog whining at the bedroom door.

He stopped six feet away and pulled ID from his pocket.

Different ID.

The State Department.

The name on the ID was Lester L. Lester, Jr. The photograph showed the guy's face below neatly combed hair and above a neatly rolled button-down collar Sorenson would have bet good money came from Brooks Brothers.

She asked, "What can I do for you, Mr. Lester?"

Mitchell asked, "Is your middle name Lester too?"

The man called Lester looked at him.

He said, "As a matter of fact, it is."

"Outstanding," Mitchell said.

"What can I do for you?" Sorenson asked again.

"I'm here to observe," Lester said.

"Because the victim was known to you?"

"Not to me personally."

"But known to the Department of State?"

"That's the gist of it."

"Who was he?"

"I'm not at liberty to say."

"Then turn yourself around and go back wherever the hell you came from. Because you're not helping here."

Lester said, "I have to stay."

Sorenson asked, "Do you have a cell phone?"

"Yes, I do."

"Then take it out and call home and get clearance to tell me what I need to know."

Lester showed no signs of doing that.

Mitchell asked, "Are your CIA pals here too?"

Lester made a big show of looking all around, very carefully.

"I don't see anyone else," he said. "Do you?"

Mitchell said, "Maybe they're hanging back in the shadows. That's what they're good at, right?"

Lester didn't reply. Then Sorenson's phone started ringing. The plain electronic sound. She answered and listened. She said, "OK, got that, thank you, sir." She clicked off the call. She looked straight at Lester and smiled. She said, "You must have driven out here pretty fast."

Lester said, "Must I have?"

Sorenson nodded. "That was my SAC on the phone. He told me you were on your way. The grapevine is still working, apparently. He told me to expect you within the next ten or so minutes."

Lester said, "There wasn't much traffic on the roads."

"And my SAC told me who the dead guy was."

Lester didn't reply.

Dawson asked Sorenson, "So who was the dead guy?"

"An embassy worker, apparently."

"One of ours?"

"Yes."

"Like a diplomat?"

"An attaché of some kind."

"Senior?"

"I didn't get that impression. But probably not junior, either. Judging by the tone of voice."

"Age?"

"Forty-two."

"Important?"

"My SAC didn't specify."

Mitchell said, "If a Special Agent-in-Charge is wide awake and on the telephone in the middle of the night, then the guy was important. Wouldn't you say?"

Dawson asked, "Where did he serve? What region? What responsibilities?"

"My SAC didn't specify. I don't think he's been told. Which might mean somewhere and something sensitive."

*The shirt was bought in Pakistan, or possibly the Middle East.*

Dawson asked, "Why was he here?"

"I don't know."

Dawson looked at Lester, and asked the same question.

Lester said, "I don't know why he was here."

"Really?"

"Yes, really. That's why I'm here. Because we don't know."

Then twenty feet away Sheriff Goodman's phone started ringing, muffled in his pocket but still loud in the silent night. All four people in the impromptu cluster turned toward the sound. Goodman answered and listened and his eyes sought Sorenson's and he started walking toward her, as if instinctively, as if compelled, finishing his call and folding his phone when he was ten feet away, and not speaking until he was another five feet closer.

"That was my dispatcher," he said. "The eyewitness is missing. The guy you talked to tonight. He never made it home."

**The short discussion** with McQueen had eaten up some time and distance, so Reacher had to take the ramp pretty fast. Then he had to brake pretty hard ahead of a tight curve. For a split second he considered hitting Alan King in the throat. He was fairly well braced in his seat, with his right foot hard on the pedal and his left hand tight on the wheel. King was waking up because of the abrupt turn and the sudden deceleration. Chances were good his neck would be in the right place at the right time.

But McQueen was still a problem, even at twenty miles an hour. Theoretically Reacher could find the lever and jam the seat back into him, and maybe swing an elbow, but the headrest was in the way, and there was collateral damage just waiting to happen, right there next to the guy on the rear bench.

A mother, separated from her child.

Two feet from McQueen, on his right. And the guy was probably right-handed. Most people were.

*They have guns.*

So Reacher just coasted onward, through the curve, to the turn at the end of the ramp. Repeats of the gas board and the motel board faced him on the far shoulder of a narrow two-lane road. Both had arrows pointing right.

Alan King yawned and said, "We're getting off here?"

Don McQueen said, "This is as good a place as any."

"For what?" Reacher said.

"For gas," McQueen said. "What else? Turn right. Follow the sign."

# Chapter 26

Reacher turned right and followed the sign. The road was narrow and dark. And dead straight, like a lot of roads in Iowa. The surrounding landscape was invisible, but it felt flat. Dormant winter fields, left and right, as far as the mind could sense. There was nothing up ahead. Just darkness. And then Missouri, presumably, a hundred miles away. Maybe a river first. The Des Moines, Reacher thought. He had studied geography in school. The river called the Des Moines met the mighty Mississippi a couple hundred miles southeast of the city called Des Moines.

He said, "This is a complete waste of time, guys. We're going to drive twenty miles and find a gas station that went out of business before they invented unleaded."

McQueen said, "There was a sign. Has to mean something."

"It means there was gas here back when you were

in grade school. Thirty cents a gallon. And Luckies at thirty cents a pack."

"I'm sure they keep those signs updated."

"You're a very trusting person."

"Not really," McQueen said.

Reacher drove on. The road surface was pitted and pot-holed and the car bounced and swayed. Not its natural element, as a vehicle. Or Reacher's, as a driver. Both had been better on the highway.

McQueen asked, "How's your head?"

Reacher said, "My head is fine. It's my nose that's busted, not my skull."

"You need another aspirin?"

"I already had that discussion with Mr. King. While you were asleep."

King said, "He elected to soldier on without. He seems very protective of Karen's personal supply."

"Aspirin is not a prescription drug," McQueen said. "She could get more at the gas station. Or Tylenol, or Advil."

"Or leeches," Reacher said. "We might find some under a dusty old pile of inner tubes and buggy whips. After we bust the padlock the bank put on thirty years ago."

"Just keep going," McQueen said. "Be patient."

So Reacher drove on, slowly south on the lumpy road, and two miles later he was proved wrong, and McQueen was proved right. They all saw a faint yellow glow in the nighttime mist, way far ahead in the distance, on the horizon, like a beacon, which grew stronger as they approached it, and which finally resolved itself into the fierce neon glare of a brand new

Shell station, all crisp white and yellow and orange, sitting like a mirage or a landed UFO on a quarter-acre bite out of a fallow cornfield. It had hi-tech pumps on two gondola islands, and lube bays, and a glassed-in store lit up so bright it must have been visible from outer space.

And it was open for business.

"You should have trusted me," McQueen said.

Reacher slowed the car to a walk and turned in. He chose the pumps farther from the store and nearer the road and eased to a stop. He put the transmission in Park and shut down the motor. He pulled the key, casually, like a reflex, like a rote habit, and dropped it in his pocket.

Alan King saw him do it, but said nothing.

Reacher said, "Same system? I get the coffee, you get the gas?"

"Works for me," McQueen said.

So Reacher opened his door and got out. He stood and stretched and arched his back and then looped around the pump islands and headed for the bright lights. He could see a kid on a stool behind the register, watching him, staring at his face. The busted nose. A universal attraction, apparently. The guy wasn't much more than twenty years old, and he looked sleepy and slow.

Reacher paused before going in, and checked back. Alan King had dipped a credit card and was getting ready to pump the gas. McQueen was still in the rear seat. Delfuenso was still next to him.

Reacher went inside. The kid behind the register looked up and nodded a cautious greeting. Reacher waited until the door sucked shut and said, "Got a pay phone?"

The kid blinked and opened his mouth and closed it again, like a goldfish.

"Not a difficult question," Reacher said. "A simple yes or no answer will suffice."

"Yes," the kid said. "We have a pay phone."

"Where is it?"

"By the restrooms," the kid said.

"Which are where?"

The kid pointed.

"In back," he said.

Reacher looked the other way, out the window.

Don McQueen's door was open.

But he was still in the car. Just sitting there, facing forward.

Reacher turned back and saw a door in the rear wall of the store. It had two stick figures on it, one in a skirt and one in pants. He stepped over to it and pulled it open. Behind it was a small lobby, with two more doors, one with the pants figure on it, and the other with the skirt. On the wall between the two was a pay phone, shiny and new, with an acoustic hood over it.

Reacher checked back. King was pumping the gas. McQueen was twisted sideways in his seat. He had both feet out of the car. They were planted on the ground. But that was all. He was stretching his legs. For comfort. He wasn't moving.

Not yet, anyway.

Reacher checked the ladies' room. No windows. No alternate exit.

He checked the men's room. No windows. No alternate exit. He pulled a wad of towels from the dispenser and came back out to the lobby and folded the towels twice and jammed them between the lobby door and its frame, on the hinge side, so that the door held itself open a few inches. A little less than four inches, to be exact. Reacher ducked back and checked the view from the phone. He could see a small sliver of the store. He could see a tiny slice of the main door. Not much, but he would know if it opened.

He hoped.

He lifted the receiver and dialed 911.

More or less instantly a dispatcher asked, "What is your current location?"

Reacher said, "Give me the FBI."

"Sir, what is your current location?"

"Don't waste time."

"Do you need fire, police, or ambulance?"

"I need the FBI."

"Sir, this is the 911 emergency service."

"And since about September the twelfth 2001 you've had a direct button for the FBI."

"How did you know that?"

"Just a lucky guess. Hit the button, and hit it now."

Reacher stared through the gap at the tiny slice of the main door. Nothing happening. Not yet. The sound in his ear changed. Dead air, then a new dial tone.

Then a new voice.

It said, "This is the FBI. What is the nature of your emergency?"

Reacher said, "I have information, probably for your field office in Omaha, Nebraska."

"What is the nature of your information?"

"Just connect me, now."

"Sir, what is your name?"

Reacher knew all about nighttime duty officers. He had talked to thousands during his years in the service. They were always either on the way down, and therefore insecure, or on the way up, and therefore ambitious. He knew what worked with them, and he knew what didn't. He had learned the right psychological approach.

He said, "Connect me now or you'll lose your job."

A pause.

Then dead air.

Then a new dial tone.

Then the outer door swept open. Reacher heard the loud swish of its rubber seal and saw part of its bright white frame flash through the limits of the narrow gap. He got a glimpse of a blue shoulder. He heard the fast click of heels on tile.

He hung up the phone.

He stepped forward and grabbed the folded towels with one hand and pushed the lobby door with the other and tossed the towels behind him and came face to face with Don McQueen.

# Chapter 27

Reacher and McQueen stepped mutely around each other, chest to chest, like guys do at restroom doors. McQueen went in and Reacher headed through the store to the coffee station, which was a complex push-button one-cup-at-a-time machine, a yard wide, all chrome and aluminum, brand new, probably Italian. Or French. European, certainly. It seemed to grind a separate batch of beans after each push of the button, and it was so slow that McQueen was out of the men's room before Reacher was through with the last cup. Which was a good thing, in that McQueen was then more or less obligated to carry two cups back to the car, which meant his hands were full, and armed men with full hands were better than armed men with empty hands, in Reacher's considered opinion.

Reacher carried the other two cups, black no sugar, one for himself and one for Karen Delfuenso. Alan King was still out of the car. The car was still next to the pump. The readout showed that less than four gallons had gone in the tank.

King said, "I'll drive from here, Mr. Reacher."

Reacher said, "Really? I haven't done my three hundred miles yet."

"Change of plan. We're going to head for the motel and hole up for the night."

"I thought you wanted to get to Chicago."

"I said our plans have changed. What part of that don't you understand?"

"Your call," Reacher said.

"Indeed," King said. "So I'll need the car key."

*Four-dimensional planning.* Reacher was on the near side of the car, and King and McQueen were on the far side. Delfuenso was still in her seat. Her door was wide open. Her head was inches away from King's right hand. It would take part of a second for King and McQueen to drop their cups of coffee. Part of another second for them to get to their guns. Reacher could throw his own cup like a scalding grenade at one head or the other, but not both. He could scramble around the trunk, or over it, but not fast enough.

No chance.

Geometry, and time.

He rested his cup on the Chevy's roof and fished in his pocket for the key.

He held it out.

*Come and get it.*

But King wasn't the dumbest guy in the world. He said, "Just drop it on the seat. I'll be right there."

Don McQueen got in the front. He twisted counterclockwise, like a friendly guy just checking all his pals were going to get properly settled and comfortable. But the position kept his right hand free and clear, close to his right pants pocket, close to the right side of his pants waistband.

King was still near the gas cap, with his own right hand free and clear, still inches from Karen Delfuenso's head.

Geometry, and time.

Reacher climbed in behind the driver's seat, and leaned over and dropped the key.

McQueen smiled at him.

King closed Delfuenso's door for her from the outside, and then he tracked around the trunk and closed Reacher's door for him. He picked up the key and climbed in and scooted his seat six inches forward. He started the engine and eased back to the road and drove onward into the darkness, south, away from the Interstate, toward the promised motel.


**The FBI emergency** response operator had stayed on the line and listened in to the aborted call to Omaha. He had heard the ring tone. He had heard the receiver go down. He was a rookie, hence the routine night duty. But he was a fast-tracked rookie, hence the D.C. assignment and the important post. He was fast-tracked because he was smart.

He was smart enough to follow up.

He called the Omaha field office and spoke to the duty agent. He asked, "Have you guys got something going on there tonight?"

The agent in Nebraska yawned and said, "Kind of. There's a single-victim knife-crime homicide in the back of beyond miles from anywhere, which doesn't sound like a very big deal, but for some reason the SAC is on it, and the CIA and the State Department are sniffing around, and we've had a bunch of roadblocks on the Interstate."

"Then you should know I put a call through to you, but the caller hung up before you answered."

"Location?"

"Caller ID and the phone company indicate a gas station in the middle of nowhere, south and east of Des Moines, Iowa."

"Did you get a name?"

"No name, but the caller was male, and in a hurry. He sounded like he was sick with a head cold. Very nasal."

"Did he say what he wanted?"

"Not specifically. He said he had information, probably for Omaha, Nebraska."

"Probably?"

"That was the word he used."

The guy in Nebraska said, "OK, thanks," and hung up.

**The dark Iowa** road ran dead straight for another eight miles to a featureless T junction. There was an immense field on the left, and another on the right, and a double-wide field ahead. Hence the mandatory turn. A repeat accommodations sign had an arrow pointing left to the motel. Another eight miles later there was a featureless crossroads with an arrow pointing right. Alan King drove on, threading through the giant checkerboard matrix of Iowa agriculture. Alongside him Don McQueen sat half turned, slumped against his window, awake and watchful. Behind McQueen Karen Delfuenso stared rigidly ahead. She wouldn't look at Reacher. She seemed disappointed in him.

Reacher himself sat still and breathed slow, in and out, just waiting.

**The night duty** agent in Nebraska wrote the words *male caller, in a hurry, head cold, nasal voice, gas station, S&E of Des Moines, Iowa* on a pad of paper, and then he scrolled through the speed dial list on his telephone console. He stopped on *Sorenson, J, cellular.*

He thought for a second.

Then he hit *Dial.*

Just in case it was important.

**At that moment** Julia Sorenson was talking to Sheriff Goodman about the missing eyewitness. The guy lived with a woman he wasn't married to, in a rented farm property eleven miles north and west of the crime scene, and there was only one practical route for him to take, and he hadn't arrived, and neither he nor his truck had been found along the way. He was not in any of Sin City's bars or lounges, and Goodman's deputies hadn't found him in town.

Then Sorenson's phone rang, and she excused herself and turned away and took the call. It was the night duty agent back at the field office. She only half listened to his preamble. Law enforcement got lots of aborted calls. Kids, pranksters, drunks, misdials, all part of the territory. But she started to pay serious attention when the guy got to the apparent source of the call. Because of her earlier gloomy and defeated conclusion: *The perpetrators were somewhere east of Des Moines.*

"Say that again?" she asked.

The guy said, "A pay phone in a gas station in the middle of nowhere, south and east of Des Moines, Iowa."

"Are we sure of that?"

"Caller ID and the phone company confirmed it."

"Who made the call?"

"No name, but the emergency operator said the voice was male."

"Anything else?"

"He was in a hurry and he sounded nasal."

"Nasal?"

"Like he had a head cold."

"Is there a recording?"

"Of the original call? I'm sure there is."

"Have it e-mailed to me. And call that gas station. Check if they have video, and if not, get a narrative and descriptions of everybody and everything."

The duty agent said, "You need to call the CIA."

Sorenson said, "Don't tell me what I need to do."

"It's just that they're calling me all the time. They want updates."

"Tell them nothing," Sorenson said. "Not yet."

Then she clicked off the call and turned back and looked Goodman in the eye and said, "Sorry, chief, but I have to go to Iowa."

# Chapter 28

Goodman got the bare bones of the story from Sorenson and said, "What about my missing eyewitness?"

Sorenson said, "You can handle that yourself for the rest of the night. But don't worry. You're about to get plenty of help. As soon as the office workers get in tomorrow I'll be replaced and you'll be knee-deep in agents. You'll have so many here you can put a couple on traffic duty. You can find out who drops gum on the sidewalk."

"Your SAC is already involved. And you haven't been replaced yet."

"He hasn't kicked it upstairs yet. Can't do that, in the middle of the night. But he will. And he'll cover his ass. Right now I bet he's writing a report, which will be in every e-mail in-box everywhere by the time the sun comes up, and the last paragraph will be a recommendation to pull me out and bring in the heavy hitters from D.C. You can take that to the bank."

"Doesn't he trust you?"

"He trusts me just fine. But this thing looks toxic. He won't want it anywhere near his own office. He prefers to look good."

"So why are you going to Iowa?"

"Because right now it's still my case."

"You really think it's them?"

"The location is right. It's about where they'd be by now."

"That's just a wild-ass guess."

"Who else would call Omaha from east of Des Moines?"

"Why would they call at all? And from a traceable pay phone?"

"A secret conscience attack, maybe. By the driver, possibly. They tell me the voice was nasal. Which could be a busted nose, not the flu. And maybe a pay phone was all he could find."

"But he hung up."

Sorenson nodded. "He changed his mind. That can happen."

Goodman said, "What about Karen Delfuenso's daughter?"

"You'll have to tell her. You'd have to anyway. This is your county, and she's your people."

"When should I tell her?"

"When she wakes up."

"That's going to be tough."

"It always is."

"Those guys will be long gone by the time you get to southeastern Iowa. It's a long way away."

"I can drive faster than they did. No more road-blocks, and I don't have to worry about tickets."

"Even so."

"Whatever, it's better than staying here, doing nothing," Sorenson said.

Sorenson checked in with Dawson and Mitchell and told them what she was going to do. She didn't offer them a ride. She expected them to follow in their own car. She thought big-deal counterterrorism agents would relish the chase. But they said they were going to stay put, right there in the wilds of Nebraska. Near the point of vulnerability. They said there was nothing to worry about in Iowa. No disrespect to that fine state, they said. But it wasn't a prime terrorist target.

Sorenson said, "They could have a base camp there. Like a hideout."

Mitchell said, "Are you serious?"

"Not really."

Dawson nodded. "We'll call St. Louis. Technically southeastern Iowa is their responsibility. They'll get involved if they need to."

Sorenson didn't speak to Lester L. Lester, Jr., of the State Department. She just ignored him completely. She got a ride with Goodman back to the old pumping station, and she got back in her car, and she followed her GPS back to the Interstate, seventy miles an hour all the way, with her lights flashing and her cell phone charging.

\* \* \*

**A deceptive exit,** Reacher thought again. Dark rural roads, and places that were shut when you got there. He had been wrong about the gas station, but in and of itself that didn't make the motel any more likely to exist. Fifty-fifty was a reasonable outcome, where truth in advertising was concerned. He had seen plenty of abandoned motels on his travels. America was full of them. They were like little time capsules, forever frozen in an earlier era, sometimes plain, sometimes adventurous in their design, always testament to the long sad decline in their owners' energies and ambitions, always evidence of the way public taste had moved on. A week in a cabin near a buggy lake was no longer enough. Now it was cruises and Vegas and the Virgin Islands. Reacher had seen travel agents' windows. He knew where vacationers went. He knew where they didn't go. He saw no reason why a motel in the wilds of Iowa would have done any business in the last thirty years.

Which was a pity, because a stop for the night would have opened up a whole new world of possibilities.

King had turned left and right, left and right, endlessly south and east through the checkerboard darkness, a total of more than thirty miles since leaving the Shell station. At each turn a copy of the accommodations board had tempted them onward, the bland little arrows looking both firm and tentative, both promising and hopeless. McQueen didn't look worried. He was awake and vigilant, and he seemed confident. He trusted the signs.

And it turned out he was right to. A mile later, for

the second time that night, Reacher was proved wrong. He saw a dull glow in the mist, far ahead on the left, and he watched as it resolved itself into separate beige pearls of light, which turned out to be dim electric bulbs in bulkhead fixtures set knee-high on the walls of a long low motel building. The design of the place was standard. There was dark brown siding, and a lobby and an office at the north end, with a Coke machine and a porte cochere, and then the building continued south in a regular rhythm, window, door, window, door, for a total of twelve rooms. Each door had two white plastic lawn chairs next to it. The low-set bulkhead fixtures were to light a sidewalk that ran the length of the building. Two rooms had cars parked outside, one an old sedan, lacy with rust, and the other an immense pick-up truck painted in a motor cycle manufacturer's colors. There was a third car parked tight against the office wall, a three-door import not much bigger than a golf cart. The night clerk's ride, presumably.

Alan King slowed the Chevy and stopped and idled on the road twenty feet from the motel's entrance. He surveyed the place, carefully, end to end, and he said, "Good enough?"

Don McQueen said, "Works for me."

King didn't seek Karen Delfuenso's opinion. There was no big three-way democratic discussion. He just rolled onward and turned in on the far side of the porte cochere and came to a stop under it, facing north, with the rooms behind him. Inconvenient, in that he would have to back up or turn around after checking in, but inevitable, in that America drives on the right and takes circles counterclockwise.

There was a night-light burning in the lobby. Reacher could see a reception counter, and a closed door behind it that no doubt led to an office. Probably the night guy was in there, asleep in a chair. There was a vase of flowers on the counter, probably fake.

Alan King said, "Mr. Reacher, would you go make the inquiry about rooms?"

Reacher said, "Obviously there are rooms. There are twelve doors and two cars."

"Then would you kindly check us in?"

Reacher said, "I'm not the best guy to do that."

"Why not?"

Reacher thought: *Because I don't want to get out of the car. Not now. Because I no longer control the car key.*

He said, "Because I don't have a credit card."

"Really?"

"Or ID. Apart from an old passport, that is. But it's been expired for years, and some people don't like that."

"You must have a driver's license, surely."

"I don't."

"But you were just driving."

"Don't tell the cops."

"Unlicensed driving is a felony."

"Probably just a misdemeanor."

"Have you ever had a license?"

"Not a civilian license, no."

"Have you ever even passed a test?"

"I guess so. Probably. In the army, possibly."

"You don't remember?"

"I remember learning. I don't remember a test, as such."

McQueen said, "I'll come with you. I have a credit card."

Which worked for Reacher. He didn't want to be out of the car alone, but equally he didn't want either King or McQueen to select the rooms alone. He wanted some influence over who went where. He opened his door. McQueen opened his door. They got out together, McQueen ten feet from the lobby, Reacher on the far side of the car. McQueen waited. Reacher looped around the trunk. Reacher paused, gestured, right-handed, open palm: *Go ahead. After you.* A precaution, not politeness. He didn't want to walk in front of a man with a gun. Not that he thought there was a serious danger of getting shot. Not then and there. Not with a night clerk and at least two motel guests within earshot.

McQueen went ahead down a decorative path made of broken paving stones jigsawed together. Reacher followed. McQueen pulled the lobby door. Reacher stepped up and held it and gestured again: *After you.*

McQueen went in. Reacher followed. The lobby had a vinyl floor and four gaudy wicker armchairs grouped around a low table. There was a higher table with push-top coffee flasks and stacks of paper cups. There was a rack on the wall with compartments for small folded brochures describing local tourist attractions. It was mostly empty.

The reception counter butted up against the side wall on the right. It ended six feet short of the wall on

the left, near the table with the coffee. There was low
TV sound behind the office door, and a rim of soft
light all around it. McQueen bellied up to the counter
on the right, and Reacher came to a stop alongside
him, on the left.

"Hello?" McQueen called.

No response.

McQueen tapped his knuckles on the counter.

"Hello?" he called again.

No response.

"Service industries," McQueen said, quietly. "Can't
beat them."

He knocked on the counter again, a little louder.

"Hello?" he said, also a little louder.

No response.

He glanced left at Reacher and said, "You better go
knock on his door."

Which would put Reacher in front of the gun for
the first time, but there was no natural way to refuse.
The route around to the door was to the left, and
Reacher was on the left. Simple as that. Choreogra-
phy. Geometry. Inevitable.

So Reacher looped around, between the end of the
counter and the table with the coffee, and he stepped
into the narrow well behind the counter. He glanced
back out through the lobby window. The Chevy was
still there, under the porte cochere. It hadn't moved. It
was idling patiently, just waiting, with white exhaust
pooling at the rear.

But McQueen had left his car door open.

Which was the first warning bell.

The second was the sound of feet on vinyl.

A fast one-two shuffle.

Exactly like the sound of a man stepping back and turning sideways.

The third warning bell was a fast composite rustle of skin and cotton and wool and metal.

Exactly like the sound of something heavy coming out of a pocket.

Reacher turned back and faced McQueen and saw nothing beyond the muzzle of a small stainless steel handgun pointing at the center of his face.

# Chapter 29

The gun was a Smith & Wesson 2213. The smallest automatic in Smith & Wesson's extensive range. Three-inch barrel, .22 Long Rifle rimfires, eight in the magazine. Dainty, but a serious weapon. McQueen had been very fast with it. Phenomenally fast. Like a magician. Like a conjuror. First it wasn't there, and then it was.

Just like that.

Reacher stood very still.

The gun was maybe eight feet away. Behind it McQueen's long right arm was locked straight and raised slightly above the horizontal. He was standing sideways on. His head was turned. One eye was closed.

His finger was white on the trigger.

Not good.

The .22 Long Rifle was one of the world's oldest rounds, and by far the most common. Annual production every year since 1887 had exceeded two billion units. For a reason. It was cheap, it was quiet, and its recoil was gentle. And it was effective. Out of a rifle it was good against rats and squirrels at four hundred and fifty feet, and against dogs and foxes at two-fifty, and against full-grown coyotes at one-fifty.

Against a human head at eight feet it would be devastating.

Even out of a short-barreled handgun.

Not good.

Not good at all.

Reacher couldn't see the Chevy anymore. McQueen was in the way. Which was not such a bad thing. At least Delfuenso would not have to watch it happen.

Which was a mercy.

But then: look on the bright side of life.

That was Reacher's innate credo.

As in: there were four basic ways of missing with a short-barreled handgun. Even at eight feet, even against a head-sized target. They were: missing high, missing low, missing left, and missing right.

Missing high was always the most likely.

All guns kick upward as they fire. Action, reaction, a basic law of physics. Inevitably new shooters with machine guns stitched a vertical line that rose forever. A classic fault. Ninety percent of training was about holding the muzzle down. Suppressors helped, because of the extra weight.

There was no reason to believe McQueen was a new shooter.

But if he was going to miss, he was going to miss high.

Laws of physics.

Four things happened at once: Reacher let out a

sudden loud inarticulate bellow, and McQueen startled and rocked back a step, and Reacher dropped vertically toward the floor, and McQueen pulled the trigger.

And missed.

Missed high, partly because Reacher's head was no longer where it had been before. Gravity had done its work. Reacher heard the roar of the shot, quieter than some, but still deafening in a closed room, and simultaneously he heard the wallboard explode above and behind his head, and then he hit the floor, knees first, then his hip, then his side, sprawling, down low behind the counter, out of sight. He had no plan. At that point he was in a strict one-step-at-a-time mode. Stay alive, and see what the next split second brings. As he fell he was aware of a vague intention to hurl the whole counter up and out, straight at McQueen, if it wasn't bolted to the floor, or else roll backward through the door into the inner office, where there had to be a window, which would be closed against the weather, but he could plunge through it elbows first, because cuts and bruises were better than a bullet in the head.

Fight or flight.

But neither thing was necessary.

The blast of the shot peaked and started to die and Reacher heard the scrape and scrabble of feet on vinyl and he grabbed the end of the counter low down near the floor and jerked himself overhand to his right, one powerful instantaneous stroke, and he got his head out in the gap, and he saw McQueen more or less falling out through the lobby door, and then sprinting back along the neat little path, and hurling himself back into the car, and the car howling away with spinning wheels and blue tire smoke. Reacher scrambled up to his knees and got there in time to see McQueen slam his door and the car rock through a wild 180 turn, back onto the road, facing south again, and then it accelerated away, hard, nose high, tail low, wheels spinning and scrabbling for grip and pouring smoke. The last thing Reacher saw through the haze was a brief flash of white in the Chevy's rear window, which was Karen Delfuenso's pale face, turning back in horror, her mouth wide open.

Reacher stayed on his knees. Silence came back. White gypsum powder drifted down on him, slowly, weightless, like talc, on his shoulders, in his hair. Tire smoke hung in the night air under the porte cochere, and it rolled slowly forward in a ghostly dissipating cloud, which followed the trajectory of the 180 turn, like a description, like an explanation, like proof, and then it disappeared completely, like it had never been there at all.

Then the office door opened a crack and a short fat man stuck his head out and looked around and said, "Just so you know, I already called the cops on you."

**Julia Sorenson heard** her phone ping over the noise of her speeding car and she opened her e-mail and found an audio attachment from the emergency operator in D.C. Her phone cradle was hooked up to her car's stereo system, which was the base Ford option and therefore nothing fancy, but it was plenty loud and clear. She turned the volume up and hit *Play* and heard a short fifteen-second recording, of two voices on the telephone, one in the Hoover Building and the other allegedly in Iowa.

*This is the FBI. What is the nature of your emergency?*

*I have information, probably for your field office in Omaha, Nebraska.*

*What is the nature of your information?*

*Just connect me, now.*

*Sir, what is your name?*

Then there was a short pause, just a beat really, and then: *Connect me now or you'll lose your job.*

Then there was another short pause, then dead air, then a new dial tone.

Then nothing.

She played it again, and listened exclusively to the caller, not the operator.

*I have information, probably for your field office in Omaha, Nebraska.*

*Just connect me, now.*

*Connect me now or you'll lose your job.*

Six seconds. Twenty-three words, spoken with urgency but also with a certain weird patience. A very nasal intonation, full of breath sounds, entirely consistent with a badly broken nose, the *M* sounds shading toward *B* sounds, *information* more like *inforbation,* and *Omaha* more like *Obaha.*

She played it again, zeroing in.

*Probably for your field office in Omaha, Nebraska. Or you'll lose your job.*

Clearly the strange urgent-but-patient blend meant

the guy was accustomed to making important operational calls, or issuing instructions of some kind, and that he knew even alert and intelligent listeners needed a chance to get from zero to sixty. But he wasn't just a businessman. Even a high-level guy used to trading millions on the phone would get a little more freaked about calling an FBI emergency line in the middle of the night. This guy sounded like it was routine to him. The *your* in *your field office* meant he wasn't actually FBI himself, at least not currently, but he seemed to know how things worked, and in a sense the *your* sounded like he considered himself a peer, or a part of the same world. *Your field office, my field office.*

The *probably* was intriguing. It was measured, and considered, and intelligent. As if the guy was in reality almost a hundred percent certain he wanted Omaha, but didn't want to derail the process with an initial assumption that could conceivably prove faulty later on. Or as if he wanted to recruit the emergency operator as a kind of partner, to let the operator own some component of the ultimate decision, to oil the wheels, to speed things along.

Her gut feeling told her again: this was a guy accustomed to making important operational calls. He had very sound bureaucratic instincts.

As in: *Or you'll lose your job.* Preceded by the very short pause for thought. This was a guy who knew exactly what to say. Who had gone through duty officers before. Who had maybe even *been* a duty officer once upon a time.

So what was he doing driving a car full of two murderers and a hostage?

And why did he make the call and then hang up prematurely?

She got no further with those questions, because right then her phone rang with a live call, the plain electronic tone blasting loud and deep and sonorous through dashboard speakers and door speakers and a subwoofer under the rear parcel shelf. She dropped the volume a notch and touched *Accept*. It was her duty officer on the line, at her field office in Omaha. The guy who hadn't picked up in time.

He said, "I have the SAC holding for you."

Sorenson slowed down to eighty. She checked the road ahead and checked her mirrors. She said, "Put him on."

There was a static click, loud and emphatic through the sound system. Then a voice said, "Sorenson?"

Sorenson said, "Yes, sir."

Her Special Agent-in-Charge. Her supervisor. Her boss. A man called Perry, fifty-four years old, a Bureau lifer, ambitious, first name Anthony, called Tony to his face, called Stony behind his back, because of the mineral lump where his heart should have been.

He said, "I called the gas station in Iowa."

"*You* did, sir?"

"I'm awake. I might as well do something useful."

"And?"

"They don't have video."

"But?"

"The night clerk seems like a smart enough kid. He came through with a pretty coherent story."

"Which was?"

"The car was a dark blue Chevy Impala. He didn't

get the plate. Four people in it, three men and a woman. Initially one man and the woman stayed in the car. A second man pumped the gas. First point of interest, he used a credit card we just found out is phony."

"Was it related to the card used at the Denver airport?"

"We don't think so. Different source, almost certainly. The second point of interest is the car took only three-point-something gallons, which the kid behind the register thought was strange. The average sale at that location is closer to eleven gallons, unless someone's filling a can for a lawn mower."

"So they either part-filled the car, which might mean they're close to home, or they topped it off, which means they'd stopped before."

"We're checking if the same card has been used anywhere else tonight. No results yet. But anyway, while the gas business was happening the third man entered the store alone and waited until the door closed and then asked for the pay phone."

"This was the driver, sir?"

"Yes. The kid described him as gigantic, with a busted nose, all raw and crusted with blood. The kid admits at first he was a little scared. The guy looked like something out of a slasher movie. Like a wild man. His clothes were dirty and his hair was a mess. But he spoke normally and ultimately he seemed pleasant enough. So the kid pointed him to the phone, which is out of sight near the restrooms. So the kid has no direct knowledge of whether the guy actually used the phone or not. Then the guy who had stayed in the car came in to use the toilet. The slasher movie guy came out and got coffee all around and then the other guy came out and they left together. The car drove away in an orderly fashion and headed south."

"Atmosphere? Anything squirrelly?"

"Nothing to report. It was the middle of the night, so they all looked a little tired and vague, but there were no bad words, no apparent tension, and no real hurry either, as far as I understand it."

"Did you listen to the emergency line recording, sir?"

"Yes, I was copied on it, obviously."

"Did anything stand out for you?"

"The word *probably*. It makes no sense. If he's one of them he knows where the crime was committed. In which case he would have said he had information for Omaha, Nebraska, period."

"You think he's not one of them?"

"I think he's low-level muscle. He drives, and he fetches coffee. He doesn't know the details."

*Bullshit, Stony,* Sorenson thought. *He doesn't sound low-level to me. He sounds smarter than you, for instance.*

She said, "Thank you, sir. That's very useful."

"Keep in touch," the SAC said, and clicked off.

Sorenson drove on for a mile, thinking, and then she eased back up to ninety miles an hour and went back to e-mail. She turned the sound system's volume up high and played the recording one more time.

*Just connect me, now.*

The big guy's first sentence had been reasonable, patient, and explanatory. *I have information, probably for your field office in Omaha, Nebraska.* A scene-setter. A preamble. But it hadn't gotten the desired results. The emergency operator hadn't jumped right to it. So the big guy had gotten impatient. *Just connect me, now.* Urgent, breathy, frustrated. Some slight wonder and incomprehension in his voice. Some slight emphasis on the last word. *Now.* A little desperate. As if to say: *I have completed the first step of the ritual dance, and I really, really don't have time for the second, and I really, really can't understand why you don't understand that.*

Not a change of heart. The big guy had hung up because he was out of time. Because the other guy had come in to use the bathroom.

The big guy was one of them. But he was a traitor.

# Chapter 30

Reacher put his hands flat on the floor and pushed himself up off his knees. He turned and looked at the fat man in the office doorway and said, "I need to borrow your car."

The fat man stared at Reacher's face.

He said, "What?"

"Your car. Right now."

"No way." The guy was about thirty, prematurely losing his hair, about five feet four high, and about five feet three wide. He was wearing a white shirt and a red sleeveless V-necked sweater. He said, "I told you, I already called the cops. They're on their way. So don't try anything stupid."

Reacher said, "How long will it take for the cops to arrive?"

"Two minutes, max. They're already rolling."

"From where?"

The guy didn't answer.

Reacher said, "County?"

The guy said, "At night we rely on the State Police."

"They were all on roadblock duty. On the Interstate. A long way west of here. Short notice. No time to organize replacements. I'd say they're two hours away, minimum. Not two minutes, maximum. If they come at all, that is. No one died here."

"A shot was fired."

"And that's a bad thing, right?"

"Of course it is."

"So they're the bad guys. Because they fired the shot. And they fired it at me. Which makes me the good guy."

"Or the even worse guy."

"Whichever," Reacher said. "If I'm the good guy you'll help me because you're on my side. If I'm the even worse guy you'll help me because you're scared of me. But either way you'll help me. So you might as well just cut to the chase and give me your keys."

"Won't do you any good."

"Why not?"

"Because I protect myself."

"Against what?"

"Against people like you."

"How?"

"No gas in my car."

"There has to be gas in your car. You're thirty miles from the gas station."

"There's a gallon or so. Good for about forty miles. And forty miles is nothing out here."

"Are you serious?"

"It's the best anti-theft protection there is. Better

than an alarm, better than a tracker, better than a fancy lock."

"You're pretty smart," Reacher said. "Or completely nuts. One or the other. What about your guests tonight? Who are they? Maybe I could borrow that pick-up truck."

The fat man just said, "Oh, man, please."

But Reacher didn't push it. He just stood there, defeated. Because of numbers. Specifically four, and three, and two. Almost four minutes had passed. King and McQueen were about to hit the next road junction. It would be a T junction, offering two choices, or a crossroads, offering three. Iowa. The checkerboard. The agricultural matrix. To be more than a field's-length behind a fleeing fugitive meant facing endlessly escalating odds of taking the wrong turn. So far Reacher had seen T junctions and crossroads in about a two-to-three ratio, spaced an average of about eight miles apart. The fat man's gallon of gas might last about sixty minutes. And at the end of that hour the odds of being on the right track would have stacked up to around six-fifty to one against.

Hopeless.

Time, and geometry.

**Sorenson's e-mail pinged** again and she found an audio file from the Iowa 911 service. It was the call that had been patched through to the FBI emergency operator.

*What is your current location?*
*Give me the FBI.*

*Sir, what is your current location?*
*Don't waste time.*
*Do you need fire, police, or ambulance?*
*I need the FBI.*
*Sir, this is the 911 emergency service.*
*And since about September the twelfth 2001 you've had a direct button for the FBI.*
*How did you know that?*
*Just a lucky guess. Hit the button, and hit it now.*

The same nasal voice. The same measured urgency. No panic, but not much patience, either. The same insight. As a matter of fact 911 dispatchers had not gotten an FBI button on September twelfth 2001. The installations had started a week or so later. But in principle the guy was right. He was clued in.

But how?

She played the file again, and got as far as *I need the FBI* when her ring tone cut in over it. Another live call. The plain electronic tone, loud and thrilling through the speakers. It was her duty officer again, at his desk in Omaha. He said, "I don't know if it means anything, but the Iowa State Police are saying they just got a 911 call about a gunshot fired in a motel lobby, about thirty-some miles south and east of that gas station."

**The fat man** hovered nervously behind the reception counter and Reacher took a look at the bullet hole in his wall. It was directly above the office door, maybe nine inches left of center, close to the ceiling, maybe an inch and a half below the crown molding. It looked like the round had hit near a stud or a screw. The impact had blasted off a large shallow flake of plaster, about the size of a teacup saucer, and the flake had left a corresponding crater. The center of the crater was drilled with the .22 hole, neat and precise, a little smaller than a pencil.

Reacher backed off and stood where McQueen had stood. He turned sideways. He bent his knees and lowered himself five inches, to make himself McQueen's height. He raised his arm and straightened it and pointed his index finger at the hole.

He closed one eye.

He shook his head.

It had been a bad miss, in his opinion. Because it would have missed even if he hadn't fallen down on the floor. It would have missed even if he had stretched up high on tiptoes. It would have missed even if he had jumped up in the air. It might have grazed a seven-five NBA star, but at six-five Reacher would have been OK under any circumstances.

*If he was going to miss, he was going to miss high.*

Civilian marksmanship was appalling, for a population obsessed with guns.

Reacher straightened up again and turned back to the fat man and said, "I need to use your phone."

# Chapter 31

Julia Sorenson drove some fast minutes uninterrupted, and then her phone rang again, loud over the speakers. Her duty officer, in Omaha. He said, "It's your lucky night. I think."

"How so?"

"The same guy is on the line again."

"The nasal guy?"

"Right now, live and in person."

"Where is he?"

"On the same phone that just called in the 911 in Iowa."

"The motel lobby thing?"

"You got it."

"How far out are the Iowa cops?"

"A long way. The roadblocks screwed them up."

"OK, put the guy on."

"You sure? Stony will want this one."

"My case," Sorenson said. "Put the guy on. I'll deal with Stony later."

She heard clicks and hiss and then a new acoustic. A room, not large. Hard surfaces. Probably an office. Laminate desks, metal cabinets. She heard the nasal voice. It said, "Hello?"

She said, "This is FBI Special Agent Julia Sorenson. What is your name, sir?"

Reacher put an elbow on the fat man's laminate desk and trapped the receiver against his shoulder. He said, "I'm not going to tell you my name. Not yet, anyway. We need to talk first."

The woman named Sorenson said, "About what?"

She was from Minnesota, Reacher thought. Originally. She sounded a little Scandinavian, like her name. And she seemed businesslike. She didn't waste words. She was direct and to the point. He said, "I need to understand my personal situation."

"Is Karen Delfuenso still alive?"

"As far as I know."

"Then it's her personal situation we should be considering."

"I am considering it," Reacher said. "That's my point. Are you going to slow me down or help me out?"

"With what?"

"Finding her."

"You're no longer with her?"

"No. They shot at me and drove off. Delfuenso is still in the car."

"Who are you?"

"I'm not going to tell you my name."

"No, I mean I need to understand your involvement."

"I have no involvement."

"You were seen driving the car."

"They asked me to."

"So you're their driver?"

"I never saw them before."

"What does that mean? You were what, a random stranger? A passerby? And they just stopped and asked you to drive their car?"

"I was hitching rides. They picked me up."

"Where?"

"In Nebraska."

"And they asked you to drive the car? Is that normal?"

"Not in my experience."

No response from Sorenson.

Reacher said, "I think they were expecting roadblocks and they wanted cover. I think they were anticipating a three-person APB, so they wanted four people in the car. I think they wanted someone else at the wheel, not one of them. Someone the cops would see first. My busted nose was a bonus. I bet that was ninety percent of the description you got. A guy with his face smashed in."

"A gorilla."

"What?"

"A gorilla with its face smashed in. Not very nice, I know."

"Not very nice to the gorilla," Reacher said. "But whatever, I was useful to them. But then they came off the Interstate. So they didn't need me anymore."

"So they shot you? Are you hurt?"

"I said they shot at me. They missed."

"Do you know where they're going?"

"No idea."

"Then how can you find Delfuenso?"

"I'll think of something."

"If they don't need you anymore, they don't need her anymore, either. Just her car."

"So we better be quick."

"I'm still an hour away."

"Are the troopers coming?"

"They're all behind me."

Reacher said, "I've lost them anyway. The roads out here are impossible. I'm going to have to come at this from a different direction."

"What were you doing in Nebraska?"

"None of your business."

"Is that where you broke your nose?"

"I don't remember."

"The sergeant at the roadblock said you admitted you'd been fighting."

"Not really. I said he should see the other guy. That was all. It was a conventional pleasantry."

"He told us you said the other guy was in a state other than Iowa."

"I can't comment on what he told you. I wasn't there for that conversation."

"Was the other guy in Nebraska?"

"You're wasting time."

"I'm not. I'm driving as fast as I can. What else can I do at the moment?"

"Drive faster still."

Sorenson asked, "Where were you going?"

Reacher said, "When?"

"When they picked you up."

"Virginia."

"Why?"

"None of your business."

"What's in Virginia?"

"Many things. It's an important state. Twelfth largest in the Union in terms of population. Thirteenth, in terms of GDP. You could look it up."

"You're not convincing me. You're not helping your personal situation."

"Why am I calling you?"

"Maybe you want a deal."

"I don't. I don't need a deal. I need to help Delfuenso if I can, and then I need to go to Virginia."

"Why would you need to help Delfuenso?"

"Why wouldn't I? I'm a human being."

No answer from Sorenson.

Reacher asked, "What did those guys do, anyway?"

"I think I won't discuss that with you. Not yet."

"I know they jacked Delfuenso's car. I know they had blood on their clothes."

"How do you know that? They bought shirts and changed."

"Delfuenso told me."

"You talked?"

"She blinked it out. In secret. A simple letter code."

"Smart woman. Brave woman, too."

"I know," Reacher said. "She warned me about the guns. I let her down."

"Evidently."

"You didn't do so great either, with the two-man APB."

"One would think a BOLO for two men would logically include more than two. By a simple inference."

"Troopers don't infer things. They don't take the initiative. Nine times out of ten it gets them in trouble."

Sorenson asked, "How is Delfuenso doing?"

Reacher said, "She's not exactly having the time of her life."

"She has a kid back home."

"I know," Reacher said. "She told me."

Sorenson asked, "Do you have access to a vehicle?"

Reacher said, "Not really. There are a couple here I might be able to borrow, but it's pointless anyway. Those guys could be anywhere by now."

"What's your name?"

"Not yet."

"OK, stay right where you are. I'll see you when I get there."

"You might," Reacher said. "Or you might not."


**Drive faster still,** the nasal guy had said, and Sorenson tried very hard to. She eased up to nearly a hundred miles an hour, which was outside her personal comfort zone. But the road was straight and wide and empty. *I never saw them before,* he had said. *I was hitching rides.* Did she believe him? Maybe. Or maybe not. It was a very neat and comprehensive explanation of the facts. Therefore perhaps suspicious in itself. Because real life was neither neat nor comprehensive. Not usually. And who hitchhiked anymore? Especially in the wintertime? The guy sounded educated. And not noticeably young. Not a normal hitchhiking demographic. Statistics. The Bureau found them to be a useful guide.

And: *They shot at me.* But: *They missed.* Either extreme good fortune, or extremely good playacting. Getting shot at by the indisputably guilty helped build credibility. Perhaps all concerned had figured that out well ahead of time.

Then her low-fuel warning pinged at her and a little lamp lit up yellow. Dumb. Not a great time to run out of gas. Not a great place, either. Iowa was a lonely state. Exits were many miles apart. Each one was an event in its own right. She took the next she saw, a no-name turn a little east of Des Moines. She could see gas station lights ahead, blue and white in the mist. The ramp led to a two-lane county road, and she saw the gas station itself a hundred feet away to the south. It was a big place, set up for trucks as well as cars. The car part had six pumps. There was a small pay hut, and a bathroom block standing alone on the edge of the lot. Across the street was a long barn-shaped building with *Food And Drink All Day All Night* painted in white on the slope of its roof.

She pumped the gas and heard the nasal voice in her head again: *I've lost them anyway. The roads out here are impossible. I'm going to have to come at this from a different direction.* Twenty-two words. Resignation, frustration, and then a new resolution. The first-person singular, used twice. The instinctive assumption of individual personal responsibility for the fate of another. And determination. And knowledge, too. She had said: *One would think a BOLO for two men would logically include more than two.* A BOLO. A be-on-the-lookout. He hadn't needed to ask what it meant. He already knew. Then he had said: *Troopers don't infer things. They don't take the initiative. Nine times out of ten it gets them in trouble.* Which was a perceptive comment. As was: *I think they were expecting roadblocks and they wanted cover.* Which matched her own thinking exactly.

Resolute, responsible, determined, knowledgeable, and perceptive.

Driving two murderers in a stolen car.

With a hostage.

*Why am I calling you?*

Who the hell was this guy?

# Chapter 32

Reacher spilled brochures out of the tourist-attraction rack in the lobby until he found one with something approximating a map. It was not an outstanding example of the cartographer's art. But it was the best the place had to offer. It was basically a hand-drawn rectangle with Kansas City at the bottom left, and St. Louis at the bottom right, and Des Moines at the top left, and Cedar Rapids at the top right. In between those four anchoring cities was a lot of white space, with a bunch of little icons describing things Reacher wasn't interested in.

He was interested in the white space itself, particularly the upper half of it. The Iowa half. Thirtieth out of fifty in population, twenty-sixth out of fifty in land area, but Iowa had a quarter of America's best-grade topsoil all to itself, and therefore it was at the head of the list when it came to corn and soybeans and hogs and cattle. Which meant spare, sparse habitation, and miles between neighbors, and lonely isolated buildings of uncertain purpose, and a kind of live-and-let-live lack of curiosity about who was doing what, and where and when and how and why they were doing it at all.

The two worst places to search were densely populated cities, and wide open countryside. Reacher had succeeded in those environments many times, but he had failed there too. Also many times.

Behind him the fat man said, "Who's going to pay for the hole in my wall?"

Reacher said, "Not me."

"Well, someone will have to."

"What are you, a socialist? Pay for it yourself. Or fix it yourself. It isn't brain surgery. Two minutes and a tub of spackle will take care of it."

"It's not right that a person should just burst in here and do a thing like that."

Reacher said, "I'm busy."

"Doing what?"

"I'm thinking."

"You're looking at a blank sheet of paper."

"You got a better map?"

"It wasn't right."

"Shit happens. Get over it."

"That bullet could have come through the wall and hit me."

"Are you kidding? Look where it is."

"But whoever fired it didn't know I was short. Not in advance. How could they? It was completely reckless. It was totally irresponsible."

"You think?"

"I could have been hurt."

"But you weren't. So don't worry about it."

"I could have been killed."

"Look where it is," Reacher said again. "It would have missed if you were standing on your own shoulders."

Then the phone rang in the office and the guy ducked back in to answer it. He came straight back out and said, "It's the FBI, for the man with the broken nose. That would be you, I suppose."

Reacher said, "Pretty soon it could be either one of us, if you don't stop yapping at me."

He took the map with him to the desk and picked up the receiver. It was the Scandinavian woman again. Originally from Minnesota. Julia Sorenson. She said, "You're still there."

"Evidently," Reacher said.

"Why?"

"I told you why. The roads here are like graph paper. Pointless trying to follow anyone more than two minutes ahead."

"Does it matter exactly which route they take? They're heading basically south. We should assume they have a destination in mind. They're not going to stay in Iowa."

Reacher said, "I don't agree."

"Why not?"

"Daylight is coming. Town and county cops will be back on duty by seven or eight in the morning. And those guys must be assuming their plate number is everywhere by now. Plus descriptions, of them and the car. They won't risk much more. They can't. So they'll hole up before dawn. Somewhere right here in Iowa."

"They could get into Missouri before the break of day."

"But they won't. They'll assume the Missouri troopers will be waiting right on the line. Troopers like to do that. Like a welcome and a warning. With the new day's BOLOs taped right on their dashboards."

"They can't stay in Iowa either," Sorenson said. "They can't really stay anywhere. If they assume their plate number is everywhere, they'll assume we're calling motel keepers too."

"They won't be using a motel. I think they have a specific place to go. A place of their own. Because their choice of exit off the Interstate was not random. I wouldn't have taken it. No sane person would have taken it. It was just a no-name back road. But they knew it well. They knew where they were going. They knew the gas station was there, and they knew this motel was here, too. No way of knowing either thing unless they've been here before."

"You could be right."

"Equally I could be wrong."

"Which is it?"

"I don't know."

"Will they hole up all day?"

"I would."

"That's risky. They'd be sitting ducks."

"Sitting ducks, yes. But not really risky. Ninety minutes after peeling out of here they'll be somewhere inside an empty five-thousand-square-mile box. You planning to go door-to-door, hoping for the best?"

"How would you do it?"

"Have you made a decision about my personal situation?"

"Not yet."

"Then you may never know how I would do it."

"Who are you?"

"Just a guy," Reacher said.

"What kind of guy?"

"Why did you call me back?"

"To try and find out what kind of guy you are."

"And what's your conclusion so far?"

"I don't know."

"I'm an innocent passerby. That's all. That's the kind of guy I am."

"Everyone always says they're innocent."

"And sometimes they're telling the truth."

"Stay right there," Sorenson said. "I'll be with you in less than an hour."

**Sorenson drove on,** somewhere between ninety and a hundred, one eye on the road ahead, the other on her GPS map. She was getting close to the no-name turn. And she could see the nasal guy's point. *No sane person would have taken it.* The landscape ahead looked infinitely dark and infinitely empty. No lights of any kind, no features, no items of interest.

*They knew where they were going.*

Then her phone rang yet again. It was Perry, her SAC. Stony, her boss. He said, "I found out a little more about the victim."

"That's good," Sorenson said. "The guy the State Department sent out wouldn't say a word."

"Mr. Lester? I went over his head. Not that State had much to conceal. Turns out the victim was a trade attaché. A salesman, basically. A dealmaker. That's all, really. His job was to oil the wheels for American exporters."

"Where did he serve?"

"I wasn't told. But they let slip he was an Arabic speaker. Draw your own conclusions."

"Why was he in Nebraska?"

"No one knows."

"Business or pleasure?"

"Not business, as far as I can tell. He was on leave between postings."

"You know that two counterterrorism guys came up from Kansas City?"

"Yes, I heard that. Might mean something. Might not. Those guys are always looking for reasons to freak out. They have a big budget to justify."

Sorenson said nothing.

Perry said, "We have a budget to justify too. I hear you made contact with the driver."

Sorenson said, "He claims he was a hitchhiker. He claims they dumped him at gunpoint. I'll be meeting with him inside an hour."

"Good. Arrest him on sight. Homicide, kidnapping, grand theft auto, breaking the speed limit, anything else you can think of. Bring him back here immediately, in handcuffs."

# Chapter 33

Sheriff Victor Goodman did the obvious, cautious thing, which was to drive the route between the old pumping station and the farm where the eyewitness lived, which was eleven miles to the north and west of town. On the way out there he drove slowly and paid careful attention to the right-hand shoulder of the road. There was ice here and there. Overall the land was pretty flat, but at a detailed level there were humps and bumps and bad cambers and ragged edges. According to a deputy who knew the guy, the eyewitness drove a well-used Ford Ranger pick-up truck. It was too old for ABS, and assuming it was unloaded it would be light and skittery at the back end. Skids and slides were possible, even likely, because it was late and the guy was probably hurrying. And a skid or a slide at speed could put the guy fifty feet into a field, easily, and maybe even tip him over, if the tires caught a rut or a furrow. So Goodman used the beam on his windshield pillar, near and far, back and forth, slowing to a walk on the curves, making sure.

He found nothing.

The house the guy lived in was a modest affair. Eighty years previously it might have anchored an independent one-man fifty-acre spread. Now it was a leftover, after two or three rounds of farm consolidations, these days either rented to or provided for a laborer. It had a sagging ridgeline and milky glass in the windows. It was dark and still. Goodman got out of his cruiser and pounded on the door and yelled and hollered.

Then he waited, and three minutes later a disheveled woman came to the door, in night clothes. The common-law wife. No, the guy was not home yet. No, he didn't make a habit of staying out all night. Yes, he always called if he was going to be late. No, she had no idea where he was.

So Goodman got back in his car and drove the same road back to the pumping station, slowly and carefully, using his pillar spot all the way, this time paying close attention to the other shoulder, and watching the first fifty feet of brittle stubble beyond it.

He saw nothing.

So then he drove other routes, in descending order of likelihood. His county was not geographically complicated. The central crossroads created four quadrants, northwest, northeast, southeast, and southwest, each one of them to some varying extent filled in with random ribbons of development. It was conceivable the guy had chosen to thread his way home through

an arbitrary and indirect route. Conceivable, but unlikely. Gas was expensive and there was no reason to
add unnecessary miles. There was no reason to think
the guy had a second lady friend willing to receive a
late-night visit. But Goodman was a thorough man, so
he checked.

But he found no old Ford Ranger pick-up trucks
parked anywhere in the northwestern quadrant. Or in
the northeastern quadrant. Or in the southwestern.

The southeastern quadrant was the least likely of
all. To get there the guy would have had to turn his
back on home, and why would he do that well after
midnight? And the southeastern quadrant was mostly
commercial, anyway. The two-lane county road leading south was lined on both sides by small strip malls.
The road leading east was the same. There were seed
merchants and dry goods stores and groceries and
gun shops and pawn shops. There was a bank. There
was a pharmacy, and a John Deere dealership. All of
those establishments closed at five o'clock each afternoon. There was angled street parking in front of the
stores, uniformly unoccupied at night, and larger lots
behind, mostly empty, and old barns used for storage,
all locked up tight.

Sheriff Goodman checked them all anyway. He
was a thorough man. He drove slowly south, looking
down the alleys between the buildings, then looping
back north through the back lots on the right, then
going south again and paying attention to the other
side of the road, before coming north again through
the back lots on the left.

He found nothing. He repeated the same procedure on the road leading east, all the way out into open country and then back again, checking both sides, checking the alleys, checking the storefronts, checking the rear lots.

And there it was.

An old Ford Ranger pick-up truck, parked neatly behind Gus Bantry's hardware store.


**Reacher folded the** inadequate map and put it in his back pocket. He checked the view out the office window. Still dark. But dawn was coming. He looked at the fat man and said, "You want to rent me a room?"

The fat man didn't answer.

Reacher said, "I could give you money and you could give me a key. You could call it running a business."

The guy responded by stepping out to the well behind the counter and unpinning a notice from the wall. It was a sheet of paper laminated in plastic, with a cursive script and pale inkjet printing spelling out a simple sentence: *Management reserves the right to refuse service.* The plastic was lightly dusted with gypsum powder, from the bullet hole.

Reacher said, "I'm the good guy here. You heard me on the phone with the federal authorities. It was an amicable conversation."

The guy said, "I can't afford any more trouble."

"You've had all the trouble you're likely to get tonight. From here on in it's going to be all about an investigation. You could have ten agents here for a week. Or more than ten, or more than a week. How does that compare to your usual winter occupancy?"

The guy paused.

Reacher said, "OK, we'll all go somewhere else."

The guy said, "Forty dollars."

"Twenty."

"Thirty."

"Don't push it. These guys have an office of budgetary responsibility. They see something they don't like, they'll call the IRS, just for fun."

"Twenty-five dollars."

"Deal," Reacher said. He dug in his other back pocket and came out with a wad of crumpled bills. He counted out twenty five bucks, a ten and two fives and five singles.

The fat man said, "A week in advance."

"Don't push it," Reacher said again.

"OK, two nights."

Reacher added a twenty and another five. He said, "I'll take a room in the middle of the row. No neighbors either side."

"Why?"

"Because I'm a solitary soul."

The fat man trawled through a drawer and came out with a brass key on a leather fob, which had the number 5 printed in faded gilt on one side, and some mailing instructions on the other. He said, "You have to sign the register."

"Why?"

"Iowa law."

Reacher put himself down as Bill Skowron, who had hit .375 for the Yankees in the World Series just weeks before Reacher was born. The fat man handed over the key and Reacher headed for his room.

**Sheriff Goodman called** Julia Sorenson on her cell. He told her he had found the eyewitness's truck.

Sorenson asked, "Any signs of a disturbance?"

Goodman said, "No, it was just parked, like normal. Behind a hardware store, real neat and tidy, just like the Mazda behind the cocktail lounge."

"Locked?"

"Yes, which is a little unusual here, to be honest. People don't normally lock their cars. Especially not twenty-year-old beaters."

"No sign of the guy himself?"

"Nothing. Like he just vanished."

"Is there a bar nearby, or a rooming house?"

"Nothing. It's a strip mall."

"I'll get some lab people to go take a look."

"It's nearly dawn."

"All the better," Sorenson said. "Daylight always helps."

"No, I mean Karen Delfuenso's kid will be waking up soon. Any news?"

"The driver called me again. They dumped him. Delfuenso was still alive, the last he saw of her."

"How long ago was that?"

"Long enough for the situation to have changed, I'm afraid."

"So I'm going to have to tell the kid."

"Just the facts. Don't say anything more until we know for sure. And call her school principal. The kid won't be fit to go today. And maybe you should keep the neighbor's kid home too, for company. Does the neighbor work days?"

"I'm pretty sure."

"Try to keep her home. Delfuenso's kid is going to need a familiar face."

"Where are you now?"

"I'm getting close. The driver is meeting me at a motel."

"Why would he do that?"

"He says he's an innocent passerby."

"Do you believe him?"

"I'm not sure."

By that point Sorenson had just passed the Shell station. She was turning right and left, right and left, endlessly south and east through the empty darkness, following the little blue accommodation boards. Her GPS showed the motel location about thirty miles ahead. She was about thirty minutes away, she thought. Her Crown Vic was doing OK across country. She was gunning it hard on the straightaways and then braking hard and hauling it like a land yacht through the turns. Like all Bureau cars it had the Police Interceptor suspension, which was better than stock. Not exactly a NASCAR prospect, but it was doing the job. Apart from the tires, that was. They were shrieking and howling and complaining loudly. She was going to need a new set. Stony was going to be thrilled.

**Reacher unlocked room** five's door and went inside and saw a standard motel arrangement. A queen bed on the left, a credenza opposite its foot, a closet in back in line with the credenza, and a bathroom in back in line with the bed. The walls were wood grain laminate a lot more orange than any natural tree, and the floor was brown carpet, and the bedspread was a color halfway between the two. The room was no kind of an aesthetic triumph. That was for damn sure. But he didn't care. He wasn't planning on using it.

He switched on the bathroom light and left the bathroom door half open. He switched on the lamp on the far-side night table. He pulled the curtains shut, all but an inch wide crack. Then he stepped out to the cold again and locked up behind him.

He crossed the front lot and crossed the road and walked west into a frozen field, fifty yards, a hundred. He hunched down in his coat and turned around and squatted down and looked back. Room five looked exactly like it had a guy in it, just sitting there, just hanging out. Reacher had survived a long and difficult life by staying alert and being appropriately cautious. He wasn't about to let the Scandinavian woman catch him unawares. He was going to hang back and stay out of sight until he was sure who she was, and who she had brought with her. Any kind of back-up or SWAT team, and he was out of there, never to return. If she was on her own, then maybe he would stroll over and introduce himself.

Or maybe he wouldn't.

He watched the road, and waited.

# Chapter 34

After a little less than thirty minutes crouching in the cold, Reacher saw headlights and blue and red strobes far away to his left, like an alien bubble rolling fast through the peaceful pre-dawn mist. About two miles away, he thought. Two minutes, at the speed it was doing. The headlights probed ahead and flicked up and down, and the strobes followed close behind. A single car, low and wide, all urgent and lonely. No back-up. No SWAT team.

So far so good.

The lights got brighter as the car got closer. Half a mile out he figured it was a Crown Victoria. A government car. A quarter of a mile out he figured it was dark blue. Two hundred yards out he figured it was the same car he had seen hours before, blasting west on the Interstate from Omaha. He fancied he could tell an individual car by its stance and its ride, like a fingerprint.

He watched as it braked hard and turned in under

the porte cochere, counterclockwise, with the string of rooms behind it, like Alan King had done. He saw the reversing lights flash white as the transmission jammed into Park. He saw a woman get out.

FBI Special Agent Julia Sorenson, presumably. The Scandinavian. She looked the part. That was for sure. She was tall, with long blonde hair. She was wearing black shoes and black pants and a black jacket with a blue shirt under it. She stood for a second and eased her back. Then she leaned into the car and slung a black pear-shaped bag over her shoulder. She took a small wallet from her pocket. ID, presumably. She looped around the hood and headed for the office door.

She took a gun off her hip.

Reacher stared left into the darkness. He saw no following vehicles. A one-two punch would have been reasonable tactics. Obvious, even. Bait, and then back-up. But it wasn't happening.

Yet.

The woman walked up the flagstone path. Fast, but not running. She pulled the lobby door. She went inside.

Sorenson saw a standard-issue rural motel lobby, with sheet vinyl on the floor and four awful wicker armchairs, and a breakfast buffet table with coffee flasks and paper cups. There was a waist-high reception counter with walk-around space on the left and none on the right. There was an office door behind the counter, with a fresh bullet hole in the wall high above it.

There was TV sound behind the office door, and a rim of light all around it. Sorenson stood in the middle of the floor and called, "Hello?"

Loud and clear and confident.

The office door opened and a short fat man came out. He had strands of thin hair plastered to his skull with product. He was wearing a red sweater vest. His eyes bounced between Sorenson's ID and her gun, back and forth, back and forth.

She said, "Where's the man with the broken nose?"

He said, "I need to know who's going to pay for the damage to my wall."

She said, "I don't know who. Not me, anyway."

"Isn't there a federal scheme? Like victim compensation or something?"

"We'll discuss that later," she said. "Where's the man with the broken nose?"

"Mr. Skowron? He's in room five. He's very rude. He called me a socialist."

"I need to borrow your master key."

"I could have been killed."

"Did you see what happened?"

The guy shook his head. "I was in the back room, resting. I heard a gunshot and I called it in. It was all over by the time I opened the door."

"I need to borrow your master key," Sorenson said again.

The guy dug in a bulging pocket and came out with a brass item on an unmarked ring. Sorenson put her

ID away and took it from him. She asked, "Who are your other guests?"

"They're here to fish. There are lakes nearby. But mostly they drink. They didn't even wake up when the gun was fired."

"Go back in the office," Sorenson said. "I'll tell you when it's safe to come out."

**Still no activity** to the left. No lights, no cars. No back-up. Reacher watched carefully, the lobby, then the road, the lobby, then the road, like a tennis umpire. He saw the woman come back out, through the door, onto the flagstone path. She still had her gun in her hand. She hadn't shot the fat man. She was clearly a person of considerable patience. She walked between the lobby and her car, past the Coke machine, and she headed down the row of rooms, on the sidewalk lit up by the bulkhead lights. She glanced at the doors as she walked. One, two, three, four.

She stopped just before room five.

She looked in through the crack between the curtains, just briefly, a duck of her head out and back. Then again, much longer, a careful survey of the sliver of the room she could see. No feet on the end of the bed. *He's in the bathroom,* she was thinking. Reacher checked left again. No lights in the north. No noise, no movement. He checked to his right too, just to be sure. The back-up could have looped around a square on the checkerboard. Which would have been smart tactics. But there were no lights in the south, either. No noise, no movement. The woman wasn't using her phone. No communication. No coordination. They wouldn't have left her exposed for so long.

She was alone.

No back-up, no SWAT team.

Reacher saw her knock on room five's door. He saw her wait, and knock again, harder. He saw her put her ear against the crack.

He stood up and started walking toward her, across the frozen dirt. He saw her put a key in the lock and turn it. He saw her enter the room, her gun up and ready. Twenty seconds later she came back out again.

She stood on the sidewalk next to the lawn chairs, glancing left, glancing right, staring straight ahead. Her gun was still in her hand, but down by her side. Reacher crunched onward over the frozen stubble. He stepped out of the field and onto the road.

She heard him. Her face turned toward him, blindly locating the sound.

"Hello," he said.

Her gun came up. A two-handed stance, feet braced. He saw her eyes lock on. He was looming up at her out of the dark. He said, "We spoke on the phone. I'm unarmed."

The gun stayed where it was.

He crossed the road. He stepped into the motel's front lot. The light from the dim bulkhead fixtures reached him.

The woman said, "Stop right there."

He stopped right there.

The gun was a Glock 17. Black, boxy, with a dull polycarbonate sheen. Behind it her head was turned slightly to the side, as if quizzically. A strand of hair was across one eye. She was a lot better-looking than Don McQueen. That was for damn sure.

She said, "Get down on the ground."

He spread his fingers and held his hands out from his sides, his palms toward her. He said, "No need to get all excited. We're on the same side here."

"I'll shoot."

"No, you won't."

"Why wouldn't I?"

Reacher looked to his left. Her car was still all lit up under the porte cochere. She hadn't killed the strobes. They were flashing red and blue from secret little mouse-fur moldings on the rear parcel shelf. Farther down the road there was nothing but darkness. In the other direction there was a new light on the horizon. Very far away. Not moving. Not a vehicle. Just a very faint orange glow, like a distant bonfire.

He said, "You won't shoot because you don't want to do the paperwork."

She said nothing.

"And it wouldn't be righteous. I'm unarmed and I'm not offering an imminent threat. You'd lose your job. You'd go to jail."

No response.

"And you want to find Karen Delfuenso. You don't have descriptions of the two guys. You don't have the names they're using. You don't know the things they let slip. But I do. You need to keep me alive long enough to ask me questions, at least."

The gun stayed where it was. But she stepped and shuffled to her left, turning all the way, keeping the front sight hard on him. She backed off twenty feet, until his path to room five's door was covered but unobstructed. At first he thought she wanted him to go inside, but she said, "Sit down, in the lawn chair."

He walked forward. The Glock's muzzle tracked him all the way, from twenty feet. A confident markswoman. McQueen had missed from eight. He stopped next to the left-hand lawn chair. He turned around. He backed up, butt-first. He sat down.

She said, "Lean back. Stick your legs out straight. Hang your arms over the sides."

He complied, and ended up about as ready for instant action as his granddad's granddad waking up from an afternoon nap. She was evidently a smart woman. A good improviser. The chair was cold against the backs of his thighs. White plastic, thoroughly chilled.

She stayed where she was, but she lowered the gun.

**He was not** what Sorenson had been expecting. Not exactly. He wasn't a gorilla and he wasn't like something out of a slasher movie. But she could see why he had been described that way. He was huge, for a start. He was one of the largest men she had ever seen outside of the NFL. He was extremely tall, and extremely broad, and long-armed, and long-legged. The lawn chair was regular size, but it looked tiny under him. It was bent and crushed out of shape. His knuckles were nearly touching the ground. His neck was thick and his hands were the size of dinner plates. His clothes were creased and dirty. His hair was matted. His facial injury was awful. His nose was split and swollen and bruising had spread under his eyes.

A wild man. But not really. Underneath everything else he seemed strangely civilized. He had moved with a kind of considered grace, calm and contained. He had spoken the same way, thinking ahead whole paragraphs and essays in the split-second pauses between sentences. *You won't shoot because you don't want to do the paperwork.* Straight to the heart of the matter. Knowledgeable, and confident. His gaze was both wise and appealing, both friendly and bleak, both frank and utterly cynical. His focus was shifting fractionally in and out, his brows rising and falling a little, the shape of his mouth always changing, as if he was constantly thinking. As if there was a computer behind his eyes, running at full speed.

She raised her gun again.

She said, "I'm sorry, but I'm under orders to arrest you on sight and take you back to Nebraska."

# Chapter 35

Sorenson's words just hung there in the cold night air. *I'm under orders to arrest you on sight and take you back to Nebraska.* The big guy paused a beat, and then he smiled, politely, generously, as if pretending to be amused by a joke he had in fact heard many times before, and he said, "Well, best of luck with that."

He didn't move. He just stayed there in the shaky chair, leaning back, legs straight out, arms dangling.

Sorenson said, "I'm serious."

He said, "They were very disorganized, weren't they?"

She said, "Who were?"

"The two guys. I expect you've got a fairly substantial forensic trail."

"Who are you?"

"I mean, jacking a car is always a sign of desperation, isn't it? You can't rely on it. There might be no traffic. You might pick the wrong victim and get shot in the face."

"What's your point?"

"They told me their names. And I think they were their real names. They didn't sound like prepared aliases. And I don't think they were. Because nothing else about those guys seemed very prepared."

"What names did they give you?"

"Alan King and Don McQueen."

"King and McQueen? Those sound totally made up."

"Exactly. If they really were made up, they'd have chosen better. And it was OK if I knew. I wasn't supposed to survive."

"What's your point?" Sorenson asked again.

"The one calling himself Alan King said he had a brother who had been in the army, name of Peter King. That might be a good place to start."

"With what?"

"Tracing them."

"Who are you?" Sorenson asked again.

"Tell me about your boss."

"Why would I?"

"He's ambitious, right? He wants a pat on the head. He thinks an arrest before the sun comes up is going to look good. And he might be right. It might look good. But flexibility would be a much better tactic here."

"Are you negotiating with me?"

"I'm just saying there's very little point in rushing back to Nebraska when Karen Delfuenso was last seen heading in the opposite direction. Your boss will understand that eventually. Delayed gratification is a good thing. It's what built the middle class."

"You're resisting arrest, technically. If I shot you now, it would be righteous."

"So go ahead. What do you think I want, to live forever?"

She didn't reply.

He said, "I'll tell you my name."

She said, "I already know your name. You signed the motel register. Your name is Skowron."

He said, "You see, *that's* a convincing alias. You bought right into it. Moose Skowron, hit .309 for the Yankees in 1960, and .375 in the postseason."

"Your name is *not* Skowron?"

"Hardly. I couldn't hit Major League pitching. But you should pay attention to 1960. The World Series in particular. The Yankees were coming off their tenth pennant in twelve years, they outscored the Pirates 55 to 27, they outhit them .338 to .256, they hit ten home runs against four, they got two complete-game shutouts from Whitey Ford, and still they lost."

"What has baseball to do with anything?"

"It's an illustration. It's a metaphor. It always is. I'm saying it's always possible to snatch defeat from the jaws of victory. That's what you would be doing if you took me back to Nebraska."

Sorenson was quiet for a second, and then she lowered her gun.

* * *

**Reacher saw the** gun go down, slowly but surely, and he thought: *It's in the bag. Nearly.* Two minutes and twenty seconds of talking. A delay and a frustration for sure, but a lot faster than shouting or yelling or fighting. A lot faster, and also a lot safer. As bad as McQueen's .22 Long Rifles would have been, Sorenson's nine-millimeter Parabellums would be worse. Much worse. He said, "My name is Reacher. First name Jack. No middle name. I used to be a cop in the army."

Sorenson asked, "And what are you now?"

"Unemployed."

"Where do you live?"

"Nowhere."

"What does that mean?"

"It means what it says. I move from place to place."

"Why?"

"Why not?"

"And you really were hitching rides?"

"I really was."

"Why are you going to Virginia?"

"Personal reasons."

"Not a good enough answer."

"It's all I can give you."

"I need more. I'm way out on a limb here."

"I'm going to Virginia to find a woman."

"Any woman?"

"One in particular."

"Who?"

"I talked to her on the phone. She sounded nice. I thought I should go check her out."

"You talked to her on the phone? You haven't actually met her?"

"Not yet."

"You're traveling halfway across the country to spend time with a woman you never met?"

"Why not? I have to be somewhere. And I don't have anywhere else I need to be. So Virginia will be as good as anyplace else."

"Do you think this woman will want to spend time with you?"

"Probably not. But nothing ventured, nothing gained."

"She must be a hell of a woman."

"She has a nice voice. That's all I know so far."

Another thirty-five seconds. Total elapsed time, two minutes fifty-five. *Getting there.* Faster than fighting. And safer. He said, "Anything else you need to know?"

"How did you break your nose?"

"Someone hit me with the blunt end of a shotgun."

"In Nebraska?"

"Yes."

"Why?"

"Who can say? Some folks are just naturally aggressive."

"If you're not who you say you are, I could lose my job. I could go to jail."

"I know that. But I am who I say I am. And you are who you are. You think Karen Delfuenso is the most important thing here. Not like your boss."

Sorenson paused.

She nodded.

She said, "So where do we start?"

*Bingo.* Three minutes and twenty-one seconds. But then Sorenson's cell phone rang, and it was all over before it had even begun.

# Chapter 36

Initially from Sorenson's point of view the ring tone was a nuisance and an interruption. It broke a spell. The big guy was well on the way to giving it all up. Who he was, what he was doing, why he was there. Every interrogation was different. Sometimes it paid to play along. Pretend to believe, pretend to cooperate, pretend to be convinced. Then his guard would drop and the truth would come. Another few minutes might have done it.

She took out her phone. It buzzed warmly against her palm. She knew it wouldn't be Stony. Stony was typing and revising and spell-checking. It would be the night duty agent, in Omaha. With high-priority information. Maybe there was something back from her facial-injury inquiries. Maybe the big guy was wanted in a dozen states. Skowron, or Reacher, or whatever the hell his name really was. In which case the call wouldn't be a nuisance or an interruption at all. It would be a shortcut instead.

She answered.

It was the night duty agent. He said, "The Iowa troopers are reporting another 911. Some farmer called in a vehicle fire on the edge of his land."

"Where?"

"About five miles south of you."

"What vehicle?"

"He can't tell. It's some distance away. He's got a big farm. A regular car, he thinks."

"Who is responding?"

"Nobody. The nearest fire department is fifty miles away. They'll let it burn out. I mean, it's wintertime in Iowa. What could it set fire to?"

She clicked off. She looked at the big guy and said, "Vehicle fire, five miles south of here."

The big guy stood up, one fast fluid movement. He crossed the motel's lot and stepped out to the middle of the road. He said, "I can see it. I saw it before."

She kept her gun in her hand. She joined him on the blacktop. She saw a light on the horizon. Miles away. A faint orange glow, like a distant bonfire.

He said, "Not good."

She said, "You think it's the Impala?"

"It would be a coincidence if it wasn't."

"We're screwed if they switched vehicles again."

He nodded.

"It would be a setback," he said.

She said, "Are you telling me the truth?"

"About what?"

"Your name, for instance."

"Jack-none-Reacher," he said. "I'm very pleased to meet you."

"You got ID?"

"I have an old passport."

"Under what name?"

"Jack-none-Reacher."

"Does the photograph look like you?"

"Younger and dumber."

"Get in the car."

"Front or back?"

"Front," she said. "For now."

**The Crown Vic** was transportation, nothing more. Not a mobile office, not a command center. Reacher got in the front seat and saw no laptop computers, no powerful radios, no array of holstered weapons. Just a phone cradle bolted to the dash, and a single extra mismatched switch. For the strobes, presumably.

Sorenson slid in alongside him and rattled the selector into gear and took off, out from under the porte cochere, counterclockwise back to the road, the same way Alan King had driven, but slower. The car bounced and yawed and settled, and then Sorenson accelerated hard. The road was dead straight. The fire was dead ahead. They were heading straight for it. It looked bright and hot. Reacher remembered a line from an old song: *Set the controls for the heart of the sun.*

Halfway there it was obvious that gasoline was involved. There was blue in the orange, and a kind of raging fierceness at the center of the fire. There would be black smoke above it, but the sky was still black in the south, so it didn't show up. In the east there were the first faint streaks of dawn, low down on the horizon. Reacher thought briefly about Chicago, and the Greyhound depot on West Harrison, and the early buses, and then he dismissed them from his mind. *Another time, another place.* He watched Sorenson drive. She had her foot hard on the gas. Slim muscles in her right thigh were standing out.

She asked, "How long were you in the army?"

He said, "Thirteen years."

"Rank?"

"I was terminal at major."

"Does your nose hurt?"

"Yes."

"I'm sorry."

"You should see the other guy."

"Were you a good cop in the army?"

"I was good enough."

"How good was that?"

"I was like old Moose Skowron, I guess. Most years I hit over .300. When it mattered I could step it up to .375."

"Did you get medals?"

"We all got medals."

"Why don't you live anywhere?"

"Do you have a house?"

"Of course."

"Is it a pure unalloyed pleasure?"

"Not entirely."

"So there's your answer."

"How do we find these guys if they switched cars again?"

"Lots of ways," Reacher said.

A mile out the fire took on a shape, wide at the base, narrow above. Half a mile out Reacher saw strange jets and fans and lobes of flame, pale blue and roaring and almost invisible. He figured the fuel line was failing, maybe at the seams or where the metal was stressed by folds and turns. He figured the tank itself was holding, but vapor was cooking off and boiling out through tiny cracks and fissures, sideways, upward, downward, like random and violent blowtorches, the tongues of flame as strong and straight as metal bars, some of them twenty or thirty feet long. Inside the fireball the car itself was a vague cherry red shape, jerking and wriggling and dancing in the boiling air. Reacher buzzed his window down and heard the distant noise. He put his hand in the freezing slipstream and felt faint warmth on his palm.

"Don't get too close," he said.

Sorenson eased up and slowed down. She said, "Do you think the tank will blow?"

"Probably not. The gas is boiling and bleeding off. There's no big pressure buildup. Combustion is too vigorous to let any kind of blowback happen. So far, anyway."

"How much gas do you think is left?"

"Now? I'm not sure. The tank was full less than forty miles ago."

"So what do we do?"

"We wait. Until it either blows up or calms down enough for us to recognize what kind of car it was."

* * *

Sorenson stopped three hundred yards from the fire, and like good cops everywhere she pulled off the road and onto the shoulder, at least a yard, and then she backed up and parallel-parked herself another whole foot into the weeds. A cautious woman. There was no chance of getting rear-ended, because there was no traffic. Reacher faced front and watched and waited. He expected a fast decision. The gas couldn't last long. On the road the car had used plenty. And that was to produce just a few puny horsepower. A hundred at most, to haul a mid-size sedan down a completely flat highway. Now the same tank was feeding a fire as intense as a phosphorous bomb. A thousand times more powerful. Like a jet engine, literally.

He asked, "Where did they jack the car, right back at the beginning? At a light?"

Beside him Sorenson shook her head. "Behind the cocktail lounge where Delfuenso works. I think they tried to steal the car first. She came out, either because of the alarm, or she was leaving anyway."

"She had her bag," Reacher said.

"Then she was leaving anyway. They stopped and bought shirts, and then they hit the road."

"And water."

"How did you know that?"

"I drank some of it. It was still cold. What were they running from?"

"They stabbed a guy to death."

"In the cocktail lounge?"

"No, in an abandoned pumping station three miles away. Some kind of strange rendezvous."

"So how did they get three miles to the cocktail lounge? Did they walk?"

"They used the victim's car."

"Why didn't they keep it?"

"It was bright red and foreign. There was an eyewitness."

"To the stabbing itself?"

"More or less. To the getaway, certainly."

"Who was the eyewitness?"

"A farm worker, about fifty."

"Was he any good to you?"

"No worse than usual. Not the sharpest knife in the drawer. Excuse the pun. He saw the dead guy go in, followed by the two perps. He saw the perps come out and drive away."

"Where was their own car? Didn't they have one?"

"No one knows."

"If they had their own car, they'd have used it, surely. They must have driven in with the guy they stabbed."

"My tech person thinks they didn't."

"Who was the guy they stabbed?"

"A trade attaché. Like a foreign-service guy. He worked in our embassies overseas. He was an Arabic speaker, apparently."

"What did they stab him with?"

"Not sure. Something big. An eight- or nine-inch blade. A hunting knife, probably."

"What was the foreign service guy doing in Nebraska?"

"No one knows. They say he was between postings. The red car was rented in Denver. At the airport. So presumably the guy flew in from somewhere and drove the rest of the way. No one has mentioned a reason why he would do that. Or from where. But the State Department is worried about it. They sent a guy."

"Already?"

"My tech team fingerprinted the dead guy, and it's been fun and games ever since. Bureau counterterrorism showed up unannounced, and the State Department guy came, and my SAC has been up all night, and the eyewitness disappeared."

"Weird," Reacher said.

In the end the fire died just as fast as the sun came up. On the left the eastern skies cracked purple and pink and gold, and dead ahead the unspent gas ran out, and the smaller blaze ebbed, and the bigger blaze came over the horizon. Cold daylight lit the scene and gave heft and form to the blackened shell. The car was parked on the shoulder, facing south, as far off the road as Sorenson was. The tires were burned away. All the glass was gone. The paint had vaporized. The sheet metal was scorched gray and purple in fantastic whorls. For twenty yards all around, the winter stubble had burned and blackened. An arc of blacktop was bubbling and smoking. There were last licks of flame here and there, low and timid and hesitant compared to what had come before.

Sorenson bumped back onto the road and drove closer. Reacher looked at the shell. Ashes to ashes. It had started out that way, all bare and shiny in the factory, and it was ending up the same way, all gutted and empty.

It was an Impala. No question about it. Reacher knew the shape of its trunk, the flat of its flanks, the hump of its roof, the pitch of its hood. He was getting a three-quarters rear view, but he was totally sure. It was Delfuenso's Chevy.

All gutted and empty.

*My car.*

Reacher stared.

It wasn't empty.

# Chapter 37

Reacher was the first to get out. He closed his door and stood next to the Crown Vic's hood, with cold on his back and heat on his face. He was five feet closer than he had been before, and therefore his angle was five feet better.

All the glass was gone. All the rubber was gone, all the plastics, all the vinyl, all the high-tech space age materials. All that was left was metal, the parts designed to be visible still curved and molded, the parts designed to be hidden all sharp and knifelike and exposed. In particular the rear parcel shelf had lost its padding and its loudspeakers and its soundproof mat and its mouse-fur covering. What was left was a stamped steel cross-member, corrugated here and there for strength, drilled here and there with holes, but otherwise as plain and brutal as a blade. Its front edge was perfectly straight.

Except it wasn't.

Reacher took three more steps. The heat was astonishing. The front of the parcel shelf looked different on the right than the left. On the right its straight edge was compromised by a humped shape completely unrelated to engineering necessity. It was an organic shape, odd and random, in no way similar to the stamped angularity all around it.

It was a human head, burned smooth and tiny by the fire.

Sorenson got out of her car.

Reacher said, "Stay there, OK?"

He turned away and took a breath from the cold side, and another, until his lungs were full. He turned back and started walking. He kept his distance, looping wide, until he was level with the side of the shell. Then he darted in, until he felt the blacktop hot and sticky under the soles of his boots.

The Chevy's rear seat was burned away completely. But the person on it wasn't. Not completely. On the right, directly behind the blackened frame of the front passenger seat, fallen down through the missing cushions to the zigzag springs below, was a shape, like a sea creature, like a seal or a porpoise or a dolphin, black in color, oozing and smooth and smoking, cooked down to half its original size. It had tiny vestigial arms, clawed up like twigs. It had no expression, because it had no face.

But it had died screaming.

That was for damn sure.


**They retreated fifty** yards north and stood silently, breathing hard, staring blankly at a spot a thousand miles beyond the far horizon. They stood like that for a whole minute, and then another, as still as statues.

Then Sorenson said, "Where are they now?"

Reacher said, "I don't know."

"And what are they driving?"

"They're not driving anything. They're being driven. They were picked up."

"By who?"

Reacher didn't answer. But he moved, finally. He glanced up at the sky and looked at the light. It was still very early. But it would do. He found the Chevy's tire tracks easily enough. They bumped down onto the shoulder through a thin skim of mud on the edge of the road about a yard wide. The mud was neither wet nor dry, and it had captured the tread prints perfectly. Like the finest plaster. The drift off the road onto the shoulder had been long and cautious. The Chevy had come in like a jumbo jet on approach. More like McQueen's driving than King's.

Reacher walked out into the dormant field. Sorenson followed him. They looped around the wreck together, as close as the heat would let them get. Once beyond it they looped back to the road, and they found more tire tracks.

A second car had driven onto the shoulder. This one at a much tighter angle. Its tread prints were captured in the skim of mud. Road tires, solid, reliable, nothing radical, nothing fancy, probably on a big sedan. But they had come steering in pretty hard. That was clear. And some little time later they had steered out again just as hard, and bumped their way south. Taken together the tracks looked like the same bite out of a big circle.

Sorenson said, "Nothing came through between you and me, right? So this guy must have gotten here hours ago."

"No, he came north," Reacher said. "Not south. He didn't come past the motel. He U-turned right here, he picked them up, and he headed back where he came from. You can see all that from the tracks."

"Are you certain?"

"What else can have happened? They didn't jack another car. That's for sure. There's no traffic out here. You could wait forever. And I doubt if they're walking. So they were picked up. This was a rendezvous. They got here first. They were waiting. They know this place. Which is how they know that back road off the Interstate."

"Who picked them up?"

"I don't know," Reacher said again. "But this thing is starting to look like a big operation. Three coordinated crews, at least."

"Why three? There were only two here. King and McQueen, plus whoever picked them up."

"Plus whoever was simultaneously disappearing your eyewitness, all the way back in Nebraska. That's what I mean by coordination. They're cleaning house. They're taking care of everyone who ever laid eyes on King and McQueen."

\* \* \*

**The break of** day brought with it a cold breeze out of the north. There was rain coming. And soon. Reacher hunched down in his coat. Sorenson's pants legs flapped like sails. She walked twenty yards into a field. To get away from the smell on the wind, Reacher figured. He followed her, with stiff stalks crunching under his feet. Just to keep her company. He didn't need to move. Right then he couldn't smell anything at all. But he had smelled similar things before, from time to time in the past, back when his nose still worked. Oil, gas, plastic, charred meat. A chemical stink, plus rotting forgotten barbecue. Worse. Any sane person would want to get out of the way.

Sorenson called the Iowa troopers and claimed the scene for the FBI. She said it was not to be approached, and nothing was to be touched, and nothing was to be moved. Then she called her own tech team and told them to make the long trip over. She told them she wanted the best crime scene analysis ever attempted, and the best autopsy ever performed.

"Waste of time," Reacher said, when she clicked off. "There's virtually nothing to be found after a fire like that."

"I just need to know," she said.

"Know what?"

"That she was dead before the fire started. If I could know that, I might be able to carry on."

**They walked back** to Sorenson's car, a long curving route around the wreck, away from the heat and the smell, and when they got twenty feet from it she did what she had to do: she cleared her throat and took a breath and pulled her gun and arrested Jack-none-Reacher, on suspicion of conspiracy, and homicide in the first degree, and kidnapping.

# Chapter 38

Sorenson was holding her Glock two-handed again, steady and straight and level, feet properly planted, weight properly braced. She was less than four yards from Reacher. Her head was turned again, to the side, just a little, the same way as it had been before, as if quizzically. The same strand of hair was over the same eye.

She said, "Look at it from my point of view. What's my alternative? What else am I supposed to do? We lost the hostage, so the game has changed. Now it moves up a level. And we need to start with an arrest, or we'll be crucified. You understand that, right?"

Reacher said, "Are you apologizing to me?"

"Yes. I suppose I am. I'm very sorry. But you know how these things work. If you are who you say you are, that is."

"I am who I say I am. You're a very suspicious woman. A person's feelings could get hurt."

"I have to be suspicious. But I'm sorry about that too."

Reacher smiled, just briefly. "I must say this is a very civilized arrest. Could be the politest ever. Apart from the gun, that is. You don't need it. Where am I going to escape to?"

"Forgive me. But I need the gun. You're a legitimate suspect. And you have valuable information. I'm sure my SAC would prefer to airbrush the Omaha field office right out of this whole thing altogether, but it's far too late for that now. So he's got to be able to show something for a night's work. Either a suspect, or a material witness. And you're one or the other. Maybe you're both."

"Suppose I don't want to go to Omaha?"

"She'll wait."

"Who will?"

"The woman in Virginia. Or maybe she won't. Or maybe she's already forgotten all about you. But whatever, that's all on hold now."

"I wasn't thinking about Virginia. I agree, that's on hold now. I was thinking about Iowa. Right here, right now. This is where the trail starts. With those tire tracks."

*Tire tracks.*

Reacher glanced behind him, at the yard-wide skim of mud on the edge of the road, but he couldn't see what he needed to see.

Sorenson said, "Where the hell do you think you are, in the movies? You're a civilian. This isn't your trail. This isn't my trail anymore, either. We lost the hostage. Remember? An innocent woman. An innocent member of the public. A carjacking victim. A *mother,* for God's sake. You get that? There's going to be a big task force now. Dozens of people. Maybe even hundreds. An Assistant SAC leading it at the very least. There's going to be media. Cable news. It's all going to be way above my pay grade. They're going to hide me away like an idiot child. So there's nothing for either one of us here in Iowa. Not now. Get used to it."

Reacher said, "The trail will go cold before the task force even gets here."

"There's nothing we can do about that."

"There is. We can stop wasting time. We can make a start."

"Have you got unemployment insurance?"

"No."

"Neither do I. So don't include me in your harebrained schemes."

"OK, I could make a start."

"How? You're a civilian. You're one man. You have no resources. What could you possibly do?"

"I could find them."

"Because?"

"I've found people before."

"And then what?"

"I could impress upon them the error of their ways."

"An eye for an eye?"

"I'm not interested in their eyes."

"I can't let that happen. It would be a crime in itself. There has to be due process. Let the law take care of it. That's the price of civilization."

"Civilization can go sit on its thumb. I liked Delfuenso. She was a nice woman. Brave too. And smart. And tough. She worked all evening at a shitty job, and still she was thinking right to the end."

"I don't dispute any of that."

"They opened the wrong door, Julia. They get what they get."

"From you? How so? Who died and made you king of the world?"

"Someone has to do it. Are you guys going to?"

Sorenson didn't answer.

Reacher said, "I'll take that as a no, shall I?"

Sorenson shrugged, and then she nodded, reluctantly, as if despite herself. She said, "There's another call I have to make."

"To who?"

"A county sheriff back in Nebraska. Delfuenso's daughter is about to wake up."

"I'm sorry."

"So I need to put the cuffs on you. I need to put you in the back of the car."

"That's not going to happen."

"This is not a game."

"It's going to rain," Reacher said. "We're going to lose the tire marks."

"Turn around," Sorenson said. "Hold your hands out behind you."

"Have you got a camera?"

"What?"

"A camera," Reacher said. "Have you got one?"

"Why?"

"We need pictures of the tire marks. Before it rains."

"Turn around," Sorenson said again.

"Let's make a deal."

"What kind of a deal?"

"You lend me your camera, and I'll take pictures of the tire marks, while you make your call to the county sheriff."

"And then what?"

"And then we'll talk some more."

"About what?"

"About my personal situation."

"What's my other option?"

"You don't have another option."

"I'm the one with the gun here."

"Except you're not going to use it. We both know that. And you have my word. I won't run. You can trust me. I swore an oath too. In the army. A bigger oath than yours."

"I have to take you back with me. You understand that, right? Omaha has to do something right tonight."

"You could say you never found me."

"The motel keeper knows I did."

"You could shoot him in the head."

"I was tempted."

"Do we have a deal?"

"You have to come back with me afterward."

"That wasn't in the deal. Not yet. Not technically. That was to be decided later. I said, and then we'll talk some more."

"If you're telling the truth, you have nothing to worry about."

"You still believe stuff like that?"

Sorenson said, "Yes, I do."

Reacher said nothing.

"Weigh it up," Sorenson said. "Think about it. Make a choice. You have no car, no phone, no contacts, no support, no help, no back-up, no budget, no facilities, no lab, no computers, and you have absolutely no idea where those guys have gone. You need food and rest. You need medical attention for your face. But I could leave you here like that. Right here, right now, alone, in the middle of nowhere, with the rain coming. Then I'd be fired, and guess what? You'd be hunted down like a dog anyway."

Reacher said, "What's my other option?"

"Come back with me to Omaha, help us out, and maybe even pick up some information as you go along. To do with as you wish."

"Information from where?"

"From who, not from where."

"OK, from who?"

"From me."

"Why would you?"

"Because I'm improvising here. I'm trying to find a way to get you in the car."

"So now you're the one offering a deal."

"And it's a good deal. You should take it."

**Reacher took his** photographs while Sorenson called the county sheriff back in Nebraska. It was a digital camera. He half-remembered maybe once taking a picture with a cellular telephone, but apart from that vague possibility the last time he had handled a camera had been back in the age of film. Not that it made much difference, he assumed. In both cases there was a lens, and a little button to press, and a little thing to look through. Except there wasn't. There was no viewfinder hole. Instead the operator had to do the whole thing on a tiny television screen. Which meant working with the camera held out at arm's length, and walking backward and forward. Like a man in a hazard suit with a Geiger counter.

But he got the two shots he wanted, and he headed back to the car. Sorenson was through with her call by then. It hadn't been fun, by the look of it. Not a barrel of laughs. She said, "OK, let's go. You can ride in the front."

He said, "Look at the pictures first."

The rain started to fall. Big heavy drops, some of them vertical, some of them sideways on the gusting wind. They got in the car, and he passed her the camera. She knew how to use it. She toggled forward, and then back again.

"You only took two pictures?" she said.

"Two was all I needed."

"Two of the same thing?"

"They're not of the same thing."

The rain hammered on the Crown Vic's roof. Sorenson looked at the first photograph, very carefully, and then the second, just as carefully. They were both close-ups of tire marks in the mud. Apparently the same tire, and the same mud. She went back and forth between them, once, twice, three times. She said, "OK, they're identical. And they're from the car that

U-turned, correct? So what are they, left and right?
Or front and rear?"

"Neither," Reacher said.

"So what are they?"

"Only one is from the car that U-turned."

"What about the other one?"

"That's from your car."

# Chapter 39

Sorenson looked at the pictures again, first one, and then the other, back and forth, over and over. The same tire, and the same mud. She said, "This doesn't necessarily mean anything."

"I agree," Reacher said. "Not necessarily."

"I was never here before."

"I believe you."

"And the Bureau doesn't have its own make of tires. I'm sure we just buy them, like anyone else. Probably from Sears. I'm sure we look for something cheap and reliable. Something generic. Whatever's on sale. Like everyone does. So these go on all the big sedans. There must be half a dozen different makes and models. Fleet vehicles, rentals, the big things old people drive. I bet there are a million tires like this in the world."

"Probably more," Reacher said.

"So what are we saying?"

"We're saying we know for sure what kind of tires

the bad guys have on their car. The same kind as yours. Which means their car is probably a big domestic sedan. It's a start."

"That's all?"

"Anything else would be speculation."

"We're allowed to speculate."

"Then I would say they are urban. Or at least suburban. Big sedans are rare in farm country. It's all pick-up trucks and four-wheel-drives out here."

"How urban?"

"From the kind of place that has taxi companies and car services. And offices and maybe an airport. The local market has to be right. I'm sure you couldn't buy tires like these out here, for instance. Why would anyone keep them in stock?"

"So you're not saying there's Bureau involvement here?"

"I'm sure there isn't."

"But?"

"Nothing."

"But?"

"But I'm pretty much a black-and-white kind of a person, and I like things confirmed yes or no, beyond a reasonable doubt."

"Then no. It's confirmed. Right now. Straight from the horse's mouth. For absolute sure. Beyond any kind of doubt. It is completely inconceivable the Bureau was involved with this. That's the worst kind of crazy thinking."

"OK," Reacher said. "Let's go. Tell me if you want me to drive for a bit. I know the way."

\* \* \*

Sorenson pulled a big wide U-turn of her own, and then she hit it hard and hurried north through the rain. They passed the motel doing about sixty. It looked different by day. The low bulkhead lights were off, and the siding looked paler.

Reacher said, "I paid for two nights in there. And I spent about thirty seconds in the room."

Sorenson said, "Why did you pay?"

"I was feeling guilty about the guy's wall."

"Not your fault."

"That was my impression at the time."

"So you shouldn't feel guilty. Not about him, anyway. I didn't like him."

"Well, I've still got his key. It's in my pocket. Maybe I'll mail it back, and maybe I won't."

Then they came to the first junction, and Sorenson braked late and made the left with all kinds of squealing and sliding on the slick surface. She came off the gas and got straightened out and hit it again.

"Sorry," she said.

Reacher said nothing. He was in no position to complain. They were still on the road. He would have been in a field.

"The tires are worn," she said. "I noticed on the way out here."

Reacher said nothing.

She said, "Which means the bad guys' tires are worn too. If the pictures are identical, that is. Which is step two. We know what kind of tires they have, and we know approximately how old they are. Maybe an older car. Maybe an older driver. Could be some old person around here, with one of those big old cars."

"I doubt it," Reacher said. "I don't think old people really love to come out in the middle of the night to watch women burn to death. Because you realize that fire was started when they were all still there? They didn't set a fuse. It wasn't spontaneous combustion. They lit it and they all stood around and watched and waited until they were sure it was going well."

"OK," Sorenson said. "It wasn't a local senior. It was someone from somewhere urban."

"With taxi companies and car services and offices and an airport," Reacher said. "And maybe with a metro-area population around a million and a half. That's something Alan King let slip. He said a million and a half people live where he lives."

"That's potentially interesting. Unless it was misdirection."

"I don't think it was. I don't think they had a script. They were generally fast and smart, but it was a random question and an instant answer. No thinking time. Too fluid for a lie. Their other lies were slower and more clumsy."

"Anything else?"

"At one point McQueen used what I felt was an odd word choice. I was skeptical about the gas station being where the highway sign said it was, and when we got there McQueen said *You should have trusted me.* I think most people would have said *believed* instead. Don't you think? You should have *believed* me?"

"What does it mean?"

"I'm not sure. In the service we were taught to listen for odd words. The Russians had language schools, with perfect accents, and slang and so on and so forth, and sometimes the only tells were odd words. So for a minute I wondered if McQueen was foreign."

Sorenson drove on and said nothing.

**She was thinking:** *The shirt was bought in Pakistan, or possibly the Middle East.* She asked, "Did McQueen have an accent?"

Reacher answered, "None at all. Very generic American."

"Did he look foreign?"

"Not really. Caucasian, six feet, maybe one-sixty, fair hair, pale blue eyes, slender, long arms and legs, kind of gangly, but when it came to pulling the gun out of his pocket and running up the path and jumping in the car he turned out to be plenty athletic. Gymnastic, even."

"OK," Sorenson said. "So the word choice was probably innocent."

"Except you have to look at the victim. He will have had dealings with foreigners."

"As a trade attaché? I suppose that's the point."

"Have you ever met a trade attaché?"

"No."

"Me neither," Reacher said. "But I met a few folks who claimed they were trade attachés."

"What does that mean?"

"How much help does Coca-Cola really need to sell its stuff around the world? Not very much, right?

Generally speaking American products speak for themselves. Yet every embassy has a trade attaché."

"What are you saying?"

"Have you ever seen a trade attaché's office? I've been in two. Both had courtyard windows, not street windows, both were lined with lead and Faraday cages, and both were swept for bugs four times a day. I know the Coke formula is a secret, but that's ridiculous."

"Cover for something?"

"Exactly," Reacher said. "Every CIA head of station on the planet calls himself a trade attaché."


**Sheriff Goodman was** dog tired. And he wasn't sure it was a good idea to take Delfuenso's daughter out of school for the day. Or for a couple of days, or a week, or a month, or whatever Special Agent Sorenson might have in mind. His attitude was the opposite. He felt work and structure and familiarity were useful crutches in stressful times. He encouraged his own people to come in as normal no matter what had happened. Bereavement, divorce, illness in the family, whatever. In his experience routine helped people cope. Obviously he had to go through the compassionate motions, telling people to take all the time they needed, stuff like that, but he always added that no one would think less of them if they stuck to their tasks. And most of them seemed grateful for it. Most of them worked on as usual, and they seemed to benefit in the long term.

But those were grown-ups, and Delfuenso's kid was a kid.

He drove out to the short row of ranch houses slowly and reluctantly. Four times in his career he had been required to tell a parent a child had died. He had never had to tell a child its parent had died. Not a ten-year-old, anyway. He didn't really know how. *Just the facts,* Sorenson had said, in an earlier conversation. *Don't say anything more until we know for sure.* Not very helpful. The facts were tough. *Hey kid, guess what? Your mom burned to death in a car.* There was no easy way to say it. Because there was no easy way for the kid to face it. She goes to bed one night all hunky-dory, and she wakes up the next morning with a different life.

Although: *Just the facts. Don't say anything more until we know for sure.*

What were the facts? What did they actually know for sure? He had seen burned bodies. House fires, barn fires. You had to get dental records. Or DNA. For the death certificate, and the insurance. A couple of days, at least. Medical opinions, that had to be signed off on and notarized. So as far as Delfuenso was concerned, nobody really knew anything *for sure.* Not yet. Except that she was missing, apparently carjacked.

And maybe a two-stage process would be better, with a ten-year-old. First, *I'm sorry, but your mom is missing.* Then, a couple of days later, when they were really sure, *I'm sorry, but your mom died.* Drip, drip. Maybe better than one massive blow. Or was that just cowardice on his own part?

He parked in front of the neighbor's house and concluded, yes, it was cowardice on his own part, no question, but it was also the best approach, probably, with a ten-year-old kid. Kids were different.

*Just the facts. Don't say anything more until we know for sure.*

He got out of his car, slow and reluctant. He closed the door and stood for a second, and then he tracked around the hood and stepped over the muddy gutter and walked up the neighbor's short driveway.

# Chapter 40

Sorenson got through the checkerboard and back to the Interstate without further incident. The car stayed on the road. The rain kept on falling. It was a gloomy day. The sky was low and the color of iron. Traffic was heavier than Reacher had seen it the night before. Each vehicle was trailing a long gray zeppelin of spray. Sorenson had her wipers on fast. She was sticking to seventy miles an hour. She asked, "What's the fastest way of finding Alan King's brother from the army?"

"King claimed he was a red leg," Reacher said. "Probably just a dagby. The Gulf, the first time around. Mother Sill will know."

"I didn't understand a word of that."

"A red leg is an artilleryman. Because way back they had red stripes on their dress pants. And their branch color is still red. A dagby is a 13B MOS. Which is a cannon crewmember's military occupational specialty. In other words, a dagby. A dumb-ass gun bunny. Mother Sill is Fort Sill, which is artillery HQ. Someone there will have a record. The Gulf the first time around was the thing with Saddam Hussein, back in 1991."

"I knew that part."

"Good."

"The brother's first name was Peter, right?"

"Correct."

"And you still think King was his real last name?"

"More likely than not. Worth a try, anyway."

"Dumb-ass gun bunny isn't very polite."

"But very necessary," Reacher said. "Unfortunately Frederick the Great once said that field artillery lends dignity to what would otherwise be a vulgar brawl. It went to their heads. They started calling themselves the kings of battle. They started to think they're the most important part of the army. Which obviously isn't true."

"Why not?"

"Because the Military Police is the most important part of the army."

"What did they call you?"

"Sir, usually."

"And?"

"Meatheads. Monkey patrol. And chimps, but that was an acronym."

"For what?"

"Completely hopeless in most policing situations."

"Where is Fort Sill?"

"Lawton, Oklahoma."

She speed-dialed her phone in its cradle. Reacher heard the ring tone loud and clear through the stereo.

A voice answered, male, low and fast and without preamble. A duty officer, probably, with Sorenson's number front and center on his caller ID, and therefore instantly on the ball and ready for business. The night guy, most likely, still there at the end of his watch. He didn't sound like a guy who had just gotten out of bed. Sorenson said to him, "I need you to call the army at Fort Sill in Lawton, Oklahoma, and get what they have on an artilleryman named Peter King, who was on active service in 1991. Present whereabouts and details of family would be especially appreciated. Give them my cell number and ask them to call me back direct, OK?"

"Understood," the guy said.

"Is Stony in his office yet?"

"Just arrived."

"What's the word?"

"Nothing is happening yet. It's weird."

"No three-ring circus?"

"Phones are quiet. No one has even asked for the night log yet."

"Weird."

"Like I said."


The eyewitness was not kept waiting at the reception desk. There was no line. He had been given a cup of coffee and he had eaten a breakfast muffin. The woman at the desk took his name and asked what kind of bed he preferred. She was a plump, motherly type, seemingly very patient and capable. The eyewitness didn't really understand her question.

He said, "Bed?"

The woman said, "We have rooms with kings, queens, and twins."

"I guess anything will do."

"Don't you have a preference?"

"What would you suggest?"

"Honestly, I think the rooms with the queens are ideal. Overall they feel a little more spacious. With the armchairs and all? Most people like those rooms the best."

"OK, I'll take one of those."

"Good," the woman said brightly. She marked it up in a book and took a key off a hook. She said, "Room fourteen. It's easy to find."

The eyewitness carried the key in his hand and left the lobby. He stood for a moment in the chill air and looked up at the sky. It was going to rain. It was probably already raining in the north. He set off down the path and saw a knee-high fingerpost for rooms eleven through fifteen. He followed the sign. The path wound its way through sad winter flowerbeds and came out at a long low block of five rooms together. Room fourteen was the last but one. There was an empty leaf-strewn swimming pool not far from it. The eyewitness thought it would make a nice facility in the summer, with blue water in it, and the flowers all around it in bloom. He had never been in a swimming pool. Lakes and rivers, yes, but never a pool.

Beyond the pool was the perimeter wall, a waist-high decorative feature made of stucco over concrete blocks. Ten feet beyond that was the security fence, all tall and black and angular and topped with canted-in rolls of razor wire. The eyewitness figured it must have been very expensive. He knew all about the price of fencing, being a farmer. Labor and materials could kill you.

He unlocked room fourteen. He stepped inside. The bed was a little wider than the one he shared at home. There were clothes on it, in neat piles. Two outfits, both the same. Blue jeans, blue shirts, blue sweaters, white undershirts, white underwear, blue socks. There were pajamas on the pillow. There were toiletries in the bathroom. Soap, shampoo, shaving cream. Some kind of lotion. Deodorant. There were razors. There was toothpaste, and a toothbrush sealed in cellophane. There was a comb. There was a bathrobe. There were lots of towels.

He looked at the bed but sat down in an armchair. He had been told lunch was available from twelve o'clock onward. Nothing to do until then. So he figured he might start his day with a nap. Just a short doze. It had been a long night.

**Reacher waited until** Sorenson was safely past a howling semi truck, and then he said, "Tell me about how the fingerprint thing worked with the dead guy."

"Standard procedure," Sorenson said. "It's the first thing they do, before decomposition starts to make it difficult. They take the prints and upload them to the database."

"By satellite?"

"No, over the regular cell phone networks."

"That's convenient."

"You bet it is. We love cell phones. We love them to death. For all kinds of reasons. I mean, can you imagine? Suppose twenty years ago Congress had proposed a law saying every citizen had to wear a radio transponder around his neck, all day and all night, so the government could track him wherever he went. Can you imagine the outrage? But instead the citizens went right ahead and did it to themselves. In their pockets and purses, not around their necks, but the outcome is the same."

"Were there prints in the bright red car?"

"Plenty. Those guys took no care at all."

"Did you upload them?"

"Of course."

"Any results?"

"Not yet," Sorenson said. "Which almost certainly means those guys aren't in the database. The software will hunt for hours, until it's sure, but it never takes this long. They must be virgins."

"Therefore not foreign," Reacher said. "There are no foreign fingerprint virgins, right? Everyone gets fingerprinted at the port of entry. Or for their visas. Unless they're illegals. They could have come over the Canadian border, I guess. People say it's full of holes."

"Except how did they get into Canada? We have access to their databases too. And Canada has no other borders. Unless they hiked across the North Pole or swam the Bering Strait."

"There's Alaska."

"But to get into Alaska from overseas you have to be fingerprinted."

"No chance of errors or glitches?"

"Not for the last ten years."

"OK, they're not foreign."

**Sorenson drove on.** She had driven the opposite way just hours before, but she didn't really recognize the terrain. The highway looked different. It was lit up a dull gray and there was no view to the sides and no horizon ahead or behind. It was like passing through an endless cloud. The rain was easing but the road was still streaming. There was spray everywhere.

By her side Reacher said, "Where did the State Department guy come from?"

She said, "I don't know. He just showed up in a car. But he was for real. I saw his ID."

"Does the State Department have field offices, like you guys?"

"I don't know. I don't think so."

"So where did he come from? Obviously not D.C., because he got there too quick."

"Good question. I'll ask my SAC. He got a message that the guy was coming. And I know he spoke to State during the night. That's how we found out the dead guy was a trade attaché."

"Or not. It feels to me like State was keeping its eye on something. Like standing by, in the vicinity. If the guy really was from State, that is. He could have been CIA too."

Sorenson said nothing. Nothing about the checked shirt from Pakistan or the Middle East, nothing about the nighttime calls from the CIA, nothing about their insistent requests for constant updates. She didn't know why, beyond a kind of basic superstition. Some things just shouldn't be mentioned out loud, and in her opinion the idea of the CIA roaming America's heartland by night was one of them.

# Chapter 41

Delfuenso's daughter was called Lucy. Sheriff Goodman met her on the neighbor's stoop. She was a thin child, dark haired and sallow, still in pajamas. She smelled faintly of sleep and a busy household. Goodman sat her down on the concrete step and sat next to her with his elbows on his knees and his hands hanging loose in front of him. Just two regular folks, chatting. Except they weren't. He started out by asking how she was, and he didn't get much of an answer. The kid was mute with incomprehension. But she was listening. He said her mom hadn't come home from work. He said no one knew where she was. He said lots of people were out looking for her.

The kid didn't really react. It was as if he had given her a piece of arcane and useless information from another world entirely, like the surface temperature of the planet Jupiter, or how AM was different from FM on the radio dial. She just nodded politely and fidgeted and shivered in the cold and wanted to go back inside.

Next Goodman spoke with the neighbor herself. He gave her the same incomplete information: Delfuenso was missing, her whereabouts were unknown, a search was continuing. He told the woman he had been advised that Lucy should stay home from school. He said maybe it would be a good idea if her own kid stayed home too. Then he asked the woman if she could stay home from work as well, to keep an eye on them both. He said familiar faces would probably be a good thing for Lucy, under the circumstances.

The neighbor hemmed and hawed and fussed a little, but in the end she said she would try to make it all work. She would do her best. She would make some calls. Goodman left her there at the door, the two kids energetic in the gloom behind her, the woman herself inert and distracted and looking worried about a dozen different things all at once.

**The rain stopped** and the clouds thinned and the Interstate went from streaming to damp to dry, all within a ten-mile stretch. Reacher started to recognize some of the road. It looked different by day. No longer a tunnel through the dark. Now it felt like an endless causeway, raised a little above the infinite flatness all around. He sat still and patient and watched the exits, most of them deceptive, some of them promising. Then he saw a really good one three or four miles ahead, vague in the distance, shapeless in the gray light, a cluster of buildings and a forest of bright signs, Exxon and Texaco and Sunoco, Subway and McDonald's and Cracker Barrel, Marriott and Red Roof and the Comfort Inn. Plus a huge billboard for an outlet mall he hadn't seen by night, because the sign was made of unlit paper, not neon.

He said, "Let's get breakfast."

Sorenson didn't answer. He felt her stiffen in her seat. He felt her get a little wary. He said, "I'm hungry. You must be, too. And I'm sure we need gas, anyway."

No response.

He said, "I'm not going to give you the slip. I wouldn't be in this car in the first place unless I wanted to be. We have a deal. You remember that, right?"

She said, "The Omaha field office has to show something for a night's work."

"I understand that. I'm coming with you, all the way."

"I have to be sure of that. So we'll eat if there's a drive-through."

"No," he said. "We'll go inside and sit at a table, like civilized people who trust each other. And I need to take a shower. And I need to buy some clothes."

"Where?"

"At the outlet mall."

"Why?"

"So I can change."

"Why do you need to change?"

"So I make a good impression."

"Were your bags still in the Impala?"

"I don't have bags."

"Why not?"

"What would I put in them?"

"Clean clothes, for instance."

"And then what, three days later?"

Sorenson nodded. "You make a good point." She was quiet for half a mile and then she slowed the car and put on her turn signal for the exit. She said, "OK, I'm trusting you, Reacher. Don't embarrass me. I'm way out on a limb here."

Reacher said nothing. They turned left off the end of the ramp and nosed into a Texaco station. Sorenson got out of the car. Reacher got out too. She didn't like that much. He shrugged. He figured if she was going to trust him at all, she might as well trust him from the very beginning. She dipped a plain Amex and started pumping. He said, "I'm going in the store. You need anything?"

She shook her head. She was worried. With good reason. A live gas hose was like a ball and chain. He was free, and she was anchored.

"I'll be back," he said, and walked away. The store was like a shabby version of the Shell station's, south and east of Des Moines. Same kind of aisles, same kind of stuff, but run-down and dirty. Same kind of clerk at the register. The guy was staring at Reacher's nose. Reacher prowled the aisles until he found the section with travel necessities. He took a tube of anti-septic cream and a small box of Band-Aids. And a small tube of toothpaste. And a bottle of aspirin. He paid in cash at the register. The clerk was still staring at his nose. Reacher said, "Mosquito bite. That's all. Nothing to worry about."

He found Sorenson waiting for him halfway be-

tween the store and the pump. Still worried. He said,
"Where do you want to get breakfast?"

She said, "Is McDonald's OK with you?"

He nodded. He needed protein and fats and sugars,
and he didn't really care where they came from. He
had no prejudice against fast food. Better than slow
food, for a traveling man. They got back in the car and
drove a hundred yards and pulled off again and
parked. They went inside to fluorescent light and cold
air and hard plastic seats. He ordered two cheeseburgers and two apple pies and a twenty-ounce cup of coffee. Sorenson said, "That's lunch, not breakfast."

Reacher said, "I'm not sure what it is. Last time I
woke up was yesterday morning."

"Me too," Sorenson said, but she ordered regular
breakfast items. Some kind of a sausage patty, with
egg, in a bun, also with a cup of coffee. They ate together across a wet laminate table. Sorenson asked,
"Where are you going to get a shower?"

"Motel," Reacher said.

"You're going to pay for a night's stay just to take a
shower?"

"No, I'm going to pay for an hour."

"They're all chains here. They're not hot-sheet
places that rent by the hour."

"But they're all run by human beings. And it's still
morning. So the maids are still around. The clerk will
take twenty bucks. He'll give a maid ten to do a room
over again, and he'll put ten in his own pocket. That's
how it usually works."

"You've done this before."

"I'd be pretty far gone if I hadn't."

"Expensive, though. With the clothes and all."

"How much do you pay for your mortgage every month? And the insurance and the oil and the maintenance and the repairs and the yard work and the taxes?"

Sorenson smiled.

"You make a good point," she said again.

Reacher finished first and headed for the men's room. There was a pay phone on the wall outside. He ignored it. There was no window. No fire exit. He used the john and washed his hands and when he got back he found two men crowding Sorenson from behind. She was still in her chair and they were one each side of her, meaty thighs close to her shoulders but not quite touching them, giving her no room at all to swivel and get out. They were talking about her to each other, over her head, coarse and boorish, wondering out loud why the pretty little lady wasn't inviting them to sit down with her. They were truckers, probably. Possibly they mistook her for a business traveler far from home. A woman executive. The black pantsuit, the blue shirt. A fish out of water. They seemed to like her hair.

Reacher stopped ten feet away and watched. He wondered which she would pull first, her ID or her Glock. He guessed ID, but would have preferred the Glock. But she pulled neither. She just sat there, taking it. She was a very patient person. Or perhaps there would be paperwork involved. Reacher didn't know the ins and outs of Bureau protocol.

Then one of the guys seemed to sense Reacher's presence and he went quiet and his head turned and his eyes locked on. His pal followed suit. They were large men, both of them bulky with the kind of flesh that wasn't quite muscle and wasn't quite flab. They had small dull eyes and unshaven faces, and bad teeth and stringy hair. They were what a doctor friend of Reacher's used to write up as PPP. A diagnosis, a message, a secret insider medical code, one professional to another, for ease of reference.

It meant Piss-Poor Protoplasm.

*Decision time, boys,* Reacher thought. *Either break eye contact and walk away, or don't.*

They didn't. They kept on staring. Not just fascination with the nose. A challenge. Some kind of a brainless hormonal imperative. Reacher felt his own kick in. Involuntary, but inevitable. Adrenaline, seasoned with an extra component, something dark and warm and primitive, something ancient and prehistoric and predatory, something that took out all the jitters and left all the power and all the calm confidence and all the absolute certainty of victory. Not like bringing a gun to a knife fight. Like bringing a plutonium bomb.

The two guys stared. Reacher stared back. Then the guy on the left said, "What are you looking at?"

Which was a challenge all by itself, with a predictable dynamic. For some unknown reason most people backed down at that point. Most people squirmed, and got defensive, and got apologetic. Not Reacher. His instinct was to double down, not back down.

He said, "I'm looking at a piece of shit."

No response.

Reacher said, "But a piece of shit with a choice. Option one, get back in your truck and get breakfast fifty miles down the road. Option two, get in an ambulance and get breakfast through a plastic tube."

No response.

"It's a limited time offer," Reacher said. "So be quick, or I'll choose for you. And to be absolutely honest, right now I'm leaning toward the ambulance and the feeding tube."

Their mouths moved and their eyes flicked from side to side. They stayed where they were. Just for a couple of seconds, just enough to save face. Then they picked option one, like Reacher knew they would. They turned and shuffled away, slowly enough to look unconcerned and a little defiant, but they kept on going. They made steady progress. They pushed out the door and disappeared into the lot. They didn't look back. Reacher breathed out and sat down again.

Sorenson said, "I don't need you to look after me."

Reacher said, "I know. And I wasn't. They were talking to me by that point. I was looking after myself."

"What would you have done if they hadn't left?"

"Moot point. Guys like that always leave."

"You sound disappointed."

"I'm perpetually disappointed. It's a disappointing world. As in, why were you just sitting there and taking it?"

"Paperwork," she said. "Arresting people is such a pain in the ass."

She took out her phone and lit it up. She checked it for bars and battery. She shut it down again.

"Expecting a call?" Reacher asked.

"You know I am," she said. "I'm waiting to be taken off this case."

"Maybe that isn't going to happen."

"It should have happened two hours ago."

"So what's your best guess?"

But she didn't get a chance to answer that question, because right then, right on cue, her phone started ringing.

# Chapter 42

**The phone hopped and buzzed.** The ring tone was thin and reedy. A plain electronic sound. Sorenson answered the call and listened. Reacher could see in her face it was not the call she was expecting. She wasn't being taken off the board. Not yet. She was being given information about the case instead. Not bad news, necessarily, judging by her expression, but not good news either. Interesting news, probably. Perplexing news, possibly.

She clicked off and looked across the wet laminate table and said, "Our medical examiners finally got around to moving the dead guy out of the old pumping station."

Reacher said, "And?"

"A hitherto unnoticed condition became readily apparent."

"Which is?"

"Just before they stabbed him to death, they broke his arm."

\* \* \*

**Sorenson told Reacher** her Bureau MEs had hoisted
the dead guy onto a wheeled gurney for the short trip
out to the meat wagon. No body bag, which was normal for that kind of situation, where a corpse was
lying in a lake of drying blood. No point getting the
bag sticky both inside and out. They had planned to
zip the guy up in the truck.

But on the way to the truck the gurney had hit a
bump and the dead guy's right arm had flopped off
the side, with the elbow turned the wrong way out.
They had used a portable X-ray machine right there
on the sidewalk, and determined that the joint was
shattered. It was inconceivable the injury could have
happened at any prior time, because the pain would
have been unbearable. No one could walk around
with a shattered elbow. Not even for a minute. Certainly no one could drive all the way from Denver.
And the injury wasn't postmortem either. There was a
little bleeding visible through the skin. And some very
slight swelling. But not much. Blood pressure had
continued after the break, but not for long.

"Defensive injury," Reacher said. "In a way. At one
remove, as it were. He pulled a weapon. A gun, or
possibly a knife of his own. In self-defense. They disarmed him with a degree of violence. I assume he was
right-handed."

"Most people are," Sorenson said. "And then they
cut him, and stabbed him, and then he bled out mo-
ments later."

"Did the eyewitness hear a scream?"

"He didn't say so."

"Busted elbows hurt bad. He must have heard something. A yelp, at least. Pretty loud, probably."

"Well, we can't ask him now."

"No weapons found at the scene? His or theirs?"

Sorenson shook her head. "They probably tossed them all down the open pipe."

"You still think he was just a trade attaché? Far from home with a knife or a gun in his pocket?"

Sorenson shook her head again.

"Something I haven't told you," she said. "The CIA has been sniffing around all night long. They called within minutes. Even before Bureau counterterrorism got there. Well before the State Department guy got there."

"What did they want?"

"Updates and information."

"There you go," Reacher said. "The dead guy was one of their own."

"So why am I still on the case? This thing should have gone nuclear by now." She checked her phone again. It had bars and battery, but it was stubbornly silent.

**They hit the** outlet mall next. Cheap stuff, in a cheap and dismal building. About a third of the units sold men's clothing. Reacher recognized some of the brands. He wasn't impressed by the discount pricing. In his opinion the steep reductions merely brought the values close to where they should have been all along.

As always his choices were limited by the availability or otherwise of the right big-and-tall sizes. But he managed to find generic blue jeans at one store, and a three-layer upper body ensemble at another: T-shirt, dress shirt, and cotton sweater, all shades of blue. Plus blue socks and white underwear at a third store, and a short blue warm-up jacket at a fourth. He figured he would keep the boots he already had. Just a few days more. They were OK.

"You like blue?" Sorenson asked him.

"I like everything to match," he said.

"Why?"

"Someone told me I should."

Total damage was seventy-seven dollars in cash, which was well within target. Three days' wear, minimum, maybe four maximum, somewhere between about twenty and twenty-five bucks a day. Cheaper than living somewhere, and easier than washing and ironing and folding and packing. That was for damn sure.

Sorenson asked, "Where do you get your money?"

Reacher said, "Here and there."

"Where and where?"

"Savings, some of it."

"And the rest?"

"I work sometimes."

"Doing what?"

"Casual labor. Whatever needs doing."

"How often?"

"Now and then."

"Which can't pay much."

"I get the rest from alternative sources."

"What does that mean?"

"Spoils of war, usually."

"What war?"

Reacher said, "I steal from bad guys."

"And you're admitting this to me?"

"I'm following your example. Federal agencies seize property all the time, right? You find coke in some guy's glove box, it's goodbye BMW. Same with houses and boats."

"That's different. That stuff reduces our expenditures. It spares the taxpayer."

"Likewise," Reacher said. "I'd be on food stamps otherwise."

He chose the Red Roof Inn for his shower. A franchise operation, with the owner on duty at the desk, and like all such guys, happy to put a little extracurricular cash in his back pocket. As expected he settled for a pair of tens, one for him and one for whichever maid was first up for favors. Reacher carried his gas station purchases into the room in one bag, and his new outfit in four others. Sorenson came in with him and checked around. She didn't say anything, but he saw she wasn't happy with the bathroom window. It wasn't big, but it was big enough. It was a ground-floor room, with a paved alley out back.

"Stay here, if you want," Reacher said. "I'll leave the shower curtain open. To keep your mind at rest."

She smiled, but she didn't reply. Not directly. Instead she said, "How long will this take?"

"Twenty-two minutes for the shower," he said. "Then three to get dry, and three to get dressed. Plus five for unforeseen eventualities. Call it thirty-three minutes total."

"That's very exact."

"Precision is a virtue."

She left and he started peeling off his old clothes. They were in pretty bad shape. He had been wearing them for days, since Bolton, South Dakota. In places they were crusted with mud, and in other places they were spotted with blood, some of it his own, and some of it not. He balled the wrecked garments up tight and stuffed them all in the bathroom trash. Then he cleaned his teeth very thoroughly and set the shower running.

He washed his hair and soaped himself up from head to foot and scrubbed and rinsed. Eight minutes. Then he got out of the shower and used a washcloth and a sink of hot water and the mirror above it to attend to his face. He soaked off the hardened smears of blood and sponged the open lacerations carefully. He rubbed a slick of soap on his upper lip and sniffed as hard as he could until he started sneezing uncontrollably. Clots of blood came out, as big as garden peas.

Then he got back in the shower and washed himself from head to foot all over again. He toweled off and dressed, and combed his hair with his fingers. He put his old passport and his ATM card in one pocket and his toothbrush in another. He put the short fat guy's motel key in his jacket. He ate aspirins and drank water from the tap. Then he found his antiseptic cream and his Band-Aids and he opened the window to let the steam out and clear the mirror.

Julia Sorenson was in the back alley, watching the window.

She was on the phone. She wasn't enjoying the call. She was arguing, but politely. With her boss, Reacher guessed. Hence the restraint. He couldn't hear what was being said on either end of the conversation, but he figured the guy was finally taking her off the board, and she was pitching to stay on. She seemed to be making all kinds of good points. Her free hand was chopping the air, pushing objections aside, moving persuasive reasons front and center. She was using the physical gestures to put animation in her voice. The telephone was a poor means of communication, in Reacher's opinion. It had no room for body language and nuance.

He looked back in the mirror and used toilet paper to dry his cuts. Then he squeezed thin worms of cream into them from the tube of antiseptic. He wiped the excess and dried the intact areas of skin. He put a Band-Aid over the biggest cut. Another over the second biggest. He dumped the trash on top of his old clothes and closed the bathroom window and headed for the bedroom. He took a look in the mirror next to the closet. The new clothes were pretty good. His hair looked OK. His face was a mess. No oil painting, that was for sure. But then, it never had been, and it was certainly a lot better than an hour ago. A whole lot better. Almost halfway human.

He stepped out to the lot. Sorenson's cruiser was right outside the door. She was leaning on the front fender. Reacher guessed she had left the alley when he closed the bathroom window. At that point she had hustled around to the front, double quick. Not to greet him. To make sure he didn't run.

She said, "You clean up pretty well."

Something in her face. Something in her voice. Not hurt. Not anger. Not necessarily even disappointment. More like confusion.

Reacher said, "What?"

"I got a call."

"I saw."

"My SAC."

"I guessed. Did he take you off the case?"

She shook her head no, then changed it to a yes. She said, "I mean, I'm off the case, yes. But not because he took me off, no."

"Then why?"

"Because there is no case. Not anymore."

"What does that mean?"

"It means that as of twenty minutes ago there is no active investigation. Which is logical, really, because as far as the Federal Bureau of Investigation is concerned nothing happened in Nebraska last night. Absolutely nothing at all."

# Chapter 43

Sorenson said, "They took it the other way. They didn't take it nuclear. They made it a black hole instead. They're erasing it from history. A CIA demand, presumably. Or State. Something squirrelly. Some kind of national security bullshit." Then her phone rang again before Reacher could reply. She checked the incoming number and asked, "Where is the 405 area code?"

"Southwestern Oklahoma," Reacher said. "Lawton, probably. It's the army."

She answered and listened for a spell and thanked whoever she was talking to. She clicked off and said, "Mother Sill confirms she had a Peter James King on active duty in 1991. He was a fister. Which I'm sure isn't what I think it is."

"Fire support team," Reacher said. "Not just a dagby after all. I sold him short. Probably a forward observer. Smart guys, most of them. The 13F MOS. Which meant he maneuvered with the lowly infantry or the humble armored divisions, rather than the kings of battle themselves. Did they confirm a brother named Alan?"

"No. Didn't deny one, either. But they'll need paperwork."

"What happened to Peter?"

"He quit as a sergeant first class in 1997."

"Same year as me. Where is he now?"

"Mother Sill doesn't know for sure. Last she heard he was working with a security company in Denver, Colorado. Which happens to be exactly where the dead guy flew into."

"Coincidence," Reacher said. "Alan King said they don't talk."

"Did you believe him?"

"He told the truth about Peter's name and service, apparently. Why wouldn't he be telling the truth about not talking to him too?"

"How many people live in Denver?"

"About six hundred thousand," Reacher said. "Between two and a half and three million in the metro area, depending on how you measure it. Too small and too big to match King's million and a half."

"How do you know stuff like that? Area codes and populations?"

"I like information. I like facts. Denver was named after James W. Denver, who was governor of the Kansas Territory at the time. It was a kiss-ass move by a land speculator called Larimer. He hoped the governor would move a county seat there and make him rich. What he didn't know was that the governor had already resigned. Mails were slow in those days. And then the new place became part of Colorado anyway, not Kansas. Area code is 303."

"Get in the car," Sorenson said.

"Want me to drive the rest of the way?"

"No, I don't. I can't arrive with you at the wheel. It's bad enough having you in the front."

"I'm not going to ride in the back."

Sorenson didn't reply to that. They climbed aboard, into their accustomed positions. Sorenson backed out of the motel lot and threaded her way back to the highway. She took the ramp and accelerated. There were rain clouds in the east. The weather was chasing them all the way. Sorenson fumbled her phone up into its cradle, where it beeped once to acknowledge it was charging, and then immediately it started to ring again, no longer thin and reedy, but loud and powerful through the sound system. Sorenson accepted the call and Reacher heard a man's voice say he was en route for the location south and east of Des Moines, Iowa, as instructed.

Sorenson clicked off and said, "My forensics team, heading for Delfuenso."

Reacher said, "Who is what we should be talking about here. How can the Bureau shut down a case where an innocent bystander died?"

"Such a thing has happened before."

"But facts don't just go away."

"We don't dispute Delfuenso died. Lots of people die every day."

"How did she die?"

"No one knows. She drove her own car to a neighboring state. It set on fire. Suicide, maybe. Maybe she took some pills and smoked a last cigarette. And dropped the cigarette. We'll never know for sure, because the evidence was lost in the fire. The pill bottle, and so on."

"That's your boss's script?"

"It's a local matter now. Sheriff Goodman will deal with it. Except he won't, because someone will sit on him too, for sure."

"What about the missing eyewitness? Is he erased too?"

Sorenson shrugged at the wheel. "A no-account local farm worker, with a history of drinking and a rented house and no stable relationships? People like that wander off all the time. Some of them come back, and some of them don't."

"That's all in the script too?"

"Everything will have a plausible explanation. Not too precise, not too vague."

Reacher said, "If the case was closed twenty minutes ago, why are you still getting calls? Like just now, from Mother Sill, and your forensics guy?"

Sorenson paused a beat. She said, "Because they both had my cell number. They called me direct. They didn't go through the field office. They haven't gotten the memo yet."

"When will they?"

"Not soon, I hope. Especially my forensics guys. I need to know how King and McQueen kept Delfuenso in the back seat. I mean, would you just sit still for that? They set the car on fire, and you just sit there and take it? Why would you? Why wouldn't you fight?"

"They shot her first. It's obvious. She was already dead."

"That's what I'm hoping."

"They may never be able to prove it."

"All I need is an indication. A balance of probabilities. Which I might get. My people are pretty good."

"Your boss will recall them, surely."

"He doesn't know they're out and about. And I'm not going to make it a point to tell him."

"Won't they check in?"

"Only with me," Sorenson said. "I'm their primary point of contact."

She drove on, another fast mile, with Reacher quiet beside her. The sun was still out behind them. It was casting shadows. The rain clouds were still low in the sky. But they were coming. The far horizon was bright. Reacher said, "If there's no case anymore, then the Omaha field office doesn't need to show anything for its night's work. Because there was no night's work. Because nothing happened in Nebraska."

Sorenson didn't answer.

Reacher said, "And if there's no case anymore, who needs a suspect or a material witness? No one did anything and no one saw anything. I mean, how could anyone, if nothing even happened?"

No response.

Reacher said, "And if there's no active investigation anymore, then there won't be any new information for you to pass on to me."

Sorenson said nothing.

Reacher asked, "So why am I still in this car?"

No answer.

Reacher asked, "Am I in the script too? A no-account unemployed and homeless veteran? With no stable relationships? Not even a rented house? People like me wander off all the time, right? Which would be very convenient for all concerned. Because I'm the last man alive who can call bullshit on this whole thing. I know what happened. I saw King and Mc-Queen. I saw Delfuenso with them. I know she didn't drive her own car to a neighboring state. I know she didn't take any pills. So are they going to erase me too?"

Sorenson said nothing.

Reacher asked, "Julia, did you discuss me with your boss while I was in the shower?"

Sorenson said, "Yes, I did."

"And what are your orders?"

"I still have to bring you in."

"Why? What's the plan?"

"I don't know," Sorenson said. "I have to bring you to the parking lot. That's all I was told."

# Chapter 44

Reacher spent a long minute revisiting a variation on an earlier problem: It was technically challenging to take out a driver from the front passenger seat, while that driver was busy doing eighty miles an hour on a public highway. More than challenging. Impossible, almost certainly, even with seat belts and airbags. Too much risk. Too many innocent parties around. People driving to work, old folks dropping in on family.

Sorenson said, "I'm sorry."

Reacher said, "My mom always told me I shouldn't put myself first. But I'm afraid I'm going to have to this time. How much trouble will you be in if you don't deliver me?"

"A lot," she said.

Which was not the answer he wanted to hear. He said, "Then I need you to swear something for me. Raise your right hand."

She did. She took it off the wheel and brought it up

near her shoulder, palm out, halfway between slow and snappy, a familiar move for a public official. Reacher swiveled in his seat and caught her wrist with his left hand, *one,* and then he leaned over and snaked his right hand under her jacket and took her Glock out of the holster on her hip, *two.* Then he sat back in his seat with the gun in the gap between his leg and the door.

*Three.*

Sorenson said, "That was sneaky."

"I apologize," Reacher said. "To you and my mom."

"It was also a crime."

"Probably."

"Are you going to shoot me?"

"Probably not."

"So how are we going to play this out?"

"You're going to let me out a block from your building. But you're going to tell them you lost me twenty miles back. So they start looking in the wrong place. Maybe we stopped at a gas station. Maybe I went to use the bathroom, and ran."

"Do I get my gun back?"

"Yes," Reacher said. "A block from your building."

Sorenson drove on and said nothing. Reacher sat quiet beside her, thinking about the feel of the skin on her wrist, and the warmth of her stomach and hip. He had brushed them with the heel of his hand, on his way to her holster. A cotton shirt, and her body under it, somewhere between hard and soft.

\* \* \*

**They stayed on** the Interstate through the southern part of Council Bluffs, Iowa, and they crossed the Missouri River on a bridge, and then they were back in the state of Nebraska, right in the city of Omaha itself. The highway speared through its heart, past a sign for a zoo, past a sign for a park, with residential quarters to the north and a ragged, tightly packed strip of industrial enterprises to the south. Then eventually the highway curved away to the left and Sorenson came off on a street that continued straight onward east to west through the center of the commercial zone. But by that point the zone had changed. It had become more like a retail park. Or an office park. There were broad lawns and trees and landscaping. Buildings were low and white, hundreds of yards apart. There were huge flat parking lots in between. Reacher had been expecting something more central and more urban. He had pictured narrow streets and brick walls and corners and alleys and doorways. He had been anticipating a regular downtown maze.

He asked, "Where exactly is your place?"

Sorenson pointed beyond the next light, diagonally, west and a little north.

"Right there," she said. "That's it."

Two hundred yards away Reacher saw the back of a sprawling white building, pretty new, four or five stories high. Behind it and to the right and left of it were wide grassy areas. Beyond it was a gigantic parking lot for the next enterprise in line. Everything was flat and empty. There was nowhere to run, and nowhere to hide.

"Keep going," he said. "This is no good."

Sorenson had already slowed the car. She said, "You told me a block away."

"These aren't blocks. These are football fields."

She rolled through the light. Directly behind the white building Reacher saw a small parking lot with staff vehicles and unmarked cars in neat lines. But there was a navy blue Crown Vic all alone some yards from them, waiting at an angle, and a black panel van next to it. There were four men stumping around in the space between the two, hunched in coats, sipping coffee, shooting the shit, just waiting.

For him, presumably.

He asked, "Do you know them?"

"Two of them," Sorenson said. "They're the counterterrorism guys that came up from Kansas City last night. Their names are Dawson and Mitchell."

"And the other two?"

"Never saw them before."

"Keep going."

"Couldn't you at least talk to them?"

"Not a good idea."

"They can't really do anything to you."

"Have you read the Patriot Act?"

"No," Sorenson said.

"Has your boss?"

"I doubt it."

"Therefore they can do whatever the hell they want to me. Because who's going to tell them otherwise?"

Sorenson slowed some more.

Reacher said, "Don't turn in, Julia. Keep on going."

"I gave them an ETA. Pretty soon they're going to come out and start looking for me."

"Call them and tell them you're broken down on the shoulder somewhere. Tell them you got a flat tire. Tell them we're still in Iowa. Or tell them we took a wrong turn and went to Wisconsin by mistake."

"They'll track my cell. Maybe they already are."

"Keep on going," Reacher said.

Sorenson accelerated gently. They passed the side of the white building. It was about a hundred yards away. It had a wide looping driveway in front of it. Its facade was modern and impressive. There was a lot of plate glass. There was no obvious activity going on. All was quiet. Reacher turned his head and watched as the building fell away behind them.

"Thank you," he said.

"Where do you want to go now?" Sorenson asked.

"A mile away will do it."

"And then what?"

"Then we say goodbye."

But they didn't get a mile away, and they didn't say goodbye. Because Sorenson's phone rang in its cradle and she answered and Reacher heard a man's voice, urgent and loud and panicked. It said, "Ms. Sorenson? This is Sheriff Victor Goodman. Karen Delfuenso's daughter is gone. She was taken away by some men."

# Chapter 45

Sorenson hit the brakes and hauled on the wheel and U-turned immediately and headed back toward the highway, fast, past the FBI building again, past its front, past its side, past its rear lot, and onward, the same way they had come minutes before. The voice on the phone told the whole long story. County Sheriff Victor Goodman, Reacher gathered, about eighty miles away. The local guy. The first responder, the night before. He sounded like a competent man, but tired and stressed and way out of his depth. He said, "I told the kid her mom was missing first thing this morning. I figured it was best to break it gently. You know, the first step, and then the second step. I told the neighbor she should keep both kids home from school today. I asked her to stay home with them. But she didn't. She was worried about her job. She left them there alone. Which she thought would be OK. But it wasn't OK. I dropped by again to touch base and only the neighbor's kid was there. All by herself. She said some men came and took Delfuenso's kid away."

Sorenson asked, "When?"

Goodman said, "This is a ten-year-old girl we're talking about here. She's pretty vague. Best guess is about an hour ago."

"How many men?"

"She doesn't really know."

"One? Two? A dozen?"

"More than one. She said men, not a man."

"Descriptions?"

"Just men."

"Black? White? Young? Old?"

"White, I'm sure, or she'd have said. This is Nebraska, after all. No idea about age. All adults look old to a ten-year-old."

"Clothing?"

"She doesn't remember."

"Vehicle?"

"She can't describe it. I'm not certain she even saw a vehicle. She claims she did, and she's calling it a car, but it could have been anything. A pick-up, or an SUV."

"Color?"

"She can't recall. If she saw it at all, that is. She might have just assumed it. She's probably never seen a pedestrian in her life. Not out there."

"Does she remember what was said?"

"She wasn't really paying attention. The doorbell rang, and Lucy Delfuenso went to answer it. The neighbor's kid says she saw men at the door, and she heard some talking, but basically she stayed in the back room. She was busy playing with something. She was really into it. About five minutes later she realized Lucy hadn't come back from the door."

"Why would Delfuenso's kid answer the door in someone else's house?"

"It doesn't feel like that to them. It's like both of them treat both places like home. They're in and out all the time."

"Have you searched the area? Including Delfuenso's own house?"

"I've got everyone on it. No sign of Lucy anywhere."

"Did you canvass the other neighbor? That gray-haired guy?"

"He wasn't there. He leaves for work at six in the morning. The fourth house didn't see anything either."

"Did you call the state troopers?"

"Sure, but I have nothing to give them."

"Missing kids get an instant response, right?"

"But what can they do? It's a small department. And it's a big state. They can't stop everyone everywhere."

"OK, we'll figure it out," Sorenson said. "I'm on my way. But in the meantime you should keep on looking."

"Of course I will. But they could be sixty miles away by now."

Sorenson didn't answer that. She just clicked off the call and howled around the on-ramp and headed west close to a hundred miles an hour.

* * *

**Ten high-speed minutes** later Reacher gave Sorenson her Glock back and asked, "Is your boss going to ignore a missing kid too?"

Sorenson put the gun back on her hip and said, "My boss is an ambitious guy. He dreams of bigger things. He wants to be an Assistant Director one day. Therefore he'll do whatever the Hoover Building tells him to do, right or wrong. Some SACs are like that. And the Hoover Building will do whatever the CIA tells it to do. Or the State Department, or Homeland Security, or the West Wing, or whoever the hell is calling the shots here."

"That's crazy."

"That's modern law enforcement. Get used to it."

"How much freedom of action are you going to get?"

"None at all, as soon as they figure out where I am."

"So don't answer your phone."

"I'm not going to. Not the first couple of times, anyway."

"And after that?"

"They'll leave voice messages. They'll send texts and e-mails. I can't go rogue. I can't disobey direct orders."

Reacher said nothing.

Sorenson said, "Well, would you? *Did* you?"

"Sometimes," Reacher said.

"And now you're a homeless unemployed veteran with no stable relationships."

"Exactly. These things are never easy. But you can make a start. You can get something done before they shut you down."

"How?"

"Motive," Reacher said. "That's what you need to think about. Who the hell snatches a dead woman's kid? And why? Especially a kid who knows nothing at all about what happened to her mom?"

"But this can't be unrelated, surely. This can't be a coincidence. This is not the father showing up after some custody battle. This is not some random pedophile on the prowl."

"Maybe it was the neighbor's kid they were looking for. Maybe they got them confused. It was the neighbor's house, after all. Is the neighbor divorced too?"

"This is not a coincidence, Reacher."

"So what is it?"

"I don't know."

"Neither do I," Reacher said. "It makes no sense at all."

Sheriff Goodman was into his thirtieth hour without sleep. He was dazed and groggy and barely upright. But he kept on going. No reason to believe the abductors had stayed in the vicinity, but he had his guys out checking any and all vacant buildings, barns, huts, shelters, and empty houses. He himself was supplementing their efforts by covering the places they weren't getting to. He had found nothing. They had found nothing. Radio traffic was full of tired and resigned negativity.

He ended up back in front of Delfuenso's neighbor's house. He parked and sat there and fought to stay awake. Fought to make himself think. He recalled how the kid had acted on the stoop, first thing that morning. Mute with incomprehension, nodding politely, fidgeting. She was a country girl. Ten years old. Not a prodigy. She would have believed any kind of halfway-legitimate adult. She would have been convinced by any kind of show of knowledge or authority. She would have bought into any kind of promise. *Come with us, little girl. We found your mommy. We'll take you to her.*

But who?

Who even knew Delfuenso was missing in the first place? His whole department, obviously, plus the neighbors and presumably some of the other locals. And the bad guys. But why would they kill the mother and then come back for the child?

Why?

He got out of his car to clear his head in the cold air. He stumped around for a minute, and then he rested on the passenger-side front fender. The heat from the engine bay kept him warm. There was rain in the east. He could see the clouds. They were scooting toward him. Then he stared straight ahead at the two houses in front of him, Delfuenso's and her neighbor's, looking for inspiration. He found none at all. He looked down at the muddy gutter. The mud was crisscrossed with his tire tracks. Like a record of futility, written there in rubber and dirt and water. He had parked on that street four separate times in the space of a few hours. First, after the sprint over from Missy Smith's place in the middle of the night. With Sorenson. Then again early in the morning, on his own, to break some of the news. Then again later, to touch base, like a good chief should, which was when he had found Lucy missing. And finally now, after the failed and fruitless local search. There were a lot of tracks. More than he would have thought, for four visits. In and out, back and forth, some straight, some curved. In a couple of places the road surface was bad enough that the mud bulged out into puddles six feet wide. Like tar pits. Apparently he had driven through both of them.

But no one else had.

He checked again, just to be sure, this time on the move, walking up and down with delicate mincing steps, staying clear of the evidence. Or the lack of it. As far as he could tell there were no tracks other than his own. There were no different marks in front of Delfuenso's house. Or in front of the neighbor's. Just his Crown Vic's familiar and undramatic Michelins. The automotive equivalent of generic aspirin. He knew them well. He was responsible for the department's budget. He ordered the tires on-line from a police supply warehouse in Michigan. Low price, no tax, full warranty. They came in on the mail truck and he had them fitted at Phil Abelson's tire shop in the next county. Phil had done a deal, a low charge in exchange for a long-term commitment. Phil was a smart guy.

Goodman got back in his car and moved it off the curb and parked it again on the hump in the middle of the road, where the blacktop was dry and pristine. He got back out and checked again, unobstructed.

He was sure.

No tracks other than his own trusty low-rent Michelins, P225/60R16s, ninety-nine bucks per, plus five for fitting and balancing.

The neighbor's kid hadn't really seen a car because there had been no car.

Lucy Delfuenso had been abducted on foot.

But what kind of sense did that make, in the wilds of Nebraska?

# Chapter 46

Sorenson came off the Interstate exactly where Reacher had gotten on about twelve hours previously. He saw the ramp he had used in the dark and the cold. He remembered the helicopter in the air, and the Impala stopping thirty feet from him, and Alan King and Don McQueen twisting in their seats to warn Karen Delfuenso. He remembered Alan King asking where he was headed. *I'm heading east,* he had said. *All the way to Virginia.*

Not exactly.

Mission not accomplished.

Sorenson continued south, into territory Reacher hadn't seen before, on a county road just as straight as anything in Iowa. But the landscape left and right was subtly different. A little rougher, a little harder. Not as picture-perfect. Twenty miles to the left clouds were rolling in from the east. There was rain in the air below them, gusting and misty and diffuse. The same rain that had fallen in Iowa, on the burned-out Impala, and the fat guy's motel. It was coming after them slowly but doggedly, like a message, like bad news that couldn't be ignored.

Evidently Sorenson had seen the eastbound on-ramp too, and she had drawn the obvious conclusion. She said, "That was where they picked you up, right?"

Reacher nodded. "I was there a fraction over an hour and a half. Fifty-six vehicles passed me by. They were the fifty-seventh."

"Suppose you hadn't been there? Suppose nobody had? They wouldn't have gotten a smokescreen."

"Delfuenso was a smokescreen all by herself."

"But suppose I had been quicker with that? Suppose it had been a three-person APB all along? Maybe with the plate number as the cherry on top."

"They had guns," Reacher said. "They could have fought their way through the roadblocks. Or they could have held a gun to Delfuenso's head. That might have worked. I don't suppose either Nebraska or Iowa gives their troopers that kind of training."

"Big risk."

"What's your point?"

"They started out south of the Interstate and they finished up south of the Interstate. They couldn't guarantee finding a hitchhiker. Not in the middle of winter. And they knew where the roadblocks were going to be, if there were going to be any at all. So why didn't they go east on country roads, directly? Why choose to risk the highway in the first place?"

"At one point they said they were heading to Chicago."

"How many people in Chicago?"

"About three million in the city, and about eight in the metro area. Area codes are 312 and 773."

"Did you believe they were heading for Chicago?"

"Not really. Not on reflection. Too far. Too ambitious for one night's drive."

"So why did they take the Interstate?"

Now the rain clouds were closer. They were moving in like a black wall. The sun had gone. Reacher felt an angry wind rocking the car. The road ahead was straight and level, well constructed, two lanes but not narrow. Turns to the left and right were infrequent, and the east-west roads were little more than paved tracks between fields. They looked desolate, like they didn't really lead anywhere.

He asked, "Have you got a map?"

Sorenson said, "Only electronic."

She fired up her GPS, and Reacher saw it find a satellite. The small screen redrew and the car became a pulsing arrow moving down a thick gray line. The small roads left and right were represented as faint gray lines.

Sorenson said, "You can zoom in and out, if you want."

Reacher found the right buttons and zoomed out. The arrow stayed the same size, but the gray lines got smaller. The north-south road they were on was a principal thoroughfare, but there was nothing equivalent running east and west until a crossroads thirty miles south of their current position.

"That's where we're going," Sorenson said. "The old pumping station is right there."

In the other direction there was no major east-west road until some distance north of the highway. Reacher said, "I guess speed might have been an issue. If they needed to get where they were going before dawn, then the Interstate might have been the only option. But I agree about the risk of exposure. And I'm not sure *how* speed was an issue, exactly. They were picked up, after all. They could have arranged the rendezvous for somewhere much closer. So altogether it would have been more logical to take off directly east from the crossroads, not north. That road looks as good as this one. I'm sure it runs all the way to Iowa."

The first fat raindrops hit the windshield. Sorenson turned her lights and wipers on. A mile to the east the rain was heavy.

**Sheriff Goodman saw** the clouds. His car was still parked in the middle of the road. He was leaning on the fender again. He had decided that snatching a kid on foot was ridiculous. A whole day's walk would get you precisely nowhere in Nebraska. So now he was wondering if the abductors had parked where he was parked, out of the mud. Maybe they were fastidious. Or maybe they had seen the mud and anticipated the danger and decided to avoid leaving tracks in the first place. Or maybe they were worried about witnesses, in which case maybe they had parked out of sight, a couple of hundred yards away. Which would still leave them exposed for a good few minutes. They would have to walk in, two or more unexplained pedestrians, and then they would have to walk out again, two or more men with a child in tow, possibly reluctant.

Then the first fat raindrops fell. Goodman watched them spatter on the mud. He checked the sky. He figured they were in for a short sharp downpour. Not uncommon. The state's immense groundwater reserves had to come from somewhere. He took a last look at the muddy gutter. Pretty soon it would be liquid, and pretty soon after that it would be skimmed over with fresh run-off from the fields, like silt, as flat and as fine as talcum powder. He wasn't concerned. The investigation would not be set back. He wasn't losing evidence, because there was no evidence to lose.

Then the rain got a little harder and he pushed off the fender. Or tried to. He got a sudden sharp pain in his shoulders. And his arms. And a savage dull pain in the center of his chest. Like heartburn. But not heartburn. He hadn't eaten anything.

He couldn't breathe. Couldn't move. His chest locked up solid. His knees gave way. He slid down the slick paint of the fender. He rested for a moment on his heels. He could feel the lip of the wheel arch digging into his back. He could smell the tire. He could smell the rain. His arms wouldn't move.

He pitched sideways and sprawled on his back. He saw black clouds above him. He felt rain on his face. His chest was being crushed. Like it had a heavy weight on it. Like one time long ago in the gym when his spotter had stepped away and he had ended up with a two-hundred-pound barbell resting below his neck. He hadn't even been able to call out. He couldn't call out now. He had no air in his lungs. He couldn't move. He fought for a minute, and then he gave it up, because he knew with sudden strange certainty he would never move again.

He relaxed.

He lost all the feeling in his legs and his arms. Like they weren't even there. He was interested. He was dying from the extremities inward. His body was racing down a list, shedding one non-essential item after another. The animal organism, immensely evolved, programmed to maintain its core function just as long as it could. Programmed to redefine that core function ruthlessly and second by second. Legs? Who needs them? Arms? What for? It was the brain that counted. The brain would be the last thing to die.

Four minutes, he thought. That was the figure that came to him. He remembered his training. People drowning in ponds, kids choking on things, you get four minutes after the heart stops. He felt his life shrinking upward and inward, into his head. That's all he was now. A head. A brain. Nothing else. That was all he ever had been. That was all any human ever was. *Cogito ergo sum. I think, therefore I am.* There was no pain. Not anymore. He was a brain, unsupported. He had no body. Like science fiction. Like a man from Mars. A space alien. He could still see. But his vision was dimming at the edges. Like an old TV. That's how it was going to happen. He understood. Finally. A question, answered. A mystery, solved. He was going to switch off like an old black-and-white TV, collapsing to a tiny spot of light that burned bright in the center of the screen, before dimming and then disappearing forever.

# Chapter 47

The wipers thrashed back and forth and the rain hammered on the roof of the car and bounced a foot off the road. Through the murk Reacher saw an oil company sign high above the plain, lit up bright. Less than half a mile away, he thought. Sorenson glanced at him and said, "OK, pay attention. This is what the locals call Sin City. This is where it starts."

She slowed the car. The gas station was on the left. But she turned right, into a lumpy gravel lot behind a no-name cinder block bar. She crunched on south and stopped behind a low beige building. There was a red Mazda parked at the back door. She said, "This is where Delfuenso worked. It's a cocktail lounge. King and McQueen drove up from the crossroads in the red car."

She rolled onward through the rain, bouncing and splashing through puddles, and she stopped again behind another low building. She said, "This is a convenience store. This is where they bought the shirts and the water." Then she bumped her way back to the road, and paused before turning. She said, "They went north from here, and you know what happened after that." But she went the other way and drove on south. Reacher saw dormant bean fields, with standing water in the plow ruts, and a sad wet quarter-mile of old farm machinery for sale, and then more bean fields. Then came low buildings with spilling rain gutters, and small forlorn strip malls. The town itself, such as it was. The GPS arrow was coming up to the crossroads. The north-south spine was about to meet the east-west spine. The map was fairly definitive. In terms of getting anywhere other than the local corner store, those two roads were the only long-distance options.

Sorenson turned west at the crossroads and a hundred yards later she stopped outside a low concrete bunker. It was maybe twenty feet long by fifteen deep and ten tall. It had a flat roof and no windows and an old metal door. It was soaked with rain, suddenly clean and tan. Reacher said, "This is the old pumping station?"

Sorenson nodded. "The dead guy was on the floor inside. King and McQueen were seen leaving in the red Mazda."

Reacher looked ahead, and behind, and left, and right. He fiddled with the GPS until he had it zoomed out to a twenty-mile radius. At that scale there was nothing on the screen except the north-south road and the east-west road. Everything else had faded away to insignificance. He said, "I think King and McQueen weren't local. It's likely they had never been here before. They probably came in off the Interstate, the same way we did. They saw the bars and the lounges. They didn't want to keep the red car, so they headed back there, which was the only kind of place they'd seen where it was likely they could find a replacement."

"OK, but why didn't they come back to the crossroads and turn east from there?"

"Two reasons," Reacher said. "They're not local, so they didn't know for sure where that road goes. I assume Delfuenso didn't have GPS or maps in her glove box. But more importantly they'll have assumed the crossroads would be roadblocked from the start. Four birds with one stone, right there. North, south, east, west, no one can go anywhere except through that crossroads. Didn't the sheriff block it?"

"No," Sorenson said. "I don't think he did."

"He should have. That was a mistake. But no big deal, because they ran away from it anyway. They went north, and they saw no obvious way east until they hit the highway. At night, in the dark, those side roads must have looked hopeless. So that's why they took the Interstate. No choice."

"OK," Sorenson said. "I'll buy that."

"The bigger question is how they got here in the first place. If they didn't drive in from Denver with the dead guy, and if they didn't have a car of their own, then they must have gotten a ride in with someone else. In other words, they were dropped off here. Just like they were picked up again later. Possibly by the same people. In which case, why didn't whoever it was just wait around for them? Why abandon them to a long and dangerous interlude? The only answer is, whatever happened in the pumping station wasn't supposed to happen. Maybe King and McQueen were supposed to get a ride with the dead guy. But they killed him instead. For some unexplained reason. Which left them improvising like crazy."

Sorenson's phone rang. Loud and dramatic through the speakers. She checked the caller ID. "Omaha," she said. "The field office."

"Don't answer it," Reacher said.

She didn't. She let it go. It rang for a long time, and then it cut off. Reacher said, "We should go see Delfuenso's house. Or her neighbor's, anyway. We should check it out. And we should talk to the neighbor's kid. Maybe she remembered something about the men. They're likely the same crew who vanished the eyewitness. Maybe the same crew who dropped King and McQueen here in the first place."

Sorenson said, "I can't remember where Delfuenso's house is. It was the middle of the night."

Her phone trilled once. A voice mail message.

"Don't listen to it," Reacher said.

She didn't. Instead she scrolled through her list of contacts until she found Sheriff Goodman's cell number. She hit *Call* and the phone dialed. Reacher heard the purr of the ring tone through the speakers, slow and sonorous, patient, no kind of urgency.

It rang for a long time, on and on.

There was no answer.

"Weird," Sorenson said.

* * *

**She backed away** from the old pumping station and turned around and headed back toward the crossroads. Before she got there she turned off into a side street. Reacher knew what she was doing. The sheriff's department wouldn't be on a main drag. It would be in back somewhere, where land was cheaper, where a big lot wouldn't be a drain on the public purse. She nosed around corners and passed all kinds of places, but none of them was a police station. She came out again south of the crossroads and tried again in another quadrant.

"There," Reacher said. He had seen a shortwave antenna on the roof of a low tan building. The building had a fenced lot big enough for a small handful of cruisers. The lot was empty, except for puddles, where the blacktop was holed by age. The whole place was old and worn, but it looked like it was maintained to a reasonable paramilitary standard. Nothing like the army, but nothing like a regular civilian establishment either.

Sorenson parked in the lot and they hustled through the downpour and found a woman behind a counter in the lobby doing double duty as receptionist and dispatcher. Sorenson showed her ID and asked where Sheriff Goodman was. The woman tried his car on the radio and got no result. She tried his cell from her landline console and got no result on that, either. She said, "Maybe he went home to take a nap. He's an old man and he's been awake for a long time."

"We need Karen Delfuenso's address," Sorenson said. "And directions."

The woman behind the counter provided both.

North and east of the crossroads, out in the empty farmland, maybe eight miles distant. Basically left and right and left and right at every opportunity. Another checkerboard. They drove out there slowly. The eastern horizon was bright. The rain was rolling out, but slower than it had rolled in. Reacher was tired. He felt hollowed out. Every cell in his body was thrilling and buzzing with exhaustion. He had been awake most of two days. Not the longest he had ever endured, but up there. He guessed Sorenson was feeling just as bad. She was pale to begin with, and she was going blue around the eyes.

Then after the final right-hand turn Reacher saw a row of four small ranch houses all alone in the emptiness. There was a cop car parked in the middle of the road. Sorenson said, "He's here after all. That's Sheriff Goodman's car. And that's Karen Delfuenso's house, second from the right."

She parked on the curb twenty feet back, and they got out.

# Chapter 48

They found Goodman where he had fallen, on his back, hard up against the front wheel of his car. His eyes were full of rainwater. New drops splashed into the tiny pools and overflowed down his cheeks like tears. His mouth was open and water was pooling in his throat. His clothes were soaked. He looked like a drowned man. His skin was already ice cold. He had no pulse. He looked slack and collapsed and empty, like only dead people can. All the invisible thousand muscular tensions of the living were gone.

*He's an old man and he's been awake for a long time.*

*Not anymore,* Reacher thought.

"How old was he?" he asked.

"Late sixties," Sorenson said. "Maybe early seventies. Too young to die, anyway. He was a nice man. A good man, like his name. Was it a heart attack?"

"Probably," Reacher said. "Stress, exhaustion, and

worry. That kind of thing. Not good for a person. Cops should get paid more."

"No argument from me on that point."

"Did he tell us what we need to know?"

"I don't think he knew what we need to know."

"I guess we should call it in."

So they got back in Sorenson's car, and she dialed the department's switchboard number on her cell. The woman behind the counter answered, and Sorenson broke the news. The woman cried. Sorenson clicked off and they waited, wet, cold, and tired, staring ahead through the windshield, not seeing much, and not saying anything.

Next on scene was a very large thirty-five-year-old man in a deputy's car. He was fair-haired and bulky and red-faced, and he was wearing a padded nylon jacket open over a uniform. The jacket had a sergeant's stripes on the sleeves. The guy came to Sorenson's window and bent down. The jacket fell open and Reacher saw a black plate with the name *Puller* over one shirt pocket and a sheriff's department star over the other. The star had the words *Chief Deputy* on it. The guy knocked on the window with fat red knuckles. Sorenson didn't lower her glass. She just pointed. The guy walked toward his chief's car with short nervous steps, like he was approaching a fortified position. Like he was expecting an armed enemy to open fire. He made it around to the passenger side and stopped. He looked down. Then he staggered away to the shoulder and bent double and threw up in the mud.

Reacher noticed the rain had stopped.

A long moment later the guy named Puller straightened up a little and stared out over the open land. He was green in the face. Not sentimental about the old man, but upset by the sight of a corpse. Reacher got out of the car. The road was still streaming, but the air felt suddenly fresh and dry. Sorenson got out on her side. The guy named Puller started back toward them and they all met as a threesome in the space between the cars.

Sorenson asked, "Are you the department's second in command?"

Puller said, "I guess so."

"Then you guess wrong. As of now you're the chief. Acting chief, anyway. And you've got things to do. You need to bring us up to speed, for instance."

"With what?"

"There's a missing kid here."

"I didn't really keep up with that."

"Why not?"

"I do traffic mostly. To and from the Interstate. Up beyond Sin City. You know, with the radar gun."

"Were you briefed on what happened here last night?"

"We all were."

"But you didn't keep up with it?"

"I do traffic mostly."

"Didn't Sheriff Goodman take you off your normal duties?"

"He took us all off."

"So why didn't you pay attention?"

"He didn't really tell me what to do."

Reacher asked, "Were you dropped on your head as a baby?"

The guy named Puller didn't answer.

Sorenson said, "Call your dispatcher and arrange for an ambulance to take the body away."

"OK."

"Then call Sheriff Goodman's family."

"OK."

"Then call the funeral home."

"From where?"

"From a telephone. Any telephone. Just make sure it's nowhere near me."

The guy named Puller walked back to his cruiser and Reacher and Sorenson walked up Delfuenso's neighbor's driveway.


**Delfuenso's neighbor was** a woman not much more than thirty. Her daughter was a ten-year-old version of the same person, still straight and slender and un-lined. The kid's name was Paula. She was camped out in the back room. No view of the road. No view of anything, except mud. She had an electronic box hooked up to the TV. All kinds of things were happening on the screen. Explosions, mostly. Tiny cartoon figures were getting vaporized in sudden puffs of smoke smaller than golf balls.

The neighbor said, "I had to go to work. I'm sorry."

Sorenson said, "I understand," like she meant it. Reacher understood too. He read the papers. He heard people talking. He knew jobs were easy to lose, and hard to get back.

The neighbor said, "I told them not to answer the door."

Sorenson looked at the kid and asked, "Paula, why did you?"

The kid said, "I didn't."

"Why did Lucy?"

"Because the man called her name."

"He called Lucy's name?"

"Yes. He said, Lucy, Lucy."

"What else did he say?"

"I didn't hear."

"Are you sure? You must have heard something."

The kid didn't answer.

Sorenson waited.

The kid asked, "Am I in trouble?"

Sorenson hesitated.

Reacher said, "Yes, kid, you are. Quite a lot of trouble, to be honest. But you can get out of all of it if you tell us everything you heard and everything you saw this morning. You do that, and you'll be completely free and clear."

A plea bargain. An incentive. A stick and a carrot. A time-honored system. Reacher had gone that route many times, back in the day. A ten-year stretch reduced to a three-to-five, probation instead of jail time, charges dropped in exchange for information. The system worked with twenty-year-olds and thirty-year-olds. It worked just fine. Reacher saw no reason why it wouldn't work just as well with a ten-year-old.

The kid said nothing.

Reacher said, "And I'll give you a dollar for candy, and my friend will give you a kiss on the head."

Bribery worked, too.

The kid said, "The man said he knew where Lucy's mom was."

"Did he?"

The kid nodded, earnestly. "He said he would take Lucy to her mom."

"What did the man look like?"

The kid was squeezing her fingers, like she could wring the answer out of her hands.

She said, "I don't know."

"But you peeked a little bit, right?"

The kid nodded again.

Reacher asked, "How many men did you see at the door?"

"Two."

"What did they look like?"

"Like you see on the TV."

"Did you see their car?"

"It was big and low."

"A regular car? Not a pick-up truck or a four-wheel-drive?"

"Regular."

"Was it muddy?"

"No, it was shiny."

"What color was it?"

The kid was wringing her hands again.

She said, "I don't know."

Sorenson's phone rang. She checked the window and mouthed, *Omaha*.

Reacher shook his head. Sorenson nodded, but she

didn't look happy. She let it ring. Eventually it stopped and Reacher looked back at the kid and said, "Thanks, Paula. You did great. You're not in trouble anymore. You're totally free and clear." He dug in his pocket and peeled a buck off his roll of bills. He handed it over. Sorenson's phone trilled once. Voice mail. Reacher said, "Now the pretty lady will give you a kiss on the forehead."

The kid giggled. Sorenson looked a little shy about it, but she went ahead and bent down and did the deed. The kid went back to her on-screen explosions. Reacher looked at her mom and said, "We need to borrow the key to Karen's house."

The woman got it from a drawer in the hallway. It was a regular house key, on a fob with a crystal pendant. Just like the car key. Reacher wondered what kind of temperature would melt crystal glass. A lower temperature than regular glass, probably. Because of whatever they put in it to make it sparkle. So the car key fob was gone forever. It was a smear of trace elements on the Impala's burned-out floor, or a tiny cloud of vapor already halfway to Oregon on the wind.

He took the key and said, "Thanks," and then he and Sorenson stepped out the door. Goodman's car was still there, but the ambulance had been and gone with the body. Puller's car was gone. And the clouds had gone too. The sky had brightened up. A watery winter sun was visible, high overhead.

Sorenson paused on the driveway and checked her voice mail list. Reacher said, "No need to listen to it. You already know what it says."

"I'm going to have to call in," she said. "The situation has changed. There's still a missing kid here and now there's no local law enforcement. Nothing competent, anyway. Not anymore."

"Call later," Reacher said. "Not yet." He looped around the wet grass and started up Delfuenso's driveway, with the door key in his hand.

Sorenson asked, "What do you expect to find in there?"

"Beds," Reacher said. "Or sofas, at least. We need to take naps. Right now we're no good to anyone. And we don't want to end up like Goodman."

# Chapter 49

Delfuenso's house was identical to her neighbor's in practically every respect. Same exact layout, same kitchen, same windows and floors and doors. Same handles, same knobs, same bathrooms. A cookie-cutter development. There were three small bedrooms. One was clearly Delfuenso's, and one was clearly her daughter's, and one was clearly a guest room.

"Your pick," Reacher said. "The guest bed, or the living room sofa."

"This is crazy," Sorenson said. "I just ignored two calls from my field office. Probably from my boss personally. So I'm effectively a fugitive now. And you think I should sleep?"

"It's an efficiency issue. Like you said, there's a missing kid. Your people aren't going to do anything about her. The locals are useless now. Therefore we'll have to deal with it. Which we can't do if we're dead on our feet from fatigue."

"They'll come after me. I'll be a sitting duck, asleep in bed."

"They're two hours away. A two-hour nap is better than nothing."

"We can't deal with it anyway. We have no idea what's going on. We have no resources."

"I know," Reacher said. "I heard you the first time. No contacts, no support, no help, no back-up, no budget, no facilities, no lab, no computers. No nothing. But what else do you want to do? The guys who have all that stuff are ignoring this whole thing. So we'll have to manage without."

"How? Where do we start?"

"With Karen Delfuenso's autopsy. The initial results. We'll know more when we get those."

"How will those help?"

"Wait and see. You could hustle them along, if you like."

"I don't need to. I know those guys. They'll be working as fast as they can."

"Where?"

"Des Moines, probably. The nearest decent morgue. They'll have walked in and commandeered it. That's how we work."

"When will we hear from them?"

"You know something, don't you?"

"Get some sleep," Reacher said. "Answer your phone if it's your tech guys, and don't if it isn't."


**Reacher used the** living room sofa. It was a compact three-seater with low arms, and it was upholstered in flowery yellow fabric. It was worse than a bed and better than the floor. He stretched out on his back and got his head comfortable and pulled his knees up to fit. He set the clock in his head for two hours, and he breathed in once, and he breathed out once, and then he fell asleep, almost instantly.

And then he was woken again almost instantly, by the phone. Not Sorenson's phone, but the house phone in the kitchen. Delfuenso's landline. It had a traditional metal bell, and it pealed slow and relaxed, six times, patient and unknowing, and then it went to the answering machine. Reacher heard Delfuenso's voice on the greeting, bright and alive, happy and energetic: "Hi, this is Karen and Lucy. We can't come to the phone right now, but please leave us a message after the tone."

Then came the tone, and then came another woman's voice. She said something about making a play date with Lucy, and then the call ended, and Reacher went back to sleep.

**He woke up** for the second time right on his two-hour deadline. His knees were numb and his back felt like it had been hit with hammers. He sat up and swiveled and put his feet on the floor. There was no sound in the house. Just still air. Far from anywhere, in the middle of winter.

He stood up and stretched and put his palms flat on the ceiling. Then he found the bathroom and rinsed his face and brushed his teeth with dinosaur toothpaste he guessed was Lucy's. Then he checked the guest room.

Sorenson was fast asleep on the bed. Her face was turned toward him and a lock of hair was across one eye, just like it had been behind her gun. One arm was up above her head and the other was folded defensively across her body. Half secure, and half insecure. An active subconscious. A conflicted state of mind. He was wondering how best to wake her when her phone rang and did it for him. The plain electronic sound, thin and accusing. One ring. Two. She stirred and her eyes opened wide and she sat bolt upright. She fumbled for the phone with sleep-numbed hands and checked the window.

"Omaha," she said.

Three rings.

She said, "I can't ignore it anymore."

Four rings.

She said, "I'm kissing my career goodbye."

Five rings.

Reacher stepped over to the bed and took the phone from her. He pressed the green button. He raised the phone to his ear. He said, "Who is this?"

A man's voice in his ear said, "Who are you?"

"I asked first."

"Where did you get this phone?"

"Take a wild-ass guess."

"Where is Special Agent Sorenson?"

"Who's asking?"

There was a long pause. Maybe the guy was hooking up a recording device or setting up some kind of a GPS locator. Or maybe he was just thinking. He said,

"My name is Perry. I'm the Federal Bureau of Investigation's Special Agent-in-Charge at the field office in Omaha, Nebraska. In other words, I'm a very senior federal law enforcement officer and I'm also Agent Sorenson's boss. Who are you?"

Reacher said, "I'm the guy who was driving the car in Iowa. And right now Agent Sorenson is my prisoner. She's a hostage, Mr. Perry."

# Chapter 50

Sorenson was going a mute kind of crazy on the bed. The guy in Reacher's ear was breathing hard. Reacher said, "I have very modest demands, Mr. Perry. If you want to get Agent Sorenson back safe and sound, all you have to do is precisely nothing. Don't call me, don't try to track me, don't try to find me, don't hassle me, don't interfere with me in any way at all."

The guy said, "Tell me what you want."

"I just did."

"I can help you. We can work together on this."

Reacher asked, "Did you take the hostage negotiator's course?"

"Yes, I did."

"It shows. You're not listening. Just stay away from me."

"What are you planning to do?"

"I'm planning to do your job."

"*My* job?"

Reacher said, "You've got dead people here, and a

missing kid. You should have told the CIA and the State Department to sit down and shut up, but you didn't. You caved instead. So stay out of my way while I fix things for you."

"Who the hell are you?"

Reacher didn't answer that. He just clicked off the call and tossed the phone on the bed.

"You're crazy," Sorenson said.

"Not really," Reacher said. "This way he's blameless and you're blameless but the job still gets done. Everyone wins."

"But he's not going to do what you told him. I know this guy, Reacher. He's not going to just sit there and take it. He's not going to let you embarrass him in front of the CIA. He's going to come after you. He's going to start a full-on manhunt."

"Let the best man win," Reacher said. "I've been hunted before. Many times. And no one ever found me."

"You don't get it. It'll be easy. He can track my phone."

"We'll leave it right there on the bed. We'll buy another one."

"He can track my *car*, for God's sake."

"We're not going to use your car."

"What, we're going to walk?"

"No, we're going to use Sheriff Goodman's car. It's right here. And he doesn't need it anymore, does he?"


**Goodman's car was** still there on the crown of the road. The keys were still in it, which was what Reacher had expected. City cops usually took their keys with them. Country cops, not so much. There was nothing more embarrassing than having some street kid steal a patrol car during an urban melee, but that kind of danger was rare in the boonies, so habits were different.

And there was an added bonus, too. They didn't need to buy a new phone. Goodman's cell was right there, charging away in a dashboard cradle identical to Sorenson's own Bureau issue. The screen was showing two missed calls. One from Sorenson's cell, and the other from the department's dispatcher.

Postmortem calls.

Reacher racked the driver's seat back and fired up the engine. The car was a police-spec Crown Vic, under the skin exactly the same as Sorenson's more discreet version. But it was older and grimier inside. The seat had been crushed into Goodman's unique shape by many hours of use. Reacher felt like he was putting on a dead man's clothes.

Sorenson asked, "Where are we going?"

Reacher said, "Anywhere with cell reception. We need to wait until we hear from your tech guys. About the autopsy. You need to call them and give them the new number."

"We're basically stealing this car, you know."

"But who's going to do anything about it? That idiot Puller?"

**Reacher turned around** in Delfuenso's empty driveway and headed back south and west toward the crossroads. He got less than half a mile before Goodman's phone rang in its cradle. A loud electronic squawk. Urgent, and nothing fancy.

The readout window showed a 402 area code.

"Omaha," Reacher said.

Sorenson craned over to read the rest of the number.

"Shit," she said. "That's my SAC's private line."

"He's calling Goodman? Why?"

"You kidnapped me. He's alerting local law enforcement all over eastern Nebraska. Iowa too, probably."

"Doesn't he know Goodman is dead?"

"I doubt it. I don't see how he could. Not yet."

"How did he get this number?"

"Database. We have lots of numbers."

"Has he spoken to Goodman before?"

"No. I don't think so. The night duty agent took a call from him. That's all. That's how this whole thing started."

"How do I work this phone?"

"You're not going to talk to him, are you?"

"We can't let everyone ignore him. He'll start to feel bad."

"But he knows your voice. You two just spoke."

"What did Goodman sound like?"

"Like a seventy-year-old guy from Nebraska."

"How do I work the phone?"

"Are you sure about this?"

"Quick, before it goes to voice mail."

"There's a microphone in the windshield pillar. Just hit the green button."

Reacher hit the green button. He heard telephone sounds over the car speakers, unnaturally loud and clear and detailed. Every hiss and every crackle was faithfully rendered. He heard Special Agent-in-Charge Perry's voice. It sounded brisk and a little tense. It said, "Is this Sheriff Goodman?"

Reacher took his right hand off the wheel and put his little finger in the corner of his mouth. Like an intrusive implement during a dental procedure. He said, "Yes, it is."

The voice filling the car said, "Sheriff, I'm Anthony Perry, the SAC at the Omaha FBI. The Bureau has an interest in a situation that may be developing in your neck of the woods."

"And what situation would that be, sir?"

"I believe you may have met Agent Sorenson from my office."

"I had that pleasure last night. A mighty fine young woman. You must be proud to have her working for you, sir."

Sorenson laid her head back and closed her eyes.

Perry said, "Well, yes, but that's beside the point right now. We picked up a report from the Nebraska State Police that a child went missing this morning."

"Sad but true, sir."

"I believe Agent Sorenson may have headed directly to you as a result."

"That's good," Reacher said. "I'll be glad of all the help I can get."

He gulped saliva past his finger.

Perry said, "Are you OK, Sheriff?"

"I'm tired," Reacher said. "I'm an old man and I've been awake for a long time."

"You haven't seen Agent Sorenson today?"

"No, not yet, but I'll be sure to watch out for her."

"It's not that simple, Sheriff. I believe she may have detoured on her way here with a male suspect. I believe that male suspect may have somehow overpowered her and may be currently holding her hostage."

"Well, sir, I can certainly see how you might describe that as a situation. Yes, indeed. But you don't need my permission to come look for her. I think you're entitled to take care of your own people. And you're always welcome here."

"No, I can't spare the manpower," Perry said. "We can't be everywhere at once. I'm asking you and your boys to be my eyes and ears down there. Can you do that for me?"

"Do what exactly?"

"Let me know immediately if you see Agent Sorenson, or her car. And if possible take her companion into custody."

"Do you have a description?"

"He's a big guy with a broken nose."

"Is he dangerous?"

"You should treat him as extremely dangerous. Don't take unnecessary risks."

"You mean shoot first and ask questions later?"

"I think that would be a very sound operating principle, under the circumstances."

"OK, you got it, Mr. Perry. You can cross my county off your list of concerns, as of right now. If he comes here, we'll deal with him."

"Thank you, Sheriff. I very much appreciate your cooperation."

"We're here to serve, sir," Reacher said. He took his finger out of his mouth and pressed the red button on the phone.

Sorenson didn't speak.

Reacher said, "What? That's a good result. This whole county is ours now. We can come and go as we please."

"But suppose we have to stray out of this county? Don't you get it? You're a wanted man. He's putting a hit on you."

"People have tried that too," Reacher said. "And I'm still here, and they're not."

**A mile later** Sorenson called her tech team to let them know she had a new cell number. Her guys didn't answer, so she had to leave a voice mail, which Reacher took to be a good sign, because it likely meant that right then they were hard at work, bent over a stainless steel mortuary table somewhere. He didn't envy them their task. Like all cops he had attended autopsies. A rite of passage, and a character thing, and sometimes important to the chain of evidence. Decomposed floaters were the worst, but badly burned people were a close second. Like carving a London broil, but not exactly.

He stopped a couple of miles short of the crossroads. He didn't want to be seen driving the dead sheriff's car. Not by local people and especially not by Puller or any of the other deputies. He didn't want controversy or radio chatter. Not at that point. At that point anonymity was his friend. He found a field entrance and backed up into the tractor ruts and left the motor running for the heat. He had about half a tank of gas. He stared straight ahead out the windshield at flat brown dirt that ran all the way to the horizon. Six months from then the car would have been hidden by green leaves, in the middle of thousands or tens of thousands of tons of produce, all made by plant DNA and rain and minerals from the earth.

Sorenson asked, "What are you thinking?"

"Right now?"

"No, about Delfuenso's autopsy."

"It'll be a yes or no answer," he said. "Either one thing or the other."

"Care to expand on that?"

"No," he said. "I might embarrass myself."

"Are you easily embarrassed?"

"I can feel a little foolish if I make grand pronouncements that turn out wrong."

"Does that happen often?"

"More often than I would like. Do you have kids?"

Sorenson shook her head. "Never happened for me."

"Did you want it to?"

"I'm not sure. You?"

"No and no. Are you easily embarrassed?"

"Not easily," Sorenson said. "Not professionally, anyway. Sometimes personally, I suppose. Like right now I wish I could shower and change. I've been wearing this shirt since I got up yesterday."

Reacher said, "I wear mine three days minimum.

And right now my nose is busted. So I can't smell anything anyway."

She smiled.

He said, "You could go shopping. You could shower at Delfuenso's house. This county is ours."

"Showering at Delfuenso's house would be creepy. A dead woman's bathroom?"

"We're driving a dead man's car."

"Where could I go shopping, anyway?"

"There must be a store in town. You could get bib overalls."

"You don't want to go to town. Otherwise you wouldn't have stopped here."

"We could go to Sin City. We know they have shirts there, at least. In the convenience store."

"Not very nice shirts."

"You'd look good in anything."

"I'll choose to ignore that," she said. Then she said, "OK, let's go to Sin City. I'll do what you did. I'll buy a shirt and you can get me an hour in a motel."

"Doesn't work that way in the afternoon. The maids will have gone home. You'd have to pay for a whole night."

"No problem. It's worth it to me."

"You're very fastidious."

"Most people are."

"We could get lunch, too."

But then Goodman's phone rang again. The same urgent electronic squawk, loud and resonant through the speakers.

The area code was 816.

"Kansas City," Reacher said.

"Don't answer it," Sorenson said.

The phone squawked on, six, seven, eight times, and then it stopped. The car went quiet again. Just the purr of the motor, and the whir of the heater.

Reacher said, "Your counterterrorism guys are from Kansas City, right?"

"They're not mine," Sorenson said.

"Dawson and Mitchell, right?"

"Yes."

"Who else would call Goodman from a Kansas City number?"

"Could be anyone. Brother, sister, daughter, son. Old college roommate. Fishing buddy."

"During work hours?"

"Why not?"

"Did Goodman even go to college?"

"I have no idea."

"I don't think his chief deputy did."

The phone trilled once. Voice mail. Sorenson leaned over and fiddled with the phone. Her hair touched Reacher's arm. The car filled with a watery, distorted sound.

"Cell phone," Sorenson said. "Weak signal. Probably indoors. Or in a moving vehicle."

Then a voice broke through and said, "Sheriff Goodman, this is Agent Dawson with FBI counterterrorism out of Kansas City. We met last night. I need you to call me back as soon as possible. And until then I need to warn you about a man traveling with Agent Sorenson out of our Omaha office. He's a dangerous fugitive and should be apprehended on sight. My partner and I are on our way to you. We'll deal with the situation after we get there, but please take care until we do. We'll be with you in about thirty minutes or less. We'll check in at the department and hope to see you there."

Then there was more watery distortion, and then there was silence.

Just the purr of the motor, and the whir of the heater.

Sorenson said, "Not our county after all."

# Chapter 51

Reacher didn't move the car. It was in as good a place as any. He said, "Clearly Omaha isn't talking to Kansas City. If your guy had known Dawson and Mitchell were on the way here he wouldn't have asked Goodman to be his eyes and ears."

"More likely the other way around," Sorenson said. "Kansas City isn't talking to Omaha. They're operating independently. Which is typical, for a bunch of counterterrorism hotshots."

"Do they think I'm a terrorist?"

"They know you were driving the car for King and McQueen. Who killed a guy you're pretty sure was CIA. Which puts you all in the relevant category, wouldn't you say?"

"There was a black guy in a pick-up truck who almost stopped for me. Not long before King and McQueen showed up. I was kind of glad at the time. I was cold and it looked like his heater was busted.

Now I wish he had stopped. I'd be in Virginia by now."

"With pneumonia, maybe."

"Let's go get you a shirt and a shower."

"But we only have half an hour. Or less."

"Until what? No one's got a beef with you. And no one will even see me."

"They think I've been kidnapped. They'll rescue me. Same thing as taking me prisoner."

"Your boss hasn't talked to them. They know nothing about the alleged kidnap. They said I was traveling with you, not holding you hostage. They'll say hi, you'll say hi, they'll ask you about the guy with the nose, you'll say you have no idea where he is. That's if they find you at all. Which they won't. They won't want a room at the motel, and even if they do, the clerk won't put them in the same room as you. That's not how motels work, generally."

"OK," Sorenson said. "Let's go."


Goodman's car had no GPS on the dash and no map in the glove box. No obvious need for either thing. Presumably Goodman had known his county like the back of his hand. Probably he had grown up there and lived there all his life. So Reacher navigated by memory and common sense and guesswork. He was about two miles north and east of the crossroads and he needed to get three miles due north of the crossroads. So he threaded basically west through the checkerboard and came out on the main drag opposite the sad line of for-sale farm junk. He paused there and checked both ways and saw nothing to worry about. No Bureau sedans, no SWAT teams, no armored trucks. No local deputies, no roadblocks, no choppers in the air. So he turned north and cruised the last mile and looped in behind the convenience store.

Sorenson detached Goodman's phone from its cradle and put it in her bag. She went in the store and five minutes later she came out again with the same kind and the same size of shirt that Delfuenso had been given, and a smaller softer packet Reacher guessed was dollar underwear and socks. The best-looking motel was on the other side of the road, so Reacher drove over there but parked some distance away. He figured it was better if Sorenson approached the place on foot. In his experience hotel keepers were habitual gossips, and he didn't want a county-wide bulletin about a stranger driving the sheriff's car. He watched Sorenson go into the office, and he saw her come out again five minutes later with a key. He watched her walk down the row of rooms, and he saw her go into one.

Thirty minutes, he figured, for a fastidious woman whose last shower had been more than thirty hours ago. Or forty minutes, possibly, if she was the kind of person who dried her hair with electricity.

He moved the car and parked it behind a bar that was closed in the daytime. Sin City as a whole was pretty quiet. The diners all had signs reading *Last Food Before the Interstate* and the gas stations had signs reading *Last Gas Before the Interstate.* He figured the Chamber of Commerce could have put up a sign saying *Last Everything Before the Interstate* without a word of a lie. But not many drivers were availing themselves of their final opportunities.

He got out of the car and locked it and walked away. He crossed the road and looped around behind Delfuenso's cocktail lounge. The red Mazda was still there. Five doors, four seats. The locks had been jimmied, presumably by Sorenson's tech team. The interior was bland and clean. The driver's seat was set for a person of average height. A rental car, typical in every respect.

*If in doubt drink coffee* was Reacher's operating principle, so he headed back across the road to the diner nearest Sorenson's motel. He got a high-backed corner booth with a blank wall behind him, and a heavy pottery mug full to the brim with a strong brew. A bad receptacle, but decent coffee. And a good tactical position. He could see the room and he could see the street. The restroom corridor was three feet from his left shoulder and there was a fire exit at the end of it. He watched out the window and saw traffic on the road. An eighteen-wheeler heading north, and a similar thing heading south. A battered pick-up truck, a boxy four-wheel-drive covered in mud, and a delivery van lacy with rust.

And then a dark blue Ford Crown Victoria, coming north.

Same make and model and color as Sorenson's car.

Needle antennas on the trunk lid, just like Sorenson's antennas.

FBI.

Two men in it.

It was going slow. Too slow. A telling percentage slower than normal caution. It was going at search speed. The driver was scanning left, and the passenger was scanning right. Reacher watched it crawl past. He thought the guys in it were two of the four he had seen in the lot behind the FBI building in Omaha. Maybe. Dawson and Mitchell. Possibly.

He sipped his coffee and measured time and speed and distance in his head. And right on cue the blue Crown Vic came back, now heading south, still going slow, the two heads in it turning as the two pairs of eyes scanned the shoulders, the buildings, the people, the cars, pausing here and there and hanging up and then jumping ahead again.

Then the car slowed some more.

And turned in.

It bumped over a broken curb and crunched over the gravel into the diner's front lot and came closer and parked with its nose a yard from Reacher's window. The two guys in it sat still. No urgency. No purpose. A coffee break, after a long and fruitless search. That was all. Reacher was pretty sure he recognized them. He was pretty sure they were Dawson and Mitchell. They were blinking and yawning and wagging their necks to ease out the kinks. They were dressed in dark blue suits and white shirts and blue ties. They looked a little ragged. A little tired. One looked a little taller and a little thinner than the other, but otherwise they were a matching pair. Both had fair hair and red faces. Both were somewhere in their early forties.

*Do they think I'm a terrorist?*

*They know you were driving the car for King and McQueen.*

They got out of the car together and stood for a moment in the cold. The driver stretched with his arms straight and his hands held low and the passenger stretched with his elbows bent high and his fists near his ears. Reacher figured they would have Glocks in shoulder holsters and cuffs on their belts. And the Patriot Act and unlimited authority and all kinds of national security bullshit to back them up.

They glanced left, glanced right, and located the diner door.

Reacher took a last sip of his coffee and trapped two dollar bills under his mug. Then he slid out of his booth and stepped into the restroom corridor. He heard the front door open and he heard two pairs of shoes on the tile. He heard the hostess take two menus out of a slot. He walked down the corridor and pushed through the door and stepped out to the back lot.

He crossed the gap between buildings and tucked in behind the motel and tracked along its rear wall. He stopped at the only bathroom window with steam on it. He tapped on the glass and waited. The window opened a crack and he heard a hairdryer shut off. Sorenson's voice said, "Reacher?"

He asked, "Are you decent?"

She said, "Relatively."

He stepped up and looked in through the crack.

She had a towel tucked tight around her. The top edge was up under her arms. The bottom edge was considerably north of her knees. Her hair was wet on one side of her part, and dry on the other. Her skin was pale pink from the steam.

She looked pretty good.

He said, "Your Kansas City pals are in the diner."

She said, "They're not my pals."

"Did your tech people call yet?"

"No."

"What's keeping them?"

"It's probably a complicated procedure."

"I hope they're good enough."

"Good enough for what?"

"To tell me what I want to know."

"That will depend on what you want to know, won't it?"

"I'll wait in the car," he said. "It's behind a bar, two buildings along."

She said, "OK."

The window closed and he heard the click of the latch, and the roar of the hairdryer starting up again. He walked on north, through the back lot, past trash bins, past a pile of discarded mattresses, past an empty rotting carton that according to the printing on the outside had once held two thousand foam cups. He crossed the open no-man's-land and slipped behind the next building, which seemed to be another cocktail lounge. He stepped over an empty bottle of no-name champagne.

And stopped.

Dead ahead of him and thirty yards away was Goodman's car, behind the bar, exactly where he had left it. But stopped tight behind it in a perfect T was another car. Facing away. A sand-colored Ford Crown Victoria. A government car for sure, but not FBI. Not the same as Sorenson's car, or Dawson and Mitchell's. It had different antennas on the trunk lid, and official U.S. license plates. Its motor was running. White exhaust was pooling around its pipes.

It was blocking Goodman's car.

Deliberately or inadvertently, Reacher wasn't sure.

There was one man in it, behind the wheel. Reacher could see the back of the guy's head. He had sandy hair, the exact same color as his car. He was wearing a sweater. He was on the phone.

A sweater meant no shoulder holster. No shoulder holster meant no gun. No gun meant the guy wasn't a plainclothes marshal or any other kind of an operational agent. Not the Justice Department, or the DEA or the ATF or the DIA or any of the many other three-letter agencies.

Ultimately the sweater meant the guy was no threat at all.

A bureaucrat, probably.

*Clothes maketh the man.*

Reacher walked on and stopped right next to the guy's window and knocked on the glass. The guy startled and peered up and out with watery blue eyes. He fumbled for his button. The window came down.

Reacher said, "Move your car, pal. You're blocking me in."

The guy took his phone away from his ear and said, "Who are you?"

Reacher said, "I'm the sheriff."

"No you're not. I met the sheriff last night. And he's dead, anyway. He died this morning. So they say."

"I'm the new sheriff. I got promoted."

"What's your name?"

"What's yours?"

The guy looked momentarily taken aback, as if suddenly conscious of a grievous etiquette offense. He said, "I'm Lester Lester, with the State Department."

Reacher said, "Your parents were very economical people, weren't they?"

"Family tradition."

"Anyway, Lester, I need to get going now."

The guy made no move.

Reacher said, "Two choices, Lester. Roll forward or backward."

The guy did neither thing. Reacher saw the wheels turning in his head. A slow process. But the guy got there in the end. He stared. *A big man. A broken nose.* He said very loudly, "You're the person we're looking for. Aren't you?"

"No point asking me. I have no idea who you're looking for."

"Get in the car."

"Why?"

"I need to take you into custody."

"Are you kidding?"

"You think the security of our nation is a joke?"

"I think involving people like you in it is."

*Very loudly.*

Reacher was suddenly aware of the phone, still in the guy's hand.

Who was he on the phone to?

The diner?

Maybe the guy wasn't so dumb after all.

# Chapter 52

Reacher wrenched the car door open and tore the phone out of the guy's hand and hurled it high in the air, right over the roof of the bar. Then he grabbed the guy by the scruff of his sweater and hauled him out of his seat and half dragged and half ran him back the way he had come, ten feet, twenty, and then he spun him around like a discus thrower and launched him toward the back wall of the cocktail lounge. Then he sprinted back and jammed himself into the guy's seat and slammed the lever into gear and stamped on the gas. Gravel sprayed all over the place and the car shot forward and he stamped on the brake and more or less fell out the door and danced around the trunk of Goodman's car to the driver's door. He blipped the fob and tore the door open and started up and backed away from the back wall of the bar and swung the wheel hard.

The sand-colored Crown Vic was still moving. He had left it in gear. He overtook it and turned tight around its hood and its slow roll caught him with a soft low-speed impact, its front end against his rear quarter. He fishtailed free and drove on through the gap between the bar and the next establishment in line. He glanced left and saw the sandy-haired guy limping as fast as he could after something, either Goodman's car or his own, he wasn't sure. After that last glimpse he looked away from the guy and focused forward and drove through the front lot and bounced over the camber of the main drag and squeezed through a gap into the back lots on the other side of the road.

Then he slowed down and took a breath and got straightened up and edged forward until he was lined up with the next gap south and had a distant view of the motel and the diner together.

No sign of Sorenson.

No action at the diner.

The blue Crown Vic was still parked. Still quiet. No one was rushing toward it. The diner door stayed resolutely closed. There was no commotion visible through the windows.

Reacher watched for a whole minute, until he was convinced.

The State Department guy had not been on the phone to the diner.

So then he watched the motel, and three minutes later Sorenson's room door opened and she stepped out. She was in the same pant suit with the new shirt under it. She had her old shirt balled up in the new shirt's wrapper. She was taking her laundry home. A different approach. Because she had a home.

She stood for a second on the walkway outside her room, glancing left and right, head high, like a woman looking for a taxicab from a city sidewalk. Then she set off north toward the bar where he had said the car was parked. He turned the wheel and eased out through the gap and crunched through the front lot and bumped over the road again and swooped around and braked to a stop right next to her. He leaned over and opened her door and she slid into her seat like it was a maneuver they had rehearsed every day of their lives.

He said, "I had to move. I had a little trouble with your Mr. Lester from the State Department."

She said, "Mr. Lester isn't mine."

Then he realized he had more trouble than he had thought. Far back in the mirror he saw Dawson and Mitchell burst out the diner door and run out into the parking lot. Both had phones to their ears. Their free hands were pumping and their jackets were flapping open. So Lester had in fact called the diner. But not deliberately. Not directly. In a very circuitous way instead. Probably he had been on the line with his people in Foggy Bottom, and his shouted *You're the person we're looking for* and the abrupt termination of the call had gotten some bright guy thinking, and that bright guy had immediately called the Hoover Building, and the Hoover Building had called Kansas City, and Kansas City had called Dawson and Mitchell on their cells, and were in fact probably still in the process of telling them *The guy you're looking for is currently kicking Lester Lester's ass about twenty yards from you.*

They saw him. Or they saw Sorenson. They froze in place and pointed and then ran for their car.

Reacher hit the gas and the sudden acceleration dumped Sorenson back in the passenger seat and the car slewed and fishtailed over the gravel. Reacher fought the wheel and bumped down over the curb at an angle and took off north up the road. He craned his neck and watched in the mirror and saw the blue Bureau car jam backward and turn and come after him.

"Hold on," he said. "I'm a lousy driver."

"Now you tell me," Sorenson said. She scrabbled around and clipped her seat belt and pulled it tight around her. Reacher kept his foot down hard. A big V-8, police spec, plenty of power and torque. Not bad at all. Except that Dawson and Mitchell had the exact same car. Same V-8, same spec, same power and torque. And maybe less weight, without the light bar on the roof and the push bars front and rear. Better aerodynamics, certainly.

Reacher knew the Interstate was fifty miles ahead, and he knew there wasn't much of anything else before that. There were some turns left and right, and there were some small stands of trees here and there, and there were occasional old wooden farm buildings standing all rotted and abandoned and unexplained in the fields. Apart from that there was just winter dirt, and it was all very flat. No dips, no valleys. No hills, no ridges.

Places to run.

No place to hide.

The road surface was bad, and the road bed had

been heaved up and down by years of winter frosts and summer droughts. Acceptable at normal speeds, but dangerous going fast. Goodman's cruiser was riding like a yacht on an ocean swell. The engine was howling and the wheel was writhing in Reacher's hands. Dawson and Mitchell were maybe four hundred yards back, but they were gaining. Reacher jammed his foot down harder. *Pedal to the metal.* A hundred miles an hour.

Places to run.

No place to hide.

*Puller,* he thought.

He said, "Do you know how to work the radio?"

Sorenson said, "I could try."

"Find out where Puller is with his radar gun. Tell him he's got a speeder heading north. A dark blue sedan."

Reacher drove on. No steering involved. The road was dead straight. The car went weightless over dips and hollows. Never airborne, but not far from it. Sorenson took the microphone out of its clip and fiddled with switches. She cleared her throat and said, "Deputy Puller, what is your location?"

Puller's voice came back over static: "Who is that?"

"This is Agent Sorenson with the FBI. Where are you now?"

"A mile shy of the county line, ma'am."

"North, south, east, or west?"

"North."

"OK, good. You have a speeder coming north toward you. A dark blue Ford Crown Victoria. Please stop the driver and caution him against his reckless and unsafe behavior."

"Will do, ma'am."

"Out," Sorenson said. She hung up the microphone. She said, "How do you stop a car doing a hundred miles an hour? We'll probably get Puller killed."

"In which case we'll be helping the gene pool." Reacher hurtled onward. Dawson and Mitchell were now three hundred yards back. About six seconds, at a hundred miles an hour. But they were still gaining. Reacher scanned far ahead. Straight road, flat dirt, low horizon. No sign of Puller.

He asked, "Did your tech team call?"

Sorenson said, "Not yet. What's on your mind?"

"Motive," Reacher said. "Who snatches a dead woman's kid? Especially a kid who saw nothing and knows nothing?"

"How can the autopsy answer *that* question?"

"It might not," Reacher said. "That's what's on my mind." His foot was hard on the boards. It was crushing the pedal. But the car was tapped out. It wouldn't go any faster. A hundred was as good as it got. They passed a turn to the left. Another, on the right. Paved, but not much more than tracks between fields.

"There," Sorenson said.

Reacher saw a dot on the horizon. A tiny smudge, vaguely black and white and gold against the brown. Puller's cruiser, waiting on the shoulder. Maybe a mile away. Thirty-six seconds. No more turns before it. Far away to the right was a copse of trees. Far away to the left was an old barn, swaybacked and gray with age.

Thirty seconds.

Twenty seconds.

"Hold tight," Reacher said.

Fifteen seconds.

He clamped the wheel tight in his hands and came off the gas and stamped on the brakes. The front end dipped radically and he and Sorenson were thrown forward and he fought to keep the car straight. Dawson and Mitchell didn't slow down. They kept on coming. Puller's car was a hundred yards ahead. Then fifty. Then thirty. Then Reacher swung the wheel hard and drove off the road into the dirt on the right and Dawson and Mitchell were launched ahead of him like a slingshot. Reacher hugged a tight bouncing circle in the dirt and saw Dawson and Mitchell passing Puller at about seventy and Puller lighting up his strobes and his siren and pulling out behind them. Reacher continued the circular turn and thumped back up on the road and headed south, fast, back the way he had come, all the way to the turn he had seen on the left, which was now on the right. He braked hard and took it and pattered over the lumpy surface and turned in on a rutted track and came to a dead stop out of sight behind the old swaybacked barn. He got out and ran to the far corner of the ramshackle structure and peered out north.

Nothing in the distance. No sign of Dawson and Mitchell. Not yet. They were still out of sight, more than a mile to the north. He counted out time and space in his head. Right then they would be slowing, stopping, turning around, hassling with Puller, showing ID, arguing, yelling, getting frustrated.

Getting delayed.

Then they would be coming back south, as fast as they could. They would have seen his tight turn on the dirt, and they would be planning on chasing him all the way back to town.

Three minutes, he figured.

Maybe three minutes and ten seconds.

He waited.

And then he saw them, right on time, far away on the main drag, hustling left to right, north to south, doing about a hundred again. An impressive sight. The big stately sedan was really picking up its skirts. Its paint was winking in the watery sun. It was planted firmly on the blacktop, squatting at the rear, straddling the center line. Reacher ran back past Goodman's car and peered out from the barn's other corner. He got a rear view of the blue Crown Vic blasting south. After ten seconds it was a tiny dot. After twenty seconds it was gone altogether.

He breathed out and walked back to the car. He got back in and closed the door. He sat slumped in the seat with his hands on his knees.

Silence. Nothing but the faithful idle of the engine, and clicks and ticks as stressed components cooled back down.

Sorenson said, "You're not such a terrible driver."

He said, "Thank you."

"What now?"

"We wait."

"Where?"

"I guess this place is as good as any."

She unzipped her black leather bag and took out Goodman's phone. She clipped it in its dashboard cradle. It chimed once to tell them it was charging.

Then it started to ring.

She leaned over and checked the window.

"My tech team," she said.

# Chapter 53

Sorenson touched the green button and Reacher heard telephone sounds over the speakers again, weirdly clear and detailed, like before. Sorenson said, "You have something for me?"

A man's voice said, "Yeah, we have some preliminary results."

The voice was tired, and a little breathless. Reacher thought the guy was walking and talking at the same time. Probably stumbling out to the fresh air and the bright sunlight, after long and unpleasant hours in a white-tiled basement room. Breathing deep, blinking, yawning and stretching. Reacher could picture the scene. A pair of institutional doors, a short flight of concrete steps, a parking lot. Maybe planters and benches. Back in the day the guy would have been pausing at that point, to light a welcome cigarette.

Sorenson said, "Go ahead."

The guy said, "You want me to be honest?"

"You usually are."

"Then I can't promise you the incineration was postmortem. It might have been. Or it might not have been. There's something that might have been damage to what might have been a rib. If I squint a bit I could see it as a gunshot wound to the chest. Which might have been enough. It's in what would have been the general area of the heart. But I wouldn't say so in court. The other side would laugh me out of the room. There's far too much heat damage for conclusions about external injuries."

"Gut feeling?"

"Right now my gut feeling is I want to retrain as a hairdresser. This thing was about the worst I've ever seen."

Sorenson was quiet for a long moment.

Then she said, "Anything else?"

"I started from the beginning, with the pelvic girdle. That's the only way to confirm gender with a case like this. And it was totally clear. The pelvic bones had been reasonably well protected by a thick layer of fat."

Reacher looked up. *Delfuenso wasn't fat. She was thin.*

Sorenson said, "And?"

"It's beyond a reasonable doubt the corpse was male."

**Sorenson ran through** the details with her guy. Like a crash course in forensic anthropology. Reacher remembered some of the words and some of the principles from the classroom. He had studied such things once, partly as a professional requirement, and partly out of interest. There were four things to look for with pelvises. First was the iliac spread. The ilia were the big bones shaped like butterfly wings, and female ilia were flared wider, and shaped more like a cradle, like cupped hands, with the anterior spines farther apart, whereas male ilia were narrower and tighter and much more straight up and down, more like a guy on a riverbank describing a foot-long trout.

Then second, the hole in the ischium was small and triangular in females, and large and round in males. And third, the angle across the pubic arch was always greater than ninety degrees in females, and rounded, and always less than ninety degrees in males, and sharp.

And the fourth was the clincher, of course: the space between the ischia was big enough in females for a baby's head to fit through. Not so with males. Not even close.

Pelvises didn't lie. They couldn't be confused one for the other. Even a million-year-old pelvis dug out of the ground in pieces was quite clearly either male or female. Short of being ground to powder, a pelvis determined gender, no question, no doubt at all, end of story, thank you and goodnight. That was what Reacher had learned in the classroom, and that was what the voice on the phone confirmed.

Sorenson said, "So it wasn't Delfuenso."

The voice on the phone said, "Correct. And I'm happy for you. But that's all I can reliably tell you. It was a male human being. Anything more than that would be pure guesswork."

Sorenson clicked off the call and turned to Reacher and said, "You knew, didn't you?"

Reacher said, "I suspected."

"Why?"

"Nothing else made sense after Lucy was taken. I figured Delfuenso might still be a captive somewhere, maybe freaking out, maybe refusing to cooperate, and the only way to shut her up was to go get her kid."

"To calm her down?"

"Or to threaten her with."

"So now we have two of them in danger."

"Or maybe we don't," Reacher said. "Maybe we have two of them as safe as houses. Because there are other potential conclusions, too. But they could be wrong conclusions. They could be embarrassingly grand pronouncements."

"Which one died? King or McQueen? Or was it someone we never heard of yet?"

"It was King, I think. He was a little fat, especially around the middle. And he would fit the theory."

"Which is what?"

"Something McQueen said when we pulled off the Interstate for gas."

"You told me this already. He said you should have trusted him."

"Before that. I was dubious about coming off there and he got a little impatient and said he was in charge."

"Maybe he was. One or the other had to be. I doubt it was a democracy."

"But there's a sound in those specific words, don't you think? *In charge?* You have Special Agents-in-Charge. We had officers in charge of this and that. A charge is something you're given. You're entrusted with it. It's authority that devolves down an official hierarchy."

"That's very subjective."

"I think a regular bad guy would have said *I'm the boss here.* Something like that."

"So what are you saying? You think McQueen is ex-military? Or ex–law enforcement?"

Reacher didn't answer that. He said, "And then he said the thing about trusting him. As if he was worthy of trust, somehow as of right. And then he shot at me and missed."

"Probably not either military or law enforcement, then. Lousy marksman."

"Maybe he was a great marksman."

"But he was in the room with you. It was what, about eight feet? How can he be a great marksman and miss from eight feet?"

"Maybe he missed on purpose."

Sorenson said nothing.

Reacher said, "I didn't really think much of it at the time. I was just happy to be alive. But it was a hell of a high shot. It was a foot over my head. Maybe more. I remember saying it would have missed the motel keeper if he'd been standing on his own shoulders. It was exaggerated. It must have been about ten degrees above the horizontal. More than eleven-point-something, to be precise."

"Don't look a gift horse in the mouth."

"I'm serious. There's more. He moved his position so he was blocking my view of the car."

"So?"

"So he was blocking their view of me. As if he needed them to think he was doing one thing, when really he was doing another thing."

"He missed. That's all. People do, sometimes."

"I think it was deliberate."

"He killed the guy in the pumping station, Reacher. He killed his own partner, apparently. He burned him to death. Why would he miss you deliberately? What makes you special?"

"Only one way to find out," Reacher said.

"Which is what?"

"Tell me your phone number."

"Why?"

"I'm going to need it."

"I left my phone in Delfuenso's house, remember?"

"You're about to go get it back. And your car. And your reputation. You're about to be a hero."

# Chapter 54

Reacher and Sorenson swapped places in Goodman's car and Sorenson drove back to town, sedately, never more than fifty miles an hour. They passed Sin City, and they passed the empty bean fields, and they passed the quarter-mile of old machinery, and more bean fields, and they turned right at the crossroads and drove a hundred yards and parked next to the old pumping station. Sorenson fiddled with Goodman's phone and brought up the list of recent calls and voice mails. She found Dawson's cell number. She dialed it and the guy answered almost instantly.

He said, "Sheriff Goodman?"

Sorenson said, "No, this is Sorenson out of Omaha. Long story with the sheriff's phone. But I have the man you're looking for. He's in my custody. You can come pick him up anytime you like."

"Where are you?"

"At the old pumping station."

"We'll be there in two minutes."

* * *

**Ninety seconds later** Reacher opened his door and said, "OK, I'm ready for my close-up." He got out into the cold and crossed the sidewalk and faced the old pumping station's concrete wall and put his fingertips on the rough surface. He shuffled his feet a yard apart and leaned forward and took his weight on his hands. *Assume the position.* Sorenson stood six feet behind him and pulled her gun and held it two-handed, trained on the center of his back.

"Looking good," she said.

"Not feeling good," he said.

"Best of luck," she said. "It's been fun hanging out with you."

"We're not done yet. I hope to see you again."

They held their poses. The concrete was cold. Then Reacher heard tires on the pavement. He heard a car come to a stop, and he heard doors open. He turned his head. The blue Crown Vic. Dawson and Mitchell. They came out fast, coats billowing, guns drawn, triumph on their faces. They talked with Sorenson briefly. Congratulations, appreciation, thanks. They said they would take over from there. Reacher turned his face back to the wall. He heard Sorenson walk away. He heard Goodman's car start up. He heard it drive off down the street.

Then there was silence. Just breathing from behind him, and the sound of cold air moving across the land.

Then either Dawson or Mitchell said, "Turn around."

Which Reacher was glad to do. His fingertips were numb and his shoulders were starting to hurt. He pushed off the wall and rocked upright and turned around. Both guys had their guns on him. They looked the same as they had through the diner window. Early forties, blue suits, white shirts, blue ties, still ragged, still tired, still flushed. Maybe a little more tired and a little more flushed than before, due to their recent exertions. Of which the worst part had probably been dealing with Puller. Fast driving was no big deal. Dealing with morons was. What was the phrase? *Like teaching Hindu to a beagle.*

The one who was a little taller and a little thinner than the other said, "My name is Dawson. My partner's name is Mitchell. We'd like you to get in the car."

Reacher said, "You understand I never met King or McQueen before last night?"

"Yes, sir. You were hitching rides. We accept that completely. No hard feelings about the evasive maneuvers in the stolen cop car just now, either. And Mr. Lester is prepared to overlook his injuries."

"What injuries?"

Mitchell said, "You hurt his leg. His feelings too, probably."

"So we're all good?"

"Peachy."

"Then why are you arresting me?"

Dawson said, "We're not arresting you. Not technically."

"You're arresting me untechnically, then?"

"Recent legislation gives us various powers. We're authorized to use all of them."

"Without telling me what they are?"

"You're required to cooperate with us in matters of

national security. And we're required to think primarily of your own personal safety."

"Safety from what?"

"You're tangled up with things you don't understand."

"So really you're doing me a favor?"

Dawson said, "That's exactly what we're doing."

Reacher got in their car. In the back. Loose, not handcuffed, not restrained in any way except for the seat belt they made him wear. They said it was Bureau policy to follow best practices for driver and passenger safety. He was pretty sure the rear doors wouldn't open from the inside, but he didn't care. He wasn't planning on jumping out.

Mitchell drove, east to the crossroads and then south into the hinterland. Dawson sat quiet alongside him. Reacher watched out the window. He wanted to study the route they were taking. The county two-lane heading south was pretty much the same as it was heading north. There was no direct equivalent of Sin City, but otherwise the terrain was familiar. Fallow winter fields, some trees, a few old barns, an occasional grocery store, an untidy yard with used tractor tires for sale. There was even a repeat of the sad quarter-mile of third-hand farm machinery, equally lame, equally rusted. There was clearly a glut on the pre-owned market.

"Where are we going?" Reacher asked, because he thought he should, sooner or later, strictly for the sake of appearances.

Dawson roused himself from a stupor and said, "You'll see."

**What Reacher saw** was the rest of Nebraska and a good part of Kansas. Almost three hundred miles in total, the first half of that distance due south from where they had started, just shy of Nebraska's east-west Interstate, all the way down to Kansas's own east-west Interstate. They stopped and got very late lunches at a McDonald's just over the state line. Dawson insisted on drive-through. The same way Sorenson had wanted to eat in Iowa. Reacher figured the FBI had an official policy. Probably a recommendation from a committee. *Don't let your prisoner starve, but don't let him get out of the car, either.* He ordered the same meal as the last time, twin cheeseburgers and apple pies and a twenty-ounce cup of coffee. He was a creature of habit where McDonald's was concerned. The meal was passed in through Mitchell's window and then passed over Mitchell's shoulder to him and he ate it quite comfortably on the back seat. There was even a cup holder there. Cop cars had gotten a lot more civilized since his day. That was for sure.

He slumbered through the rest of the two-lane mileage. *Slumber* was his word for a not-quite-asleep, not-quite-awake state of semi-consciousness he liked a lot. Even if he hadn't, it would have been hard to resist. He was tired, the car was warm, the seat was comfortable, the ride was soft. And neither Dawson nor Mitchell was talking. Neither one said a single word. There was no big three-way conversation. Not that Reacher wanted one. Silence was golden, in his opinion.

Then they turned east on the Interstate, toward Kansas City, Missouri. Reacher knew his American history. Kansas City was first settled by Americans in 1831. It was first incorporated in 1853. It was called the City of Fountains, or the Paris of the Plains. It had a decent baseball team, World Champions in 1985. George Brett, Frank White, Bret Saberhagen.

Its area code was 816.

Its population was counted several different ways. Local boosters liked to bump it up by ranging far and wide.

But most agreed its metro area was home to about a million and a half people.

# Chapter 55

The Interstate's architecture and its appearance and its grammar were the same as its parallel twin a hundred and fifty miles to the north. It was equally straight and wide and level. Its exits were equally infrequent. They were preceded by the same blue boards, part information, part temptation. Some exits were for real, and some were deceptive. The blue Crown Vic hummed along. Dawson and Mitchell stayed resolutely silent. Reacher sat straight and comfortable, held in place by his belt. He watched the shoulder, and he watched the road ahead. It was getting dark in the east. The day was nearly over. The sun had come up over the burned-out Impala, and now it was disappearing somewhere far behind him.

Then he felt the car slow fractionally ahead of an exit sign to a place with a name he didn't recognize. The blue boards showed gas and food but no accommodation. But that deficiency was recent. The accommodations board was blank, but newly blank. There was a neat rectangle of new blue paint on it, not quite the same shade as the old blue paint. A bankruptcy, possibly, or a corporate realignment, or the death of a mom or a pop or of both.

Or something more complicated, maybe.

Up ahead the exit itself looked somewhere halfway between for-real and deceptive. Plausible, but not wildly attractive. There was no gas station sign immediately visible. No lurid colors announcing fast food. But the way the land lay in the gathering gloom suggested there might be something worthwhile over the next ridge or around the next bend.

Mitchell checked his mirror and put on his turn signal and slowed some more. *Best practices for driver and passenger safety.* He eased off the gas and hugged the white line and took the exit gently and smoothly. He kept his turn signal going and paused and yielded at the end of the ramp and turned right on a two-lane local road. South again, maybe a hundred miles short of the Paris of the Plains, out into open country.

They passed a gas station a mile later, and a no-name diner a mile after that. Then a last blue board stood all alone on the shoulder, completely blank except for one horizontal patch of new blue paint and one vertical patch of new blue paint. A short motel name and an arrow pointing straight ahead, both of them recently concealed.

Left and right of the road was nothing but dormant agriculture. Just like Iowa. Wheat, sorghum, and sunflowers. Nothing doing right then, but in six months it would all be as high as an elephant's eye, on some of the best prairie topsoil in the world. For long miles there was no habitation to be seen. Whatever farm buildings were left were all more distant than the darkening horizons.

Mitchell drove more than twenty miles through the lonely country, and then he slowed again. Reacher peered ahead into the gloom, looking for lights. He saw none at all. Then the road jinked right and left around a stand of bare trees and fell away into a broad shallow valley and the last gloomy glow from the west showed a motel about a mile away, laid out like a model on a table.

It was a fair-sized place. It had a central block, maybe for the office and the dining room, and a bunch of satellite blocks, with maybe five or six rooms in each. The blocks were all low-built but long, and they were all roofed with what looked like Spanish tiles, and they were all faced with what looked like pale stucco. There was an empty swimming pool, and there were cement paths, and parking areas, and bare flowerbeds. The whole compound was ringed by a low decorative wall done up in the same pale stucco as the buildings. From a distance the overall effect was like a seaside place. Not exactly Miami, not exactly California, not exactly Long Island, but a kind of landlocked fever-dream interpretation of all three mixed together.

And despite the blanked-out signs, the place looked open for business.

There were lights on in the main office block, and four of the windows in the satellite blocks were lit up too. There was steam drifting from what might have been a kitchen vent. There were two cars parked far apart in two different lots. Both were sedans, both were long and low, both were dark in color. Fords, Reacher thought. Crown Victorias, probably.

Exactly like the car he was riding in.

He said, "Is that place where we're going?"

Mitchell drove on in silence, and Dawson didn't answer either.

As they got closer Reacher expected to see more of the place. More details. But he didn't. He couldn't. The details never resolved. Something was obscuring his view. Not just the evening gloom. From half a mile out there seemed to be some kind of a low haze all around the edges of the compound. Like a force field, walling it in.

From a quarter-mile out, he saw what it was.

It was a security fence, maybe eight or ten feet high, made of dense metal mesh painted flat black, with rolls of razor wire canted inward at the top at an angle of forty-five degrees. It followed every twist and turn of the low stucco wall, all the way around the compound, but set ten feet farther out, like that innocent architectural frivolity's sinister cousin.

Canted inward at the top.

It was for keeping people in, not keeping them out.

**Dawson made a** call on his cell and by the time Mitchell got close to the fence a motorized gate was already opening. He drove on through and Reacher turned in his seat and saw the gate closing again behind them. Mitchell kept on going, along a worn concrete roadway, tight around a circle, and he stopped next to the office. He didn't sit back and sigh and stretch like his journey was over. He didn't switch off the motor. He kept the car in gear and his foot on the brake. Reacher unclipped his belt and tried his door. He had been right. It wouldn't open from the inside.

Dawson got out and opened it for him from the outside. He didn't say anything. He just pointed with his chin, toward the office door. Reacher slid out and stood up straight in the evening chill. Dawson got back in and closed his door and the car drove off. It moved quietly away from next to Reacher's hip and completed its trip around the circle and headed back along the worn concrete roadway to the gate. The gate was already opening before the car got there and it drove on through without stopping. It paused for a second and then turned right on the two-lane and headed back north, the way it had come.

The gate closed behind it, not fast, not slow, but silent.

**Reacher stepped into** the motel office. It looked like a hundred others he had seen. It was very similar to the fat man's place from early that morning. There was a reception counter, and lobby furniture, and a table with space for coffee and breakfast muffins. There was vinyl on the floor, and pictures on the walls, and lighting chosen more for a small electric bill than adequate illumination.

There was a plump, motherly woman behind the counter. She was smiling, in a kind, welcoming fashion. She said, "Mr. Reacher?"

Reacher said, "Yes."

"We've been expecting you."

"Have you?"

She nodded. She said, "We have rooms with kings, queens, and twins, but I've gone right ahead and put you in a room with a queen."

"Have you?" Reacher said again.

The woman nodded again. She said, "I think the rooms with the queens are the nicest. They feel more spacious, with the armchairs and all. Most people like those rooms the best."

"Most people? How many guests do you get?"

"Oh, we have quite the procession."

He said, "I guess I'm happy with a queen. I'm on my own."

"Yes," she said. "I know."

She wrote in a book and took a key off a hook. She said, "Room twenty. It's easy to find. Just follow the signs. They're all lit up at night. Dinner starts in an hour."

Reacher put the key in his pocket and went back outside. It was nearly full dark. As promised he saw knee-high fingerposts lit up by nearby spotlights set on spikes in the ground. He followed the sign for rooms sixteen through twenty. The path was brushed concrete and it wound its curving way around empty flowerbeds and it came out at a long low block of five rooms together. Room twenty was the last room in line. The empty swimming pool was not far from it, and beyond the pool was the decorative wall faced with stucco, and beyond that was the security fence. Up close it looked tall and black and angular. The mesh was a matrix of flat steel blades welded into rectangles smaller than postage stamps. Too small to put a finger in. Way too small for a foothold. Plus loops of razor wire overhanging the whole thing. It was a very efficient fence.

Reacher unlocked his door and let himself in. As promised he saw a queen bed, and armchairs. There were clothes on the bed, in two neat piles. Two outfits, both the same. Blue jeans, blue button-down shirts, blue cotton sweaters, white undershirts, white underwear, blue socks. Every garment looked to be exactly the right size. Not easy to find, at short notice.

*We've been expecting you.*

There were pajamas on the pillow. There were toiletries in the bathroom. Soap, shampoo, conditioner, shaving cream. Some kind of skin lotion. Deodorant. There were disposable razors. There was toothpaste, and a new full-size toothbrush sealed in cellophane. There was a hairbrush and a comb, like the toothbrush brand new and still sealed. There was a bathrobe on a hook. There were little hotel slippers in a packet. There were all kinds of towels on the rails, and a bath mat.

Just like the Four Seasons.

But there was no television in the room, and no telephone.

He locked up again, and went out exploring.

**Overall the whole** compound was roughly rectangular, indented here and there for the sake of interest and variety. A complicated network of brushed concrete paths wound in and out and visited everywhere of significance, including five separate accommodation blocks, and the main building, and the pool, and a mini golf installation way in one far corner. There were raised flowerbeds everywhere, edged with lower versions of the low stucco wall. In the gaps and the angles between the buildings and the walls and the flowerbeds there was crushed stone. A simpler network of concrete roadways connected the gate to the turning circle near the office, and then onward to five separate five-space parking lots near each of the accommodation blocks, and to a delivery bay behind the main building.

Four rooms were lit up inside. Two of them were near the two parked cars, and two of them weren't. The parked cars were Ford Crown Victorias, police spec, with needle antennas on their trunk lids. Reacher checked their dark interiors through their windows, and saw empty cell phone cradles on their dashboards, just like Sorenson's.

He stood for a minute in the dark and listened hard. He heard nothing. Total silence. No traffic. No airplanes. Just vast nighttime emptiness all around. Common sense and dead reckoning told him he was in Kansas, somewhere on the axis between Topeka and Wichita, probably halfway between the two, or maybe slightly nearer Topeka, possibly someplace near the Tallgrass Prairie Preserve. But as far as physical evidence was concerned he could have been on the dark side of the moon. The sky felt heavy and cloud-covered and there was no world beyond the dense mesh fence.

He turned and strolled back the way he had come, past one of the lit-up windows, and then he more or less bumped into a guy coming out of a room marked *14.* The guy was a lean, hardscrabble type, of medium height, not young but not yet ancient, with a lined and seamed face like he spent all his time outside in the weather.

*A farm worker, about fifty.*

The guy smiled like he had a shared secret and said, "Hi."

Reacher said, "You're the eyewitness."

The guy said, "The what?"

*Not the sharpest knife in the drawer.*

Reacher said, "You saw the red car."

"Maybe I did, and maybe I didn't. But we're not allowed to talk about any of that. Not even to each other. Didn't they tell you?"

The guy was wearing new blue jeans, and a new blue button-down shirt under a new blue cotton sweater. Exactly like the clothes on Reacher's bed, but smaller. His hair was clean and brushed. He had a fresh shave. He looked like a guy on vacation.

Reacher asked him, "When did you get here?"

The guy said, "Early this morning."

"With Dawson and Mitchell, or with someone else?"

"I didn't get their names. And we're not allowed to talk about it, anyway. Didn't they tell you?"

"Who's supposed to tell me?"

"Didn't you get a visit?"

"Not yet."

"When did you get here?"

"Just now. A few minutes ago."

"They'll come pretty soon, then. They'll come to your room and they'll tell you the rules." The guy shuffled in place on the path. Like he was impatient about something. Like he had somewhere else to be.

Reacher asked him, "Where are you going now?"

The guy said, "To the dining room, man. Where else? They got beer there. A whole bunch of different brands. Long neck bottles, good and cold. I mean, no work all day and free food and free beer? Does it get any better than that?"

Reacher said nothing.

The guy said, "You coming?"

"Later, maybe."

"No rush," the guy said. "I'm planning to snag a few, but they got plenty. They ain't going to run out anytime soon. You can trust me on that." And then he hustled onward along the winding path, at first all lit up from the waist down by the fingerpost spotlights, and then eventually out of sight.

Reacher stayed where he was. Room fourteen. One of the two lit-up rooms without a Bureau car parked nearby. The other was room five. He turned around and backtracked, all the way past the six-through-ten block, around a flowerbed, across the gap to the next block, to the first door in line. Room five. He was planning to knock, but he didn't need to. When he was still six feet away the door burst open and a girl ran out, all arms and legs and energy. A thin kid, dark haired and pale, maybe ten years old, all jacked up on excitement, and smiling wide. Then she saw Reacher's giant bulk in the gloom on the walkway and she froze in place and her smile changed to puzzlement and her hands came up over her mouth, so that Reacher could see nothing of her face except two huge eyes.

He said, "Hello, Lucy."

# Chapter 56

Delfuenso herself came out straight after that. She must have heard his voice. She stopped on the walkway all backlit by warm light from the room behind her. She looked in great shape. She looked rested, and happy, and relieved, and relaxed. She was wearing a woman's version of the place's standard-issue clothing. New blue jeans, and a new blue blouse under a new blue sweater of a different style, lighter and tighter and shorter than the men's. Her hair was clean and styled, and her face was bright and fresh. Clearly she had found piles of clothes on her bed, and toiletries in her bathroom.

*We've been expecting you.*

She said, "Lucy, this is Mr. Reacher. He was with me part of the time."

The kid said, "Hello, Mr. Reacher."

"Hello, Lucy," Reacher said again.

The kid said, "You broke your nose."

"Technically someone broke it for me."

"Does it hurt?"

"Not much anymore."

Delfuenso said, "Lucy was on her way to try the mini golf."

"It's too dark," Reacher said. "I was just there."

The kid pondered that new information. Her face went serious and contemplative. She said, "Then can I go look for something else? I don't think I've seen everything yet."

"Sure," her mother said. "Go see what you can find." So the kid scuttled away along the path and Delfuenso looked at Reacher and said, "I guess the fence makes it safe for her to run around on her own. And there's no water in the pool."

Reacher said, "Can we talk?"

"About what?"

"Last night. And today."

"We're not allowed to talk about that."

"Do you always do what you're told?"

"No, not always. But I think I will about this kind of stuff."

"What kind of stuff?"

"National security. We can't tell anyone about anything."

"I was there with you."

"For some of it. Not for all of it."

"Will you answer questions for me? That's not the same as telling me things."

"They brought you here. They'll tell you what's happening."

Reacher said, "I don't think they know what's happening."

\* \* \*

**They had just** thirty minutes before dinner and Delfuenso was nervous about talking, so they used the closest clandestine location they could find, which was Delfuenso's room itself. It was identical to Reacher's, except for two twin beds instead of a single queen, which made it cramped, because of two large armchairs. Reacher sat down in one, and Delfuenso lifted her bag off the other. The bag with the aspirins. It looked heavy. Maybe she still had her bottle of water in it.

He said, "What did you think had happened, back at that motel?"

She dumped her bag on the bed. It bounced once, and settled. She sat down in her chair.

"We're not allowed to talk about that," she said again.

"Says who?"

"They made it clear. We're here for our own protection. Talking could put us at risk."

"How could it?"

"They didn't say exactly. They just said we're tangled up in things we don't understand, and we're here because they want to keep us safe. We're sequestered, like a jury. Something to do with the Patriot Act."

"Sequestered? That's bullshit. You're locked up. You can't leave."

"I don't want to leave. It's kind of fun here. I haven't had a vacation in years."

"What about your job?"

"They said they'll square that away with my boss. School too, for Lucy. They said they can make it OK. A thing like this, everyone has to pull together."

"Did they say how long you have to stay here?"

"Until it's over. Not too long, probably. But I hope it's at least a week."

Reacher said nothing.

Delfuenso said, "Your nose looks a little better."

"Does it?" Reacher said, although he didn't want to. He didn't want to talk about his nose. But he figured a little conversation might not hurt. *A delay and a frustration, but faster than shouting or yelling or fighting.*

Delfuenso said, "It looked really awful before. I was staring at it in the car for hours. You cleaned it up."

He nodded.

She said, "In fact, you cleaned your whole self up. You took a shower, didn't you?"

"It's not that rare of an occurrence."

"Well, I wondered."

"I bought new clothes too."

"You needn't have. They give you clothes here. They said we're allowed to keep them. Both sets, if we want. And the toiletries."

He asked, "What happened after you left that motel in Iowa?"

She didn't answer.

He said, "You know what happened. They know what happened. How can it hurt if I know what happened too? I'm in here with you. I can't go anywhere. I can't talk to anyone else."

Delfuenso thought for a long moment. Her face went exactly like her daughter's, serious and contemplative. Then she shrugged and said, "That part was pretty awful. After you went inside with McQueen, I mean. I couldn't see much. He was in the way. But I saw the flash and heard the shot. He came running out and I couldn't see you anymore. I assumed you were dead. And then McQueen told us you were."

"Did he?"

Delfuenso nodded. "King asked if he got you, and McQueen said yes, right between the eyes. They kind of laughed about it. I was terrified. I assumed they would do the same to me. I mean, why wouldn't they? We were no use to them anymore. I started screaming. King told me to shut up. So I did. It was pathetic. I thought if I did what he told me, he wouldn't shoot me. I really learned something in that minute. People will do anything to stay alive, even if it's just ten more seconds."

"Then what happened?"

"We drove around some. Like figures of eight, around the fields. They were staying close for some reason. King was driving. He stopped about ten miles west. I assumed this was it. I assumed my time had come. But he said he wanted to have some fun first. He told me to take my shirt off. The blue one they bought for me. And I was going to. Like I said, people will do anything to stay alive. King got out of the car. He got in next to me in the back. He kind of chased me across the seat. Then McQueen got out and opened my door and pulled me out and King kind of started to follow after me and McQueen shot him. Just like that. Just pulled his gun and shot him."

"In the chest?"

Delfuenso nodded. "Right in the heart."

"And then?"

"McQueen calmed me down and told me he was an FBI agent working undercover with the bad guys. Pretending to be one of them."

"OK," Reacher said. "Rather him than me. That's a tough job."

"I know."

"Do you?"

"I mean, I've seen it in the movies."

"Then what?"

"McQueen told me he had fired over your head and you were still alive and perfectly OK. He said he was sorry I had to see what happened to King but he couldn't figure out any other way to save me. Not right then. He said he had to act a part to a certain extent but couldn't let things go too far."

"And then?"

"He made some calls on his cell and he belted King in where he was, which was where I had been sitting, and then we drove off. I was in the front. We parked again about five miles east and two new guys came and picked us up in their own car. They set fire to mine. They said they had to do that, because the bad guys would expect McQueen to obscure the evidence, and they might check to make sure he had. They said they would get me a new car. Which is great, because that old one had a bad transmission."

"These new guys were FBI too?"

"Yes. From Kansas City. They showed me ID. McQueen didn't have ID, because he was undercover."

"And they brought you straight here?"

She nodded again. "I said I wouldn't stay without Lucy, so they went to get her too."

"Where did McQueen go?"

"He came here with me and left again immediately. He said he had to get back in position. He said he had some explaining to do. I think he's going to tell them you killed King."

"Me?"

"That's what they were discussing. Like they picked up a stranger to change the numbers but the stranger tried to rob them. I think he's going to say you killed King and escaped."

"Did they say what kind of bad guys these are?"

Delfuenso shook her head.

"No," she said. "But they seem very worried about them."


**Dinner came next,** and it was a very strange meal. They walked over to the main building together like a little family, Reacher and Delfuenso side by side with Lucy skipping and tripping between them. The dining room was a large square space with twenty tables and eighty chairs, all of them serviceable pine items thickly varnished to a high syrup shine. The room was like many other rooms Reacher had seen, but it was completely empty apart from the eyewitness, who was sitting alone at a corner table behind a miniature thicket of three empty beer bottles, all different. He was working on a fourth, and he jabbed its neck in the air in an enthusiastic greeting. A happy man. Maybe he hadn't had a vacation in years either. Or ever.

The motherly woman from the reception desk brought menus. Reacher wondered if she was FBI too, and concluded she probably was. As it happened the three guests she had right then were contented enough, at least for the moment, but he imagined others might find the situation stressful or annoying, in which case he figured she would need some kind of official weight to back up her naturally patient manner.

The menu offered just two choices, cheeseburger or chicken, presumably both microwaved straight out of a freezer. FBI agents tended to come out of law school or law enforcement, not out of restaurant kitchens. Reacher chose the cheeseburger, his fifth of the day, and Delfuenso and her daughter followed suit.

Then before the meals arrived two more people came in. Both men, both in blue suits and white shirts and blue ties. The owners of the parked Crown Vics, obviously. The resident agents. The babysitters. They looked alert and alive and solidly competent.

Delfuenso said, "They're the two who brought me here."

Lucy said, "They're the two who brought *me* here. From Paula's house."

The two men scanned the room and headed straight for Reacher. The one on the right said, "Sir, we'd ap-

preciate it if you'd eat your dinner at our table tonight."

Reacher said, "Why?"

"We need to introduce ourselves."

"And?"

"We need to tell you the rules."

# Chapter 57

The two Bureau suits led Reacher to a four-place table in the opposite corner of the room to where the eyewitness had stationed himself. Reacher took the corner chair, his back to the wall, the whole room in view. Pure habit. No real reason. No danger of any kind. That dining room was probably the safest place in Kansas.

The two agents sat down, one on his left and one on his right. They leaned in, intently, elbows on the table. They were maybe a little younger than McQueen or Sorenson. Late thirties, or dead-on forty. Not rookies, but not old-timers, either. Both were dark and wiry. One was going bald faster than the other. They said their names were Bale and Trapattoni. They said they were close colleagues of Dawson and Mitchell. Same field office, same job. They said they had read Reacher's record from the military. They said they knew all about him.

Reacher said nothing about that.

Bale was the guy losing his hair. He asked, "You happy here?"

Reacher said, "Why would I be?"

"Why wouldn't you be?"

"I took an oath to protect the Constitution. So did you, I guess."

"And?"

"I'm being deprived of my liberty without due process of law. That's a Fifth Amendment offense, right there. And you're a party to it."

"This isn't a prison."

"I guess the fence maker didn't get that memo."

"So you're not happy?"

Reacher said, "Actually I'm fine. I like you guys. I like the FBI. I like the way you think. I can't help it. You're doing wrong, but you're doing wrong right. You put everyone together, so there are mutual witnesses to everything that goes on here. You could have thrown us in solitary somewhere and done whatever the hell you liked to us. But you couldn't do that. Because deep down you're on the side of the angels. I can't take that away from you. You even left the mini golf here. When did you buy this place?"

Trapattoni said, "Three years ago."

"Was it a Kansas City initiative?"

"Yes, it was. Counterterrorism, central region."

"Why did you need it?"

"There was an emerging requirement."

"For what?"

"For a place to keep people safe."

"I think it's a place for keeping yourselves safe."

"How so?"

"I think you take witnesses away from local law enforcement whenever your undercover operations get messy. So that no questions are ever answered."

"You don't think undercover agents deserve to be kept safe?"

"I think they deserve all the help they can get."

"So?"

"I'm wondering how many undercover operations you run. This place could take fifty people at a time. That's a lot of witnesses."

"I can't comment on how many operations we run."

"Has this place ever been full?"

"No."

"Has it ever been empty?"

"No."

"In three years? That's quite a few operations."

"It's a big job."

Reacher said, "So tell me the rules."

Bale said, "There are two of them."

"Try me. I can count that high."

"You'll be our guest here until the operation is concluded. That's non-negotiable. And you won't discuss what you've seen of the operation so far with the other guests. Or with anyone else. Not even any tiny little part of it. Not now and not ever. That's non-negotiable too."

"That's it?"

"It's for your own good. They saw you too. Only one of those guys in the Impala was on the side of the angels."

"King died."

"But not before he used his phone a couple of times.

From the gas stations, we think. The times of the calls coincide with the use of the credit card."

"You were tapping his phone?"

"Having an undercover man brings many advantages."

"What did he say about me?"

"They have your name and your description. Bear that in mind when you think bad thoughts about the fence maker."

"Who are these guys?"

No answer.

"Is McQueen going to be OK?"

"Don't worry about him."

"I can't help it."

"We put seven months into this. He's not going to quit now."

"I'm not worried about him quitting. I'm worried about someone else making that decision for him. He's got some explaining to do tonight."

"We can't discuss it," Bale said. "Just remember the rules."

And that was it. Bale sat back. Trapattoni sat back. The conversation was over. And right on cue the food came. Reacher figured the motherly type had been watching through a spy hole. Or listening on a headset.


**Delfuenso and her** daughter were long gone and the eyewitness was finishing up his seventh bottle of beer by the time Reacher left the dining room. He walked along the lit-up path toward his temporary quarters and he stopped in the chill air and looked up at the sky. There were no stars. No moon. Ideal conditions for a little clandestine activity, except there was no way out but the gate, and there was no way of opening it, and there were no telephones.

Then the eyewitness came stumbling out of the dining room and up the path. The knee-high finger-post lights gave Reacher a pretty good view of the guy's legs working not quite right. He was more than buzzed, but not yet falling down. He was taking slow and elaborately precise steps, left, right, putting his feet down flat, striding shorter than normal, looking down and concentrating hard. Reacher backtracked until his shins were in a pool of light. Full disclosure. He didn't want to give the guy a heart attack.

The guy came on slowly, left foot, right foot, and then he saw Reacher's legs and stopped. No big shock. No great surprise.

The guy gave an amiable grin.

Reacher said, "Were you this drunk when you saw the red car?"

The guy thought about it and said, "Approximately."

"Who talked to you about it?"

"Sheriff Goodman and the blonde lady from the FBI."

"What didn't you tell them?"

"I told them everything."

"No, you didn't," Reacher said. "No eyewitness ever does. You left things out. Things you weren't sure about, things that might have sounded stupid, things you were doing that you shouldn't have been doing."

"I was looking for my truck."

"Where was it?"

"I couldn't remember. That's why I was looking for it."

"Did you tell them that part?"

"They didn't ask."

"And you were going to drive home like that?"

"It's not far. I know the turns."

"And?"

"I got caught short. I stopped to take a leak."

"Where?"

"In back of the old pumping station. I didn't tell them that part, either."

Reacher nodded. *Things you were doing that you shouldn't have been doing.* Public urination, and drunk driving. Illegal in every town in America. He said, "So you didn't really see them. Not if you were behind the building."

The guy said, "No, I saw them real close. I was all done by then. I was all zipped up and coming out."

"Did they see you?"

"I don't think so. It was pretty dark. There was a shadow."

"How far away were you?"

"Ten feet, maybe."

Reacher asked, "What did you notice?"

"I told the sheriff," the guy said. "And the blonde lady."

"You answered their questions. That's not the same thing."

"I don't remember."

"Concentrate."

The guy closed his eyes. He swayed back and forth on his heels. He raised his hand and held it palm-out, as if he was steadying himself against the old concrete building. He was using physical cues. He was thinking himself back into the moment.

He said, "The first guy was hurrying. He wanted to get in there first. He was unzipping his coat."

"Had they been in a group of three before that? Walking together?"

"I can't be sure. But I think so. It felt like that. Like suddenly the first guy had bolted ahead, and the other two guys were hustling to keep up."

"Suits, right?"

"No coats at all."

"Anything in their hands?"

"Nothing."

"What did you do when all three of them were inside?"

"I headed back across the road."

"Why?"

"I needed to find my truck. And I didn't want to stick around."

"Why not?"

"Bad feeling."

"From the guys in the suits?"

"More from the first guy. In the green coat. I didn't like him."

Reacher asked, "Did you hear anything?"

The guy said, "A little shouting and yelling. Like they were fighting."

"Where were you when the guys in the suits came out again?"

"On the other sidewalk."

"Anything else?"

The guy said, "I shouldn't be talking about this. They told me not to." And then he stepped around Reacher, carefully and elaborately and precisely, and he carried on along the path. Reacher started after him, and then he stopped. Because he heard the soft whisper of a car on the road. A quarter-mile away, maybe. He turned and saw lights in the distance, vague diffuse beams bouncing and stabbing through the mist.

Then the gate began to open, not fast, not slow, and silent.

# Chapter 58

Evidently Julia Sorenson had not gotten her phone back. Or her car. Or her reputation. She had not become a hero. Reacher saw a shiny black Crown Vic pull in off the two-lane and drive through the still-moving gate. Its headlight beams turned in a wide arc and it hissed over the concrete roadway and came to a stop on the circle near the main office door. A guy Reacher hadn't seen before got out of the front passenger seat and opened the rear passenger door. He didn't seem to say anything. He just pointed with his chin. Like Dawson had.

Julia Sorenson slid out of the back and stood up and stood still. She looked tired in the low light, and a little defeated. A little round-shouldered. The night breeze caught her coat and flapped it open. She was still wearing the new shirt. But her holster was empty. She had surrendered her weapon.

The guy from the front closed her door behind her and slid back in his seat. The car drove off and left her standing there alone. The gate started to open again. The car drove through it, and paused a beat, and turned right, and drove back the way it had come.

The gate closed again behind it. Reacher watched the car until its lights were gone and its whisper had died away to silence. Then he turned around and watched Sorenson.

She stood still for a moment more, and then she went inside. Reacher counted out time in his head, for the greeting from the motherly type at the reception desk, and the smile and the welcome, and the kings and the queens and the twins, and the armchairs, and the floor space, and the majority preferences. All that kind of stuff. *We've been expecting you.* Four minutes, he figured. Maybe less, if the conversation went faster, which he figured it might, because it would be one agent to another. Or maybe more than four minutes, if Sorenson was up on her high horse and asking all kinds of outraged and resentful questions.

It took four minutes exactly. Sorenson came out with a key in her hand. She looked resigned. She checked the numbers on the low fingerposts and set off in Reacher's direction. Then she checked again at the next fork and headed off at a shallow angle down a different path.

"Julia," Reacher called, softly.

She stopped walking.

She called, "Reacher?"

"Over here."

She stepped off the path and walked over the crushed stone to him. He asked, "What happened with you?"

She said, "We're not supposed to communicate."

"Or what? They're going to lock us up?"

"Well, we can't talk out here. Where can we go?"

**They went to** Reacher's room. Sorenson took a good look around it and said, "This is completely bizarre. It's just like a regular motel."

Reacher said, "It is a regular motel. Or it was. The Kansas City field office bought it three years ago. They told me. You never heard about it?"

"Not a word. Are the others here too?"

Reacher nodded. "Delfuenso and her kid, and the eyewitness. Safe and sound. They're all having a good time, actually."

"Even though they're locked up?"

"They've been told they're sequestered. Like a jury. For their own good. Not the same thing as being locked up. They're all treating it like a vacation. Mini golf and free beer."

"Is it legal?"

"I don't know. I'm not a lawyer. But it probably is. Except that it probably shouldn't be. You know how these things are."

"Who brought them here?" she said. "Who burned in the car?"

"Alan King burned in the car," Reacher said. "But he was shot in the heart first. By McQueen. McQueen is one of you, undercover. Out of Kansas City. Which is why Dawson and Mitchell came straight up to baby-sit you at the pumping station. They were doing damage control. McQueen burned the car and he and Delfuenso were picked up by part of his Bureau support team. In a Bureau sedan, like the tire marks showed, again out of Kansas City. McQueen came here with them but left again immediately. Apparently he said he had to get back in position."

"Poor guy. He's going to be under a hell of a lot of pressure. With King dead? How is he going to explain that?"

"With great difficulty, I would think."

"But you were right. He missed you deliberately. He fired over your head."

"But there was nothing he could fake when it came time to punch Delfuenso's ticket. So he offed King instead."

"Good man. I hope he's OK."

"What happened with you?" Reacher asked again.

Sorenson sat down on the bed. She said, "Me? It started out OK. In fact, it started out just fine. I drove back to Delfuenso's place and got my phone and got back in my own car and called my SAC. I told him I had managed to overpower you and hand you over to the Kansas City boys. My SAC was very impressed. And he was very pleased. But I couldn't quite let it go. I asked a few too many questions. He didn't like that so much. I could tell. Then at one point he changed completely. He wasn't pleased anymore. Not pleased at all. I could hear it in his voice."

"At what point?"

"I checked the glove box when I locked up Goodman's car. Purely out of habit. I didn't want any unsecured weapons left in it, and who knows what a country sheriff keeps in his glove box? But as it happened there was nothing in there except a notebook and a pen. So I looked through the notebook, naturally. Turns out Sheriff Goodman was a very thorough guy. He'd been doing his research overnight, and he'd been making notes about Karen Delfuenso. I guess he figured the more the merrier, when it came to information. I guess he thought it would help, if we didn't get her back fast, although I can't see how it would."

"And?"

"There was something in there that struck me as odd, so I asked my SAC about it. Except I didn't actually ask about it. I just mentioned it, really. But whichever, that was when he went all weird on me."

"What something was odd?"

"I took Delfuenso to be a long-term resident. Maybe not necessarily a fourth generation farm girl or anything, but I got the impression she'd been there a good long time. Certainly I figured Lucy would have been born and raised there."

"But she wasn't?"

"They've only been there seven months. The neighbor on the other side said they moved there after a divorce. So it seems to have been a much more recent divorce than I thought."

"Are we even sure she was married in the first place?" Reacher said.

"There's a kid."

"That doesn't imply marriage."

"Why wouldn't she have been married?"

"She copes on her own," Reacher said. "She copes really well. Like she's always been obliged to. And she's smart. Looking after some guy would drive her crazy."

"Smart women shouldn't get married?"

"Are you married?"

She didn't answer that. She said, "I don't care if it was a wedding with a thousand guests on a beach in Hawaii or a one-night stand in a motel in New Jersey. The point isn't that she was a single mom. The point is she's a single mom who moved to town just seven months ago."

Reacher said, "The Kansas City boys told me this operation is seven months old."

"That's impossible."

"Why would they lie?"

"No, I mean Delfuenso can't be connected. How could she be? It has to be a coincidence. It has to be. Because we've already got one coincidence."

Reacher said, "So now we have two coincidences?"

"Which is one too many."

"What's the first coincidence?"

Sorenson said, "You remember Alan King's brother?"

"Peter King? The fister?"

"Apparently my night guy put a search on him. Just to be helpful. Right after he got off the phone with Mother Sill, the first time. DMVs, the postal service, the banks, the credit card companies. The cell phone companies, if we can get away with it, which is usually always. And the results came back this evening."

"And what were they?"

"It looks like Peter King left Denver and moved to Kansas City."

"When?"

"Seven months ago."

# Chapter 59

Reacher moved in his chair and ran his fingers through his hair and said, "Alan King told me his brother wasn't speaking to him."

Sorenson said, "Did Alan King live in Kansas City?"

"I think so."

"Maybe he didn't. And even if he did, maybe they never met. Kansas City is a big enough place."

"I know," Reacher said. "Metro area population is a million and a half."

"Is it?"

"Area code is 816."

"OK."

Reacher said, "So now we have three coincidences. Seven months ago Delfuenso moved to the back of beyond in Nebraska, and simultaneously Peter King moved to Kansas City, Missouri, where his brother might or might not have been living, and where his brother might or might not have been even speaking

to him, and simultaneously your central region coun-
terrorism people, who are based in Kansas City,
Missouri, decided to start up a complex undercover
operation that seems to be centered on a spot very
close to Delfuenso's new quarters in the back of beyond in Nebraska."

"We can't have three coincidences. That's too
many."

"I would agree," Reacher said. "Theoretically. But
we don't have three coincidences. We have two proven
links."

"Proven how?"

Reacher leaned forward in his chair and put his
palm on the bed. He pressed down and tested the
mattress for softness and yield.

He said, "First, Peter King was definitely Alan King's
brother. And Alan King was definitely a bad guy. Because an undercover FBI agent found it necessary to
shoot him in the heart and burn him up in a fire.
Which is a pretty basic definition for being a bad guy,
wouldn't you say?"

"And second?"

Reacher said, "Your SAC had you brought here because you found out about Delfuenso's move seven
months ago. And this place is for people who stumble
on evidence of undercover operations. Therefore Delfuenso's move was part of an undercover operation."

"What part?"

Reacher said, "Let's go ask her."

* * *

**Reacher stopped short** of Delfuenso's door, and
Sorenson stepped up and knocked softly. There was a
long minute's delay, and then there was the rattle of a
chain. The door opened a crack on dim light inside
and Delfuenso's voice whispered, "Who is it?"

Reacher figured she was whispering because her
kid had just gone to sleep.

Sorenson said, "Karen Delfuenso?"

Delfuenso whispered, "Yes?"

Sorenson said, "I'm Julia Sorenson from the FBI
field office in Omaha. I was working on getting you
back last night."

And then Delfuenso shushed her, quite impatiently,
like Reacher knew she would. Because her ten-year-
old had just gotten to sleep. Delfuenso came out and
bustled Sorenson away from the door, like Reacher
knew she would, over to a place more than ten feet
away, where it was safe to make a noise.

"I'm sorry," Sorenson said. "I didn't mean to be a
nuisance. I just wanted to introduce myself. I just
wanted to see you were OK."

"I'm fine," Delfuenso said, and more than ten feet
behind her Reacher slipped into the room.


**He had been** in the room once before, so he was
safely familiar with its layout, even in the dark, and it
was dark. There was no light anywhere except an orange neon bulb inside a light switch in the bathroom.
Its faint glow showed Lucy asleep in the bed farther
from the door. She was on her side, fetal, rolled into
the blankets. The sheet was up to her chin. Her hair

was spilled on the pillow, black on white. Reacher found Delfuenso's bag on the other bed. Nearer the door, nearer the armchairs. He had seen her lift it off the chair and dump it on the bed. It had looked heavy. And the mattresses were soft and yielding. Not like trampolines. Not like drum skins. But even so the bag had bounced. Like she still had her bottle of water in it.

He stepped slow and quiet on the carpet and carried the bag to the bathroom. He spread a folded bath towel on the vanity counter, one-handed, patting it into place directly under the dim glow from the light switch. He emptied the bag on the towel. A precaution against noise, which worked to some extent, but not completely. There was no loud clattering, but there were plenty of sharp thumps.

He waited. And listened. Lucy slept on, breathing low and quiet.

He raked through the things on the towel. There was all kinds of stuff. Makeup, a hairbrush, two plastic combs. A slim glass bottle of scent. Two packs of gum, both half gone. A wallet, containing three dollars and no credit cards and a seven-month-old Nebraska driver's license. It was made out to Delfuenso at the address Reacher had visited. She was forty-one years old. There was an emery board for her fingernails, and a steakhouse toothpick still in its paper wrapper, and seventy-one cents in loose coins, and a ballpoint pen, and a house key on a chain with a crystal pendant.

He saw the pack of aspirins. There was no bottle of water. There was nothing large and heavy except a bible. A hardcover King James version, smaller than an encyclopedia, bigger than a novel. Fairly thick. Dark red cardboard on the front, dark red cardboard on the back. Gold printing on the spine, gold printing on the front. *Holy Bible*. It looked like it didn't get much use. It looked like it hadn't been opened very often.

In fact, it was impossible to open. The pages were all crinkled and gummed together, by some kind of yellowish fluid, dried long ago. A spillage, possibly. Inside the bag. Pineapple juice, maybe, or orange. Or grapefruit. Something like that. Something sugary. A small carton with a straw, or a drinking cup for the kid, dumped in there and overturned.

So why keep the bible? Was there a taboo against trashing damaged bibles and replacing them? Reacher didn't know. He was no kind of a theologian.

It was very heavy, for a book.

He used his nails and tried to separate the front cover from the first endpaper page. Not possible. It was gummed solid. Evenly, and uniformly. Reacher pictured the spilled juice, pulsing out around the hole for the straw or through the spout of the cup, flooding the bag, soaking the good book evenly and uniformly.

Not possible.

Spilled juice would leave a random stain, probably large, but it wouldn't cover the whole book equally. Some part of it would be untouched. What got wet would swell, and the rest would stay the same. Reacher had seen books in that condition. Frozen pipes, blood-stains. Damage was never uniform.

He used one of Delfuenso's combs and forced it

end-on between the pages. He slid it up and down and levered it back and forth until he had made two fingertip-sized recesses in the pulp. Then he put the book spine-down on the vanity counter and bent over and hooked his nails in the recesses and jerked left and right.

Paper tore and the book fell open.

Everything from Exodus to Jude had been hollowed out with a razor. A custom-shaped cavity had been created. Very neat work. The cavity was roughly rectangular, maybe seven inches by six, maybe two inches deep. Not much of the paper had been left at the top and the bottom and the sides of the book. Hence the glue. Walls had been built, thin but solid. The whole thing was like a jewelry box with its lid stuck shut.

But it contained no jewelry.

The cavity was shaped and sized and contoured specifically for its current contents, which were a Glock 19 automatic pistol, and an Apple cellular telephone with matching charger, and a slim ID wallet.

The Glock 19 was a compact version of the familiar Glock 17. Four-inch barrel, smaller and lighter all around. Often considered a better fit for a woman's hand.

Always considered easier to conceal.

It was loaded with eighteen nine-millimeter Parabellums, seventeen in the magazine and one in the chamber, ready to go. No manual safety on a Glock. Point and shoot.

The phone was switched off. Just a blank screen on the front, and a shiny black casing on the back, with a silver apple, partly bitten. Reacher had no idea how to

turn the phone on. There would be a button somewhere, or a combination of buttons, to be pressed in
sequence or held down for a certain small number of
seconds. The charger was a neat white cube, very
small, with blades for an outlet, and a long white wire
tipped with a complex rectangular plug.

The ID wallet was made of fine black leather.
Reacher flipped it open. It was like a tiny book in itself. The left-hand page was a colored engraving of a
shield. *Department of Justice. Federal Bureau of Investigation.* The right-hand page was a photo ID. Delfuenso's face was on it. A little pale from the flash, a
little green from fluorescent tubes overhead. But it
was her. The picture was overlapped with an official
seal. *Department of Justice* again. Holographic. The
words *Federal Bureau of Investigation* ran side to side
across the whole width of the card.

Special Agent Karen Delfuenso.

Reacher repacked the cavity and squeezed the cov-
ers down over the damage he had caused. He carried
the book in his hand, slow and quiet past the sleeping
girl, out through the door, toward the two women still
huddled ten feet away. Sorenson was talking inanely,
just burning time, and Delfuenso was looking a little
exasperated and impatient with her. They both heard
the scuff of Reacher's boots on the concrete. They
both turned toward him.

Reacher raised the bible and said, "Let us pray."

# Chapter 60

They left Lucy sleeping alone. Delfuenso thought it was safe enough. The whole place was secure, and she said the kid wasn't the type who woke up in the night scared or disoriented. They went to Sorenson's room, which was number nine. Closer than Reacher's. Sorenson hadn't been in it yet. She hadn't gotten that far. She had been on her way to open it up when Reacher had called out to her in the dark.

She unlocked her door with her key and all three of them stepped inside. Reacher saw an identical version of his own billet. Two armchairs, a queen bed, two neat piles of clothing, but the feminine selection, the same as Delfuenso was wearing. No doubt the bathroom was equally provisioned with lotions and potions and towels.

Delfuenso sat down in an armchair and Reacher handed her the bible. She cradled it in her lap, with both hands on it, like it was a purse and she was afraid of bag snatchers. Sorenson sat on the bed. Her room, her entitlement. Reacher took the second armchair.

He said, "Obviously I have a million questions."

Delfuenso said, "You've put us all in a very difficult situation. You should have left my bag alone. What you did was almost certainly illegal."

Reacher said, "Grow up."

Sorenson looked at Delfuenso and asked, "Didn't they search you here? Or on the way here?"

Delfuenso said, "No, they didn't."

"Me neither," Reacher said. "Not even a little bit."

"Then that's a serious deficiency," Sorenson said. "Wouldn't you agree? I thought Kansas City was supposed to be good at this stuff."

Delfuenso shrugged. "I was playing the part of the random helpless victim, so I'm not surprised they gave me a pass. They should have searched Reacher, though. His position was never very clear."

"Kansas City doesn't know who you are?" Reacher asked.

"Of course they don't," Delfuenso said. "Or I wouldn't be here in their damn prison camp, would I?"

"So who are you?"

"That's not something I'm willing to discuss."

"Did King and McQueen come in south from the Interstate? To the old pumping station?"

"Why do you want to know?"

"Because it's the key fact here."

"No, they came north out of Kansas."

"How?"

"They were driven. By an accomplice."

"Had they been there before? To that crossroads?"

"Has anyone?"

"So they never saw Sin City. They didn't know anything about it. They didn't know they could jack a car there. But still, that's where they went. Why?"

Delfuenso didn't answer.

Reacher said, "Because you were McQueen's emergency contact. That's why. In case things went wrong. But you weren't put there by Kansas City. Because Kansas City doesn't know who you are. So who put you there?"

Delfuenso didn't answer.

Reacher said, "Someone else put you there, obviously. Someone higher up the food chain, clearly, to be going over Kansas City's head in secret. I'm guessing the Hoover Building. Some big cheese in a suit, all burdened down with worries."

Delfuenso said nothing.

Reacher said, "Which begs the question, what exactly was the nature of those worries?"

Delfuenso said, "Were you really a military cop?"

Reacher didn't answer.

Sorenson said, "Yes, he was. I've seen his file. He was decorated six times. Silver Star, Defense Superior Service Medal, Legion of Merit, Soldier's Medal, Bronze Star, and a Purple Heart."

"We all got medals," Reacher said. "Don't read too much into it."

Delfuenso said, "There's a problem with Kansas City."

Reacher said, "What kind of a problem?"

"Poor performance."

"How poor?"

"They're getting people killed."

**Delfuenso ran it** down for them. She spoke for ten minutes straight. The central region was always busy. There were valuable targets within its jurisdiction. Important civilian infrastructure, and military establishments, including factory sites. There was always terrorist chatter, too, both domestic and foreign, on the Internet, some of which was aimed at that infrastructure and those establishments and factories. Most of which was fantasy dreaming or empty boasts or idle wouldn't-that-be-cool speculation. But some of it was real. Enough of it to worry about, anyway.

So the Kansas City boys went proactive, and got into a sequence of four undercover penetrations. They got agents inside four separate targets. The operations were textbook smooth at the beginning. Then they fell apart. None of them produced intelligence. Two of them produced dead undercover agents.

But still. Notwithstanding. The central region was always busy. The Internet chatter never let up. Then one day there was a new voice. It talked about liquid measure of some kind. Gallons, hundreds of gallons, thousands of gallons. With a regular emphasis on Nebraska's water table. No one knew what any of it meant. No one could decipher any specific intent. But the chatter intensified daily. Thousands of gallons, hundreds of thousands, millions of gallons, and eventually tens of millions.

So a fifth undercover operation was planned. The

new voice was contacted by a lone federal dissident entirely invented by Kansas City. The federal dissident offered to join forces with the new voice and help. Background questions were asked, and answers were invented. Bona fides were established. After a long and cautious delay the new voice agreed to meet with the federal dissident. And so the operation came slowly to life.

But at the same time an operation-within-an-operation had been planned by the Hoover Building. Like spying on the spies. Under the guise of a routine higher-level review it had been suggested that Kansas City bring in an agent entirely unknown in the Midwest. For the undercover position. In theory, for extra safety and security. In reality, the Hoover Building wanted a guaranteed reliable man at the heart of the operation. The name they put forward was Special Agent Donald McQueen, most recently of the San Diego field office.

And as a backstop and as an on-the-ground observer they moved Karen Delfuenso from the main counterterrorism unit in D.C. They moved her in secret. The whole nine yards, like witness protection. She rented a house. She got a job. Her kid came with her and enrolled in school.

"That's a big deal," Sorenson said. "Were you happy with that?"

"Happy enough," Delfuenso said. "You know how it is. We go where we're told. And I like moving around. I want Lucy to see something of the world."

"Did she know why you were moving?"

"Not specifically. Only generically. She knows I

have a gun and a badge. But she doesn't ask questions. She's used to it."

"But she could have blown your cover. She could have talked in school."

"And said what? Mommy's got a gun? Every mommy in Nebraska has a gun. Or Mommy's a secret agent? All kids make up stories like that. It's expected. Especially when their mommy is really a cocktail waitress, half naked from the waist up all night long."

Then Delfuenso went on with the story. McQueen made contact early on. He played it slow and careful and built up trust and credibility. The new voice turned out to be a medium-sized group of white Americans in an uneasy alliance with a medium-sized group of foreigners from the Middle East. The group called itself Wadiah. Its leader was a man with a code name of his own, and so far McQueen had been denied access to him. The foreigners from the Middle East were thought to be Syrians.

"What's their aim?" Reacher asked.

"We don't know yet," Delfuenso said.

"That's a weird ethnic mixture."

"I agree."

"Is McQueen going to be OK?"

"That depends on whether you're a glass-half-full type of guy, or a glass-half-empty. They lost two out of four so far. So on the face of it his odds are about fifty-fifty."

"Not good."

"Which is why some big cheese in a suit was all burdened down with worries."

"And that's without him having to explain what happened to King."

"Tell me about it," Delfuenso said.

**Sorenson made hot** tea with a plug-in kettle from a cupboard and water from the bathroom. She brought it over on a tray. Reacher thanked her but looked at Delfuenso and asked, "Why did you do all that blinking in the car?"

Delfuenso took her tea and asked back, "Did I have you fooled?"

"Totally. I thought you were a random victim. Brave and smart, for sure, but regular-person brave and smart, not law enforcement."

"And that's exactly what I needed you to think. Mc-Queen knew who I was, obviously, but King didn't. So I had to play a part for him. I had to play a part all night, in fact, because it was pretty obvious I was going to end up face to face with either Wadiah or the Kansas City FBI. And neither one of them could be allowed to know who I was."

"I get that. I know you had to act a part. But you didn't have to blink."

"My aim was to get out of there as fast as I could. The sooner the better. By any means available. So I thought if I enlisted you I might get out quicker. You looked like a capable guy. I thought you might get the chance to stage something along the way. But you didn't. So sure enough I ended up face to face with the Kansas City boys, who put me in here, because I played my part so well they think I'm nobody."

"So what really happened last night?"

"You saw most of it."

"But not all of it. And I didn't understand any of it. And I'm interested in the conversation you had with McQueen after he shot King in the heart. You must have had at least half an hour alone with him, before you were picked up."

"Closer to forty minutes. And it wasn't McQueen who shot King in the heart. He passed me his gun around the seat. I told you different because I was still playing the part back then. Also I made up all that stuff about screaming and wailing."

"So what really happened tonight?"

"You tell me."

Reacher shrugged.

"I have no idea," he said. "But I don't think either King or McQueen was carrying the knife. Too big for a suit pocket. There was nothing in their hands. I suppose one of them could have had it strapped to his forearm, but that seems unlikely. I think the other guy had it. And I think he was always planning to use it. He was unzipping his coat as he walked into the bunker."

"You spoke to the eyewitness."

"I'm sure he'll deny it. He's following the rules. For the free beer."

Delfuenso said, "These things are always co-productions. King and McQueen went on behalf of Wadiah to meet with some other guy appearing on behalf of some other group. Funding, probably, or some other kind of cooperation. Or logistics. Or supply. It was supposed to be a love-in. The plan was King and

McQueen should get a ride there, and then the new guy would take them onward to his HQ. Like a ritual dance. But it went to rat shit immediately. The new guy started shouting something at them and then he pulled out a knife and tried to kill them. McQueen disarmed him."

"And broke his arm in the process."

"Did he?"

Sorenson said, "The medical examiner told us. At lunchtime today."

Reacher said, "And then what?"

Delfuenso said, "And then McQueen killed the guy. In self-defense. Almost a reflex."

"Bullshit," Reacher said. "He killed him to shut him up. The guy was shouting. Who knew what he was going to say next? Too big a risk to take. Could be the guy is based in San Diego and he's seen McQueen going in and out of the FBI building there. And McQueen wouldn't want King to hear that."

"It was a justifiable homicide."

"Did he do it well?"

"Is that your benchmark for justifiable?"

"Style points can help. If the decision is close."

"I don't know how well he did it."

"I do," Sorenson said. "I saw the body. And he did it pretty well. Lateral slash on the forehead to blind the guy, and the knife up under the ribs, like one, two."

"Happy now?" Delfuenso asked.

"That's a little old-school," Reacher said. "Don't you think? The forehead thing used to be considered cool. Flamboyant, even. But it was always completely unnecessary. Might as well make the second move first. If you've got a nine-inch blade up to the hilt in someone's gut, does it really bother you that he's still got twenty-twenty vision?"

"Whatever, it was justifiable."

"I agree. No argument from me. Either way. What happened next?"

"They ran for it. They didn't like the red car. They figured either the local cops or the other group of bad guys would come looking for it. Or both. McQueen knew where I was. He always knew my whereabouts. So he drove up to Sin City, but like he didn't really know where he was going, and he kind of pretended to spot my Chevy, and right away King agreed it would be a good car to steal."

"But they didn't just steal it."

"They couldn't get it open. It's a late model. All kinds of security. They set the alarm off. I looked out the window in the ladies' room. They were just standing there. So I figured if I went out back like I had just finished work they could rob me at gunpoint and take the key. That was what I was expecting. McQueen too, he said. Maybe a tap on the head, at worst. But King had other ideas. He didn't want to leave a witness. So he went for the whole hijack thing. He took the cocktail waitress along for the ride. And so the act began."

"Did McQueen know the guy in the bunker?"

"No. He told me he'd never seen him before."

"So you don't know who he was either. And you weren't getting a real-time news feed all night and all day. Not like we were. And Kansas City won't have told you, because you're nobody."

"Told me what?"

Sorenson said, "As far as we know, the dead guy was a CIA head of station."

Delfuenso was quiet for a moment. Then she said, "I need guidance on this." She opened her bible and took out the cell phone and the charger. She got everything plugged in. She held a button down for two long seconds. The screen lit up. With a text message already on it. All in capital letters.

"Emergency," she said. "McQueen just dropped off the radar."

# Chapter 61

Delfuenso called whatever secret number was stored in her phone, and she got the latest update. To say McQueen had dropped off the radar was just a figure of speech. In reality his GPS signals had disappeared off a computer screen. He was carrying two chips, one in his phone, and one sewn in the back of his belt. For seven months they had recorded his every move. Now an hour ago they had blinked off and disappeared, never to return. Both of them. Seconds apart. The likelihood of two near-simultaneous failures was so remote it wasn't even worth considering. McQueen was in trouble.

Reacher asked, "Where was he last recorded?"

Delfuenso said, "At his normal location."

"Which is where?"

"A Wadiah hideout."

"Which is where?"

"Near Kansas City."

Reacher asked, "Do your people have a plan?"

Delfuenso said, "We're not going to involve the Kansas City boys. That was decided a long time ago. They're walled off, as of this minute. Because they can't help us with a problem like this. Their track record tells us they probably caused it."

"So what's the plan?"

"A SWAT team direct from Quantico."

"When?"

"Rapid deployment."

"How rapid?"

"They'll be in Kansas City in eight hours."

"That's rapid?"

"It's a big country. There's a lot to organize."

"Eight hours is way too long."

"I know it is."

"But we're right here. The three of us. We're a hundred miles from Kansas City. Which is two hours. Not eight."

**There was no** discussion. Not that Reacher expected there to be. An undercover agent was down, and he figured the FBI's unwritten codes would be at least half as strong as the army's. Undercover was the toughest job in the world, and the only way to make it bearable was to make it so the guy in the field knew he was watched over by people who would react instantly if he ran into trouble.

They gave themselves three minutes to prepare. Reacher didn't need them. He hadn't unpacked. His toothbrush was still in his pocket. He was good to go.

Delfuenso spent her time writing a note for Lucy. Sorenson spent her time getting out of her pant suit and into the free stuff from the piles on her bed. She said she felt it was going to be a denim kind of night.

Then in a brief before-the-storm pause Delfuenso looked straight at Reacher and said, "Remember, Wadiah has your name and your description."

Reacher said, "I know."

"And McQueen has almost certainly told them it was you who killed King. Remember that too."

"What are you, my mother? Don't worry about me."


**At that point** they had just one weapon between them, which was the Glock 19 from Delfuenso's bible. She carried it in her right hand, with her ID wallet open and ready in her left. Her phone was in her pants pocket. First port of call was Trapattoni's room. His light was still on. He answered Delfuenso's knock within seconds. He was confused by her ID. Like the ground had suddenly shifted under his feet. Not a cocktail waitress. Not an innocent victim. Not anymore. And apparently her ID was better than his. Higher up the food chain. Like an ace of trumps. Maybe because it had been issued by the Hoover Building, not by a regional field office. Reacher didn't really understand the nuances. But the guy fell in line immediately. He grabbed his suit coat, no questions asked, and he hustled with them all the way over to Bale's quarters.

Bale put up more of a fight. Apparently he had a

bigger ego. The visit started out the same way. Light still on, a fast answer to the knock, genuine surprise at the ID thrust under his nose. Then the guy started to argue. He said he knew nothing about any of this. He hadn't been informed. He hadn't been briefed. Delfuenso wasn't in his chain of command. She was an agent of equal rank, that's all, Hoover Building or no Hoover Building. She couldn't tell him what to do.

The guy was immovable. He was all the way up on his high horse.

Which put Delfuenso on the spot. She couldn't put the guy on the line with the mothership. The Hoover Building was not going to back her up. Not then. Too cautious. The suits were not going to approve a half-assed nighttime guerilla excursion by two women agents and a civilian. Too much risk, too much liability. Way outside the box. All that was left was the power of personal persuasion. Agent to agent. Face to face. And it wasn't working.

So Reacher hit the guy. Not hard. Just a pop to the solar plexus, left-handed. No big deal. Just enough to fold him up a little. Then it was easy to pin his arms behind his back while Sorenson took his gun out of his shoulder holster, and his spare magazine off his belt, and his cell phone out of one pocket, and his car key out of another. Trapattoni gave up the same four items voluntarily. And with a degree of haste and alacrity.

Reacher put Bale in one armchair, and Trapattoni joined him in the other.

Delfuenso said, "Your job is to stay here and attend to your duties. You still have two guests, one of which is my daughter. I expect her to be kept safe and treated well."

No answer.

Reacher said, "You gave up your service weapons. Where I come from, that's a real big no-no. I'm sure it's the same with you. Do what you're told, and no one will ever know about it. Step out of line, and I'll make sure everyone knows about it. You'll be a laughingstock. Robbed by two women? You'll be a punch line. You won't get a job as a dog catcher."

There was no answer, but Reacher sensed surrender.

**They checked both** cars and chose the one with more gas, which was Bale's. Delfuenso drove. Sorenson sat next to her in the front. Reacher sprawled in the back. A hundred yards later the motherly type in the office played it Trapattoni's way, not Bale's. She volunteered to look after Lucy, and she hit the button for the gate at the first time of asking. Delfuenso and Sorenson and Reacher got back in Bale's car and drove away. Around the traffic circle, along the concrete roadway, and out through the gate.

They turned right, north toward the Interstate.

The gate closed again behind them.

A car, three phones, a Glock 19, two Glock 17s, and eighty-eight rounds of nine-millimeter ammunition.

Good to go.

# Chapter 62

The twenty-plus miles of dark rural two-lane was hard going at speed, so there was no meaningful conversation until they were through the cloverleaf and heading east on the highway. Bale's car drove straight and steady, just like Sorenson's, just like the Impala. Quiet and smooth and unburstable, even at close to a hundred miles an hour. Impressive, Reacher thought.

Delfuenso asked, "What exactly does a CIA head of station do for a living?"

Reacher said, "He's responsible for a chunk of foreign territory. He lives near and works out of its biggest embassy. He deals with defectors and runs the local agents who work for us."

Then he said, "Or she."

Delfuenso asked, "Are there any women CIA heads of station?"

"I have no idea. I was in the army."

"Did you have female superiors?"

"Whenever fortune felt like smiling on me."

"Local agents who work for us? What kind?"

"The usual kind. Foreign nationals who because of blackmail, bribes, or ideology betray their countries to us. Now and then the head of station meets with the most important of them."

"How?"

"Just like in the movies. A lonely café, a back street, a city park, packages on the shelf in a phone booth."

"Why do they meet?"

"The blackmailed need to hear the threats over again, and the bribed need their bags of money, and the ideologues need to be stroked. And the heads of station need to collect their information."

"How often do they meet?"

"Could be once a week, could be once a month, whatever the individual agent needs."

"And the rest of the time this guy is posing as a trade attaché?"

"Or a cultural attaché. Or anything else that doesn't sound like very much work."

"And this is Russia and the Middle East and Pakistan and places like that, right?"

"I sincerely hope so," Reacher said.

"So why would a guy like that try to kill an FBI agent in Nebraska?"

Sorenson said, "He was an Arabic speaker. So maybe one of the Syrians from Wadiah had been one of his agents, back in Syria. Or maybe he still was. Maybe it was all to do with something they started overseas. But no Syrian came to that meet in the bunker, so maybe the CIA guy got suspicious. I mean, from his point of view everyone except his own guy is a bad guy, right?"

"Except that the CIA isn't allowed to operate inside America."

"Well, maybe it's super-covert. Maybe they were going to terminate the guy. Because of unfinished business or something. They're not going to share that with us."

Delfuenso said, "But the guy could tell the difference between McQueen and his best Syrian buddy, right? Or what? If he couldn't terminate the right guy, he might as well just go right ahead and terminate the wrong guy instead? Did I miss that on the CIA web site?"

Reacher said, "They weren't going to terminate anyone. They wouldn't send a head of station to do that. They have specialists. They call them wet boys. That's who they would have sent. And a wet boy wouldn't have brought his Boy Scout knife. He'd have brought an altogether different kind of knife. And taken an altogether different kind of approach. We wouldn't even have identified the dead guy yet. Not by fingerprints or face or dental work, anyway."

Sorenson said, "OK, so it was just a regular meet. No drama. The CIA head of station was running his agent."

"But his agent didn't show. So why didn't he just bullshit his way out of there? Why pull the knife?"

"Maybe he's not a good bullshitter."

"He's a CIA head of station. There are no better bullshitters."

"Maybe he knew McQueen from somewhere."

"McQueen didn't know him."

"It doesn't have to be a two-way street. So maybe the guy knew McQueen was FBI, and then he sees him inside a terrorist organization, in which case I guess most people are going to think *traitor* well before they think *undercover.*"

"So it was all an innocent accident? Mistaken identity?"

"Some things are simpler than they appear."

Reacher nodded.

"I know," he said.

Delfuenso said, "But none of this explains why a CIA head of station showed up posing as a member of a terrorist group. That's who King and McQueen were sent to meet, don't forget."

"Maybe he was undercover too," Sorenson said.

"The CIA isn't allowed to operate inside America."

"This is the modern world, Karen."

"Two simultaneous undercover operations in the same place at the same time? What would be the odds?"

"Not too long," Reacher said. "Not necessarily. All it takes is two people to get interested in the same interesting thing."

"Would they use a head of station for that kind of work?"

"They might. He would be unknown back here. He'd have the skills. He'd be used to the life. He'd speak the language. As far as the paperwork goes, they might say he's between postings."

Delfuenso said, "If they killed my guy, I'd burn

their house down. So why haven't we heard from them?"

"You probably have," Reacher said. "But not personally. Right now it's probably still one-on-one, in some back room in Washington. Two old white guys in suits. With cigars."

**The clock in** Reacher's head and the mileage boards counting down toward Kansas City showed they were going to beat their two-hour deadline by a decent margin. The trip was going to take an hour forty, or an hour forty-five, max. Not that there wouldn't be a few extra miles at the end. The bad guys were unlikely to be hiding out in whatever the highway people took to be the exact center of the city. Reacher didn't expect them to be holding their meetings in the lobby of a downtown hotel.

"It's a suburban house," Delfuenso said, like she could hear him thinking. "South of the city, and a little east."

"How far out of town?"

"Maybe twelve miles."

An hour fifty-three, he thought, door to door.

He said, "What kind of neighborhood?"

"Decent. And crowded."

"That's awkward."

"Potentially."

"But well chosen, I suppose."

Delfuenso nodded at the wheel. "Wadiah is smarter than most of what we see."

\* \* \*

**The Paris of** the Plains got a mile closer every forty seconds, and Sorenson asked, "What do you know about Peter King?"

Delfuenso said, "Where did you hear that name?"

"Reacher heard Alan King say it."

Delfuenso glanced at Reacher in the mirror and nodded.

"Yes," she said. "I remember that. And then he made the slip about a million and a half people living where he lived. Right after claiming he was based in Nebraska. Right after claiming he'd been driving three hours despite a full tank and bottles of cold water."

Sorenson said, "We know Peter King moved from Denver to Kansas City, seven months ago."

"You know more than you should."

"Was his move a coincidence?"

"There are no coincidences. Not in law enforcement. You know that."

"Is he a cop or an agent?"

"Why would he be?"

"I'm just trying to give him the benefit of the doubt. That's all. He served his country."

"Then sadly no, Peter King is not a cop or an agent."

"Is he connected to Wadiah?"

"We think so."

"How closely connected?"

"We think he might be their leader."

"I see."

"Because in terms of their organizational chart there's only a couple of roles we can't put a name to, and there's only a couple of names we can't assign a role to. One of those roles is leader, and one of those names is Peter King. So to connect the two seems like a fairly logical assumption."

"With a brother he doesn't talk to in the ranks?"

"He doesn't talk to anyone in the ranks. Not if he's the leader. That's not how these cells operate. The leader talks to his trusted lieutenants only, two or three of them at the most. Then there's a chain of command, rigorously compartmentalized, for security."

"Even so, it's still weird."

Delfuenso nodded. "McQueen got to know Alan King pretty well. There's some kind of strange sibling dynamic going on there. Alan is the kid brother. Or was, I should say now. Very needy guy. Always craving his big brother's approval. Obsessed by the guy. Which is why he mentioned him last night, I guess. There was no other reason to. Apparently there was some unspoken issue, stretching back more than twenty years. Peter was holding Alan accountable for something. Some kind of lapse or betrayal or disgrace. In return Alan was always trying to prove himself. And McQueen got the impression Peter *wanted* Alan to prove himself. Like a redemption thing. Tough love, but love nonetheless. You know how it is with family. Blood is thicker than water, and all that kind of shit. From what we know about him, Peter is going to be mighty pissed that Alan is dead."

"Which must be why McQueen is in trouble. Tonight of all nights."

Delfuenso nodded again.

"Exactly," she said. "Let's hope he's managing to convince him it was Reacher who did it, and there was nothing he could do to stop it."

**The plain west-east** Interstate that had run so serenely all the way through the state of Kansas splintered into a whole mess of beltways and thruways about ten miles short of the line. Delfuenso turned south, still on the Kansas side, and then she headed east again on a federal road with a new number, and they entered Missouri in the overtaking lane at ninety miles an hour, following a sign to a place called Lee's Summit. But they turned north well before they got there, toward a new place called Raytown, but they never got there, either. They turned off before it slid into view, heading now north and west, into multiple acres of suburban sprawl backed by what Reacher took to be a large park. By day it might have been pretty. By night it was just a big black hole. By that point Delfuenso was driving slow and cautious, nosing the silent car through uncertain turns, pausing hesitantly, moving briskly through patches of light, slowing again in patches of darkness, as if unsure of her destination, or scared of it.

Reacher asked her, "Have you been here before?"

She said, "None of us has, except McQueen. Too soon for that. This phase of an operation is all about standing back and seeing what develops. But I'm copied on the file. I know the address. I've seen the house on Google Maps. So I know the general situation."

The general situation was going to be American

suburbia, plain and simple. That was clear. There were municipal sidewalks left and right, mossy concrete, heaved up here and there by tree roots, studded less often by city fireplugs. And Reacher could see houses, regularly spaced in lots, most of them modest, some of them small, a few of them large, all of them dark and fast asleep. Most of them had white siding. Some were painted a color. Most of them were one-story, much wider than they were high. Some had eyebrow windows at the eaves, for upstairs bonus rooms. All had mailboxes and foundation plantings, and lawns, and driveways. Most had cars parked, at least one or two, or sometimes three. Some had children's bikes outside, dumped and dewy, and soccer goals, or hockey goals, or basketball hoops. Some had flagpoles, with Old Glories hanging limp and gray in the still night air.

"Not what I expected," Reacher said.

"I told you," Delfuenso said. "A decent, crowded neighborhood."

"Syrians don't stand out here?"

"The pale ones say they're Italians. The dark ones have been telling people they're Indians. From the subcontinent. You know, Delhi and Mumbai and places like that. Most people can't tell the difference. They say they work tech jobs in the city." Then she slowed, and came to a stop on the curb. She said, "OK, I think we're about two blocks away. How do you want to do this?"

Reacher had stormed houses before. More than once, less than twenty times, probably. But usually with a full company of MPs, divided into squads, some of them in back, some of them out front, some of them held in reserve in armored trucks with heavy firepower, all of them equipped with working radios. And all of them usually in places cordoned off and cleared of noncombatants. And usually with a bunch of medics standing by. He felt underequipped, and vulnerable.

He said, "We could set fire to the place. That usually works pretty good. They all come running out sooner or later. Except that McQueen could be tied up or locked in or otherwise incapacitated. So we better put one of us in the cellar door, if there is one, and one of us through the front, and one of us through the back. How are your marksmanship skills?"

"Pretty good," Delfuenso said.

"Not bad," Sorenson said.

"OK, you'll have your guns up and out in front of you. Shoot anything that moves. Except if it's me or McQueen. Use head shots for certainty. Aim at the center of the face. Save rounds. No double taps. We'll have the advantage for about four seconds. We can't let it turn into a siege."

Delfuenso said, "You don't want to try a decoy approach? I could go to the door and pretend to be lost or something."

"No," Reacher said. "Because then after they shoot you in the head Sorenson and I will have to do all the work on our own."

"Have you done this kind of thing before?"

"Haven't you?"

"No, this is strictly a SWAT function."

"It's usually about fifty-fifty," Reacher said. "In

terms of a happy ending, I mean. That's been my experience."

"Maybe we should wait for Quantico."

"Let's at least go take a look."

They slid out of Bale's car, stealthy and quiet, guns in their hands. They were the only things moving. Dark blue clothing, nearly invisible in the moonlight. They went single file on the sidewalk, instinctively six or eight feet from each other, the whole length of the first block, and across the street without pausing, at that kind of time in that kind of place more likely to come down with a rare disease than get run over by moving traffic. They walked the length of the second block, but slowed toward its end, and bunched up a little, as if discussion might be neccacary Delfuenso had said she knew the house from above, in two dimensions on the computer screen, and she had said she hoped she would know it in three dimensions on the ground. It was all going to depend on what the block looked like from the side. From a human's point of view, not a satellite camera's.

They stopped on the corner and Delfuenso peered up the street to their right. It rose on a slight slope, and then it dropped away again. The first few houses were visible. The rest weren't.

"This is it," Delfuenso said.

"Which house?"

"The second house over the hill on the left."

"You sure? We can't see it yet."

"The satellite pictures," she said. "I looked at the

neighbors. Up and down the street. And the corners. I know this is the right street. No fire hydrant. Every other corner has had one. This one doesn't. *W* for without a fire hydrant, *W* for Wadiah. That's how I planned to remember it."

Reacher glanced around. No fire hydrant.

"Good work," he said.

Sorenson volunteered to go in through the cellar door. If there was one. If not, she would find a side window and break in from there. Reacher was OK with that. The third angle would help, but it wouldn't be decisive. Clearly the most dangerous spot would be the front, and clearly the most effective spot would be the back. Only two real choices. Risk and reward.

He said, "I'll be the back door man."

Delfuenso said, "Then I'll take the front."

"But don't tell them you're lost. Shoot them in the face instead. Before they even say hello."

"We should give Sorenson a head start. If there is a cellar door, I mean. That's a slower way in."

"We will," Reacher said. "When we get there."

And then they moved off together, walking fast, up the street to their right.

# Chapter 63

They stayed off the sidewalk and walked in the road. No point in wasting what little tree cover there was. Reacher stopped them when he figured they were about seven feet below the crest of the rise. From there he and Sorenson would go yard to yard behind the houses, and Delfuenso would pause a long moment and then walk on alone. She would give them that head start because of their sideways detour and their tougher going. Fences, hedges, dogs. Maybe even barbed wire. This was Missouri, after all. The Southern Wire Company of St. Louis had once been the world's biggest manufacturer of bootleg cattle wire. Three cents a pound. Enough to go round.

But Delfuenso's approach was always going to be the most dangerous. Lookouts were always posted out front. Not always posted out back. If any approach was going to be spotted, it was going to be hers. Then it would depend on their paranoia level. Which might be high, by that point. Was she just an innocent pedestrian, or was everything a threat now?

There was no barbed wire. No dogs. Suburban pets were too pampered to spend the night outside. Suburban yards were too fancy for wire. But there were hedges and fences. Some of the fences were high and some of the hedges had thorns. But they got through OK. Sorenson was very agile over the fences. Better than Reacher. And thorny hedges could be backed through. Cheap denim was a tough material.

It was going to be hard to tell exactly when they would hit the top of the hill, because they were on flat rolled lawns in yards built up with all kinds of terraced landscaping. But there was a weak moon in the sky and Reacher could see the power lines through the gaps between houses, and he saw them peak on one particular pole, in a very shallow inverted V, and he took that to mean they were at the crest of the rise.

*The second house over the hill on the left.*

Sorenson got it. She used her hands and mimed it out, *one, two,* and then she pointed at the *two* as if to say *That's the target.* Reacher nodded and they moved on, through the yard they were in, over a picket fence with rabbit wire stapled to it, into the next yard, which belonged to the target's next-door neighbor. It was crowded with stuff. There was a gas grill, and lawn chairs, and many and various wheeled vehicles. They were the kind small children sit astride and either pedal or scoot. One was in the shape of a tennis shoe. Reacher stopped and looked at the house. Three bedrooms, probably. Two of them full of kids. Thin walls. Nothing but siding and sheetrock. Better to shoot in the other direction. Unless the other neighbor was an orphanage.

They moved on, to the last fence. They looked over at their target.

Their target was a two-story house.

It was about half as wide and twice as high as any of its neighbors. It had dark red siding. It had what looked like a full-width kitchen across the back. Then would come a front central hallway, probably, with rooms either side. And a staircase. Probably four rooms on the second floor. About the size of any other house, really, but split in half and stacked.

Not good. Not good at all. Two-story houses were about eight times as difficult as one-story houses. That had been Reacher's experience.

Sorenson looked a question at him.

He winked. Left eye.

They climbed the fence. Into the target's yard. It was minimally maintained. Rough grass, no flower-beds. No trees. No ornamental plantings. No grills, no chairs, no toys.

But there was a cellar door.

And it was wide open.

It was the traditional kind of cellar door. Made of pressed metal, maybe five feet long by four feet wide, split down the middle into two halves, built at a very shallow angle into the ground, the top end hard up against the foundation of the house and about a foot and a half higher than the bottom end. It gave onto a short flight of rough wooden steps.

There was no light in the basement. Reacher walked left and right and saw no light anywhere in the house, except behind a small pebble-glass window on the ground floor, on the left-hand side of the building. A powder room, presumably. Occupied, possibly. Worst case, all kinds of fanatics sleeping four to every room, with one of them awake and in the toilet.

Dining room, living room, maybe four rooms upstairs.

Worst case, maybe twenty-four people.

He walked back to Sorenson and she held forked fingers under her eyes and then put them together and pointed them down through the cellar door: *I'm going to take a look down there.* He nodded. She took the wooden steps slowly and carefully, putting her weight near the outer ends, where creaks were less likely. She reached the concrete floor and ducked her head and disappeared under the house.

Reacher waited. Forty seconds. A whole minute.

Sorenson came back. The duck of the head, the reappearance in the well at the foot of the steps. In the moonlight she looked a little out of breath. But she nodded. *OK. It's clear.* Reacher pointed at her, and tapped his left wrist, and then touched his ear. *Wait until you hear us at the doors.*

Sorenson disappeared again.

Reacher backed away until he could see down the side of the house to the street. Delfuenso was waiting there. In the shadows. She was leaning on a sidewalk tree. She was practically merged with it. He waved. She pushed off the tree. She mimed: *What's happening?* A cupped hand, brought up to her shoulder, her elbow tucked in. He shrugged. A big exaggerated gesture: *I'm not sure.* She held her thumb sideways: *Yes or no?*

He held his thumb up.

*Yes.*

She nodded. She took a breath. She held her palms out to him, both hands, including the gun, and she spread all her fingers: *In ten.*

She curled a finger down: *In nine.*

Another finger: *In eight.*

Then she scooted sideways out of the picture, toward the front door, and Reacher did the same thing, toward the back.

*Seven. Six. Five. Four.*

*Three.*

*Two.*

*One.*

Delfuenso had been counting faster than Reacher He heard a hammering on the front door while his foot was still in the air. The hammering sounded like the butt of a Glock on a steel plate. A steel front door. Reinforced. A security measure. He wondered what kind of resistance the back door was about to offer him.

Not much, as it turned out.

He smashed his boot heel an inch above the knob, accelerating all the way, punching hard through the last final fraction, and the door burst inward and then Reacher was right there in the kitchen, a little fast, but otherwise with no more trouble than stepping over some kind of small hurdle in his way. The hammering continued at the front. The kitchen was cold and empty. Recently used, but currently deserted. Reacher stepped into the hallway, ready to find someone on the way to answer the door, ready to shoot that someone in the back.

The hallway was deserted.

The hammering continued. Loud enough to wake the dead. Reacher prowled the hallway, his gun stiff-armed way out in front of him, his torso jerking violently left and right from the hips, like a crazy disco dance. The house-storming shuffle. There was a dining room on the left. It was full of stuff and full of furniture. But it was empty of people.

There was a parlor on the right.

Full of stuff. Full of furniture.

Empty of people.

There were two more doors off the hallway. One had a bar of light under it. The pebble-glass window. The powder room. Occupied, possibly. Reacher took a long step and raised his boot and smashed it through the lock. The lock proved no stronger than the kitchen's. The door crashed open and Reacher stepped back with his finger tight on the trigger.

The powder room was empty.

The light was on, but there was no one home.

Then Sorenson stepped in through the final door, leading with her Glock.

"Don't shoot," Reacher said. "It's me."

He saw the cellar stairs behind her. Empty. No one there.

*Ground floor all clear.*

He said, "Let Delfuenso in. I'm going to check up-stairs."

He went up. His least favorite situation. He hated the stairs. Everyone did. Everything was against you, including gravity. Your enemy had the high ground and the better angle. And the limitless possibilities of concealment. And the immense satisfaction of seeing you lead with your head.

Not good, but Reacher went up those particular stairs happily enough, because by that point he was certain the house was empty. He had busted into houses before. The vibe was wrong. There was no heartbeat. It felt still and quiet. It felt abandoned.

And it was.

There were four bedrooms with four walk-in closets and two bathrooms, and Reacher checked them all, jerking left and right again, pirouetting like a damn paramilitary ballerina. There should have been music playing, with sudden orchestral climaxes.

All the bedrooms and closets and bathrooms were empty.

There was junk, there were beds, there were clothes, there was furniture.

But there were no people.

*Ground floor all clear.*

*Second floor all clear.*

Nobody home.


**Which in some** small portion of everyone's mind is a very welcome result. Human nature. Relief. Anticlimax. Peace with honor. But Reacher and Sorenson and Delfuenso met in the central hallway and admitted to nothing but frustration. If McQueen wasn't there, he had to be somewhere else just as bad, if not worse. He had been evacuated in a hurry.

"They must have a bigger place somewhere," Reacher said. "Surely. They're supposed to be two medium-sized groups working together. This place is too small for them, apart from anything else. This place is just a pied-à-terre, or officers' quarters, or guest quarters. Something like that. Some kind of extra facility."

"Could be a mail drop," Sorenson said.

"McQueen lived here," Delfuenso said. "We know that for sure. He told us so, and we have seven months of GPS to prove it."

Reacher walked up and down the hallway, turning lights on as he went. He lit up the dining room and he lit up the parlor. He lit up the kitchen. He said, "Start looking. If they're back and forth between two places regularly, they'll have left some kind of a trace. However well they cleaned up."

And they had cleaned up pretty well. That was clear. They had done a decent job. But not in any conventional sense. There was considerable disarray. There were used dishes in the sink. The beds were unmade. Sofa cushions had not been plumped, old newspapers had not been removed, the trash had not been taken out. Mugs had not been washed, ashtrays had not been emptied, clothes had not been folded and put away. The occupants had gotten out fast.

But they had prioritized. They had taken a lot of stuff with them. That was where their clean-up effort had been spent. Mail, paperwork, bills, bureaucracy, officialdom. No trace of any such items had been left behind. No names. No papers large or small. No scraps. No notes, no doodles, no messages. Not that Reacher was expecting to find a treasure map with *OUR HQ* and an arrow on it, in bright red ink. But most people leave something behind. Some small unconsidered item. A toll receipt, a matchbook, a cinema ticket. In the trash, dropped in a corner, under a sofa cushion. These guys hadn't. They were pretty good. Careful, meticulous, alert and aware. Very disciplined. That was clear. Disciplined on an ongoing day-to-day basis, too. Not just high days and holidays. Good security. Further progress was going to depend on a random mistake.

Then Sorenson called from the kitchen.

With the random mistake.

# Chapter 64

Sorenson had seven big-size McDonald's paper sacks lined up on the kitchen counter. Take-out food. The bags were used and stained and crumpled. Sorenson had emptied them all. There were soda cups and milk shake cups and burger clamshells and apple pie wrappers. There were cheeseburger papers and register receipts. There was old lettuce going brown, and chopped onion going slimy, and ketchup packets going crusted.

Sorenson said, "They like McDonald's."

"Not a crime in itself," Reacher said. "I like McDonald's."

"But it's a good plan B," Delfuenso said. "We could leave them alone and they'll die anyway in five years from heart attacks."

"They like McDonald's," Sorenson said again. "My guess is pretty much every day they sent a gofer to the nearest drive-through for a couple of sacks. I bet there's a drive-through not more than five minutes from here."

"This is America, after all," Delfuenso said.

"And maybe you get the taste for it. So when you're stationed at your other camp, maybe you look for a drive-through near there, too. And maybe once in a while if you have to make the trip all the way from A to B, you stop at the drive-through near A and you load up with a little something for the ride. And then if you have to make the trip all the way back again from B to A, maybe you stop at the drive-through near B and you do the same thing."

"And you cross-pollute your garbage," Reacher said.

Sorenson nodded.

"Exactly," she said. "You buy a burger and fries and a soda, and you eat it in the car along the way, except maybe you don't finish the soda, so you carry the sack into the house at the end of the trip and you finish it right here. In this kitchen. And then you dump the sack in the trash. Which is hygienic, but the bad news is you just linked two geographic areas that should have stayed separate."

Reacher asked, "What do the register receipts tell us?"

"Six of them are from one place and the seventh is different."

"Where is the seventh from?"

"I don't know. It's not an address. It's a code number."

* * *

**Sorenson couldn't go** through her field office. As far as her field office was concerned she was quarantined in the motel in Kansas, at the central region's express request. So she got on-line on Trapattoni's phone and found a PR number for McDonald's. She wasn't optimistic. Any jerk could call from a cell phone and say she was with the FBI. She was expecting a long and tedious runaround.

So Reacher asked Delfuenso, "How is McQueen's GPS data recorded?"

"Screen shots," she said. "Lines and points of light on a map. You can choose the interval. A week, a day, an hour, whatever you want."

"Can they do seven months?"

"I don't see why not."

"How would you get it if you needed to see it?"

"By e-mail. To my phone, if necessary."

"We need to see it."

"They think I'm holed up in that motel."

"Doesn't matter. You don't have to tell them you aren't. Just tell them you're going crazy doing nothing and you want to help out. Tell them you have a theory and you want to work on it. Tell them you might as well do something while you're sitting there. Tell them you'll get right back to them if it pans out."

"What theory?"

"Doesn't matter. Be shy about it. Just tell them you need the data."

Delfuenso dialed her phone, and Sorenson got put on hold for the second time.

* * *

**By that point** they were two hours and nearly thirty minutes into it. Reacher figured Quantico would be well into the process of gearing up. He wasn't exactly sure how FBI SWAT teams worked. Maybe they had pre-packed trucks ready for the drive out to Andrews Air Force Base. Or maybe they used helicopters. Or maybe they stored their stuff at Andrews permanently, all ready to go. Then would come the long flight west. Well over a thousand miles. In an Air Force C-17, he figured. He doubted that the FBI had heavy jets of its own. Then the landing, at Kansas City's own municipal airport, way to the northwest, or at Richards-Gebaur Air Force Base, about twenty miles south. If Richards-Gebaur was still in business. He wasn't sure. Plenty of places had been abandoned, right at the time his own career was coming to an end. A systemic problem. In which case Whiteman Air Force Base would be the only alternative, sixty miles to the east. Then would come more trucks or helicopters, and then painstaking tactical preparations, and then finally action.

*Eight hours. It's a big country. There's a lot to organize.*

The choice of airport would depend on where McQueen was. Sorenson was still talking her way through a corporate maze. Delfuenso was staring at her phone, willing an e-mail to arrive. Time was ticking away. Reacher figured they might end up doing nothing more than guiding the Quantico team in on target. Like forward observers. Like Peter King.

Better than nothing.

\* \* \*

**Sorenson got her** information first. Such as it was. There had been no real opposition from the McDonald's main office. No real secrecy or obfuscation. Just confusion, and a certain amount of incompetence, and a lot of hold music and phone tag. Eventually she had ended up talking to a minimum-wage server at the franchise in question. A burger flipper. On a wall phone, probably. She could hear tile echo and raw fries being plunged into hot oil. She asked the server for his location.

"I'm in the kitchen," the boy said.

"No, I mean, where is your restaurant?"

The boy didn't answer. Like he didn't know how. Sorenson thought she could hear him chewing his lip. She thought he wanted to say, *Well, the restaurant is on the other side of the counter. You know, like, from the kitchen.*

She asked him, "What is your mailing address?"

He said, "Mine?"

"No, the restaurant's."

"I don't know. I never mailed anything to the restaurant."

"Where is it located?"

"The restaurant?"

"Yes, the restaurant."

"Just past Lacey's. You can't miss it."

"Where is Lacey's?"

"Just past the Texaco."

"On what road?"

"Right here on Route 65."

"What's the name of the town you're in?"

"I don't think it has a name."

"Unincorporated land?"

"I don't know what that is."

"OK, what's the nearest town with a name?"

"Big town?"

"We could start with that."

"That would be Kansas City, I guess."

Then there was some yelling. A manager, Sorenson thought. Something about clean-up time.

The kid said, "Ma'am, I got to go," and hung up the phone.


Sorenson put her phone on the kitchen counter and Reacher looked a question at her and she said, "Route 65, near something called Lacey's, just past a Texaco station."

Reacher said nothing.

Sorenson got back on-line on her phone and called up a map. She made all kinds of pinching and spreading and wiping motions with her fingertips. On and on. Her face was falling all the time. She said, "Terrific. Route 65 runs all the way through the state, north to south, from Iowa to Arkansas. It's nearly three hundred miles long."

"Any sign of Lacey's?"

"This is a map. Not the business pages. Lacey's is probably a store of some kind. Or a bait shop. Or a bar." But she stayed with it. She went ahead and searched on-line. She typed *Lacey's + Kansas City.* Nothing. Then *Lacey's + Missouri.*

She said, "It's a small grocery chain."

She dabbed her finger against the glass to follow a link. The phone was slow. Then the site came up and she started with the wiping and the pinching and the spreading again. She said, "They have three locations on Route 65. Each one about twenty miles apart. Like an arc. They're all about sixty miles from the city."

Two hours and forty minutes into it.

"Making progress," Reacher said.

Then Delfuenso's phone pinged, for an incoming e-mail.

# Chapter 65

The seven-month screen shot was laid over a grayed-out satellite image of five contiguous central states. Kansas, Nebraska, Iowa, Illinois, and Missouri. More than three hundred and forty thousand square miles. More than twenty-six million people.

McQueen's movements among those miles and those people were recorded as thin amber lines. His recent jaunt up from Kansas to Nebraska to Iowa and back again to Kansas showed up as a faint jagged rectangle. There were some other long spidery lines. But not many. He had made very few other long-haul trips. Most of his movements had been concentrated close to Kansas City itself. At that position on the map the amber lines overlaid one another like a manic scribble. Almost a solid mass. The lines were bright where they repeated one over the other. Some spots looked like holes burned in the screen.

Reacher asked, "Can you zoom in?"

Delfuenso did the spreading thing with her fingers,

like Sorenson had. She expanded the manic scribble. She centered it on the screen. She zoomed it some more. She centered it again. The solid mass became a knotted tangle of movements. The bright lines dimmed as they separated.

But two spots still burned stubbornly hot. Two locations, each one visited maybe hundreds of times. The inch of space between them was a river of light. A journey back and forth, made maybe hundreds of times. One spot was southwest of the other. Like a seven on a clock face, and a two.

"Point A and point B," Reacher said. "Can't be anything else."

Sorenson got the map back on her screen. She put her phone next to Delfuenso's. She zoomed and wiped until she matched the state line, where the die-straight border between Kansas and Missouri suddenly looped off course, to follow the banks of the Missouri River. She said, "OK, point A is right here, on this street, basically. In this house, obviously." Then she scrolled north and east, both phones at once, both index fingers moving in lockstep, precise and delicate. She said, "And point B is very close to the northernmost Lacey's store."

Sixty miles. Through mazy suburbs, and along dark country roads.

Two hours and fifty minutes into it.

Plus another hour, now.

Maybe more.

"Let's go," Reacher said.

\* \* \*

**Bale's car had** GPS, which helped. Sorenson read the address for the northernmost Lacey's off her phone, and Delfuenso entered it in the machine. Then she lit up the strobes and took off, loud and fast. No more need for stealth. Not around point A, anyway. Point B would be a different matter. She said she would deal with that when they got there.

The same satellites that had tracked McQueen got the car out of town after almost no time at all in the mazy suburbs. Score one for technology, Reacher thought. The cold hard logic in the circuits sent them what he was sure was the wrong way, down a bland street he was certain was a dead end. But then a concealed right and a shallow left brought them to one of the beltway on-ramps, and six fast miles after that they turned east on I-70, along the southern edge of Independence, Missouri. President Harry S Truman's hometown. Reacher's favorite president. The highway was straight and empty, and a hundred miles an hour was easy. Reacher began to feel a little more optimistic. They were going to make it to point B within about fifty minutes, total. Which was good. Because even if the Quantico guys were already in the air by then, which they had to be, they still had a long way to come.

They left the highway at a small road in the middle of nowhere, but by that point Reacher was trusting the system. He was watching the arrow, and the gray lines. He saw how Route 65 dog-legged north of where they were. It jogged east toward a town called Marshall. Some historical reason, presumably. The GPS was cutting the corner. It was going to join Route 65 right after a famous Civil War battlefield site. Reacher knew his American history. That particular field had seen a nine-hour artillery duel. The Kings of Battle. With observers. And crude incendiary rounds. The Confederate gunners had heated their cannonballs in fires, hoping to set things ablaze. The Union gunners had worn red stripes on their pants.

Out his window the moonlight showed fields on both sides of the road, all churned up by animals, all fenced in with wire. There were gates and water troughs and giant piles of feed covered over with tarpaulins, and weighted down with old car tires.

"Farm country again," Sorenson said. "Is that what it's going to be? A farm?"

"A farm would make sense," Reacher said. "Somewhere isolated. With barns, and so on. For vehicles. And for storage. And for dormitories, maybe. For many dormitories, possibly. I don't know how many people there are in two medium-sized groups."

"Not too many," Delfuenso said. "Not necessarily. Half a dozen is called medium. Up to maybe fifteen or twenty. So it'll be somewhere between twelve and forty."

"That's enough," Sorenson said. "Don't you think?"

Reacher said nothing. They had eighty-eight rounds of ammunition. The last figures he had seen in the army showed that an average infantryman records one enemy fatality for every fifteen thousand combat rounds expended. In which case, for forty opponents, they would need six hundred thousand rounds. Not eighty-eight. Alternatively they would need to be a lot smarter than an average infantryman.

\* \* \*

**Route 65 wore** its status lightly. It was three hundred miles long and it split the state, but in person it looked like any other country road. Maybe a little wider, maybe a little better surfaced, but otherwise it had nothing to recommend it. Almost immediately it crossed the mighty Missouri on an iron trestle. But that was its only point of interest. After the bridge it ran north through the darkness, anonymously, never really deviating, never really staying straight. Then Sorenson said, "OK, we're about ten miles south. I don't know which way the kid at the McDonald's was orienting himself. I don't know if we're going to see the Texaco station and the Lacey's store first, or whether we're going to hit the McDonald's first."

Delfuenso killed the strobes. Five miles after that, she started to slow. Two miles later, she killed the rest of her lights. The world shrank around them, instantly dark blue and misty. There was no Texaco sign ahead. No blaze of light from a supermarket window. No red neon, no golden arches.

"Keep going," Sorenson said.

Delfuenso crept onward, at maybe twenty miles an hour. Not as hard as it looked. The yellow line in the center of the road showed up gray and kept them on course. There was some forward visibility. Not much, but enough for twenty miles an hour. People could run faster.

Still no Texaco, no Lacey's, no McDonald's. Or no McDonald's, no Lacey's, no Texaco, depending on what the order was going to be. Reacher looked left and right, as far as he could into the fields. They were dark and flat and empty. Nothing to see. Not that he expected a neon sign saying *Last Terrorist Hideout Before the Interstate.* But twelve or forty people usually put on some kind of a show. Maybe the glow of an outhouse lamp around a warped door, or a lookout's cigarette, or a locked car's alarm flashing gently on the dash, or the blue haze of an insomniac's television behind a badly drawn drape.

But there was nothing.

Delfuenso said, "We must have gone wrong somewhere."

Sorenson said, "No, this is the right road. The Lacey's should be dead ahead."

"Are those web site maps always accurate?"

"Government GPS is always accurate. Point B is dead ahead, too."

Reacher said, "So make a note, in case you have to talk to Quantico. Tell them Whiteman Air Force Base would be the best place to land."

"Talk to Quantico? You mean, if we fail to get the job done and I'm the only survivor?"

"Obviously there's a number of possible outcomes."

"And that's one of them?"

"That's two of them. We might fail to get the job done with no survivors."

# Chapter 66

A fast-food restaurant and a grocery store and a gas station put out a lot of electric light, so they had been expecting to see a glow a mile or so before they got there. But as it turned out they were already halfway past the McDonald's before they even noticed it. It was closed for the night. As was Lacey's, the grocery store. As was the Texaco station.

Reacher hoped they weren't on the blue boards on the highway. Or it would be a classic deceptive exit. The gas station looked like a ghost ship. No lights anywhere. Just a tangle of strange dark shapes rising up out of the ground. The grocery store was a sullen gray mass, as big as a hill, but angular. And without the red and yellow neon and the fluorescent tubes inside, the McDonald's was just another small A-frame silhouette against the sky. It could have been any kind of a low-rent operation, all closed up and done for the day.

"I heard the manager shouting in the background,"

Sorenson said. "Something about clean-up time. I guess that's what they do when they're about to close."

Reacher said, "So where's point B?"


**Sorenson did her** twin-phone thing again. She calibrated them against the Interstate. She got them both lined up. She scaled them the same. She took a breath and said, "If the grocery store web site is accurate, then point B is about a mile northwest of our current position."

"That's out in the fields," Reacher said.

"It's a farm," Delfuenso said. "I knew it would be."

They left the car parked sideways across three spaces in Lacey's front lot. They tracked around the dark bulk of the building and came out at the back. Just reconnaissance at that point. Just purely. Strictly a preliminary survey. An immediate attack would have been pinning a lot of hopes on a grocery store's web site. For one thing, the symbol the web site had used to mark the spot would scale up to about a mile wide.

Reacher had seen from Bale's GPS that Route 65 was strictly a north-south deal. So he lined himself up with it and faced the way they had been driving. Then he made a forty-five-degree turn to his left and pointed. He said, "That's northwest. What do you see?"

Not much, was the consensus. And it was true. But it was equally true there was even less to see in any other direction. Somehow the dark was darker due west and due north. As if there really was something there in the northwest quarter. Invisible, but there. They strained their eyes, they relaxed, they defocused, they looked away, they tried peripheral vision. They saw nothing. But it felt like a substantial kind of nothing.

Reacher said, "Can you do Google Maps?"

Sorenson said, "Cell service is not good enough out here."

So they went back to the car and Reacher fiddled with Bale's GPS. He zoomed it in, and in, until he was sure all the little roads were there. Then he moved their current position to the right of the screen.

The space behind Lacey's was bounded on the right by Route 65, and on the left by a small road running parallel, and at the top by one east-west two-lane, and at the bottom by another. An empty box, more or less square, but not quite. Technically it was a parallelogram, because the roads at the top and the bottom sloped down a little from right to left. It wasn't a particularly big empty box. But it wasn't small either. Exact scale was hard to determine on the GPS screen, but worst case, the box was a mile on a side. Best case, it might have been two miles by two. Reacher said, "That's somewhere between six hundred and forty and two thousand five hundred and sixty acres. Is that too big for a single farm?"

Sorenson said, "There are just over two million individual farms in the United States, working almost a billion acres, for an average farm size of close to five hundred acres. Statistics. We find them useful."

"But an average is just an average, right? If there's a bunch of moms and pops working five or ten acres, then someone is working twenty-five hundred."

"Livestock, maybe. Or industrial corn."

"There's livestock here. I saw the hoof marks."

"You think it's all one farm?"

"Maximum of five," Reacher said. "Shouldn't take too long to check them all."

Delfuenso's phone buzzed. The secret phone. From her bible. It was set on silent, but it didn't sound very silent to Reacher. Whatever little motor produced the vibration was whining away like a dentist's drill. Delfuenso answered and listened for a long minute. Then she acknowledged and hung up.

"My boss," she said. "With a new factor for my theory. He wondered if it might be pertinent."

"What theory?" Reacher said.

"The thing I claimed to be working on to get the GPS data. The thing I had to be shy about."

"What new factor?"

"Now the State Department spokespeople are denying the dead guy in the pumping station was anything to do with them. They're saying he was just a guy. Definitely not a consular official, or any other kind of employee. Double definitely not, fingers in their ears, la, la, la."

"But he was fingerprinted. He's in the system now."

"An understandable error. Forensics is always quick and dirty in the field."

"Bullshit," Sorenson said. "My people are good."

"I know they are."

"So?"

"So maybe it's State's spin control that's quick and dirty."

Reacher nodded. "Why don't they just take out an

ad in the paper? This way they're practically proving the guy was CIA."

"To us, maybe. But we knew already. This way the rest of the world can sleep easy at night."

"Or is it a legal thing? This way they can deny they were operating inside America."

"Everyone knows they operate inside America. They gave up hiding that a long time ago."

"Then they're proving something else, too. This guy wasn't just CIA. He was bent CIA. He wasn't undercover. He was guest starring. Why else deny him?"

"You think a CIA head of station was a double agent?"

"They can count that high over there. Being a triple agent might pose a challenge."

"I don't like the idea of a CIA insider talking to Wadiah."

"Didn't happen," Reacher said. "Your guy knifed him too soon for talking."

"They'd been together before. They must have been. At least for a few minutes. I think they walked to that bunker as a threesome."

*Like suddenly the first guy had bolted ahead, and the other two guys were hustling to keep up.*

"Probably," Reacher said.

"So they must have talked."

"Probably."

"I want to know what they said."

"We'll ask McQueen. When we find him."

"Tell me the answer to that word game. Where you have to speak for a minute without using the letter *A*."

"Is that how you want to remember me?"

"I could win a couple of bar bets."

"That was a game with Alan King."

"I overheard."

"Later," Reacher said. "When we've found Mc-Queen. He'll want to hear it too."

"He was asleep."

"I doubt he ever sleeps."

"How many acres was it?"

"Doesn't matter about acres. This is about buildings. We'll know it when we see it."

And they saw it and knew it exactly ten minutes later, after six hundred yards on foot.

# Chapter 67

**They formed up in back of the grocery store,** where they had stood before. They aligned themselves with the road, for reference, and they turned forty-five degrees left, as before. Northwest. Reacher took a last look at McQueen's GPS tracks. At maximum magnification they hooked around an angle, like an upside-down letter *J*. Clearly there was a vehicle entrance off the top east-west two-lane. McQueen had driven north on Route 65, past the McDonald's, past the Lacey's store, past the Texaco station, and then he had turned left, and left again, into a driveway. He had done all that enough times to burn the evidence into a photograph. And its bright end point was just about right on the diagonal across the parallelogram. About halfway along its length. Which in terms of miles would be half of the square root of two, at the pessimistic end of the scale, or half of the square root of eight, at the optimistic end. Close to thirteen hundred yards, or close to twenty-five hundred. Either twenty minutes' walk, or forty. Or somewhere in between. They would be coming up on whatever it was from the rear three-quarter direction. Not bad. Better than the front, certainly, and better than head-on toward the back. Not as good as sideways-on. If any house had a blank wall, it would be on the side. Or a wall with token windows, maybe with pebble glass, powder rooms or bathrooms. Like the place in the suburbs, sixty miles away.

They separated laterally as much as they dared. Delfuenso started out way to the left, and Sorenson started out way to the right. Reacher was in the middle, and he could see both of them, but only just. They couldn't see each other. Delfuenso set out first. Then minutes later Sorenson walked out into the dirt. Reacher came last. Three targets, widely separated side to side, widely separated front to back. Dark clothes, dark night. Maybe not yet smarter than the average infantryman, but not any dumber, either.

There was heavy mud underfoot, all churned up and lumpy and unreliable. Some of it felt slick and slippery. Animal dung, Reacher assumed, although he still couldn't smell anything. He kept his eyes fixed on an imaginary spot on the horizon, to keep his progress straight. He had Bale's Glock in his right hand, down by his side. Ahead of him and far to his left he could just about see Delfuenso. A shadowy figure, barely there at all. But she was making decent progress. Short steps, energetic, really working it. He could see Sorenson a little better. She wasn't so far ahead. And she was marginally paler than Delfuenso. Blonde, not dark. The moon was still out in places, but it was low in the sky and not bright.

Safe enough.

So far.

The mud kept their speed low. Reacher revised his estimates. Not twenty minutes or forty. It would take closer to thirty minutes or sixty. Frustrating, but not a disaster. The Quantico guys were still at thirty-five thousand feet. Probably somewhere over West Virginia. Still hours away. He trudged onward, slipping and sliding.

Then he began to slow. Because the blank view ahead of him seemed to be solidifying. Just a sense. There was some kind of substance there. Still invisible. Not a small distant farmhouse, presumably. Something hulkier. Maybe a giant barn. Sheet metal, or corrugated tin. Painted black. Blacker than the night itself.

On his left Delfuenso was slowing too. She was sensing the same thing. And on his right Sorenson was altering course a little. Her line was drifting closer to his. Delfuenso was edging in, too. There was something ahead of them, and instinct was telling them not to face it alone.

Reacher walked on, staring ahead. Seeing nothing. His vision was as good as anyone else's. He had never worn eyeglasses. He could read in dim light. And in the black of night the human eye was supposed to be able to see a candle flame a mile away. Maybe more. And initial adaptation to the dark was supposed to happen within four seconds. The iris was supposed to open wide. To the max. And then retinal chemistry was supposed to kick in over the next few minutes. Like turning up a volume knob. But Reacher could see nothing ahead. It was like he was blind. Except that in this case seeing nothing felt like a version of seeing something. There was something there.

A breeze came up and flapped his pants. The air felt suddenly cold. Ahead on his right Sorenson was waiting for him. And Delfuenso was cutting in toward him. They were abandoning their separation. They were making one big target. Bad tactics. They met up a minute later. They regrouped. All three of them together, way out in the field, like they had been at the beginning, behind Lacey's loading dock.

"This is weird," Sorenson whispered. "There's a big shape out there."

"What shape?" Reacher asked. Maybe her eyes were better than his.

"Like a big patch of nothing. Like a hole in the air."

"That's what I'm seeing," Reacher said. "A big patch of nothing."

"But a low patch of nothing," Delfuenso said. The breeze blew again and she shivered. She said, "Start high. Look at the sky. Then move down. You can see an edge. Where one kind of nothing changes to another kind of nothing."

Reacher looked at the sky. Ahead of them in the north and the west it was padded with thick black cloud. No light at all. Way behind them in the southeast was a patch of thinner gray. Sullen moonlight, through a fissure. Not much. But there was wind up there. The thinner clouds were moving. Maybe the fissure would open wider. Or maybe it would close up altogether.

He faced front again and started high and moved his gaze down. Looking for Delfuenso's edge. Looking hard. But not seeing it. There was no other kind of nothing. It was all the same kind of nothing to him.

He asked, "How low?"

"Above the horizon, but not by much."

"I can't even see the horizon."

"I'm not imagining it."

"I'm sure you're not. We'll have to get closer. You up for that?"

"Yes," Delfuenso said.

Sorenson nodded, blonde hair moving in the dark.

They walked on, staying close. Ten yards. Twenty yards.

Staring ahead.

Seeing nothing.

Thirty yards.

And then they saw it. Maybe the greater proximity did the trick, or maybe the wind moved the cloud and threw a couple of extra moonbeams down to earth. Or maybe both.

It wasn't a farm.

# Chapter 68

It looked like a capsized battleship. Like a hull, upside down and beached. It was black, and hard, and strangely rounded in places. It was long and low. It was deep. It was maybe hundreds of feet from side to side, and hundreds of feet from front to back. It was maybe forty feet tall. It was about the size of the Lacey's supermarket. But far more substantial. Lacey's was a cheap and cynical commercial structure. Lacey's looked like it would blow away in a storm. And plenty of similar establishments had.

But this thing out in the field looked bombproof. Something about the way it was hunched down in the earth suggested concrete many feet thick. The radiused haunches where walls met roofs suggested immense strength. Its corners were rounded. There were no doors or windows. There seemed to be a waist-high railing all around the edge of the roof. Tubular steel.

They walked closer. Forty yards later they had a

better view. Reacher glanced back. Behind them the wind was nibbling at the fissure in the clouds. The moon was coming out. Which was both good and bad. He wanted a little more light, but not too much more. Too much more could be a problem.

He faced front again and started to see detail up ahead. The building wasn't black. Not exclusively. It was also dark brown and dark green. Dull flat nonreflective paint, thickly applied in giant random slashes and spikes and daggers.

Camouflage.

A U.S. Army pattern, dating back to the 1960s, to the best of Reacher's recollection.

Delfuenso whispered, "What is it?"

"Not sure," Reacher said. "An abandoned military installation, obviously. The fence is gone. Some farmer got a hundred extra acres. I don't know what it was originally. It's blastproof, clearly. Could have been for storage of air-defense missiles, possibly. Or it could have been an ammunition factory. In which case the concrete is protecting the outside from the inside, not the other way around. I would have to see the main doors to know more. Missile storage needs big doors, for the transporters. An ammunition factory would have smaller doors."

"Abandoned when?"

"That's a very old camouflage pattern. So the place hasn't been painted in fifty years. It was abandoned after Vietnam, maybe. Which might make it more likely it was an ammunition factory. We didn't need so many bullets or shells after that. But we cut back a little on missiles too. So it could be either."

"Why is it still here?"

"These places can't be demolished. How would you do it? They were built to take on a lot more than a wrecking ball."

"How do people get a place like this?"

"Maybe they bought it. The DoD is happy to take what it can get. Or maybe they're squatting. No one checks on places like this. Not anymore. No manpower. There are too many of them. Your granddad's tax dollars at work."

"It's huge."

"I know it is. You want to revise your personnel estimate? You could get more than forty people in there. You could get four hundred."

"You could get four thousand in there."

"Didn't McQueen give you a figure?"

"A terrorist headcount is a moving target. He never saw everyone at once. I'm still betting on a couple of dozen, tops."

"They must be rattling around in there."

"How do we do this?"

"Very carefully."

"Where do we start?"

Reacher glanced at her. And then at Sorenson. *The guy in the field knew he was watched over by people who would react instantly if he ran into trouble.* But *instantly* was a big word. They were very close to four hours into a mission launched because eight hours had seemed ludicrously long. Was four hours an instant? Not even close.

So was eight hours so much worse?

He said, "The smart money is on very careful surveillance. We need to study that place from all four sides."

Delfuenso said, "That would take hours."

"So be it."

"You mean we should wait for Quantico."

"It's an option."

"But not a good one," Delfuenso said. "Especially not for Don McQueen."

"I agree."

"So the dumb money is on attacking without adequate preparation. Is that our choice?"

"Call it half-assed preparation."

"To be honest, in what way are we even minimally prepared?"

"We're tooled up," Reacher said. "We're awake, and they might not be."

Sorenson said, "If we don't do something now, there's no point doing anything at all. That's our situation, right? And that's a military kind of problem, isn't it? Did you train for this stuff?"

"I trained for all kinds of things. Usually by starting with a little history. Back in the day the Soviets had some pretty big missiles. That thing in front of us was built to stand up to one. We have three handguns."

"But suppose you were the inside man?"

"I'm all in favor of helping McQueen."

Delfuenso said, "Just not with us?"

"There were certain things I never had to say to my own people. Because it was right there in the job description."

"What certain things?"

"You could get killed or maimed, doing this."

"Is there a way we can reduce that risk? Without taking hours?"

"Yes, there is," Reacher said.

**They invested seven** minutes in talking through the contingencies. There was no point in making a plan. No plan could survive the first exchange of fire. No plan ever did. Except in this case it was impossible to make a plan, anyway. Because there was no information.

They turned away from the building and sat down in a line in the dirt and talked. *This might happen, that might happen.* They agreed on some rules of thumb. They nailed down some basic procedures. Reacher was reasonably optimistic about getting close to the concrete. Neither a missile hangar nor an ammunition factory needed gun ports. And there was no way to drill your own. Even with a missile. So the place was not bristling with guns. Therefore the approach from distance would be safe enough. After that, there would be plenty of things to worry about. There would be sentries on the roof, presumably. Behind the tubular steel railing. On a walkway. Or maybe a running track. But not many sentries. And all of them so far untested. Reacher knew his history. Sentries were sometimes more trouble than they were worth.

They ran out of things to say. There was an awkward silence. No doubt the FBI had appropriate banter for the occasion. The army sure did. But private jokes are private jokes. They don't translate between cultures. So none were made. All three of them just stood up mute and turned around and paced off distances and got into their starting positions. They looked ahead through the dark and identified their personal targets.

"Ready?" Reacher said.

Sorenson said, "Good to go."

Delfuenso said, "Yes."

"Remember, speed and direction. No deviation from either. Now go."

They stood up.

They started walking.

All went well, until Sorenson was shot in the head.

# Chapter 69

Reacher heard it all in reverse order. Because of the speed of sound, and because of how close he was to Sorenson, and because of how far he was from the building. He heard the wet punch of the bullet finding its target, and a split second later he heard the supersonic crack of the bullet's flight through the air, and a split second after that he heard the boom of the rifle that fired it from four hundred yards away. By which time he was already on the ground. He moved on the first sound, throwing himself down, and before he even hit the dirt he had some early conclusions, thoughts not so much developing as flashing fully formed in his mind: He knew it was a sniper rifle, probably an M14 or equivalent, probably a .308, and he knew it had no night scope, or he himself would have been the first target, given human nature, and therefore he knew Sorenson had been spotted simply because she was pale in the moonlight, her skin and her hair just marginally more visible than his or Delfuenso's.

He knew all of that, instantly and instinctively. And he knew Sorenson was dead. He knew it for sure. There was no mistaking the sound. He had heard such sounds before. It had been a head shot, through and through, in and out, 168 grains at more than twenty-six hundred feet per second, hitting with more than twenty-six hundred foot-pounds of energy, dropping more than twenty-six inches from four hundred yards, like a curveball finding the strike zone.

Not survivable.

Not even remotely.

He waited.

There was no second shot.

He moved his hands. He rubbed dirt on them, front and back. He dragged dirt up to his face and smeared it on.

He moved his head.

He couldn't see Delfuenso.

Which was good. She was on the ground somewhere, head down and invisible. He looked the other way. He saw a faint gleam in the dirt. Small and pale. Sorenson's hand. Either her right or her left, depending on how she had fallen.

He knew there would be no answer, but even so, he whispered, "Julia?"

There was no answer.

So he whispered, "Delfuenso?"

No answer.

"Delfuenso? Karen? Are you there?"

A breathy voice came back in the dark: "Reacher? Are you hit?"

He said, "Sorenson was."

"Bad?"

"Worse than bad." He started crawling, elbows and knees, head down. The back part of his brain told him he must look like a bug on a bed sheet. The front part told him no, if he was visible he would be dead already. He risked a glance ahead, one eye, and adjusted course a fraction. He stopped an arm's length from the pale gleam in the dirt. He reached out and found Sorenson's hand. It was still warm. He found her wrist. He laid two fingers on it.

*You could get killed or maimed doing this.*

*I don't need you to look after me.*

There was no pulse. Just limp, clammy skin. *All the invisible thousand muscular tensions of the living were gone.* He crawled half a yard closer. He followed her arm, to her shoulder, to her neck.

No pulse.

Her neck was slick with slippery blood and gelatinous brain tissue and gritty with bone fragments. Her jaw was still there. And her nose. And her eyes, once blue and amused and quizzical. There was nothing left above her eyes. She had been hit in the center of the forehead. The top of her head had come off. Hair and all. Her scalp would be hanging down somewhere, attached by a thread of skin. He had seen such things before.

He checked her neck one more time.

No pulse.

He wiped his hand in the dirt and patted around

for her pistol. He couldn't find it. It could have been anywhere. Black polycarbonate, in the dead of night. He gave up on it. He found her shoulder again, and the small of her back, and he slipped his hand under her sweater and moved it around and took the spare magazine off her belt. Her hip was still warm. *A cotton shirt, and her body under it, somewhere between hard and soft.* He lay on his belly and stuffed the magazine in his pocket. Then he backed away, elbows and knees, and he turned like a crab and crawled over to Delfuenso's position. A long way. Thirty or forty yards.

Delfuenso whispered, "Is she dead?"

He said, "Instantaneous."

There was a long, long pause.

Then Delfuenso said, "Shit, I really liked her."

"Me too," Reacher said.

"A person like that is the best of the Bureau."

Something wild in her voice.

"Shit happens," Reacher said. "Get over it."

"Is that how you army people react to things?"

"How do you FBI people react to things?"

She didn't answer.

She said, "So what now?"

"You should go back to the car," Reacher said. "Keep low all the way. Call Quantico and update them. Remember, tell them Whiteman Air Force Base is their best shot. Maybe you should call Omaha, too. Her SAC is a guy called Tony Perry. I talked to him once. And I think the night duty agent was a friend of hers. So break it gently. Also her tech guy. He should hear it personally."

"Aren't you coming with me?"

"No," Reacher said. "I'm going to find that sniper."

"You can't do that alone."

"You can't come with me. You have a kid."

"I can't let you. I'm ordering you to withdraw."

"That's not going to happen."

"Let Quantico take care of it."

"McQueen can't wait that long."

"You'll be killed. There could be hundreds of them in there."

"You said two dozen."

"Even so. Two dozen men. They're trained for this kind of thing."

"And now we're about to find out how well they're trained. Maybe they were great in high school, but let's see if they can hit a Major League fastball."

"They could be vicious."

"They don't know the meaning of the word. Not yet."

"I can't let you do it. You won't survive. I might as well shoot you now."

"You can't stop me. I'm a civilian."

"Therefore McQueen and Sorenson are nothing to you. Let us look after our own."

"I would," Reacher said. "But I don't hear any SWAT planes in the air."

"They're close."

"They're over Ohio. Maybe Indiana. That's not close."

"How does it help if you get shot too?"

"It doesn't. But I might not."

"There's a number of possible outcomes, right?"

"Yes," he said. "There are."

"And that's definitely one of them."

"Yes," he said again. "It is."

"So why?"

"Because I liked Sorenson. I liked her a lot. She was fair and decent to me."

"So come to her memorial service. Write to the newspaper. Start a fund for a statue. You don't have to go into battle for her."

"Battle offers me better odds."

"In what way?"

"It gives me some kind of a chance to survive the night."

"How are those better odds? If you come back with me, you're guaranteed to survive the night."

"No," Reacher said. "If I come back with you, I'm guaranteed to die of shame."

There was no more conversation. No more argument. No more back and forth. Just an awkward silence. No doubt the FBI had appropriate banter for the occasion. The army sure did. But private jokes are private. So neither Reacher nor Delfuenso said anything. She just looked at his face. He wasn't sure why. It was all smeared with dirt. With cowshit, probably. Maybe it was just as well his nose wasn't working.

Delfuenso said, "Good luck."

Then she backed away, elbows and knees, and she crabbed through a turn and set off back the way they had come, toward Lacey's store. Reacher watched her until she was lost to sight. He waited a minute more, to be sure she wasn't going to break her word and double back. He knew she wanted to. But she didn't. Because of Lucy, presumably. *You have a kid.* It was about the only line she hadn't argued with, in all of their long conversation.

He waited a minute more, to be doubly sure, and then he turned around the other way and crawled forward into the darkness.

# Chapter 70

West Point had talked for hundreds of hours about tactics and strategy, and Reacher had paid attention, in a theoretical way. But in a practical way he preferred his own methods. Which were based entirely on the other guys. No point in thinking about himself all the time. He knew his own strengths, which were few, and his own weaknesses, which were many. It was the other guys that mattered. What were their strengths?

Well, they were good shooters. Or at least one of them was. That was clear. A head shot at four hundred yards in the dark of night was by no means extraordinary, but it was thoroughly competent.

But apart from that, they wouldn't have much. And their weaknesses would be significant. Mostly caused by fear. They would be so accustomed to secrecy and paranoia their perceptions would be permanently altered. As in: Reacher was betting that right then they were making two very bad decisions. First, they were overthinking his approach. They were assuming anyone originally with Sorenson would now either quit or track around ninety or more degrees and come at them from a different direction. They were briefly considering a double bluff from such a person, but paranoia prefers triple bluffs to doubles, so they were focusing their main attentions on the three new angles, not the one old angle. The southeast approach was now considered sterile, as far as they were concerned. No doubt they would post a guy or two anyway, but they wouldn't be their best guys, and they would be spending most of their time craning over their shoulders toward where they thought the real action was.

And therefore second, they were about to send out a party into that safe and sterile corridor, to haul away Sorenson's body. Because they were worried about who she was. And because they couldn't leave her lying out there. It wasn't their land. Some farmer's granddaddy had given it up to the DoD, way back in the day, and then these many years later the granddaddy's grandson had gotten it back again, and he was working it, starting early every morning, like farmers do. So for secrecy's sake the body had to go. And real soon. Paranoia waits for no man. Five or ten minutes, Reacher thought. They would come out one of the larger doors on the north side. Two of them, probably. In a vehicle. They would drive straight over.

They would stop ten feet from where Reacher had dug himself into the dirt.

* * *

**It was eight** minutes, and they did exactly what Reacher was expecting. A pick-up truck came looping around out of the north, on the same trajectory but at a tighter angle than McQueen's upside-down-J-shape GPS tracks. It was a gray truck. Primer, maybe. Hard to see in the moonlight. But there. Not a crew cab. Just a regular pick-up. It headed straight over, bouncing on the dirt. It was showing no lights. Secrecy, and paranoia. The cab was dark and shadowed. No detail to be seen inside. But there would be two guys minimum. Maximum of three. More likely two.

The truck slowed and two guys hung their heads out the windows, looking for what they had come for. Sorenson's hair was clotting black by then, but there was still enough white skin to guide them in. Still enough of a gleam in the pale moonlight. They acquired their target and rolled through the last twenty yards and backed up with their tailgate near where she lay. They got out together and stood still for a moment.

Two of them. Not three. The dome light in the cab proved it.

Unarmed. Nothing held in their hands, nothing slung on their backs.

They walked toward her.

Reacher was not a superstitious man, nor was he spiritual in any way, nor did he care for ancient taboos. But it was important to him they didn't touch her.

They shuffled around and looked down, in a head-scratching kind of a way. Like any two grunts anywhere, handed a task. They were Syrians, Reacher figured. But pale. The alleged Italians. They looked stunted. Small, wiry frames. Thin necks.

They got themselves set. They planted their feet. They didn't speak. They didn't need to. Their job was pretty obvious. The mechanics were self-evident. The geometry was what it was. The one on the left would do half the work, and the one on the right would do the other half. They would pick up what they could, and the dawn birds would take care of the rest.

They bent their knees.

And the ground behind them opened like a folk tale and a giant nightmare figure rose up out of it, shedding dirt and slime like a waterfall, and it took one long step and smashed its right fist into the back of the left-hand guy's neck, a huge, vicious, downward-clubbing blow, like the apparition was driving a rail-road spike with its knuckles, and then after the impact there was a long, elegant follow-through, the huge fist sweeping way down past the knee, then immediately whipping back up, the same route, like a convulsion, the giant figure jerking at the waist, its elbow smashing the right-hand guy square in the throat.

Then Reacher knelt on the first guy's chest, and pinched the guy's nose shut with the fingers of one hand, and jammed the other hand palm-down over the guy's mouth.

No struggle. Already dead.

The second guy struggled. But not for long.

Reacher wiped his hands in the dirt and headed for the pick-up truck.

# Chapter 71

Their guns were in the truck, dumped on the seats. Two Colt submachine guns, with canvas slings. Like M16 rifles, basically, but shorter and chambered for the nine-millimeter Parabellum. American made, nine hundred rounds a minute, twenty round magazines, your choice of full auto or three-round bursts or single shots. Reacher didn't like them much. America had never really gotten into the submachine gun business. Not in a convincing way. There were many better choices to be had from Europe. Steyr, or Heckler and Koch. Just ask Delta Force. Or Quantico, for that matter. The guys on the plane wouldn't be armed with Colts. That was for damn sure.

But still. Something was better than nothing. Reacher checked them over. They were loaded and they seemed to work. He closed the passenger door and tracked around to the driver's side. He pushed the seat back and got in. The engine was still running. The truck was a Ford. Nothing fancy. He wound both windows down and tucked his Glock under his right thigh and piled both Colts on the passenger seat.

Good to go.

He counted to three and put the truck in gear and moved off slowly. The ground that had felt churned up and lumpy and unreliable underfoot felt just as bad under the wheels. The truck shuddered and slipped and bounced on stiff, load-ready springs. He followed the same course the two guys had used on the way out. A straight line, basically, to the top corner of the building. Its huge bulk stayed shadowy and indistinct most of the way. But as he got closer he saw more of it. Then suddenly it was right there, out his open window. Like driving past a docked ocean liner. Poured concrete, no doubt reinforced inside by thick steel bars, and shaped by temporary wooden formwork. He could see the wood grain here and there, preserved forever. The curves had been made by stepping flat planks around a radius. What looked smooth from a distance looked brutal and discontinuous up close. In places wet concrete had been forced out through gaps between boards. The building looked like it was lined with unfinished seams. The camouflage paint was thick and cross-hatched with brush strokes. Not a tidy job. But then, camouflage talent was all about pattern, viewed from afar. Not application, viewed from up close.

He slowed and took a breath and hauled on the wheel and made the turn around the top corner and saw the north face of the building for the first time. It was a blank concrete wall with three giant protuberances coming out of it. Like squat semicircular concrete tunnels, parallel, each one straight and maybe a hundred feet long. Like elongated igloo entrances. For air raid protection. There would be blast doors at both ends of the tunnels, never to be open at the same time. Trucks would drive in through the first door, and then pause in a kind of quarantine. The first door would close behind them, and the second door would open in front of them. Then the trucks would drive on. Getting out would be the same procedure in reverse. The interior of the structure would never be exposed to external pressure waves.

Missile storage, Reacher thought. The Cold War. Anything, anywhere, anytime. If the military wanted it, the military got it. In fact, the military got it whether it wanted it or not.

First question: which of the three entrance tunnels was currently in use?

Which was an easy question to answer. The moonlight showed tire tracks quite clearly. The soft earth was beaten down into two ruts, in and out of the center tunnel. Practically a highway.

Reacher held his curve, wide and easy, and then he bumped down into an established track that would bring him head-on to the center door. Which was closed. It had a frame wider than the mouth of the tunnel. Like an airplane hangar. The door would open in two halves, like a theater curtain, rolling on big iron wheels and rails.

Open how? There was no radio in the car. No surveillance camera near the door. No light beam to be tripped, no call button, no intercom. Reacher drove slowly forward, unsure, with the door ahead of him like a high steel wall. Behind the railing on the roof he could see sentries. Five of them, long guns over their shoulders on slings, peering out into the middle distance in what looked like a fairly desultory fashion. Sentry duty was arduous and boring. Not what the average adventurer signs up for. No excitement. No glamour.

Reacher came to a stop with the pick-up's grille a yard from the door.

The door started to open.

The two halves broke some kind of a seal between them and set off grinding back along their tracks, driven by what sounded like truck engines straining under the load. The whole assembly must have weighed hundreds of tons. Blastproof. Whatever the military wanted. The gap widened. Two feet. Three. There was dim light in the tunnel. Weak bulbs, in wire cages, strung out along the ceiling. Reacher tugged the Glock out from under his leg. He held it, low down and out of sight.

The doors stopped when the gap got to be about seven feet wide. Enough for a passenger vehicle. Reacher took a breath and counted to three and put his left hand on the wheel and touched the gas and rolled inside.

And saw four things: a guy right next to him, right next to a big red button near the first door, and a guy a hundred feet away, right next to a big red button near the second door.

His earlier advice to Delfuenso: *Shoot them in the face, before they even say hello.*

Which he did, with the first guy. Although not technically in the face. He raised the Glock a little higher and drilled the guy through the center of the forehead, about where Sorenson had gotten hers.

*Save rounds. No double taps.* Which was OK. The first one had worked just fine. The guy was in some kind of a baggy green uniform. He had a handgun on his belt, in a big flapped holster. Not like any military thing Reacher had ever seen. More like folk art.

Reacher looked up again. The second guy was too far away. A hundred feet was too long for a handgun. So he stepped out of the truck and hit the big red button. The giant door started to close again behind him. He waited. The second guy waited. Still a hundred feet away. Still too far for a handgun. So Reacher got back in the truck and put his seat belt on. Then he stamped on the gas and accelerated. Straight at the second guy. Who froze for a fatal second. Who fumbled with his big flapped holster. Who gave up on it and ran. Away from his door. No way to open it in a hurry. Not an escape hatch. The mechanism was too slow. The guy was going to take his chances loose inside the tunnel. Which was dumb. The guy wasn't thinking strategically. He wasn't thinking himself into his opponent's frame of mind. He was going to duck and dive and dodge, and then dart away and hug the side wall. He was going to assume no driver would risk wrecking his vehicle against the concrete.

Reacher drove on, left-handed.

And sure enough, the guy feinted one way, and feinted the other, and then slammed himself flat against the wall, like a bullfighter, assuming Reacher would swing close but swerve away before contact.

Mistake.

Reacher ran straight into him at about thirty miles an hour, smashing the front of the truck mercilessly into the concrete, taking the guy between the knees and the waist, crushing him, seeing the shock on his face, and then the hood panel folded up from the crash like a concertina and he didn't see him anymore. Reacher was slammed against his seat belt and the windshield shattered and the truck came up on its front wheels and then crashed back down and Reacher was thrown back hard against the cushion. All kinds of smoke and steam rose up. The noise had been short but loud and it had brought ferocious echoes off the concrete, tearing, crushing metal, breaking glass, harsh clangs from separating components. Bumpers, Reacher thought, and headlight bezels and hub caps. Things like that.

The tunnel went quiet. Reacher sat still for a second. He figured very little would have been heard beyond the second door. If anything at all. The door was designed to be effective against a hundred-megaton atom bomb. The pop of a single nine-millimeter round and the sound of a car crash would be nothing to it.

He forced open his distorted door and climbed out of the wreckage. He stepped around to what was left of the hood. The second guy was about cut in half. Bleeding badly from every hole he had. He was dark haired and dark skinned. Foreign, for sure. *But we all bleed the same color red.* No doubt about that. The truth of that statement was plain to see. Reacher put the guy out of his misery. A single shot, close range, behind the ear. An unnecessary round expended, but good manners had a price.

**The Colt submachine** guns were all tangled in the passenger foot well, thrown there by the crash. Reacher lined them up straight and hung one on his left shoulder, and one on his right. He swapped out the Glock's two-gone magazine for the fresh one he had taken from Sorenson's belt. Two rounds can make a difference.

Then he walked the rest of the tunnel and pushed the big red button.

# Chapter 72

Reacher heard a whine like a starter motor, and a cough, and then two huge truck engines burst into life and the second door started to open. Up close and on foot it was a different experience. The truck engines were as big and as loud as anything they put on a Mack or a Peterbilt. The doors were huge and thick, like buildings all their own.

And up close and on foot they seemed to move faster. Or maybe that was an illusion. Which would be understandable. Because the gap was going to be man-sized a long time before it was vehicle-sized. Everything was relative. Ten more seconds and the gap would be big enough to step out on stage.

The big diesels dug in, and the gap grew two feet wide.

Then two and a half.

Reacher raised the Glock.

He stepped through the gap.

No one there.

\* \* \*

Reacher was in an empty garage. The space was maybe forty feet by forty. It had a sad old pick-up truck in one corner, gray primer, down at the front on a flat tire, but that was it in terms of vehicle content. The rest was all empty space and oil stains. All the way to the back wall, which was a recent installation in plywood. The side walls and the ceiling were the original concrete. And in fact the side walls and the ceiling were all more or less the same thing. Like a tunnel, continuing on from the entrance tunnel, forty feet wide and probably four hundred feet long, but now interrupted by the new partition.

There were three ways out of the garage, not counting the door Reacher had just come in through, which would be a fourth. There was a new door dead ahead in the plywood partition, and there was an original door in each of the side walls. In those two original spots the tunnel's vaulted curve was straightened out by a door frame cast so thick and so deep it was almost a tunnel in itself. Reacher pictured the complexity of the lumber formwork, and the anxious DoD engineers inspecting it, and the immense stress it was under until the mass of concrete had set.

The original door on the right was taped over.

It had a sheet of heavy see-through plastic laid over it, fixed at the edges with what looked like a whole roll of duct tape.

Purpose unknown.

But Reacher's motto was *If in doubt, turn left,* so he went the other way. Through the other original door, in the left-hand side wall. The door itself was a stout old item faced in some kind of faded laminate. Probably a real big deal fifty years ago. Some kind of a new wonder material. The handle was a plain steel affair, but thick and solid. Probably cost a thousand dollars all on its own.

Reacher turned the thick steel handle and pushed the door and stepped into a square room made from two old walls and two new. Some kind of a crew room. Comfortable chairs, low to the ground. A man in one of the chairs. Not McQueen. He started to get up. He went back down easily enough. Center mass, not a head shot. Safer. More to aim at. Instantaneous brain death not required. Not in that situation. The guy's finger was not on a launch button.

The crew room had a second door, and Reacher kept the Glock hard on it until he was sure no one was coming to the rescue. Then he moved on, through that second door, into a long narrow internal hallway that ran away from him to the right, four hundred feet or more. He was beginning to see the layout. The building inside was three parallel chambers, long and thin, like three cigars laid side by side. Corresponding with the three entrances. All full of missiles, way back when. Then empty, just three long echoing vaults. Now colonized and boxed off with plywood. Long central hallways, rooms to the left, rooms to the right, repeated three times over. Which was ironic. What goes around comes around. The modern DoD had started out exactly the same way. Massive expansion at the start of World War Two had left it scrambling.

It burrowed into whatever unsuitable old building it could find.

The bad news was, there were a lot of new rooms. Possibly forty per chamber. A total of a hundred and twenty. Plus or minus. Quantico would arrive before he was halfway through the search. Which would be a problem. They would have gotten Delfuenso's call well before then. She would have told them to land at Whiteman and head north locked and loaded and ready to rock and roll. The crossfire was not going to be pretty.

And the even worse news was plywood was not a good insulator of sound. Which meant the last gunshot had been clearly audible throughout fully one-third of the facility. So Reacher ducked back the way he had come, through the crew room, past the dead guy in the low-slung chair, and into the garage again. The big mechanized doors were still standing open. Like pulled drapes. Beyond them was the hundred-foot entrance tunnel, still with the two dead guys and the wrecked pick-up in it. Reacher found the inside button and hit it. The starter whined and the big diesels caught and the doors began to close. The noise was deafening. Which was exactly what Reacher wanted. Given a choice he liked his rear flank protected, and he wanted plenty of audible warning if someone tried to come in after him.

Then he walked the depth of the garage space and tried the new door in the plywood end partition. It opened into the same kind of long, narrow central corridor. Rooms to the left, rooms to the right. The center vault, colonized just like the first vault. Some of the doors had blue spots on them. Plastic circles, cut out and glued on. The second room on the left and the second room on the right both had one. That pattern repeated every three rooms as far as the eye could see.

Reacher checked behind him. The door he had come through had two blue spots.

He listened hard and heard nothing. He took a breath and counted to three and set off walking. To the second door on the right. A cheap store-bought item. With a thin chrome handle. And a blue spot, at eye level.

He turned the thin chrome handle. He pushed open the door. A room, of decent size. Empty. No people. No furniture. No nothing, except what had been there all along, which was another original door through the side wall. It was identical to the first two he had seen, with the complex cast frame like a tunnel all its own, and the pale old laminate facing, and the heavy steel handle. Clearly the blue spot meant a way through, side to side. A shortcut, from chamber to chamber. For busy people. The garage door got two blue spots because it had ways through both left and right. The lateral access was an efficiency measure. Both now, apparently, and certainly back when missiles roamed the earth. It would have been time-consuming for a technician to walk the whole length of the building and go outside and then come back in down a different tunnel. Far better to facilitate a little cross-town traffic. Maybe every sixty feet or so. Some guy with a clipboard would have figured that out, long ago. The architects would have gotten to work, with drafting tables and sharpened pencils, and load factors calculated with slide rules and guesswork.

Reacher was in a room on the right-hand side of the row. And just like the door he had seen on the right in the garage, this door on the right was also covered over with thick see-through plastic, which was also stuck down very carefully at the edges with duct tape. Lots of it.

Purpose unknown.

He had two motel keys in his pocket. One from the fat man's place in Iowa, and one from the FBI's quarantine spot in Kansas. The fat man's key was sharper. The tang at the end had been left pretty rough by the key cutting process. Maybe the key was a replacement. Maybe some guest had headed home with the original still in his pocket, and maybe the fat man's policy was to use the cheapest services he could find.

Reacher pressed the see-through plastic against the faded old laminate behind it, and he scratched at it with the tip of the key. The key snagged and jumped and made pulls and blisters. The blisters went thin and puffy and the second go-round with the key started a hole in one of them. Reacher got the tip of the key in the hole and sawed away at it, cutting where he could, stretching and tearing where he couldn't. When the slit reached three inches long he put the key back in his pocket and hooked his fingers in the slit, palms out, and he forced his hands apart.

The plastic was tough. Some kind of heavy grade. Not like the tissue-thin stuff he had seen painters use as drop cloths. More like shrink-wrap. He had seen people struggling with it. Supermarkets should sell switchblades, right next to the salami. He got the slit about twelve inches long and the tension went out of it. He had to start a new cut with the key. He learned from that experience. He changed his technique, to a rhythmic cut-yank-cut-yank sequence, with the key in his mouth between cuts. Eventually he got it done, more or less all the way from top to bottom, very stretched and ragged, but big enough to force himself through.

He put his arm through the hole and turned the heavy steel handle and pushed the door with his fingertips. Nothing but darkness beyond. And cold air. And a silent acoustic suggestive of vast space and hard walls.

He turned sideways and forced himself through the slit in the plastic, leading with the Glock, then his right foot, then his right shoulder, ducking his head, pulling his left arm and his left foot after him. He used touch and feel, tracing the shape of the cast frame around the door, closing the door behind him, searching for a light switch. He knew there would be one. Those old-time architects with their drafting tables and their sharpened pencils would have been plenty thorough. The electrical plans would have been a whole separate sheaf of blueprints.

He found an electric conduit on the wall. Steel

pipe, thickly painted, cold to the touch, covered in dust. He traced it back to a square metal box, maybe four inches by four, with a dimple on its front face, and a cold brass toggle in the dimple.

He turned the lights on.

# Chapter 73

The third chamber was not subdivided. It was in its original state. It was a tunnel, roughly semicircular in section, forty feet wide, maybe four hundred feet long, just over head high at the side walls, perhaps thirty feet tall at the peak of the vaulted ceiling. It was formed from concrete, poured and cast like the outside, with wood grain showing here and there, with stepped curves, with thin ragged ribs and seams where the formwork had leaked. It was unpainted, but no longer raw. It was mellow and faded and dusty, after many patient decades. It had a blank wall at the far end, and it had blastproof doors at the near end, with a mechanism exactly like the one Reacher had used in the center chamber.

It was not empty.

All along the center of the space was a nose-to-tail line of enormous flatbed semi trailers. No tractor units. Just the trailers, one after the other, like a traffic jam on the highway. Each trailer was close to fifty feet long and twelve feet wide. There were eight of them. Each of them had four load-bearing axles at the rear, and two huge cantilevered arms at the front, first rearing up at a steep angle, and then reaching forward at a shallower angle, ready to latch into the tractor unit, like gigantic insect antennas.

They were all painted the color of sand. Desert camouflage base coat. Reacher knew exactly what they were. They were components from the army's HET system. Heavy Equipment Transporter. This particular type of trailer was called the M747. Its matching tractor unit was called the M746. Both had been built by the Oshkosh Corporation in Wisconsin. Both had been taken out of front-line service after the Gulf War in 1991. Neither had proved sufficiently durable. Their task had been to haul Abrams battle tanks around. Battle tanks were built for tank battles, not for driving from A to B on public roads. Roads got ruined, tracks wore out, between-maintenance hours were wasted unproductively. Hence tank transporters. But Abrams tanks weighed more than sixty tons, and wear and tear on the HETs was prodigious. Back to the drawing board. The old-generation hardware was relegated to lighter duties.

But in this case, not much lighter.

Each of the eight trailers was loaded with a nose-to-tail pair of flasks or vats or containers. For some kind of liquid, clearly. But really big. Tens of thousands of gallons. Each unit was the size of four Volkswagens stacked two on two, like bricks. The size of a small room. They were made of steel, rolled and folded and hydroformed, and welded, like squat fat bottles, with a protective frame all around, the function of the bottle and the function of the frame so well integrated it was hard to see where one finished and the other began. Overall they were like rounded-off cubes, about twelve feet long, by twelve feet wide, by twelve feet high, reinforced in places for strength and durability. The steel looked thick and solid. Maybe it was backed with an extra mineral layer. An innovation.

But not a recent invention. Because nothing in the chamber was recent. There was a thick layer of dust over everything. Over the massive containers, over the flatbed trailers, over the concrete floor. Gray, and spectral, and undisturbed. Under the trailers most of the tires looked soft. Some of them were flat completely. There were cobwebs. The scene was archaeological. Like breaking through into a Pharaoh's tomb. The first to lay eyes on it for five thousand years.

Or twenty years, maybe. The physical evidence was there. The age of the equipment. The dust. The perished rubber. The still air. The chill. It was perfectly possible to believe those trailers had been backed in two decades ago, and detached from their tractor units, never to move again, and then walled off, and left behind, and forgotten.

Eight trailers. Sixteen containers. Sixty-four Volkswagens. The steel was painted bright yellow, now faded a little by dust and time. On the side of each one, at a modest size, no bigger than a basketball, was stenciled a design first sketched in 1946, by a bunch of smart guys at the University of California Radiation

Laboratory. Smart guys with time on their hands, designing a symbol, coming up with what they thought was stuff coming out of an atom. Most people thought it was three fat propeller blades, black on yellow.

Nuclear waste.

# Chapter 74

Reacher killed the lights and squeezed back through the slit in the plastic. He crossed the empty room and stepped out to the corridor. And saw three people. All men. They were walking away from him, talking as they went, piles of three-ring binders in their arms. Shirtsleeves. Dark pants. Unarmed. None of them was McQueen.

Reacher let them go. The cost outweighed the gain. Too noisy, for no real reason. They opened a blue-spot door on the left, way far up the corridor. Clearly heading sideways into the first chamber. Four spots down, one room over, one room back. Or whatever. Like map coordinates. Not unlike getting around the Pentagon.

They had come out of a room ahead and on the left of where Reacher was standing. Its door was open, and it hadn't been before. Reacher took a breath and counted to three and walked the thirty feet. The room was an office, maybe twenty feet by seventeen, with one concrete wall and three plywood walls. All four walls were full of shelves. The floor was full of desks. Both desks and shelves were full of paper. Loose, in stacks, clipped together, in rubber bands, in binders. The paper was full of numbers. Six, seven, and eight figure numbers, of no great interest or appeal, just raw material to be added and subtracted and multiplied. Which they had been. Most of the papers were like ledger pages.

No computers.

All paper.

More footsteps in the corridor.

Reacher listened hard. He heard a door open. He heard it close. He heard nothing else. He stepped back out to the hallway. He figured if McQueen was being held prisoner somewhere, it would be deep in the bowels. Four hundred feet away, potentially. Way in the back, far from the outside world. In one of two chambers. A complex search pattern. And the long central hallways were deathtraps. Nowhere to run, nowhere to hide. Apart from the rooms with blue spots. But there weren't many of them. And worrying about sideways escape routes didn't do much for sustained forward motion.

*That's a military kind of problem, isn't it? Did you train for this stuff?*

Not exactly. Not without people and ordnance and helicopters and radios and fire support. Which he didn't have.

He checked the room opposite. Another office, twenty feet by seventeen, shelves, desks, papers, numbers. Lots of numbers. Six, seven, and eight figures, all of them added and subtracted. All of them carefully recorded and accounted for. He checked the room next door. Same exact thing. Desks, shelves, papers, and numbers. He retraced his steps and headed back to the first room he had come from. The room with the lateral door.

He heard more footsteps in the hallway.

He stepped inside the room and closed the door.

Now he heard lots of footsteps in the hallway.

People, running.

People, shouting.

He went Glock-first through the slit in the plastic and closed the door behind him.

**The shortest distance** between two points was a straight line. Reacher hustled the length of the third chamber, four hundred feet, past all the abandoned trailers, past all the huge sinister bottles. Dust came up from under his feet. It was like walking in thin snow. For the first time he was glad about his busted nose. His nasal passages were lined with scab tissue. Without it he would be sneezing like crazy.

The last original door was ten feet from the end of the tunnel. Exactly in line with the last yellow bottle. Exactly in line with its radiation symbol. Reacher pulled it open and took out the fat man's motel key and fought his way through the plastic skin. Cut, rip, cut, rip. Easier in that direction. The plastic bellied out into the room and he could keep plenty of tension on it. The space beyond was empty. It had been built like a room, but it was being used like a lobby.

He listened at the door to the corridor. He heard sounds, but they were distant. They were the sounds of chaos and confusion. A hurried search, combing the length of the building, moving away from him. He was behind the front lines. Way in the back, far from the outside world.

He opened the door. He peered out. Hundreds of feet to his left men were going room to room. Five of them, maybe, searching, in and out, in and out. Moving away from him.

The door opposite had a blue spot. It would be empty. Built like a room, used like a lobby. So Reacher started one room down, across the corridor. No blue spot. He crept over to it, slow and silent. He opened the door. An office. Shelves, desks, paper. A man behind one of the desks. Reacher shot him in the head. The blast of the gunshot ripped through the chamber, barely muffled at all by the plywood partitions. Reacher stepped back to the door. He peered out. Hundreds of feet away the five searchers were frozen in place, bodies moving one way, eyes the other. Reacher put the Glock in his pocket and took the Colt off his shoulder. The submachine gun. He clicked it to full auto and held it high and sighted down the barrel. He pulled the trigger and fought the muzzle climb. Twenty rounds at the rate of nine hundred a minute. Less than a second and a half. Smooth as a sewing machine. All five men went down. Probably three dead, one wounded, one panicking. Not that Reacher was keeping score. He already knew the score. He was winning. So far.

He dropped the empty gun and slipped the other Colt off his other shoulder. He thought: *Time to visit the first chamber. Time to keep them guessing.* He ducked back to the door with the blue spot. He opened it. He went in. Built like a room, used like a lobby.

But not empty.

There was a staircase in it.

It was a metal thing, like a ladder, steep, like something from a warship. It led into a vertical tunnel through the roof concrete. At the top of the vertical tunnel was a square steel hatch, massive, with cantilevered arms and springs and a rotary locking wheel, like in a submarine. It was closed. Reacher figured it would be domed on the outside, designed to seat itself tighter under the pulsing pressure of a blast wave.

The locking wheel drove pegs through a complicated sequence of gears, into clips all around the rim. The wheel was in the unlocked position. That was obvious. None of the pegs was engaged. Clearly the guys on the roof had closed the hatch behind them, to hide the light from below. To preserve their night vision, and for secrecy. But they had left it unlocked, so they could get back in. Common sense.

The smart move would have been to shin up the ladder and spin the locking wheel so that whoever was out there stayed out there. That way Reacher could have continued his inside activities undisturbed.

But the sniper was out there. With his M14, and his one-gone magazine, and probably a big smug smile on his face.

Reacher turned out the lobby light. He waited four seconds in the dark, for his irises to open wide. Then another minute, for his retinal chemistry to kick in. Then he found the handrail by feel and started climbing.

# Chapter 75

Reacher got to the top of the ladder and felt around in the dark and used an after-image of what he had seen. He figured the hatch might weigh a few tons. Maybe more, if it was some kind of a sophisticated steel-and-concrete sandwich construction. Which it might be, because of radiation concerns. Those old-time architects would have been well schooled in such things. Possibly by the pointy-heads at the University of California. No point in designing a hatch to survive a blast if it was going to leak gamma rays afterward. But no human could lift several tons while standing on a ladder. Which meant the bulk of the weight would be counterbalanced by the springs. Which meant the hatch should open with a decent push.

He pushed.

The hatch rose two inches. Accompanied by deep twanging and grinding from the springs.

Loud.

He waited.

A band of not-quite-black showed around three sides of the rim. He figured the sentries would be standing at the edge railing. Which would put three-quarters of them some distance away. The roof was the size of Yankee Stadium. Only those on the south side were close.

He pushed again, harder.

The hatch rose another foot.

More twanging and grinding.

No reaction.

He pushed again. The hatch opened all the way. Ninety degrees, like a door. He looked up and saw a square of dark Missouri sky. The hatch was hinged on the north side of the square. The ladder was bolted to the east side. Which meant he would come out with his front and his back and his right-hand side all vulnerable.

Which meant he should come out fast. Which was not easy to do. No way of keeping his finger on the trigger. The moment of maximum danger. Every mission had one. He hated stairs. He hated leading with his head.

He clamped the Colt in his right hand, between the flat of his thumb and his palm. He jumped his left hand up, rung by rung. He got the Colt out and put his knuckles on the roof, like an ape. He twisted at the waist and got his left hand flat on the concrete.

He took a breath and counted to three and vaulted out.

He got up in a crouch and held the Colt high, jerking it side to side as he scanned around. The house-storming shuffle, all over again.

He was close to the edge of the roof, on the south side. To his half left was the sterile southeastern corridor. No one there. To his right was the west, with a lone shadowy figure far away at the rail, looking away from him. He turned north and saw five figures staring out where Bale's GPS had shown the two-lane. They thought Sorenson's approach had been a cross-country diversion. They thought the main attack was coming from the road.

Overthinking, and paranoia.

He clicked the second Colt to single shots and moved behind the upright hatch. It would give him partial three-quarters cover from the west and the north. He rested his left elbow on it. He sighted in on the guy in the west. Two hundred feet, maybe. An easy shot with any kind of a rifle. An easy shot with any kind of an H&K sub, which were generally as good as rifles, at short to medium distances. Unknown, with the Colt. But better than the Glock. A handgun at two hundred feet was the same thing as crossing your fingers and making a wish.

Reacher was a good long-distance marksman. He had won competitions. But not under conditions like he faced at that moment. He needed to see two things at once. His current target, and the reaction from the other five guys three hundred feet and seventy degrees farther on, when they heard the shot. He needed to see their vague silhouettes turn toward the sound. He needed to identify the shape of the M14. He needed to know which one of them was the sniper.

Because the sniper was next.

He rested the front sight on the guy in the west. He

breathed out and kept his lungs empty. Calm and quiet. Calm and quiet. He could feel his heart, but the front sight wasn't moving. He was good to go.

He eased his trigger finger tighter. And tighter. Smooth, microscopic, relentless. Flesh on metal on metal. He felt the break coming.

The gun fired.

Bright flash, loud sound.

Bull's-eye.

The guy in the west jerked slightly and fell down vertically.

The five guys in the north spun around.

The sniper was the middle guy. Third from the left, third from the right. Reacher saw the M14 in his hands. Slope arms, out in front of him, turning with him. A familiar shape. Forty-seven inches long, the dull gleam of walnut in the moonlight. Almost four hundred feet away. Reacher moved around the raised hatch lid, slow and easy, no rush at all, and he sighted in, and he breathed in and breathed out, and out, and out, and he fired again.

A miss.

But not a disaster. The round drifted a little left and down and caught the next guy low in the throat.

Reacher leaned a fraction clockwise to compensate and fired again. But by that point the four survivors were all moving. A nine-millimeter Parabellum takes a third of a second to travel four hundred feet, and a third of a second is long enough for a guy to move enough.

A miss.

No one went down.

One in the chamber, seventeen in the box. Reacher moved his thumb and switched to triples. His preferred option, with a B-grade weapon. Quantity, not quality. A random little triangle, like jabbing with a three-legged stool. He aimed generally right and fired.

The right-hand guy went down.

Three survivors. From left to right, numbers one, three, and four. They all knelt and fired back. Wild misses, except for the M14. The .308 came close. But not very. Which was telling. The guy was OK with no pressure at all. But in the heat of the moment he wasn't the best in the world. Reacher figured they could put that on the guy's tombstone: *Great against unsuspecting women in the dark. Otherwise, not so much.*

Reacher fired again, at numbers three and four, the sniper and his immediate neighbor, like a composite target. A triple.

Number four went down.

Not the sniper.

Two survivors.

Reacher had one in the chamber, and eleven in the box. Plus the Glock and two spare magazines, one of them full and one of them two short. He could use the Glock's rounds in the Colt, if he had to. Same nine-millimeter Parabellums. The magic of standardization. He had no idea what the two survivors had left. The M14 was most likely using a twenty-round magazine. The other guy's gun might have been anything. A long duel was a possibility. Up close and personal. Within sight. An infantry slugfest. The real kings of battle. A vulgar brawl, which was the kind of fight Reacher liked best.

Numbers one and three were still kneeling. Not close together. Reacher heaved the hatch lid closed and lay down behind it. He clicked back to singles. He wrapped himself around the dome of the hatch and got himself comfortable. The sniper fired at him. Better this time. The round hit the hatch and clanged away, a giant ricochet that might have made it all the way to Lacey's store.

Reacher lay still, calm and quiet, and comfortable. He fired back.

And hit the sniper.

Very low on the left side, he thought. Maybe in the hip. Nothing but a flesh wound. Not fatal, but certainly a distraction. The guy spun away and went down prone. Smaller target. The other guy followed suit. He went down flat and started blazing away. Some kind of an attempt at covering fire. Dangerous only to people in the next county, but at least the guy was showing some kind of solidarity. Reacher sighted in on the muzzle flash, and took his time. He aimed a little high and a little right, to allow for what seemed like persistent drift, and he tried to skip one off the concrete and up into the guy's face. Too dark to see if it worked, but certainly the guy stopped firing. Maybe he was only reloading. Or taking a nap. But he looked very still. Then a distant car drove left to right on the two-lane, maybe six hundred yards away, with its lights on bright, and the moving bubble in the mist backlit the situation for a second, and Reacher came to the conclusion the guy was permanently out of action. He was sprawled in an odd position.

Reacher moved his aim a fraction, back to the wounded sniper. One in the chamber, nine in the box. Ten chances, a static target, four hundred feet. He used the same high-and-right compensation and fired again. And again. And again. He felt he was hitting. But he couldn't see for sure. There was no answering fire. Then the same car came back the other way on the two-lane. Lost, maybe. Or worried about the gunshots. Not a cop, probably. No blue lights, no red lights, and no sane cop would parade back and forth in the line of fire. The moving bubble of light framed the view for a second. Soft, and vague. The sniper wasn't moving. He looked hunched, head down, and inert.

Reacher fired again. And again.

One in the chamber, four in the box. He had all the visual information he was going to get. He could fire a thousand times and be no surer than he already was. He came out from behind the dome and started a low crawl north. Elbows and toes. Slow, and painful on the concrete. No reaction from up ahead. No incoming rounds. Reacher held his fire. No point in identifying his position with the muzzle flash.

He stopped a hundred and fifty feet away. Just for a moment. To assess and evaluate. Still no movement. Just vague shapes, humped and low. Then the same car drove by on the two-lane. For a third time. Same bright lights. Same moving bubble. Reacher started to worry a little about who it was. Nosy neighbors could be a problem. Nine-millimeter rounds fired in the open were not loud, but they would be audible at a reasonable distance. The car's lights showed an unchanged situation. No movement. No sign of life. Possibly a trap.

Reacher crawled onward. Slow and easy. He would hear the hatch behind him if a new player wanted to join in the fun. The springs were loud. The sentries must have heard them too, when he had come up the ladder, but at that point the sentries hadn't known there were hostiles already inside the building. Maybe they thought they were getting reinforcements. Or a cup of coffee and a sandwich. In that respect they hadn't been paranoid enough.

Reacher stopped again fifty feet out. There was no movement ahead. Nothing at all. He stood up and walked the rest of the way. And found the five humped shapes, more or less all in a line in the dark. Five men. Four dead. The sniper was still breathing. He must have been hit three or four times. Still alive. Lucky.

But not very.

Reacher kicked the M14 away and slung the Colt back on his shoulder. He grabbed the guy by the belt and dragged him to the rail. He lifted him over, by his belt and the collar of his coat. Then he dropped him. The guy bounced once on the stepped concrete radius and fell forty feet to the ground.

*Let's see if they can hit a Major League fastball.*
*Strike three, pal.*

Reacher turned and jogged the four hundred feet back to the domed hatch. He heaved the lid open and felt with his feet for the ladder.

# Chapter 76

If **Delfuenso had been correct about no more** than two dozen opponents, then there were nine of them left, with maybe one of those nine wounded. The guy in the corridor, one of the five searchers. He had gone down pretty heavily. More than just gravity. Out of the fight, almost certainly. Which left eight still vertical. Better than a poke in the eye. A decent rate of attrition. So far. Reacher opened the blue-spot door and peered out into the corridor.

No one there.

He went room to room, one at a time, from the back of the building to the front, and he saw the same things everywhere: desks and shelves and paper. No people. It took him the best part of ten minutes to clear the second chamber. He entered the first through the garage. He started again, room to room, moving in the opposite direction, front to back.

Desks, shelves, paper.

No people.

Not in the first room, not in the second, not in the third or the fourth or the fifth. He guessed they must all be clustered in the far back corner. Safety in numbers. A defensible position. Unless they were all playing an elaborate game of cat and mouse, moving from chamber to chamber around him. Which was unlikely. But possible.

The third room on the left had been done up like a kitchen. A stove, a refrigerator, a sink. Drawers full of knives and forks and spoons. Food storage. The room opposite was a dining hall. Trestle tables and benches. Beyond that were bedrooms. Like dormitories. Bunk beds, eight to a room. Three rooms in total. Plus two more, each with just one bed. Privacy, but no luxury. The beds were plain iron cots. Rough sheets, coarse blankets. After that came washrooms and toilets. After that came yet more offices. Desks and shelves and paper.

So Delfuenso had been more or less exactly right. There were accommodations for a total of twenty-six people, max. The wrong side of two dozen, but not by much. One of them would be McQueen, presumably.

Therefore there were nine hostiles still vertical, somewhere.

Then it was eight, because the next room had a guy working feverishly at a desk. Reacher shot him point blank and instantly in the chest, with the Glock, and then it was seven, because the sound of the gunshot stirred things up and he caught another guy running for safety in the corridor, and shot him in the back.

Then everything went quiet again. No sound anywhere, even accounting for the fact Reacher was a little deaf after firing so often in an enclosed space. The next room was empty. As was the next. Which was the halfway point in the chamber. Twenty more rooms to go. Ten on each side. Three more blue spots, all on the right. All leading through to the middle chamber. Built like rooms, used like lobbies. Therefore there were still seventeen viable targets ahead. Slow progress. The Quantico team was probably in Illinois airspace by then. Maybe talking to St. Louis air traffic control, getting permission to proceed, setting a course for the approach to Whiteman.

The next room on the left was empty.

Desks, shelves, paper.

No people.

The next room on the right had Don McQueen in it.

McQueen was tied to a chair. He had a black eye and was bleeding from a cut on the cheek. He was dressed in coarse black denim. Like prison garb. No belt. No GPS chip.

There was a man behind the chair.

The man behind the chair had a gun to McQueen's head.

The man behind the chair was Alan King.

Living and breathing.

Alive again.

# Chapter 77

Except the man behind the chair was not Alan King. He was a slightly different version of the exact same guy. Marginally older, a little harder, maybe half an inch taller, maybe a pound or two lighter. But otherwise identical.

"Peter King," Reacher said.

"Stay where you are," King said. "Or I'll shoot your man."

Reacher said, "He's not mine."

Peter King's gun was a Beretta M9. Army issue. Better than the Glock, in Reacher's private opinion. Its muzzle was tight in the hollow behind McQueen's right ear. A dangerous place for it to be. Therefore, job one: make the Beretta move.

Peter King said, "I need you to place your weapons on the floor."

"I guess you do," Reacher said. "But I'm not going to."

"I'll shoot your man."

"He's not mine. I already told you that."

"Makes no difference to me. I'll shoot him anyway."

Reacher raised the Glock.

"Go right ahead," he said. "Then I'll shoot you. You pull your trigger, I'll pull mine. There's only one definite here. Which is that I'm going to walk out of this room, and you're not. The only question is whether McQueen is going to come out with me, or stay in with you. You understand that, right? What were you, a forward observer?"

King nodded.

Reacher said, "Then you've hung out with real soldiers long enough to have some basic grasp of short-term tactics."

"You're not going to give this guy up. You've gone to a lot of trouble to find him."

"I'd prefer to take him with me, sure. But it's not a dealbreaker."

"Who are you?"

"Just a guy, hitching rides."

"McQueen claims you killed my brother."

*Job one: make the Beretta move.*

"The woman killed your brother," Reacher said. "The cocktail waitress. Even then it wasn't a fair fight. Your brother was a useless tub of lard."

King said nothing.

Reacher said, "I bet he burned real well. All that fat? I bet he went up like a lamb chop on a barbecue."

King said nothing.

Reacher said, "You would too, probably. You're not much thinner. Is it a genetic thing? Was your momma fat as well as ugly?"

No reaction.

None at all.

"What do you care about your brother anyway?" Reacher asked. "Story is you weren't even talking to him. Which I guess I can understand. He must have been a real disappointment. What did he do? Wet the bed all the time? Or did he interfere with the family dog?"

King didn't answer.

Reacher asked, "What kind of a dog was it? Did it yelp?"

The Beretta didn't move.

Stalemate.

"Tell me," Reacher said. "I'd like to understand. I'd like to know what came between you. I'd like to know what made you cut him off for twenty long years. Because I had a brother once. He's dead now, unfortunately. We were both busy all the time. But we talked when we could. We got along pretty well. We had fun. We were there for each other, when we needed to be. I never made him ashamed, and he never made me ashamed."

Silence in the room. One concrete wall, three plywood walls, a weird, dull acoustic.

Then King said, "It was more than twenty years."

"What was?"

"Alan was a coward."

"How so?"

"He ratted someone out."

"You?"

"His best friend."

"Doing what? Knocking over a package store?"

"Doesn't matter what they were doing," King said. "Alan walked, and his best friend didn't."

"And you would never do that, right?"

"No, I wouldn't."

"Because you're a man."

"You got that right," King said.

"So face me like a man," Reacher said. "Take your gun out of McQueen's ear and count to three and go for it."

"What, like a duel?"

"Call it whatever you want. But stop using an innocent man for a shield. That's a pussy's trick."

"He's not an innocent man. He's a federal agent."

"He's tied to a chair. You can get back to him afterward."

"You think you're going to lose?"

"There are two possible outcomes here. Both should be considered."

No answer.

"Pussy," Reacher said.

"We count to three, right?"

"If you can."

"Then we fire?"

"One of us does."

"Start with your gun down by your side."

"You first."

"On three," King said. "Guns down. You and me both. Then we count to three again. Then we fire."

Reacher watched the guy's eyes. They were OK.

"Works for me," he said.

King said, "One."

Reacher waited.

King said, "Two."

Reacher waited.

King said, "Three."

Reacher lowered his gun, loose and easy against his thigh.

King did the same thing.

McQueen breathed out and leaned away.

Reacher watched King's eyes.

King took a breath and said, "OK."

Reacher said, "Ready when you are."

"On three, right?"

"Go for it."

King said, "One."

Strategy. It was the other guy that mattered. Reacher knew as sure as he knew anything that King was going to fire on two. It was a cast-iron certainty. The first count had been a decoy and a reassurance. One, two, three, guns down. It had set a rhythm and a precedent. An expectation. It had established trust. For a reason. King had it all figured out. He was a man with a plan. It was right there in his eyes. He was a smart guy.

But not smart enough.

He wasn't thinking strategically. He wasn't thinking himself into his opponent's frame of mind.

Reacher raised the Glock and shot him in the face, right after the one.

# Chapter 78

After that it got harder, not easier. First Reacher couldn't get McQueen out of the chair. He was tied to it with thin cord pulled very tight and the knots were hard as stones. And second, the survivors somewhere in the rooms beyond had finally gotten the message. They must have heard the shot close by and as soon as King didn't come out all triumphant they started up with a half-assed version of Custer's last stand. Either that or they were all planning to run for it. And either thing would put live bodies in the way. Reacher heard them all crowding together in the corridor. He heard the snick of slides being pulled. Automatic weapons, being checked and readied. He heard an urgent muffled conference, not far from the door, half in English and half in Arabic.

He asked, "What does *Wadiah* mean, anyway?"

McQueen said, "Safekeeping."

"I thought so."

"You speak Arabic?"

"The odd word."

"Don't you have a knife?"

"I have a toothbrush."

"That won't help."

"It's good against plaque."

"Just get me out of this damn chair."

"I'm trying."

The cord was too tough to break. It was some kind of a blend, maybe cotton and nylon, woven tight, about a quarter of an inch across. Probably tested against all kinds of strains and weights.

Reacher said, "I have a key."

McQueen said, "I'm not in handcuffs, for God's sake."

Reacher pulled out the fat man's key. He nicked at the rope with the rough-edged tang, down by McQueen's right hand. The tang cut some fibers. Maybe two or three. Out of maybe ten thousand. Reacher said, "Put some tension on it. As much as you can. You're FBI, right? Make like you're trying to lift your pension."

McQueen's shoulder and biceps bunched and the cord went hard as iron. Reacher sawed at it. Not back and forth. He had to pluck at it. The key worked only one way. But it made progress. Outside the door the voices were loud. Two factions. Doubt and questions, resolve and encouragement. Reacher was rooting for the doubt. Just for a little while longer. McQueen kept the pressure on. Fibers snapped and severed, first a few, then several, then many, then an eighth of an inch, then most of them, then only a few remained, and finally McQueen tore his right hand loose.

Reacher picked up Peter King's Beretta from the floor. He put it in McQueen's right hand. McQueen said, "That Colt on your shoulder would be better. These corridors are pretty long."

Reacher said, "It only has five rounds left in it. I'm planning to use it as a club." He started on McQueen's left wrist, plucking, cutting, fibers popping under the strain. McQueen said, "You could reload it."

Reacher said, "No time. We don't want to be caught with our pants down."

"How many in your Glock?"

"Thirteen."

"Unlucky."

"True." Reacher stopped sawing and swapped out the magazine for the full one he had taken from Bale, in the motel room in Kansas, about a million years ago. Click, click, hand to hand, not a blur like the showboats could do it, but no more than a second and a half. He started sawing again. The voices were still loud in the corridor.

Reacher said, "Do you have an accurate head-count?"

McQueen said, "Twenty-four tonight, not including me."

"Six left, then."

"Is that all? Jesus."

"I've been here at least twenty minutes."

"Who the hell are you?"

"Just a guy, hitching rides."

"Well, good work, whoever you are."

"Did you have a private room, when you were here?"

"No, those were for Peter King and the big boss."

"I thought Peter King was the big boss."

"No, King was number two."

"So who's the big boss?"

"I don't know. I never met him."

"Where is he now?"

"I have no idea."

The door opened. McQueen fired from his chair. A dark shape fell backward. Reacher stepped across and kicked the door shut again. He said, "Five left."

McQueen said, "How would you do it?"

"If I was them? I'd open every door in the corridor and put a guy in the first five rooms with blue spots. They'd see us before we saw them. We couldn't go anywhere at all."

"That's what I'm worried about."

"Are they smart enough?"

"I don't know," McQueen said. "They're plenty smart in some ways."

"I'm certainly getting that feeling."

"How? You know what this is all about?"

Reacher said, "I think I've figured most of it out."

"So you understand we absolutely need to capture this building intact, right?"

"Speak for yourself. All I absolutely need to do is get to Virginia."

"What's in Virginia?"

"Many things. It's an important state. Twelfth largest in terms of population, and thirteenth in terms of GDP."

McQueen's left hand came free. Reacher gave him

the Colt and crouched down and started work on his
ankles, from behind.

**The ankle ropes** went slower. The tough fibers were
doing the work the hardware store guy should have
done with his buffing wheel. The key was getting
smooth. Not good. So Reacher adapted his technique.
He used the last of the burr on the tang to tug up part
of the knot, and he used the key from the FBI's motel
in Kansas as a spike to force the knot apart. A different approach, and slower, but it got the job done a
small fraction at a time. Five minutes later McQueen
was three-quarters free, and five minutes after that he
was out of the chair completely. He was trailing brace-
lets of severed rope from his wrists. He had the Colt
submachine gun in his left hand and Peter King's Beretta in his right. Good to go. They were about two
hundred feet from the first mechanized door, and
three hundred feet from the second. Three hundred
feet from the sweet night air. Three hundred feet from
safety.

"Ready?" Reacher said.

McQueen nodded.

Reacher opened the door to the corridor.

# Chapter 79

The escape went bad immediately. The three hundred feet might as well have been three thousand miles. The five survivors had done the smart thing. All the room doors were standing open, along the whole length of the corridor, to the left and the right. Whichever way Reacher and McQueen went they risked getting fired on from inside as they passed. Or not. It was unpredictable. It was a lottery. Five hostiles, thirty-nine doors, not counting the one they were coming out of. Standard infantry tactics would have been to roll grenades into every room, at an angle, as they approached, or to blast through one plywood wall after another with anti-tank weapons. But they had no grenades, and no anti-tank weapons. They had two handguns and an almost-empty submachine gun.

Problem.

Reacher said, "We need a diversion."

McQueen said, "What kind?"

"We could set the place on fire."

"We absolutely cannot do that. We need to preserve the paperwork."

"I don't have any matches, anyway. We'd have to try to get to the kitchen and use the stove. In which case we might as well try to get all the way out."

"We should go sideways. There's a clear run through the third chamber."

"Pick a door," Reacher said. He couldn't see the blue spots. All the doors were folded back into the rooms. He knew there were six doors with blue spots. Built like rooms, used like lobbies. There were five bad guys. Therefore one way through was clear. A sixteen percent chance. Sixteen point six, recurring forever, to be totally accurate.

"Back to back?" McQueen asked.

"Who leads?" Reacher said.

"Doesn't really matter."

"It might," Reacher said. He wasn't pinning much hope on a sixteen percent chance. They were likely to run into someone in whichever lateral lobby they chose. One of the five. The resulting gunfire would alert the other four. If they gave chase, then the backward-facing guy would have to do most of the hard work. But if the four survivors did the smart thing and made lateral loops of their own, one by one, like outflanking maneuvers, then the forward-facing guy would take most of the load.

"You lead," Reacher said.

McQueen stepped out into the corridor. Reacher stepped out behind him, walking backward, and they moved together, slow and quiet and cautious, back to back, almost touching, but not quite. From that point on it was all about trust. Reacher desperately wanted to glance back over his shoulder, and he knew McQueen felt the same, but neither man did. Each was responsible for a hundred and eighty degrees, no more, no less. They made it twenty feet, to the next pair of doors, one on the left and one on the right, and McQueen slowed and took a breath. Both doors were open.

No blue spots.

Nobody in the rooms.

Onward.

Another twenty feet. Another pair of doors. One on the left, one on the right.

Smarter than smart.

The bad guys had people in both rooms.

Reacher and McQueen pivoted ninety degrees, instantly, Reacher firing right, McQueen firing left, and way up at the far end of the corridor a third guy stepped out and way down at the bottom end a fourth guy stepped out and Reacher and McQueen were caught in a literal crossfire, with incoming rounds from all four points of the compass. Reacher hit the guy in the room ahead of him and the guy went down and McQueen bundled in after Reacher and slammed the door. They stood there together, stooped and panting, with the dead guy on the floor between them.

"You hit?" Reacher asked.

"No," McQueen said.

That was the good news. The rest of the news was all bad. Ahead of them was a blastproof concrete wall probably ten feet thick. To their left and their right and behind them were plywood partitions just half an inch thick. And outside of a thin cheap door with no lock were four hostiles who knew exactly where they were.

Reacher said, "They don't even need to come in. They can fire through the walls. Or the door."

"I know," McQueen said.

And they did. Immediately. The first round came through the door. It punched out an ugly scab of wood that spun sideways and missed McQueen by an inch. The second round came through the wall. The plywood was tougher. But not much. The bullet came right through, but it had shattered into fragments. One of them nicked Reacher on the back of his hand. No big deal, in the grand scheme of things, but the cut started a fat trickle of blood. He stepped close to the splintered hole and put the Glock's muzzle hard on it and fired back, twice, at different angles. McQueen did the same thing at the door. Reacher heard feet wheeling away.

Temporary relief, but ultimately only a stalemate.

Reacher stepped to the side wall and raised his boot high and kicked it, the same way a firefighter kicks down a door. The wall cracked and gave a little. He figured they could kick their way through eventually. But there was no point. They were on the wrong side of the corridor for the old lateral doors. All the blue spots were on the opposite side. And slow and noisy progress from one rat trap to another would gain them absolutely nothing.

Not good.

And then it got worse.

The building filled with a faint diesel roar. The outer door, opening, at the far end of the hundred-foot entrance tunnel. Reacher pictured the seal breaking, the big diesels rumbling, the two halves of the door grinding back along their tracks, the gap between them widening slowly and unstoppably. Far too soon for Quantico. They were still in the air, surely. Over Missouri by that point, hopefully, maybe even on approach to Whiteman, maybe even right then lowering the landing gear, but Whiteman was all of sixty miles away, and they still had complex preparations and transfers to make.

So, not the cavalry.

More bad guys.

He said, "They're bringing in reinforcements."

McQueen nodded, and said nothing.

Reacher said, "How many, do you think?"

"Could be dozens. Hundreds, even. There's a network. Everything's a co-production now."

Reacher said, "OK."

"I'm very sorry," McQueen said. "Thank you for everything you tried to do."

They shook hands, mute and awkward in the miserable plywood room, McQueen still trailing frayed cords from his wrists, Reacher's hand bloody from his cut.

The diesel noise started up again. The outer door closing, to allow the inner door to open, the ancient fail-safe circuits still obedient.

McQueen said, "I assume they'll lead them straight here."

Reacher nodded. "So at least let's not wait for them. Let's make them work for it."

"The third chamber is the place to be. They'll be a little less willing to shoot in there."

Reacher nodded again. The flatbed trailers, the giant yellow flasks. The radiation symbols. He said, "Don't stop for me. No matter what. Better that one of us gets out than neither."

McQueen said, "Likewise."

"I'll go first. I'll go left and through. You go right."

"You want the Colt back?"

"You keep it. It drifts left and down. Remember that." Reacher cannibalized his part-gone magazines and put a full load in his Glock. One in the chamber, seventeen in the box. Some of the brass ended up smeared with his blood. Which seemed appropriate. Some old guy once said the meaning of life is that it ends. Which was inescapably true. No one lives forever. In his head Reacher had always known he would die. Every human does. But in his heart he had never really imagined it. Never imagined the time and the place and the details and the particulars.

He smiled.

He said, "On three?"

McQueen nodded.

He said, "One."

The diesels sounded louder. The inner door, opening.

McQueen said, "Two."

Reacher stepped over to the splintered threshold.

McQueen said, "Three."

* * *

**Reacher burst out** at full speed, through the door, through some kind of final mental barrier, into the corridor, ice cold and careless, in his mind already dead like his father and his mother and his brother, bargaining for nothing more at all except the chance to take someone with him, or two of them, or three, and a guy to his left heard the noise and stepped out of a room and Reacher shot him, a triple tap, chest, chest, head, and then he plunged onward, across the narrow space, into a blue-spot room, a guy right in front of him going down the same way, chest, chest, head, and then Reacher was through the ancient door, into another plywood room, which was empty, with gunfire behind him, and out into the center chamber's corridor, a shape running toward him from the right, firing, and into the next blue-spot room, with footsteps behind him, and then it was all over, finally and utterly and completely and definitively, because of the taped plastic sheet over the old door ahead of him, and because the Glock jammed and wouldn't fire anymore.

A tired spring in the magazine, maybe, or his blood on the shell casings, already sticky and all fouled up.

The world went very quiet.

He turned around, slowly, and he put his back on the plastic sheet. Two men had guns on him. One pale face, one dark. The odd ethnic mixture. They were shoulder to shoulder in the doorway. The last two survivors from the original headcount. Both for him. Which was OK. It meant McQueen was getting a clear run, at least for the moment.

Their guns were Smith & Wesson 2213s, stainless

steel, the exact same thing as McQueen had used in the fat man's motel lobby. Wadiah's standard issue, apparently. Maybe a bulk purchase, at a discount price. Three-inch barrels, eight .22 Long Rifle rimfires in the magazines. But not aimed high this time. Not high at all. Aimed right at the center of his chest.

The white guy smiled.

The Arab smiled.

The white guy closed one eye and sighted down the three-inch barrel.

The Arab closed one eye.

Reacher kept both eyes open.

Their trigger fingers tightened.

No sound anywhere. Reacher willed McQueen to make it. *Get to the garage. Hide in the sad old truck. Let the reinforcements move past you. Hit the button and close the door. Then run like hell.*

Their trigger fingers tightened some more.

They tightened all the way.

Then: two shots. Very close and very loud. A ragged little volley. Like a loose double tap. The white guy fell to his knees. Then he pitched forward on his face. The Arab sprawled sideways. His face was all gone, replaced by a gaping exit wound. Shot in the back of the head.

And behind them both, suddenly revealed, still on her feet, a Glock 19 in her hand, was a small slender figure.

Karen Delfuenso.

# Chapter 80

Delfuenso had driven Bale's Crown Vic all the way inside and parked it in the garage. McQueen was already in the front passenger seat. Delfuenso said it was her that Reacher had seen on the two-lane, driving back and forth, with her bright lights on. At first she had meant it just as moral support, but later she had realized the backlight might be useful. Hence the triple trip. She had seen Reacher's muzzle flash on the roof. She had buzzed her windows down and heard the shots. When the subsequent long delay became unbearable she had found her way inside.

Reacher said, "Thank you."

She said, "You're welcome."

She got a first-aid kit out of the trunk. Bureau issue. She said every unmarked car had one. Standard practice. A matter of policy. She cleaned the cut on his hand and bound it up. Then they got in the car. She backed up and turned around and rolled through into the entrance tunnel. Reacher got out again and hit the red button. The inner door started to close, to allow the outer door to open. The ancient fail-safe circuits, still obedient. Then they came out of the tunnel into the sweet night air, and they bumped across the dirt, where the farmer's grandson had torn out the DoD's old approach road. They made it back to the two-lane, and turned right, and right again, and they parked sideways across three bays in Laccy's front lot, exactly where they had started.

Reacher asked her, "Do you have an ETA for Quantico?"

She said, "There was a delay. They're still about three hours out."

"Would you drive me back to the cloverleaf?"

"When?"

"Now."

"Why?"

"I want to get to Virginia."

"Quantico will want to talk to you."

"I don't have time for that."

"They'll need to know what you know."

"I don't know anything."

"Is that going to be your official position?"

"It always is."

"And what's your unofficial position?"

"Same thing. I don't know anything."

"Bullshit," McQueen said to her. "He told me he had it all worked out."

"I don't believe him," Delfuenso said. "I don't have it all worked out. Not yet. Not all of it, anyway. Obviously I saw the nuclear waste. So I assume they were planning a strike somewhere. Maybe soon. Maybe into Nebraska's aquifers."

"Not possible," Reacher said. "Those trailers aren't going anywhere. Not now, not soon, not ever. They haven't moved for twenty years. Their tires are rotted and I bet their axles are rusted solid. It would take the Corps of Engineers a year just to get them out of the tunnel."

"Why are they in there at all? That place wasn't built to house that kind of stuff."

"They had to put it somewhere. No one wants it in their own back yard. It was probably just temporary. But they never figured out a permanent solution. So I guess they just forgot about it. Out of sight, out of mind."

"But why would Wadiah want it, if it can't be moved? If it can't be moved, it can't be used."

"They were never going to use it. It's strictly window dressing. It's purely for show."

"What show?"

"I'm not saying another word," Reacher said. "Quantico will say I'm not allowed to know. They'll call me a security risk. They'll try to keep me in that motel in Kansas for the rest of my life. Which would drive me crazy. Which would give everyone a problem."

"Privately, then," Delfuenso said. "Strictly between us."

Reacher said nothing.

"You owe me," Delfuenso said.

"Then I get a ride to the cloverleaf?"

"Deal."

"It's the law of unintended consequences," Reacher said.

"In what way?"

"It's a bank," Reacher said.

**"Wadiah is a** banking organization," Reacher said. "The United States has done a pretty good job of shutting down terrorist banking, all over the world. The bad guys can't move money anywhere, and they can't keep money anywhere. So they had to invent an alternative. A parallel system. I guess a bunch of entrepreneurs spotted an opening. Some Americans, some Syrians. *Wadiah* is the Arabic word for safekeeping. It also means a type of Islamic bank account. As in, you put money in it, and they keep that money safe for you."

"There's money in that building?" Delfuenso said. "Where?"

"There's no money in any bank. Not in yours, not in mine. Not really, apart from a few bucks in a drawer. Most money is purely theoretical. It's all in computers, backed by trust and confidence. Sometimes they have gold in a vault downstairs, to make themselves look serious. You know, to suggest capital reserves, like in the Fed in New York, or Fort Knox."

"The nuclear waste?" Delfuenso said. "It's a capital reserve? Their version of the gold in Fort Knox? Is that what you're saying?"

"Exactly," Reacher said. "It sits there and backs their currency. Which they invented. They don't deal in dollars or pounds or euros or yen. Remember the on-line chatter? They were talking about gallons. That's what they call their currency unit. They buy and sell in gallons. This bomb costs a hundred gallons, that bomb costs five hundred gallons. Wadiah keeps track of the deals. They take deposits, they process payments, they shuffle balances from one account to another, they make a profit from their fees. Like any bank. Except they don't use computers, because we can hack computers. It's all on paper. Which is why McQueen wouldn't let me burn the place down. Because you guys need names and addresses. It's like a regular terrorist encyclopedia in there."

Delfuenso looked at McQueen. She said, "Is he right?"

McQueen said, "Apart from one minor point."

"Which is?"

"Those tanks are empty. They're completely harmless. They were built but never used. They're surplus. That's why they're in there. Surplus equipment in a surplus building."

"Did Wadiah know they were empty?"

"Sure," McQueen said. "Not that they ever admitted it to their clients."

Delfuenso smiled, just briefly.

"I'm living the dream," she said. "I just shot a couple of crooked bankers."


**Delfuenso started the** car again and rolled slowly south. Reacher sprawled in the back. Delfuenso and McQueen talked in the front, professionally, one agent to another, assessing the operation, evaluating the result. They ran through all the details, from the inside perspective, and from the outside. She told him about Sorenson. They agreed her fate was the only item in the debit column. Other than that they agreed the outcome was more than satisfactory. Spectacular, even. A major score. A treasure trove of information, and a complex system dismantled. Then McQueen told her the only remaining loose end was the identity of the big boss. Not Peter King, as previously thought. Delfuenso blinked and stopped the car on a lonely curb in the middle of nowhere.

She said, "I got some news from Quantico. When I called them about Whiteman. We heard from the State Department again. But not from their PR people this time. I think this one is genuine."

"What did they say?"

"They have no staffer named Lester L. Lester, Jr. Never did. They never heard of him."

"CIA?"

"Likewise. Never heard of him. And we can believe them. Because right now all their cards are on the table. They're depending on us to keep quiet about the guy in the old pumping station."

"Who was he?"

"He had worked in Pakistan and all over the Middle East. Except he wasn't running agents. They were running him. He had gone native. He was Wadiah's mole inside Langley."

Delfuenso moved off the curb and started south again.

McQueen said, "Why did he attack us?"

"He attacked you personally. He had your name.

Kansas City's security is poor, and the CIA watches what we do. They knew we had a mole inside Wadiah. Their mole reported back. The big boss told him to deal with you. So he lured you to a remote location for a meaningless meeting. Simple as that."

"You did well," Reacher said, from the back seat. "Fast reactions. The smart money would have been on the other guy."

McQueen said, "Thank you."

"The forehead thing was a bit retro, though."

"It was the way it came out. That's all. I bent his arm and grabbed the knife, and the blade ended up pretty high, so I thought, why the hell not? Just for old times' sake."

**They came off** Route 65 where it turned east, onto the small rural road, ready to cut the corner back to the Interstate exit. They passed the Civil War battlefield site, where Americans had fired cannons at Americans for nine long hours. McQueen turned in his seat and looked at Reacher and said, "One last thing."

Reacher said, "What?"

"Tell me how you talk for a minute without using the letter *A*."

Delfuenso said, "You were asleep."

McQueen said, "I haven't slept for seven months."

Reacher said, "Easy. Just start counting. One, two, three, four, five, six. And so on. You don't hit a letter *A* until you get to a hundred and one. You can even do it real fast and still get nowhere near ninety-nine inside a minute."

Delfuenso eased to a stop next to a ragged grassy shoulder. No one spoke. No doubt the FBI had appropriate banter for the occasion. The army sure did. But private jokes are private. So they all sat quiet for a minute. Then Reacher got out and walked away, without looking back, past the first ramp west toward Independence and Kansas City, and onward over the bridge to the eastbound ramp. He put one foot on the shoulder and one in the traffic lane, and he stuck out his thumb, and he smiled and tried to look friendly.

No one knows suspense like
#1 *New York Times* bestselling author Lee Child.

And there's no bigger name in suspense
than Jack Reacher.

If you enjoyed *A Wanted Man*,
please keep reading for the
Jack Reacher short story

# "Deep Down"

and then for an exciting preview of

# Never Go Back

**A JACK REACHER NOVEL**

Coming in hardcover and eBook
from Delacorte Press
Fall 2013

# Deep Down

Reacher's designated handler told him it wasn't going to be easy. There were going to be difficulties. Numerous and various. A real challenge. The guy had no kind of a bedside manner. Normally handlers started with the good news.

*Maybe there isn't any,* Reacher thought.

The handler was an Intelligence colonel named Cornelius Christopher, but that was the only thing wrong with him. He looked like a decent guy. Despite the fancy name he seemed to have turned out fairly plain and pragmatic. Reacher would have liked him, except he had never met him before. Going undercover with a handler you never met before led to inefficiency. Or worse.

Christopher asked, "How much did they tell you yesterday?"

Reacher said, "I was in Frankfurt yesterday. Which is in Germany. No one told me anything. Except to get on a plane to Dulles, and then report to this office."

"I see," Christopher said.

"What should they have told me?"

"You really know nothing about this?"

"Some local trouble with staff officers."

"So they did tell you something."

"No one told me anything. But I'm an investigator. I do this stuff for a living. And some things are fairly obvious. I'm a relatively new guy who has so far been posted almost exclusively overseas. Therefore I'm almost certainly unknown to the kind of staff officer who doesn't get out much."

"Out of where?"

"The Beltway, for instance. Call it a two-mile radius from this very office. Maybe they also have a fishing cottage on a lake somewhere. But that's not the kind of place I'm likely to have been."

"You're not very happy, are you?"

"I've had more promising days."

"What's your problem?"

"When does this thing start?"

"This afternoon."

"Well, that's my problem, right there. I've got a handler I never met before and a situation I know nothing about."

"Scared?"

"It's bad workmanship. It's shoddy and confused. It shows no pride. Because you guys are always the same. There's a clue in the title, remember?"

"What title?"

"Your title. Military Intelligence. Ideally both of those words should mean something to you. But surely at least one of them does. One at a time, if you wish. On alternate days, if you want."

"Feel free to give me your honest opinion."

Reacher said, "So what do I need to know?"


**And at that** same minute a car backed out of a driveway, in a distant location, slowly, a front-wheel-drive car, with a yelp as the tires turned. Not the shriek of speed. The opposite. A suburban sound, rubber on a tended blacktop driveway, like the smell of the sprinkler on the summer air.

Then the car paused and the driver selected a forward gear and the car rolled south, gently over the speed bumps that the driver himself had argued should be put in, for the safety of the children.

Then the car turned a little west, toward the highway, ready to join the mighty flow toward the capital.

**Colonel Cornelius Christopher** sat forward and made a space on his desk, paired hands coming together back to back, and then sweeping apart, pushing clutter aside. The move was emphatic. But purely metaphorical. There was nothing on the desk. No clutter. A good man-manager, Reacher thought. *He let me have my say, and now we're moving right along.*

Christopher said, "There's no danger. It's going to be all talking."

Reacher said, "Talking about what?"

"You were right, it's about staff officers. There are four of them. One of them is bad. They're all political liaison people. To the House and the Senate. They practically live there. You know the type. Going places, fast track, better not to get in their way."

"Specifically?"

"The army is asking for a new sniper rifle. We're giving evidence to some new pre-committee. Begging, basically. Our legislative overseers. In fact, not even really. They sent senior staffers instead. We're not even talking to elected officials."

"Now you don't sound very happy."

"I'm not here to be happy. The liaison officers are sitting in on these hearings, obviously. And one of them is leaking. Design criteria, load, range, size, shape, weight, and budget."

"Leaking to who?"

"A likely bidder located overseas, we assume. A foreign manufacturer, in other words. Someone that wants the business. Someone that likes a rigged game."

"Is the business worth it? How many sniper rifles do we buy? And how much do we pay for them?"

"It's the implied endorsement. They can sell copies for five grand each to the freak market. The price of a decent used car. As many as they want. Like selling crack."

"Who else is at these hearings?"

"There's our four liaison and the four staffers we're pitching to, plus our procurement guy and the Marine procurement guy, plus a Ranger sniper and a Marine sniper for color commentary."

"The Marines are involved?"

"In a minority way. They didn't bring their own liaison, for instance. But it's definitely a joint project. No other way of doing a thing like this."

"So why wouldn't it be the Marines leaking? Their procurement guy or their sniper? Why assume it's our guys?"

"The leaks are via a fax machine inside the Capitol Building. Which is where our liaison guys have their offices."

"How certain are you of that?"

"Completely."

"Could be the staffers. They're in the Capitol Building, presumably."

"Different phone network. Our legislative overseers are on some new super-duper thing. Our offices are still steam-powered."

"OK," Reacher said. "So it's one of our guys."

"I'm afraid so," Christopher said.

"Motive?"

"Money," Christopher said. "Got to be. I can't see anyone forming a deep ideological attachment to a European firearms manufacturer. Can you? And money is always a factor for officers like these. They're mixing with corporate lawyers and lobbyists all the time. Easy to feel like the poor relation."

"Can't we just watch their fax machine?"

"Not inside the Capitol Building. Our legislative overseers don't like surveillance. Too many unintended consequences."

"Are they sending to an overseas fax number?"

"No, it's a local number. But these guys hire local people. As agents and lobbyists."

"So my job is what?"

"To find out which one of our guys is the bad apple. By talking to them."

"Where?"

"In the committee, at first. The Ranger sniper has been recalled. Personal reasons. You're going to take his place."

"As what?"

"Another Ranger sniper."

"With a real Marine sniper in the room? I'll be asked for opinions. He'll nail me in a second."

"So be Delta Force, not Rangers. Be mysterious. Don't say anything. Be all weird and silent. Grow a beard."

"Before this afternoon?"

"Don't worry about it. We've seen your file. You know which end of a rifle is which. We have confidence in you."

"Thank you."

"There's one other thing."

"Which is?"

"Our liaison guys are not guys. They're women."

"All of them?"

"All four."

"Does that make a difference?"

"I sincerely hope so. Some of the talking is going to have to be social. That's easier with women. You can do it one on one. Men always want to drink in groups."

"So I'm here to take women to bars, and ask them what they want to drink, and by the way are they leaking military secrets overseas? Is that the idea?"

"You'll have to be more subtle than that. But yes, it's a kind of interrogation. That's all. Which you're supposed to be good at. You're supposed to do this stuff for a living."

"In which case why not arrest them all and interrogate them properly?"

"Because three of the four are innocent. Where there's smoke there's fire, and so on. Their careers would be hurt."

"That never stopped you before."

"We never had fast track people before. Not like this. Going places. We wouldn't cripple them all. One of them would survive, and she'd get her revenge."

Reacher said, "I'm just trying to establish the rules of engagement."

"Anything that wouldn't get thrown out of court for blatant illegality."

"Blatant?"

"Flashing red with a siren. That kind of blatant."

"That bad?"

"We can't tolerate this kind of thing. Not with a foreign manufacturer. We have politicians to please, and they have donors to protect. American donors."

"Who like a rigged game."

"There's two different kinds of rigged. Our kind, and their kind."

"Understood," Reacher said.

"There's no danger," Christopher said again. "It's all just talking."

"So what are the difficulties? What's not going to be easy?"

"That's complicated," Christopher said.

The front-wheel-drive car joined the traffic stream on the highway. It became just one of thousands, all heading the same way, all fast and focused and linear and metallic, like giant rounds fired from giant chain gun barrels somewhere far behind them. Which was a mental image the driver liked very much. He was a bullet, implacable and relentless, singular in his purpose. He was heading for his target. His aim was true.

Across the barrier no one was heading in the other direction. The morning flow was all one way, high speed and crowded, toward the distant city.

Christopher did the thing with his hands again, clearing metaphorical clutter off his desk, and out of the conversation. Ready for a new topic. The difficulties. He said, "It's a speed issue. We have to be quick. And at the same time we have to keep things normal for the Marine Corps. We can't let them suspect we have a leak. So we can't stop talking, or they'll guess. But we can't let much more stuff go overseas. So you can't waste time."

Reacher said, "What, this is going to be like speed dating?"

"You're new in town, so why wouldn't you?"

"I would," Reacher said. "Believe me. It would be like a dream come true. But it takes two to tango. And I'm a realistic guy. On a good day I could get a woman to look at me. Maybe. But four women all at once is not very likely."

Christopher nodded.

"That's the complication," he said. "That's the difficulty we were worrying about. Plus, these women are scary. West Pointers, off-the-charts IQs. Fast track. Going places. You can imagine."

"I don't have to imagine. I was at West Point."

"We know. We checked. You didn't overlap with any of them."

"Are any of them married?"

"No, fortunately. Fast track women don't get married. Not until the time is right."

"Any serious relationships?"

"Same answer."

"Are they older or younger than me?"

"Older. Twenty-nine and thirty."

"Then that's another negative. Most women date older men. And what rank am I going to be?"

"You're going in as a sergeant. Most snipers are."

"Women like that don't want enlisted men."

Christopher nodded again. "I said at the beginning this wasn't going to be easy. But think logically. You might not need to go through all four. You might hit lucky the very first time. Or the second. And you might just know anyway. We have to assume the guilty one will resist any kind of contact. It could be that three say yes and one says no. In which case she's the one."

"They'll all resist contact. They'll all say no."

"Maybe one slightly more emphatically than the others."

"I'm not sure I could tell the difference. It always feels about the same to me. My social antenna must not be very well developed."

"We don't see another way of doing this."

Reacher nodded.

He asked, "Did you get me a uniform?"

"We got you a suit."

"Why?"

"Because you're going to be a Ranger. Or Delta. And they like to show up in civvies. It makes them feel like secret agents."

"It won't fit."

"The suit? It'll fit. Your height and weight are in your file. It was easy. It was like ordering anything. Except bigger."

"Have you got bios on these women?"

"Detailed," Christopher said. "Plus transcripts of everything said at the hearings so far. You should probably read those first. The way they talk will tell you more than the bios."

**Five miles west,** across the Potomac River, a thirty-year-old woman belted a fanny pack low on her hips and moved it around until it was comfortable, in its accustomed position. Then she bent forward and flipped her hair back and slid a toweling band in place, easing it back, and back, until it was seated just right. Then she kicked the hallway baseboard for luck, left toes, right toes, and then she opened her door and stepped out and ran in place for a moment, just gently, warming up, loosening, getting ready, facing it down.

Five miles.

Thirty minutes.

Possible.

It would depend on the lights, fundamentally. If more than half of the crosswalks were green, she would make it. Fifty-one percent. That was all she needed. Less than that, she wouldn't. Simple arithmetic. A fact of life. No disgrace.

Except it was. Failure was always a disgrace.

She took a breath, and another, and she hit her watch, and she ran down her path, and left onto the sidewalk, and she settled in for the first unbroken stretch. Long, easy strides, relaxed but pushing just a little, breathing well, moving well, her hair swinging behind her in a perfect circular rhythmic pattern, symmetrical, like a metronome.

The first crosswalk was green.


**Reacher started with** the transcripts. The precommittee hearings. There were records of two separate sessions, the first two weeks ago, and the second one week ago. Hence the rush. The third session was due.

The transcripts were exactly what transcripts should be. Every vocal sound uttered in the room had been transcribed onto paper. Every *um* and *er* and *you know*, every false start, every repetition, every unfinished sentence, every stutter and stammer, every hopeless tangle and broken train of thought. Reading the pages was almost like hearing the voices. But not quite. There was a semi-real quality. Speech never hit paper just right, however good the transcriber.

The first to speak was one of the Senate staffers. Reacher could picture the guy. Not young. Disrespectful to send a kid, unless the kid was a hotshot, and hotshots didn't get sent to waste time listening for sixteen hours before saying no to the army. So it would be an older guy, solid and substantial and been-there-forever, but a clear B-lister all the same, because A-listers didn't get sent to waste time listening for sixteen hours before saying no to the army, either.

This particular example of a senior B-lister sounded puffed-up and bossy. He started out by making himself chairman of the board. He just announced it. No one objected. Not that Reacher expected anyone to. Presumably the guy had a dynamic of his own going on with the other staffers, and why would the army or the jarheads care which one of the assholes did what? So the guy went ahead and formally recited the purpose of the meeting, which he said was to examine available courses of action in the light of the perceived requirement for a new infantry weapon, namely a sniper rifle.

Reacher didn't like that sentence at all. Because of the word *perceived*. Clearly that was how the argument was going to go. *You don't really need this. Yes, we do. Why?* Which was the big bureaucratic elephant trap, right there. The on-the-ground snipers would drift the wrong way. Had they ever missed a shot because of inferior equipment? Hell no, sir, we *never* miss our shots. Hell, we can use *anything.* Hell, we could make our own damn sniper rifles out of your granddaddy's old varmint gun and a length of rainwater gutter and a roll of goddamned *duct tape.*

*Sir.*

And the procurement officers would drift too far the other way, until they started sounding like gun nuts or

NRA members writing a letter to Santa Claus. So it was a ritual dance. There was no way of winning. It was 1986 and it was all about planes and missiles and computers and laser-guided integrated systems. Firearms were boring. They were going to lose. But not after their wet-dream sniper rifle specification leaked overseas. The foreign manufacturer could gear up ahead of the next attempt. Or go right ahead and build the thing and sell it to the Soviets.

Reacher turned the pages, and it went pretty much as he had guessed it would. The puffed-up bossy guy asked why they needed the new rifle, and no one answered. The bossy guy asked them to pretend he was an idiot and knew nothing about the subject. Not a big ask, Reacher thought. Then the army procurement guy spoke up and the typist must have nearly worn out his *m* key: *Um. Erm. Umm.* (Pause) *I'm . . . I'm . . . I'm . . .*

The bossy guy said they could come back to that. Then he asked what exactly they were looking for, and things got back on solid ground with long back-and-forths about what qualities a sniper rifle needed. Cold shot accuracy was head of the list, of course. Often a sniper gets just one chance, which by definition will be out of a cold barrel. It has to hit. So the barrel is all about perfectly uniform internal dimensions, and heavy match-grade steel, with the right twist, and maybe some fluting for stiffness and reduced weight, the whole thing properly bedded into the stock, which shouldn't swell or shrink depending on the weather, or be too heavy to carry twenty miles. And so on.

The liaison women spoke often and at length. The first up was identified by the initials *C.R.* She said, "This is extremely high-tech metalwork we're talking about here. And we'll need groundbreaking optics. Maybe we could incorporate laser range finding. This could be very exciting. It could be a great research opportunity for somebody."

A smart woman. Whole sentences. And good sentences. She was trying to make it radical, not boring, and she was hinting at big dollars getting spent in someone's district, which would be an IOU any senator would be happy to tuck away in his vest pocket. A good tactical approach.

But it didn't work. The chairman of the board asked, "Who's going to pay for all that?"

At which point the transcriber had written: *Pause.*

Reacher switched to the bio stack and found that C.R. was Christine Richardson. From Orange County, California. Private prep school, private high school, West Point. She was thirty years old and already a lieutenant colonel. Fast track, and the political shop was a greased rail anyway. Nice work, if you could get it.

The thirty-year-old woman with the fanny pack and the headband made it through three crosswalks on green and got held up at the next three on red. The seventh turned green before she got there, but it was choked with walkers, and they were slow to get going, so she got hung up behind them, running in place for two whole seconds, then pushing through, dodging left, dodging right, refusing to cut away diagonally, because then the distance would be less than the full five miles, which would be cheating, and she never cheated. At least not with running. She made it through the crowd to the opposite corner, and she turned right, and she logged the junction in her mind as half-red and half-green, which seemed fair to her, and which meant so far she was running exactly fifty-fifty, three and a half green, three and a half red, which was not a catastrophe, but which was not great either, because she liked to bank plenty of greens well before she got closer to the center, where things were always stickier.

She ran on, another unbroken stretch, her strides still long and easy, still relaxed, but pushing now just a little more, picking up the pace, still breathing well, still moving well, her hair still swinging behind her in its perfect pattern, still symmetrical, still like a metronome.

The next crosswalk was red.

**The man in** the car got snarled up in traffic where 270 approached the Beltway. Inevitable, and expected. Orderly deceleration by all concerned, the flow hanging together, still like the thousand-round burst from the distant chain gun, but fully subsonic now, slow and fat and stealthy in the air. 355 to Wisconsin Avenue would be jammed, so he decided to stay on until 16th Street, east of Rock Creek Park. It wouldn't be a racetrack, but it would be better. And it would drop him down all the way to Scott Circle, and then Mass Ave ran all the way to the Capitol.

He was a bullet, and he was still on target.

**From the other** side of the office Cornelius Christopher said, "OK, library hour is over. Go get your suit now. You can take the documents with you, but not out of the building."

The supply office was two floors down, not exactly full of exploding fountain pens or cameras concealed in buttonhole flowers, but full of distantly related stuff, and certainly full of all the items needed to turn an honest man into a fake. The suit was well chosen. Not remotely expensive or up to date, but not tacky, either. Some kind of gray sharkskin weave, probably some man-made fiber in there, or a lot, wide lapels like five years ago. Exactly what an enlisted man would wear to a bank interview or a bail hearing. It was artfully creased here and there, from years in an imaginary closet, and there was even room dust on the collar. It looked like it was going to fit, except the arms and the shoulders. Reacher's file figures showed six-five and two-fifty, and he was reasonably in proportion, like a regular guy enlarged, except for arms as long as a gorilla's, and shoulders like basketballs stuffed in a sack.

There was a button-down shirt that was going to be way too small in the neck, but that was OK, because soldiers in suits were supposed to look awkward and uncomfortable. The shirt was blue and there was a red tie with it, with small blue crests on it. It could have come from a rifle club somewhere. It was a good choice. The undershirt and the boxers were standard white PX items, which was fine, because Reacher had never heard of anyone buying that kind of stuff anywhere else. There was a pair of black PX socks, and a pair of black dress-uniform shoes. They looked to be the right size.

The supply guy said, "Try it all on. If there's a problem, we can do some alterations. If not, you should keep it on. Get used to it, and wear it in some. You'd already be on a bus or a plane by now, if you were really coming in from somewhere."

The shirtsleeves ended up half-staff, and the neck couldn't get close to buttoning, but the effect was OK. Every sergeant in civvies Reacher had ever seen wrenched his tie loose after about ten minutes. The suit coat was tight across the shoulders, and the sleeves stopped short of the knobs on the side of his wrists. He stood back and checked a mirror.

Perfect. A sergeant's salary was embarrassingly close to the poverty line. And sergeants didn't read *GQ*. Not usually. The whole ensemble looked exactly like a hundred dollars grudgingly spent at the outlet mall ahead of a sister-in-law's second wedding.

The supply guy said, "Keep it on. It'll do."

Reacher was supposed to supply his own pocket junk, so next up was ID. It had his real name and his photograph on it, but a master sergeant's rank, and an infantry unit sufficiently generic to be plausible for a guy deployed with Special Forces, shooting individuals one at a time from a mile away.

"How do I communicate with the colonel?" Reacher asked.

"Try the telephone," the supply guy said.

"Sometimes hard to find a phone in a hurry."

"There's no danger," the supply guy said. "It's all just talking."


**The woman with** the fanny pack and the headband crossed the Potomac on the Francis Scott Key Bridge, high above the water, running hard, die straight, through the hot swampy air, a glorious unbroken sprint, heading for Georgetown but not planning to get there. She was going to turn right on M Street, which became Pennsylvania Avenue, all the way to Washington Circle, and then New Hampshire Avenue to Dupont Circle, and then Mass Ave the rest of the way to the Capitol itself.

A crazy route, geographically, but any other option was either less or more than five miles, and five miles was what she ran. To the inch. Anyone else would have used her car's odometer, on a quiet Sunday morning, but she had bought a surveyor's wheel, a big yellow thing on a stick, and she had walked with it four separate times before she came up with eight thousand eight hundred yards exactly, and not a single step less or more. Precision was important.

She ran on. By that point she could feel a wide sweat stripe all the way down her back, and her throat was starting to burn. Pollution, hanging over the sluggish river, a visible cloud. But she dug in and pushed on, long, long strides, fast cadence, arms pumping. Her headband was soaked. But she was ahead of schedule. Just. Many variables to come, but she had a chance of making it. Five miles in thirty minutes. Eight thousand eight hundred yards in one thousand eight hundred seconds. Fourteen and two-thirds feet a second. Not an international distance, so there was no world record. No national record, no Olympic record. But the greats might have done it in twenty-four minutes. So thirty was acceptable. For her, with traffic, and lights, and office workers in the way.

She pushed on, breathing hard, still moving well, right up there in the zone.


**The traffic on** 16th Street was stop-start heavy, frustration on every block, past Juniper Street, and Iris, and Hemlock, and Holly, and Geranium, and Floral. Then past Walter Reed, with the park green and serene on the right. The driver was no longer a bullet. He was shrapnel at best, subject to aerodynamic forces, jinking right and left between the lanes to win some fractional advantage on the dead-straight road. A Southern town, built for horses and buggies, perspiring gentlemen in hats and vests flicking mosquitoes away, now sclerotic with jammed vehicles, superheated air shimmering above their hoods, expensive paint winking in the sun.

He still had a long way to go. He was going to be late.

**Reacher walked the** corridors until he smelled an office with a coffee machine going. He ducked in and helped himself to a cup, practicing a sergeant's manner, on the surface quiet and deferential, with ramrod competence showing underneath. But the office was empty, so his acting was wasted, and the coffee was burnt and stewed. But he took it with him anyway, in one hand, the sheaf of documents in the other, all the way back to Cornelius Christopher's office.

Christopher said, "You look the part."

Reacher said, "Do I?"

"Your file says you're pretty good with a long gun."

"I do my best."

"You could have been a real sniper."

"Too much waiting around. Too much mud. The best snipers are always country boys."

"And you're a city boy?"

"I'm a nowhere boy. I grew up on Marine bases."

"Yet you joined the army?"

"I'm naturally contrary."

"Did you finish your reading?"

"Not yet."

"We checked for financial irregularities," Christopher said. "Or financial excesses, I suppose. But they're all living within their means. Appropriate accommodations, four-cylinder cars, good clothes but small wardrobes, modest jewelry, no vacations, not that they'd take a vacation anyway. Not fast track people. Not if they want to be Chief of Staff one day. Or a defense industry lobbyist."

Reacher put the thirty-year-old Lieutenant Colonel Christine Richardson to the bottom of the pile, and started in on the second of the women, twenty-nine years old and a mere major, name of Briony Walker, the daughter of a retired naval officer, brought up mostly in Seattle and San Diego, public elementary school, public high school, valedictorian, West Point.

Christopher said, "I hope it's not her."

Reacher said, "Why?"

"The naval connection."

"You like the navy?"

"Not much, but it's still a military family."

The third candidate was another thirty-year-old light colonel, this one called Darwen DeWitt, and right there Reacher knew she wasn't the product of a military family. Not with a name like that. In fact she was the daughter of a Houston businessman who owned about a hundred dent-repair franchises. Private education all the way, softball star, West Point.

The fourth was Alice Vaz, age thirty, lieutenant colonel, granddaughter of another lieutenant colonel, except this one had been called Mikhail Vasilyevich and he had been a lieutenant colonel in the Red Army. A Soviet. His son, Alice's father, had gotten out of Hungary just in time, with a pregnant wife, and Alice had been born in the United States. A citizen. California, public elementary, public high, West Point.

"Notice anything definitive?" Christopher asked.

Reacher said, "Their names are perfectly alphabetical. Alice, Briony, Christine, and Darwen."

"OK, apart from that."

"Two of them are rich girls. What does that do to your money motive?"

"Maybe taking money is a habit with rich people. Maybe that's how they get rich in the first place. Did you notice anything else?"

"No."

"Neither did we."

**The woman with** the fanny pack and the headband was on New Hampshire Avenue, gunning hard up the rise, the hubbub of Dupont Circle already visible in the haze ahead. She was up two greens on the crosswalks and she could see it already, reaching the Capitol steps, slamming her hand on her wrist to stop the watch, gasping for air, once, twice, bent over, hands on knees, then raising her head, then bringing her arm up slowly, and blinking the sweat from her eyes and focusing on the pale LCD readout and seeing the magic numbers: twenty-nine something.

She could do it.

She hammered on, striding short because of the gradient, really breathing, really hurting, but still moving well.

**The man in** the car was still on 16th Street. He had the air on high, but even so he could feel sweat on his back. Vinyl upholstery, and a four-cylinder motor with no power to spare for a big compressor. He was just past Harvard Street, getting to where young and rent-strapped aides were forced to live. No cars for them. They were walking to work, right alongside him, about the same speed.

He watched one, a girl, in pantyhose despite the heat, the nylon scissoring fast, ugly white athletic sneakers on her feet, with tube socks, her dress shoes no doubt in the big bag she was carrying, along with briefing papers and position papers and talking points, maybe with a makeup kit, hoping against hope everyone else would be busy and she would get to go on the television news for a comment.

There were male versions too, dressed out of a Brooks Brothers sale, heads high, striding out. Every block brought more of them, twos and threes, until both sidewalks were full of them, all heading the same way, power walking, almost an army, an unstoppable force, clean-living and idealistic young people setting out to do good for their country.

They were going to get to work before him. The traffic was awful.


The transcript showed that the second pre-committee hearing had picked up more or less exactly where the first had left off, solidly on the safe grounds of technical discussions, about minutiae like actions and stocks and bedding and triggers and scopes. It was as if a collective but unspoken agreement had been reached, to avoid unpleasant issues, and to run out the clock with the kind of things shooters liked to talk about.

The four liaison women poked and prodded and drew the men out endlessly, going over things again and again, refining details until Reacher could practically see the new weapon in his mind's eye. Three of them were doing it just to keep the ball rolling, and the fourth was lapping it all up, no doubt picturing her contact in a foreign boardroom reading her fax, unable to believe the precision of the specification he was being handed.

Who was the fourth?

Christine Richardson and Darwen DeWitt did most of the talking. The transcript looked like a movie screenplay where C.R. and D.D. were the big stars. They each got plenty of ink. But their approaches were different. Richardson was rah-rah for the army, every question and every point laying a kind of guilt trip on the politicians for not rushing to make the world a safer place. DeWitt showed more concern for the Congressional point of view. She was almost a fifth skeptic. Devil's advocate, maybe, or perhaps her sympathies genuinely lay elsewhere. Perhaps her Houston dent-repair upbringing had made her a fiscal conservative. But wherever she was coming from, she laid bare the details of the secret spec as much as anyone.

Briony Walker and Alice Vaz said less. Walker was all about accuracy. The naval family. She wanted the rifle to be like the guns on her daddy's ships, artillery instruments, infallible when properly aimed. And she was weirdly interested in the end results. She asked about head shots and chest shots, about how it felt to wait while the bullet flew, about what they saw through the scope afterward. The effect was almost pornographic.

Alice Vaz asked mostly wider questions. The others debated rifle stocks made of composite materials, which wouldn't shrink or swell no matter the conditions, and she asked about the conditions. Where in the world was this rifle likely to go? How hot? How cold? How high? How wet? She didn't get clear answers, and after a spell she gave up. There were no A.V. attributions in the last twenty pages of the transcript.

Christopher asked, "Gut feeling?"

Reacher said, "Just from this?"

"Why not?"

"Then I would say it's Christine Richardson. She sounds like the prime mover. She wants everything spelled out every which way. No secrets with that woman."

"I could say she's trying to sell it. I could say she thinks the political guys will find that stuff interesting."

"No, she knows they don't. But she keeps on talking anyway. She won't let them leave anything vague or unspecified. Why is that?"

"Maybe she has OCD."

"What's that?"

"Obsessive compulsive disorder. Like alphabetizing your underwear."

"How do you alphabetize underwear?"

"Figure of speech."

"So you're happy with Richardson?"

"No," Christopher said. "We think it's her too. From the externalities in the transcripts, at least. The issue is going to be proving it."


**The woman with** the fanny pack and the headband was on Mass Ave, approaching Scott Circle, and the man in the car was on 16th Street, approaching Scott Circle. Their average speeds for the last many minutes had been more or less identical, at ten miles an hour, her progress steady and resolute and relentless, his frustratingly stop-start-fast-fast-slow. She was pushing hard, ready for an iconic athletic breakthrough, desperate for it, and he was agitated about the time, anxious about being late, wishing he could have parked and taken the

Metro without getting back at the end of the day to find all his wheels had been stolen.

It happened like this: she was on the left-hand sidewalk, on Mass Ave, and he was at right angles to her, in 16th Street's extreme right lane, wanting to come off into the circle. She was looking straight ahead, watching the traffic, watching the upcoming crosswalk lights, trying to time it, suddenly convinced that if she got held up there her bid was over. He was looking beyond the three cars ahead, to the far left, diametrically away from her, watching the traffic coming into the circle, which would have prior right of way. He was looking for an upcoming gap, trying to time it, hoping to roll up to the line and squirt on through, one unbroken move.

She sprinted, hard, hard, hard, and he moved up, craning left, looking for the gap that would be his, seeing half a gap, rolling, rolling, the cars ahead of him clearing, the gap tightening, not really a gap at all, but his last chance, so he went for it, hitting the gas, wrenching the wheel, smashing into her as she sprinted into the space she had been sure would remain, because surely no driver would try to use it.

She went up in the air and down on his windshield rail, impossibly loud metallic thumps and crashes, and he braked hard and she spun on the shiny roof and clattered over the inclined tailgate and landed head first on the blacktop.

**Reacher butted all** the paperwork into a neat stack and put it back on Christopher's desk. Christopher said, "Almost time to get down to business. Do you know the committee room number?"

Reacher said, "Yes."

"Do you know where it is?"

"No."

"Good. I'm not going to tell you. I want you wandering around like a little lost country boy. I want everything about this thing to be realistic from the get-go."

"Nothing about this thing is realistic. And nothing about this thing is going to work."

"Look on the bright side. You might get lucky. One of them might be into rough trade. All on the army's dime, too."

Reacher said nothing. He used the door on F Street and turned right and left onto New Jersey Avenue, and then the Capitol Building was right there in front of him, half a mile ahead, big and white and shining in the sun. He looped around into the plaza and went up the steps. A Capitol cop looked at his ID and gave him a barrage of directions so confusing that Reacher knew he would need a couple of refreshers along the way. Which he got, first from another guard, and then from a page.

The designated committee room had an impressive door made from polished mahogany; and inside, it had an impressive table made from the same wood. Around the table were seated four people. One was the transcriber. He was in shirtsleeves and had a court-reporter machine in front of him. The other three were clearly the army procurement officer, and the Marine Corps procurement officer, and the Marine sniper. The two officers were in uniform, and the sniper was in a cheap suit. Probably a Recon Marine. A Delta wannabe. The officers shook hands, and the sniper gave a millimetric nod, which Reacher returned, equally briefly, which for two alleged snipers was effusive, and for a dogface and a jarhead meeting for the first time was practically like rolling around on the floor in an ecstatic bear hug.

There was no one else in the room. No political staffers, none of the liaison women. The clock in Reacher's head said the meeting was due to start inside a minute. The clock on the wall was a minute fast, so the meeting was already underway, according to Capitol time. But nothing was happening. No one seemed to care. The Marine sniper was mute, and the procurement guys were clearly as happy to waste time sitting quiet as to waste it talking up a storm about a lost cause.

The clock ticked. No one spoke. The jarhead stared into space, infinitely still. The officers moved in their chairs and got comfortable. Reacher copied the jarhead.

Then eventually the staffers came in, followed by three women in army Class A uniform. Three women, not four. *Class A uniform, female officer, the nameplate is adjusted to individual figure differences and centered horizontally on the right side between one and two inches above the top button of the coat.* Reacher scanned the black plastic rectangles. DeWitt, Vaz, and Walker were there. Richardson was not. A and B and D were present, but C was missing. No Christine.

The four staffers looked a little upset, and the three women looked very unhappy. They all sat down, in what were clearly their accustomed places, leaving one chair empty, and the guy at the head of the table said, "Gentlemen, I'm afraid we have some very upsetting news. Earlier today Colonel Richardson was struck by a car as she was running to work. At Scott Circle."

Reacher's first thought was: *Running? Why? Was she late?* But then he understood. Jogging, fitness, shower and dress at the office. He had seen people do that.

The guy at the head of the table said, "The driver of the car is a postal worker from the Capitol mail room. Eyewitness accounts suggest risks were taken by both parties."

The army procurement officer asked, "But how is she? How's Christine?"

The guy at the head of the table said, "She died at the scene."

Silence in the room.

The guy said, "Head trauma. From when she hit the windshield rail, or from when she finally fell to the ground."

Silence. No sound in the room, except the patter of the transcriber's machine, as he caught up with what had been said. Then even he went quiet.

The guy at the head of the table said, "Accordingly, I suggest we close down this process and resume it at a more suitable time."

The army procurement officer asked, "When?"

"Let's schedule it for the next round of budget discussions."

"When are those?"

"A year or so."

Silence.

Then Briony Walker said, "No, sir. We have a duty to fulfill. The process must be completed. Colonel Richardson would have wanted it no other way."

No answer.

Walker said, "The army deserves to have its case made properly and its needs and requirements placed in the record. People would quickly forget our reason for abandoning this process. They would assume we had not been truly interested. So I propose we complete our mission by making certain every detail and every parameter have been adequately clarified and accurately recorded. Then at least our legislators will know exactly what they are approving. Or rejecting, as the case may be."

The guy at the head of the table said, "Does anyone wish to speak against the proposal?"

No answer.

"Very well," the guy said. "We will do as Major Walker suggests, and spend the rest of the day going over everything one more time. Just in case there's something we missed."

**And go over** it they did. Reacher recognized the sequence of individual discussions from the transcripts. They started at the beginning and worked their way through. Most items were simply reiterated and reconfirmed, but there were some lingering live debates. Briony Walker was all out for bolt action. The naval family. The accuracy issue. A bolt action was operated manually, as gently as you liked, so the gun stayed still afterward, with no microscopic tremors running through it. On the other hand a semi-automatic action was operated by gunpowder explosions, and was absolutely guaranteed to put tremors into the gun afterward. Perhaps for a critical length of time.

"How long?" one of the staffers asked.

"Would be critical?" Walker asked back.

"No, how long do these tremors last?"

"Some fractions of a second, possibly."

"How big are they?"

"Certainly big enough to hurt accuracy at a thousand yards or more."

The staffer looked across the table and said, "Gentlemen?"

The army procurement guy looked at his Marine counterpart, who looked at his sniper, who stared into space. Then everyone looked at Reacher.

Reacher said, "What was the first item you discussed?"

The staffer said, "Cold shot accuracy."

"Which is important why?"

"Because a sniper will often get just one opportunity."

"With a bullet that was chambered when?"

"I think we heard testimony that it can have been several hours previously. Long waits seem to be part of the job."

"Which means any tremors will have disappeared long ago. You could chamber the round with a hammer. If you assume the money shots are always going to be singles, and widely spaced, possibly by hours or even days, then the action doesn't matter."

"So you'd accept a semi-automatic sniper rifle?"

"No, sir," Reacher said. "Major Walker is correct. Possibly the money shots won't always be the first shots. And accuracy is always worth pursuing wherever possible. And bolt actions are rugged, reliable, simple, and easy to maintain. They're also cheap."

So then came a debate about which bolt action was best. The classic Remington had fans in the room, but so did Winchester and Sako and Ruger. And at that point Alice Vaz started up with more of her big-picture questions. She said, "The way to understand our requirements, for not only actions but also stocks and bedding, it seems to me, is to understand where and how this rifle will actually be used. At what altitude? At what barometric pressures? In what extremes of temperature and humidity? What new environments might it face?"

So to shut her up the army procurement guy ran through just about everything in the War Plans locker. No names and no specific details, of course, but all the meteorological implications. High altitude plus freezing mist, extreme dry heat with sand infiltration, rain forest humidity and high ambient temperature, in snow many degrees below zero, in downpours, and so on.

Then one of the staffers insisted that the steel for the barrel had to be domestic. Which was not a huge problem. Then another insisted that the optics had to be domestic too. Which was a bigger problem. Reacher watched the women seated opposite. Darwen DeWitt wasn't saying much. Which was a surprise after her star turns the first two times out. She was a little more than medium height, and still lithe, like the teenage softball star she had been. She was dark-haired and pale-skinned, with features more likely to be called strong than pretty, but she was spared from being plain by mobile and expressive eyes. They were dark, and they moved constantly but slowly, and they blazed with intelligence and some kind of inner fire. Maybe she was burning off surplus IQ, to stop her head from exploding.

Briony Walker was the navy daughter, and she looked it, neat and controlled and severe, except for an unruly head of hair, untamed even by what looked like a recent and enthusiastic haircut. She too had an animated face, and she too had a lot going on behind her eyes.

Alice Vaz was the best looking. Reacher didn't know the word. *Elfin,* maybe? *Gamine*? Probably somewhere in between. She had darker skin than the other two, and a cap of short dark hair, and the kind of eyes that switch between a twinkle and a death ray in, well, the blink of an eye. She was smaller than the other two, and slight, in a European kind of way, and maybe smarter, too. Ultimately she was controlling the conversation, by hemming it in with questions too boring to answer. She was making the others focus.

The meeting dragged on. Reacher made no further contributions beyond an occasional grunt of assent. Eventually conversation dried up and the guy at the head of the table asked if everyone agreed the army's needs and requirements were now properly in the record. All hands went up. The guy repeated the question, this time personally to and directly at Briony Walker, possibly a courtesy, possibly out of spite, her own words fed back to her. But Walker took no offense. She just agreed, yes, she was completely satisfied.

Whereupon the four staffers stood up and left the room, hustling and bustling and without a word, as if to take time out to say goodbye would hopelessly overburden their busy schedules. The women stood up, but the next out of the room was the army procurement guy, who just clapped his Marine buddy on the shoulder and disappeared. Whereupon the Marine clapped his NCO on the shoulder and they walked out together, leaving just Reacher and the women in the room.


**But it didn't** stay that way for long. The women were already in a huddle. Not exactly leaning in, face to face, a tight little triangle, shoulder to shoulder, touching each other, like regular women. But maybe the West Point version. They drifted in lockstep to the door, there was a polite glance from Alice Vaz, and then they were gone.

Reacher stayed where he was. No big rush. Nothing

he could have done about it. Maybe there were guys who could have pulled it off. *Hey, I'm sorry about your dead buddy that I never met, but can I separate you from your grieving pals and take you out and buy you a drink?* Reacher was not one of those guys.

But the women weren't going anywhere. He was sure of that.

He got up and stepped out and saw them where the corridor widened into a lobby. They were still together in their tight huddle. Not going anywhere. Just talking. Lots of social rules. They would end up in a bar, for sure, but not yet.

Reacher drifted back to a bank of pay phones and dialed. He leaned on the wall. He saw Briony Walker glance at him, then glance away. Just the out-of-towner making a call. Maybe to his local buddies, telling them he's done for the day, asking them where the action is at night.

Christopher said, "Yes?"

Reacher said, "Did you hear about Christine Richardson?"

"Yes, we did."

"So it's going to be a little harder now."

"It might be over now. If Richardson was the leak all along."

"Suppose she wasn't?"

"Then it might be easier, not harder. With the other three. Emotion helps. Loose lips sink ships."

"It wasn't a fun afternoon. Romance is on no one's mind. They're talking to each other. There's no way into a conversation like that."

"Exploit any opportunity you can."

"You're not in the Capitol, but you're monitoring their fax line, right?"

"Correct."

"Including tonight?"

"Of course. What do you know?"

"It's not DeWitt."

"How do you know?"

"She was upset. She's thirty years old and she never had anyone die before."

"It's natural to be upset."

"But if she had a secret agenda she'd have gotten over it. To do her work. But she didn't. She hardly said a word. She sat there like the whole thing had no purpose. Which was absolutely the appropriate reaction for anyone without an agenda of her own."

"Had either of the other two gotten over it?"

"Alice Vaz was all over it. Briony Walker likewise. And Walker made a real big fuss about going through it all one more time. With every detail stated for the record."

"So she could check if she missed anything in her last two faxes?"

"That's a possible interpretation."

"What did Vaz do?"

"Same thing she did in the transcripts. Big geography. She should quit and run a travel agency."

"What are you going to do?"

"I don't know yet. Just monitor that fax line for me."

**Reacher hung up** the phone. The women were still in the lobby, still talking, still not going anywhere. He set off toward them, just strolling, like a man with an hour to kill, like a stranger in town drawn toward the only faces he knew. Plan A was to keep the pretense going, maybe getting into the group via Briony Walker's interest in gunshot wounds. Maybe she was a sniper groupie. He could offer some opinions. Head shot or chest shot? *Well, ma'am, I favor the throat shot. If you hit it just right you can make their heads come off.*

Plan B was to abandon the pretense and come clean as an MP captain undercover for MI, and see where that road led. Which might be all the way home. If he made out Richardson had been the prime suspect, then whoever worked hardest to reinforce that conclusion would be the guilty one. If no one worked hard, then Richardson had been the guilty one all along.

He strolled on.

Plan A or Plan B?

They made the decision for him.

They handed it to him on a plate.

They were civilized women, and reflexively polite in the way that military people always are. He was heading close to them. He wasn't going to pass by on the other side. So he had to be acknowledged. Briony Walker looked straight at him, but Darwen DeWitt was the first to speak. She said, "We weren't introduced. I guess it wasn't that kind of an afternoon."

"No, ma'am," Reacher said. "I guess it wasn't." He said his name. He saw each of the three file it away in her memory.

He said, "I was sorry to hear about Colonel Richardson."

DeWitt nodded. "It was a shock."

"Did you know her well?"

"We all came up together. We expected to carry on together."

"Brother officers," Reacher said. "Or sisters, I guess."

"We all felt that way."

Reacher nodded. They could all afford to feel that

way. No rivalry. Not yet. They faced no significant bottleneck until the leap from Brigadier General to Major General. From one star to two. Then a little rivalry might bite.

Briony Walker said, "It must have happened to you, sergeant. You must have lost people."

"Ma'am, one or two."

"And what do you do on days like that?"

"Well, ma'am, typically we would go to a bar and toast their journey. Usually starts out quiet, and ends up happy. Which is important. For the good of the unit."

Alice Vaz said, "What unit?"

"I'm not at liberty to say, ma'am."

"What bar?"

"Whatever is close at hand."

DeWitt said, "The Hyatt is a block away."


**They walked over** to the Hyatt. But not exactly together. Not a foursome. More accurately a threesome and a singleton in a loose association, held together only by Reacher playing dumb enough to miss the hints he should get lost. The women were too polite to make it more explicit. But even so the walk was excruciatingly embarrassing. Out of the grounds, across Constitution, onto New Jersey Avenue, across Louisiana and D Street, and then they were there, at the Hyatt's door. Reacher stepped up promptly and held it open. Because immediate action was required, right there, right then. Indecisive loitering on the sidewalk would have led to heavier hints.

They shuffled past him, first Vaz, then DeWitt, and finally Walker. Reacher fell in behind them. They found the bar. Not the kind of place Reacher was used to. For one thing, there was no bar. Not as such. Just low tables, low chairs, and waiter service. It was a lounge.

Walker looked at Reacher and asked, "What should we drink?"

Reacher said, "Pitchers of beer, but I doubt if they have those here."

A waiter came and the women ordered white wine spritzers. It was summer. Reacher ordered hot coffee, black, no sweeteners required. He preferred not to clutter a table with jugs and bowls and spoons. The women murmured among themselves, a trio, with occasional guilty glances at him, unable to get rid of him, unable to be rude to him.

He asked, "Do those meetings usually go like that? Apart from the thing with Colonel Richardson, I mean."

Vaz said, "Your first?"

Reacher said, "And hopefully my last, ma'am."

Walker said, "No, it was worth it, It was a good at-bat. They can't say no to everything. So we just made it fractionally more likely they'll say yes to something else, sometime soon."

"You like your job?"

"Do you like yours, sergeant?"

"Yes, ma'am, most of the time."

"I could give the same answer."

The waiter brought the drinks, and the women returned to their three-way private conversation. Reacher's coffee was in a wide, shallow cup, and there wasn't much of it. He was a couple of mouthfuls away from the next awkward moment. They hadn't gotten rid of him leaving the Capitol, and they hadn't gotten rid of him entering the hotel. The end of the first round of drinks was their next obvious opportunity. All it would take was an order: *Sergeant, you're dismissed.* No way of fighting that, not even under Plan B. *Captain, you're dismissed* worked just as well, when said by majors and lieutenant colonels.

**But it was** Darwen DeWitt who left after the first round of drinks. She was still not talking much, and she clearly wasn't enjoying herself. She was finding no catharsis. She said she had work to do, and she got up. There were no hugs. Just tight nods and brave smiles and meaningful glances, and then she was gone. Vaz and Walker looked at Reacher, and Reacher looked right back at Walker and Vaz. No one spoke. Then the waiter came back right on cue, and Vaz and Walker ordered more spritzers, and Reacher ordered more coffee.

The second spritzer loosened Walker up a little. She asked Reacher what he felt when he pulled the trigger on a live human being. Reacher quoted a guy he knew. He said recoil against his shoulder. Walker asked what was the longest kill he had ever made. Truth was about eleven feet, at that stage, because he was a cop, but he said six hundred yards, because he was supposed to be a sniper. She asked with what. Truth was a Beretta M9, but he said an M21, an ART II scope, and a 7.62 NATO round.

Alice Vaz asked, "Where was this?"

Reacher said, "Ma'am, I'm not at liberty to say."

"Which sounds like a Special Forces scenario."

"I guess it does."

"Six hundred yards is fairly close range for you guys."

"Practically point blank, ma'am."

"Black bag for CIA, or legitimate, for us?"

"Ma'am, I'm not at liberty to say."

And those twin denials seemed to create some credibility. Both women gradually abandoned their defensive body language. Not that it was replaced by personal interest. It was replaced by professional interest, which came across in a poignant way. Neither woman had a realistic hope in her lifetime of becoming a battlefield commander. Both were forced to take a different route. But both seemed to look across the divide with concern. In an ideal world they would be fighting. In which case they would want the best available weapons. No question about that. In which case simple ethics demanded the best available weapons for those currently doing the fighting in the less than perfect world. Simple justice. And simple preparedness, too. Their sisters might never get there, but their daughters would one day.

Walker asked Reacher his private opinion about the rifle design. Were there things that should be added? Taken away? Reacher said, "Ma'am, I think they got it about right," partly because that was the kind of thing a sergeant would say to an officer, and partly because it was true. Walker seemed happy with the answer.

Then both Walker and Vaz got up to use the restroom. Reacher could have used a pit stop too, but he didn't want to follow directly behind them. That would have been too weird, right after the walk from the Capitol. So he waited. He saw Vaz use a pay phone on her way. There was a line of them in wooden hutches on the lounge's back wall. Vaz used the center phone. Walker didn't wait for her. She went on ahead. Vaz spoke for less than ten seconds and then hung up and continued on her way to the restroom.

**Walker never came** back from the restroom. Vaz sat down alone and unconcerned and said Walker had gone back to the office. She had used the D Street door. She had a lot to do. And did Reacher want another drink?

Reacher and Vaz, alone together. Walker, on her own, on the loose.

Reacher said, "You buying?"

Vaz said, "Sure."

Reacher said, "Then yes."

"Then follow me," Vaz said. "I know a better place than this."


**The better place** was tucked in close to the tracks out the back of Union Station. It was better in the sense it had an actual bar. It was worse in every other way. In particular it was in a lousy neighborhood, full of ugly brick and ramshackle buildings, with dark streets and all kinds of alleyways and yards all over the place, with more wires overhead than trees. The bar itself felt like a waterfront establishment, mysteriously landlocked, low and wide and made a warren by subdivision into many different room-sized areas. Reacher sat with his back to a corner, where he could see both front and rear doors at once. Vaz sat next to him, not close, but not far away, either. She looked good. Better than she had a right to. Class A uniform, female officer, was generally no kind of a flattering outfit. It was essentially tubular. Maybe Vaz's was tailored. It had to be. The jacket was waisted. It went in and out properly. The skirt was tight. And a little short. Just a fraction, but detectable by the human eye unaided.

Vaz said, "I hope not to be in this shop much longer."

"Where next?"

"War Plans, I hope."

"Do they cash this shop's checks?"

"You mean, can I take my credits with me? Absolutely. Politics and War Plans? They're practically the same thing."

"So when?"

"As soon as possible."

"But you're worried this business with Colonel Richardson will slow things down. No one likes a fuss, right? And the shop is understaffed now. Maybe they can't let you go."

"You're pretty smart, for a sergeant."

"Rank has nothing to do with being smart, ma'am."

"Tell me about yourself."

"You first."

"Nothing to tell," Vaz said. "California girl, West Point cadet, first I wanted to see the world, and then I wanted to control it. You?"

"Marine Corps boy, West Point cadet, first I wanted to see the world, and then I wanted to survive it."

"I don't remember many West Point cadets who became sergeants afterward."

"Some did. From time to time. In a way."

"I see."

"Do you?"

"You're an undercover operator," Vaz said. "I always knew the day would come."

"When what?"

"When you finally figured it out. As in, your procurement office is riddled with corruption, and has been for years. As in, you don't need a new sniper rifle. You know that. But those guys have already sold stock in the new model. Maybe the money is already spent. So they have to make it happen. Any way they can. I mean, did you hear some of the arguments they were making?"

"Where is their office?"

"Who? Procurement is a big department."

"The guy I saw today, for instance."

"His office is in the Capitol Building."

"With a fax machine?"

"Of course."

"Did any of the others know this?"

"In the political shop? We all did. Why do you think Walker made them go through the whole thing again today? Because she wanted to generate a third fax."

"Why?"

"An extra piece of evidence for you. We knew you'd catch up with it eventually."

"Why didn't one of you drop a dime before?"

"Not our place."

"You mean the cost-benefit ratio wasn't right. One of you would have to step up, and it's conceivable she could lose. Because anything can happen in a military court. In which case she's out of the running right from that moment. Because she was once on the losing side. You couldn't risk that kind of mistake. Not having come so far."

"The running for what?"

"For whatever it is you all plan to be."

"For a spell we thought the previous sniper could be the undercover guy. The one you replaced. Like entrapment. He was letting the officer push him to want more and more. But in the end we thought he was just a sniper. So we'd have nailed you for the real undercover guy in about a minute, except no one was really paying attention this afternoon."

"Because of Richardson? What did she think was happening?"

"The same as we all did. Procurement is a swamp and you'd notice sooner or later."

"What is it you plan to be?"

"Respected. Perhaps within a closed community, but by someone."

"Has your life lacked respect so far?"

"You have no idea," Vaz said. She turned toward him, moving on the bench, her knees coming close to his, dark nylon over dark skin. She said, "I'm proceeding on the assumption that I can trust my impression that you're younger than me. And in a branch with much less generous and accelerated promotion. And that therefore I outrank you."

"I'm a captain," Reacher said. "Ma'am."

"Therefore if our chains of command were in any way related, it would be inappropriate for us to have a close relationship. Therefore the question is, are our chains of command in any way related?"

"I think they're about as far apart as chains of command can be."

"Wait there," she said. "I'll be right back."

And she got up and threaded her way through the cluttered space, heading for the restroom corridor in back. Five minutes, minimum, Reacher thought. He followed her as far as a pay phone on the wall. The phone was a scratched old item and the wall behind it was dark with smoke and grime.

He dialed, and said his name.

Cornelius Christopher said, "Yes?"

Reacher said, "I'm done."

"What does that mean? You're quitting?"

"No, it means the job is done."

"What do you know?"

"Walker must be back at the Capitol by now. Any faxes yet?"

"No."

"You were wrong. No one is leaking to a foreign fire-arms manufacturer. No one ever was. Why would any-one need to? Everyone knows what a good sniper rifle should be. It's self-explanatory. It's obvious. The basic principles have been understood for a century. No one needs to gather secret intelligence. Because they already know."

"So what's the story?"

"I'm waiting for the final proof. I should have it in five minutes or less."

"Proof of what?"

"It's Alice Vaz," Reacher said. "Think about the tran-scripts. Her big-picture questions. She asked a couple more this afternoon. She wanted it spelled out exactly where this new rifle will be used. She asked what new environments it might face."

"So?"

"She was trying to get into War Plans through the back door. And the procurement guy fell for it. No de-tails, but he gave plenty of weather clues. Anyone could reverse-engineer our entire slate of global intentions from what he said."

"Like what?"

"He said high altitude plus freezing mist."

"Afghanistan," Christopher said. "We're going to have to go there sooner or later."

"And extreme dry heat with sand infiltration."

"The Middle East. Iraq, most likely."

"And rain forest humidity and high ambient tempera-ture."

"South America. Colombia, and so on. The drug wars."

"And in snow many degrees below zero."

"If we have to go to the Soviet Union."

"You see? She got a summary of all our future plans from the guy. Exactly the kind of oblique data that enemy intelligence analysts love."

"Are you sure?"

"I gave her two seconds to react and she came up with blaming procurement for being corrupt. It was almost plausible. She's very smart."

"Which enemy? Which foreign intelligence?"

"The Soviets, of course. A local fax number, probably in their embassy."

"She's their asset?"

"In a big, big way. Think about it. She's on the fast track. She's going right to the top. Which is what? The Joint Chiefs, at least. But maybe more. A woman like this could be President of the United States."

"But how did they recruit her? And when?"

"Probably before she was born. Her granddaddy was some big Red Army hero. So maybe her daddy wasn't a real refugee. Maybe the KGB shuffled him to Hungary so he could get out and look like a dissident. Whereupon his daughter could be born an American and become a real deep down sleeper. She was probably groomed for the fast track from birth. These people play a long game."

"That's a lot of assumptions."

"The proof will be here in about three minutes. Or not."

"But why risk wasting a super-high-value asset on this? Because if you're right, then this is useful, but it's not life-changing. This is not the hydrogen bomb."

"I think this was kind of accidental. I think it came up in the normal course of her duties. But she couldn't resist phoning it in. Habit, or a sense of obligation. If she's a true believer."

"What's the proof you're getting in five minutes? Or is it three?"

"It's two minutes now, probably," Reacher said. "She made a brief call from the Hyatt hotel. Think about it. She's a huge asset. Maybe their biggest ever. She's headed all the way to the top. Which could be anywhere. And right now she's stopping in War Plans next, which is a real big prize in itself. So she has to be protected. Like no one has ever been protected before. And she was suspicious of me somehow. Maybe routine paranoia. I was new. I was hanging around. So she called for help. She told the embassy's wet boys where I'd be, and when. And then she lured me into the trap. Right now I'm supposed to believe I'm about to get in her pants."

"Soviet wet boys are coming for you?"

"One minute now, probably. I'm about to be a mugging gone wrong. I'm going to be found dead on a street corner."

"Where are you?"

"In the badlands behind Union Station."

"I can't get anyone there in less than a minute."

"I didn't expect you would."

"Are you going to be OK?"

"That depends on how many they send."

"Can you arrest Vaz before they get there?"

"She's long gone. I'm sure she went straight out the bathroom window. You'll have to pick her up. She'll be heading for her office."

Then a man stepped in through the bar's rear door.

"Got to go," Reacher said. "It's starting."

**Reacher hung up** the phone. The guy at the rear door was compact and hard-edged, dressed in black, moving easily. He looked vaguely similar to Vaz in terms of ethnic background. But he was a decade older. Nothing in his hands. Not yet. Not inside a public bar. Reacher guessed the point of the guy coming in the back was to chase him out the front, where the main force would be gathered. Easier to set up a mugging gone wrong on a public street, rather than in a private yard in back of a bar. Because it wasn't a great street. Not a great neighborhood. Broken lighting, plenty of shadows, plenty of doorways, passersby habituated by instinct and long experience to look away and say nothing.

The guy was scanning the room. Vaz had spent very little time on the phone. Very few words. Probably not more than *big guy, very tall, gray suit*. Reacher felt the guy's eyes on him. He practically heard the check marks. *Big guy, right there. Very tall, no question. Gray suit, here's our boy.* The guy started away from the door.

Reacher started toward it.

A wise man asked, what's the best time to plant a tree? A wise man answered, fifty years ago. As in, what's the best time to make a decision? A wise man answers, five seconds before the first punch is thrown.

The guy in black weighed maybe one-ninety, and he was doing about two miles an hour. Reacher weighed two-fifty, and he was doing about three miles an hour. Therefore closing speed was five miles an hour, and impact, should it happen, would involve some multiple of four hundred forty pounds a square inch.

Impact did happen.

But not at five miles an hour. Closing speed was dramatically increased by a sudden drive off Reacher's back foot and the vicious clubbing swing of his elbow. Which therefore connected with a real big multiple of their combined bodyweights. Reacher caught the guy on the perfect cheekbone-nose-cheekbone line and the cracking and splintering was clearly audible over the wooden thud of feet on the floor. The guy went down like a motorcycle rider hitting a clothesline. Reacher walked on by and stepped out the back door.

Nobody or somebody?

That was the only question. And there is no bigger difference than nothing or something. Had they posted all of the main force at the front? Or had they left a lone guy as back-up?

They had left a guy. Dark hair, dark eyes, thicker coat than his pal. Smart as a whip, probably, but any human given instructions is at a disadvantage. *Your target is a big guy, very tall, gray suit.* And however smart you are, however quick, that lethal one, two, three question-and-answer drumbeat occupies precious mental milliseconds, at least *big guy check, very tall check, gray suit check*, like that, and the problem comes when the big guy in the gray suit occupies those same precious milliseconds by walking straight toward you and breaking your skull with his elbow.

Reacher walked on, to where an arch led from the yard to the alley.

**The alley was** wide enough for two horses and a beer cart axle. At the right-hand end was an arch to another private yard. At the left-hand end was the street. Reacher's shoes were quiet. Class A uniform shoes. Therefore man-made soles. No one wanted leather welts. More to polish. Reacher stopped short of the street and put his back against the left-hand wall. In a movie there would be a busted shard of mirror at his feet. He could edge it out and check the view. But he wasn't in a movie. So he inched around, and peered out, one eye.

Thirty feet away. Four guys. Therefore a total of six dispatched. Six wet boys in a foreign embassy. Permanently. For her. *Like no one has ever been protected before. A woman like this could be President of the United States.* They had two cars parked on the far side of the street. Diplomatic plates. Probably never paid their parking fines. The guys were in a rough arc near the bar's door, their backs to Reacher, just standing there semi-animated, like guys sometimes do for a spell, outside a bar.

There was no busted shard of mirror, but there was a broken quarter brick, about the size of a baseball. In no way reflective, but the need for a mirror was past. Reacher picked it up, and stepped out to the street, and turned left.


**Thirty feet was** ten paces, and Reacher kept a steady speed through the first five of them, and then he wound up and threw the brick fragment at the nearer car and accelerated hard so that the brick shattered the rear windshield and the four heads snapped toward the sound and Reacher's elbow hit the first of those heads all in a tight little one-two-three sequence, less than a second beginning to end.

The first guy went down, obviously, vertically beneath Reacher's scything follow-through, and then Reacher spun back off the bounce and drove the same elbow backward into the next guy's head. Which left two guys still on their feet, one close, one inconveniently distant, so Reacher feinted toward the farther one and then pivoted back and head-butted the nearer one, like he was trying to drive a fencepost into dry baked earth with his head. Which left one still on his feet, which the guy put to good use by running for it.

Reacher let him go. There were things Reacher didn't like to do. Running was one of them.

**Twenty-four hours later** Reacher was back in Frankfurt, where he stayed for a week, before moving on to Korea for a regular tour. Neither he nor anyone in the world heard anything more about Alice Vaz. He had no idea whether his analysis had been right or wrong, close or wildly inaccurate. But a month after his arrival in Seoul he heard he was being considered for a medal. The Legion of Merit, to be specific, and for no discernible reason, other than what might be gleaned from the notes in the manual: *Awarded for exceptionally meritorious conduct in the performance of outstanding services to the United States.*

# Never Go Back

## Chapter 1

Eventually they put Reacher in a car and drove him to a motel a mile away, where the night clerk gave him a room, which had all the features Reacher expected, because he had seen such rooms a thousand times before. There was a raucous through-the-wall heater, which would be too noisy to sleep with, which would save the owner money on electricity. There were low-watt bulbs in all the fixtures, likewise. There was a low-pile carpet that after cleaning would dry in hours, so the room could rent again the same day. Not that the carpet would be cleaned often. It was dark and patterned and ideal for concealing stains. As was the bedspread. No doubt the shower would be weak and strangled, and the towels thin, and the soap small, and the shampoo cheap. The furniture was made of wood, all dark and bruised, and the television set was small and old, and the curtains were gray with grime.

All as expected. Nothing he hadn't seen a thousand times before.

But still dismal.

So before even putting the key in his pocket he turned

around and went back out to the lot. The air was cold, and a little damp. The middle of the evening, in the middle of winter, in the northeastern corner of Virginia. The lazy Potomac was not far away. Beyond it in the east, D.C.'s glow lit up the clouds. The nation's capital, where all kinds of things were going on.

The car that had let him out was already driving away. Reacher watched its tail lights grow faint in the mist. After a moment they disappeared completely, and the world went quiet and still. Just for a minute. Then another car showed up, brisk and confident, like it knew where it was going. It turned into the lot. It was a plain sedan, dark in color. Almost certainly a government vehicle. It aimed for the motel office, but its headlight beams swung across Reacher's immobile form, and it changed its direction, and it came straight at him.

Visitors. Purpose unknown, but the news would be either good or bad.

The car stopped parallel with the building, as far in front of Reacher as his room door was behind him, leaving him alone in the center of a space about the size of a boxing ring. Two men got out of the car. Despite the chill they were dressed in T-shirts, tight and white, above the kind of athletic pants sprinters peel off seconds before a race. Both men looked more than six feet and two hundred pounds. Smaller than Reacher, but not by much. Both were military. That was clear. Reacher could tell by their haircuts. No civilian barber would be as pragmatic or brutal. The market wouldn't allow it.

The guy from the passenger side tracked around the hood and formed up with the driver. The two of them stood there, side by side. Both wore sneakers on their feet, big and white and shapeless. Neither had been in the Middle East recently. No sunburn, no squint lines, no stress and strain in their eyes. Both were young, somewhere south of thirty. Technically Reacher was old enough to be their father. They were NCOs, he thought. Specialists, probably, not sergeants. They didn't look like sergeants. Not wise enough. The opposite, in fact. They had dull, blank faces.

The guy from the passenger side said, "Are you Jack Reacher?"

Reacher said, "Who's asking?"

"We are."

"And who are you?"

"Your legal advisors."

Which they weren't, obviously. Reacher knew that. Army lawyers don't travel in pairs and breathe through their mouths. They were something else. Bad news, not good. In which case immediate action was always the best bet. Easy enough to mime sudden comprehension and an eager approach and a hand raised in welcome, and easy enough to let the eager approach become unstoppable momentum, and to turn the raised hand into a scything blow, elbow into the left-hand guy's face, hard and downward, followed by a stamp of the right foot, as if killing an imaginary cockroach had been the whole point of the manic exercise, whereupon the bounce off the stamp would set up the same elbow backhand into the right-hand guy's throat, one, two, three, smack, stamp, smack, game over.

Easy enough. And always the safest approach. Reacher's mantra was: *Get your retaliation in first.* Especially when outnumbered two-to-one against guys with youth and energy on their side.

But. He wasn't sure. Not completely. Not yet. And he couldn't afford a mistake of that nature. Not then. Not under the circumstances. He was inhibited. He let the moment pass.

He said, "So what's your legal advice?"

"Conduct unbecoming," the guy said. "You brought the unit into disrepute. A court martial would hurt us all. So you should get the hell out of town, right now. And you should never come back again."

"No one mentioned a court martial."

"Not yet. But they will. So don't stick around for it."

"I'm under orders."

"They couldn't find you before. They won't find you now. The army doesn't use skip tracers. And no skip tracer could find you anyway. Not the way you seem to live."

Reacher said nothing.

The guy said, "So that's our legal advice."

Reacher said, "Noted."

"You need to do more than note it."

"Do I?"

"Because we're offering an incentive."

"What kind?"

"Every night we find you still here, we're going to kick your ass."

"Are you?"

"Starting tonight. So you'll get the right general idea about what to do."

Reacher said, "You ever bought an electrical appliance?"

"What's that got to do with anything?"

"I saw one once, in a store. It had a yellow label on the back. It said if you messed with it you ran the risk of death or serious injury."

"So?"

"Pretend I've got the same kind of label."

"We're not worried about you, old man."

*Old man.* For no good reason Reacher saw an image of his father in his mind. Somewhere sunny. Okinawa, possibly. Stan Reacher, born in Laconia, New Hampshire, a Marine captain serving in Japan, with a wife and two teenage sons. Reacher and his brother had called him *the old man,* and he had seemed old, even though at that point he must have been ten years younger than Reacher was that night.

"Turn around," Reacher said. "Go back wherever you came from. You're in over your heads."

"Not how we see it."

"I used to do this for a living," Reacher said. "But you know that, right?"

No response.

"I know all the moves," Reacher said. "I invented some of them."

No reply.

Reacher still had his key in his hand. Rule of thumb: don't attack a guy who just came through a door that locks. A bunch is better, but even a single key makes a pretty good weapon. Socket the head against the palm, poke the shaft out between the index and middle fingers, and you've got a fairly decent knuckleduster.

But. They were just dumb kids. No need to get all bent out of shape. No need for torn flesh and broken bones.

Reacher put his key in his pocket.

Their sneakers meant they had no plans to kick him. No one kicks things with soft white athletic shoes. No point. Unless they were aiming to deliver blows with their feet merely for the points value alone. Like one of those martial arts fetishes with a name like something off a Chinese food menu. Tai Kwon Do, and so on. All very well at the Olympic Games, but hopeless on the street. Lifting your leg like a dog at a hydrant was just begging to get beat. Begging to get tipped over and kicked into unconsciousness.

Did these guys even know that? Were they looking at his own feet? Reacher was wearing a pair of heavy boots. Comfortable, and durable. He had bought them in South Dakota. He planned to keep on wearing them all winter long.

He said, "I'm going inside now."

No response.

He said, "Goodnight."

No response.

Reacher half turned, and half stepped back, toward his door, a fluid quarter circle, shoulders and all, and like he knew they would, the two guys moved toward him, faster than he was moving, off-script and involuntary, ready to grab him.

Reacher kept it going long enough to let their momentum establish, and then he whipped back through the reverse quarter circle toward them, by which time he was moving just as fast as they were, two hundred and fifty pounds about to collide head-on with four hundred, and he kept on twisting and threw a long left hook at the left-hand guy. It caught him as designed, hard on the ear, and the guy's head snapped sideways and bounced off his partner's shoulder, by which time Reacher was already throwing a right-hand uppercut under the partner's chin. It hit like a how-to diagram and the guy's head went up and back the same way his buddy's had bounced around, and almost in the same second. Like they were puppets and the puppeteer had sneezed.

Both of them stayed on their feet. The left-hand guy

was wobbling around like a man on a ship and the right-hand guy was stumbling backward. The left-hand guy was all unstable and up on his heels and his center mass was open and unprotected. Reacher popped a clubbing right into his solar plexus, hard enough to drive the breath out of him, soft enough not to cause lasting neurological damage. The guy folded up and crouched and hugged his knees. Reacher stepped past him and went after the right-hand guy, who saw him coming and swung a feeble right of his own. Reacher clouted it aside with his left forearm and repeated the clubbing right to the solar plexus.

The guy folded in half, just the same.

After that it was easy enough to nudge them around until they were facing in the right direction, and then to use the flat of his boot sole to shove them toward their car, first one, and then the other. They hit head-on, hard, and they went down flat. They left shallow dents in the door panels. They lay there, gasping, still conscious.

A dented car to explain, and headaches in the morning. That was all. Merciful, under the circumstances. Benevolent. Considerate. Soft, even.

*Old man.*

*Old enough to be their father.*

By that point Reacher had been in Virginia less than three hours.

# Chapter 2

Reacher had finally made it, all the way from the snows of South Dakota. But not quickly. He had gotten hung up in Nebraska, twice, and then onward progress had been just as slow. Missouri had been a long wait and then a silver Ford, driven east by a bony man who talked all the way from Kansas City to Columbia, and who then fell silent. Illinois was a fast black Porsche, which Reacher guessed was stolen, and then it was two men with knives at a rest stop. They had wanted money, and Reacher guessed they were still in the hospital. Indiana was two days going nowhere, and then a dented blue Cadillac, driven slowly by a dignified old gentleman in a bow tie the same blue as his car. Ohio was four days in a small town, and then a red crew-cab Silverado, with a young married couple and their dog, driving all day in search of work. Which in Reacher's opinion was a possibility for two of them. The dog would not find easy employment. It was likely to remain forever on the debit side of the ledger. It was a big useless mutt, pale in color, about four years old, trusting and friendly. And it had hair to spare, even though it was the middle of winter. Reacher ended up covered in a fine golden down.

Then came an illogical loop north and east into Pennsylvania, but it was the only ride Reacher could get. He spent a day near Pittsburgh, and another near York, and then a black guy about twenty years old drove him to Baltimore, Maryland, in a white Buick about thirty years old. Slow progress, overall.

But from Baltimore it was easy. Baltimore sat astride I-95, and D.C. was the next stop south, and the part of Virginia Reacher was aiming for was more or less inside the D.C. bubble, not much further west of Arlington Cemetery than the White House was east. Reacher made the trip from Baltimore on a bus, and got out in D.C. at the depot behind Union Station, and walked through the city, on K Street to Washington Circle, and then 23rd Street to the Lincoln Memorial, and then over the bridge to the cemetery. There was a bus stop outside the gates. A local service, mostly for the gardeners. Reacher's general destination was a place called Rock Creek, one of many spots in the region with the same name, because there were rocks and creeks everywhere, and settlers had been both isolated from one another and equally descriptive in their naming habits. No doubt back in the days of mud and knee britches and wigs it had been a pretty little colonial village, but later it had become just another crossroads in a hundred square miles of expensive houses and cheap office parks. Reacher watched out the bus window, and noted the familiar sights, and catalogued the new additions, and waited.

His specific destination was a sturdy building put up about sixty years before by the nearby Department of Defense, for some long-forgotten original purpose.

About forty years after that the military police had bid on it, in error, as it turned out. Some officer was thinking of a different Rock Creek. But he got the building anyway. It sat empty for a spell, and then it was given to the newly-formed 110th MP Special Unit as its HQ.

It was the closest thing to a home base Reacher had ever had.

The bus let him out two blocks away, on a corner, at the bottom of a short hill he had walked many times. The road coming down toward him was a three-lane, with cracked concrete sidewalks and mature trees in pits. The HQ building was ahead on the left, in a broad lot behind a high stone wall. Only its roof was visible, made of gray slate, with moss growing on its northern hip.

There was a driveway entrance off the three-lane, which came through the high stone wall between two brick pillars, which in Reacher's time had been purely decorative, with no gates hung off them. But gates had been installed since then. They were heavy steel items with steel wheels which ran in radiused tracks butchered into the old blacktop. Security, in theory, but not in practice, because the gates were standing open. Inside them, just beyond the end of their swing, was a sentry hutch, which was also new. It was occupied by a private first class wearing the new Army Combat Uniform, which Reacher thought looked like pajamas. Late afternoon was turning into early evening, and the light was fading.

Reacher stopped at the sentry hutch and the private gave him an inquiring look and Reacher said, "I'm here to visit with your CO."

The guy said, "You mean Major Turner?"

Reacher said, "How many COs do you have?"

"Just one, sir."

"First name Susan?"

"Yes, sir. Major Susan Turner, sir."

"That's the one."

"What name shall I give?"

"Reacher."

"What's the nature of your business?"

"Personal."

"Wait one, sir." The guy picked up a phone and called ahead. *A Mr. Reacher to see Major Turner.* The call went on longer than Reacher expected. At one point the guy covered the mouthpiece with his palm and asked, "Are you the same Reacher that was CO here once? Major Jack Reacher?"

"Yes," Reacher said.

"And you spoke to Major Turner from somewhere in South Dakota?"

"Yes," Reacher said.

The guy repeated the two affirmative answers into the phone, and listened some more. Then he hung up and said, "Sir, please go ahead." He started to give directions, and then he stopped, and said, "I guess you know the way."

"I guess I do," Reacher said. He walked on, and ten paces later he heard a grinding noise, and he stopped and glanced back.

The gates were closing behind him.


**The building ahead** of him was classic 1950s DoD architecture. Long and low, two stories, brick, stone, slate, green metal window frames, green tubular handrails at the steps up to the doors. The 1950s had been a golden age for the DoD. Budgets had been immense.

Army, Navy, Air Force, Marines, the military had gotten whatever it wanted. And more. There were cars parked in the lot. Some were army sedans, plain and dark and well-used. Some were POVs, personally-owned vehicles, brighter in color but generally older. There was a lone Humvee, dark green, huge and menacing next to a small red two-seater. Reacher wondered if the two-seater was Susan Turner's. He figured it could be. On the phone she had sounded like a woman who might drive such a thing.

He went up the short flight of stone steps to the door. Same steps, same door, but repainted since his time. More than once, probably. The army had a lot of paint, and was always happy to use it. Inside the door the place looked more or less the same as it always had. There was a lobby, with a stone staircase on the right to the second floor, and a reception desk on the left. Then the lobby narrowed to a corridor that ran the length of the building, with offices left and right. The office doors were half glazed with reeded glass. The lights were on in the corridor. It was winter, and the building had always been dark.

There was a woman at the reception desk, in the same ACU pajamas as the guy at the gate, but with a sergeant's stripes on the tab in the center of her chest. Like an aiming point, Reacher thought. Up, up, up, fire. He much preferred the old woodland-pattern battle-dress uniform. The woman was black, and didn't look happy to see him. She was agitated about something.

He said, "Jack Reacher for Major Turner."

The woman stopped and started a couple of times, as if she had plenty she wanted to say, but in the end all she managed was, "You better head on up to her office. You know where it is?"

Reacher nodded. He knew where it was. It had been his office once. He said, "Thank you, sergeant."

He went up the stairs. Same worn stone, same metal handrail. He had been up those stairs a thousand times. They folded around once and came out directly above the center of the lobby at the end of the long second-floor corridor. The lights were on in the corridor. The same linoleum was on the floor. The office doors to the left and right had the same reeded glass as the first-floor doors.

His office was third on the left.

No, Susan Turner's was.

He made sure his shirt was tucked in and he brushed his hair with his fingers. He had no idea what he was going to say. He had liked her voice on the phone. That was all. He had sensed an interesting person behind it. He wanted to meet that person. Simple as that. He took two steps and stopped. She was going to think he was crazy.

But, nothing ventured, nothing gained. He shrugged to himself and moved on again. Third on the left. The door was the same as it always had been, but painted. Solid below, glass above, the reeded pattern splitting the dull view through into distorted vertical slices. There was a corporate-style name plate on the wall near the handle: *Maj. S. R. Turner, Commanding Officer.* That was new. In Reacher's day his name had been stenciled on the wood, below the glass, with even more economy: *Maj. Reacher, CO.*

He knocked.

He heard a vague vocal sound inside. It might have been *Enter.* So he took a breath and opened the door and stepped inside.

He had been expecting changes. But there weren't

many. The linoleum on the floor was the same, polished to a subtle sheen and a murky color. The desk was the same, steel like a battleship, painted but worn back to shiny metal here and there. The chairs were the same, both behind the desk and in front of it, utilitarian mid-century items that might have sold for a lot of money in some hipster store in New York or San Francisco. The file cabinets were the same. The light fixture was the same, a contoured white glass bowl hung off three little chains.

The differences were mostly predictable and driven by the march of time. There were three console telephones on the desk, where before there had been one old rotary-dial item, heavy and black. There were two computers, one a desktop and one a laptop, where before there had been an in-tray and an out-tray and a lot of paper. The map on the wall was new and up to date, and the light fixture was burning green and sickly, with a modern bulb, all fluorescent and energy saving. Progress, even at the Department of the Army.

Only two things in the office were unexpected and unpredictable.

First, the person behind the desk was not a major, but a lieutenant colonel.

And second, he wasn't a woman, but a man.

# Chapter 3

**The man behind the desk was wearing the same** ACU pajamas as everyone clse, but they looked worse on him than most. Like fancy dress. Like a Halloween party. Not because he was particularly out of shape, but because he looked serious and managerial and desk-bound. As if his weapon of choice would be a propelling pencil, not an M16. He was wearing steel eyeglasses and had steel-gray haircut and combed like a schoolboy's. His tapes and his tags confirmed he was indeed a lieutenant colonel in the U.S. Army, and that his name was Morgan.

Reacher said, "I'm sorry, colonel. I was looking for Major Turner."

The guy named Morgan said, "Sit down, Mr. Reacher."

Command presence was a rare and valuable thing, much prized by the military. And the guy named Morgan had plenty of it. Like his hair and his glasses, his voice was steel. No bullshit, no bluster, no bullying. Just a brisk assumption that all reasonable men would do exactly what he told them to, because there would be no real practical alternative.

Reacher sat down, in the visitor chair nearer the window. It had springy bent-tube legs, and it gave and bounced a little under his weight. He remembered the feeling. He had sat in it before, for one reason or another.

Morgan said, "Please tell me exactly why you're here."

And at that point Reacher thought he was about to get a death message. Susan Turner was dead. Afghanistan, possibly. Or a car wreck.

He said, "Where is Major Turner?"

Morgan said, "Not here."

"Where, then?"

"We might get to that. But first I need to understand your interest."

"In what?"

"In Major Turner."

"I have no interest in Major Turner."

"Yet you asked for her by name at the gate."

"It's a personal matter."

"As in?"

Reacher said, "I talked to her on the phone. She sounded interesting. I thought I might drop by and ask her out to dinner. The field manual doesn't prohibit her from saying yes."

"Or no, as the case may be."

"Indeed."

Morgan asked, "What did you talk about on the phone?"

"This and that."

"What exactly?"

"It was a private conversation, colonel. And I don't know who you are."

"I'm commander of the 110th Special Unit."

"Not Major Turner?"

"Not anymore."

"I thought this was a major's job. Not a light colonel's."

"This is a temporary command. I'm a troubleshooter. I get sent in to clean up the mess."

"And there's a mess here? Is that what you're saying?"

Morgan ignored the question. He asked, "Did you specifically arrange to meet with Major Turner?"

"Not specifically," Reacher said.

"Did she request your presence here?"

"Not specifically," Reacher said again.

"Yes or no?"

"Neither. I think it was just a vague intention on both our parts. If I happened to be in the area. That kind of a thing."

"And here you are, in the area. Why?"

"Why not? I have to be somewhere."

"Are you saying you came all the way from South Dakota on the basis of a vague intention?"

Reacher said, "I liked her voice. You got a problem with that?"

"You're unemployed, is that correct?"

"Currently."

"Since when?"

"Since I left the army."

"That's disgraceful."

Reacher asked, "Where is Major Turner?"

Morgan said, "This interview is not about Major Turner."

"Then what's it about?"

"This interview is about you."

"Me?"

"Completely unrelated to Major Turner. But she

pulled your file. Perhaps she was curious about you. There was a flag on your file. It should have triggered when she pulled it. Which would have saved us some time. Unfortunately the flag malfunctioned and didn't trigger until she returned it. But better late than never. Because here you are."

"What are you talking about?"

"Did you know a man named Juan Rodriguez?"

"No. Who is he?"

"At one time he was of interest to the 110th. Now he's dead. Do you know a woman named Candice Fox?"

"No. Is she dead too?"

"Ms. Fox is still alive, happily. Or not happily, as it turns out. You sure you don't remember her?"

"What's this all about?"

"You're in trouble, Reacher."

"For what?"

"The Secretary of the Army has been given medical evidence showing Mr. Rodriguez died as a direct result of a beating he suffered sixteen years ago. Given there's no statute of limitations in such cases, he was technically a homicide victim."

"You saying one of my people did that? Sixteen years ago?"

"No, that's not what I'm saying."

"That's good. So what's making Ms. Fox unhappy?"

"That's not my topic. Someone else will talk to you about that."

"They'll have to be quick. I won't be sticking around for long. Not if Major Turner isn't here. I don't remember any other real attractions in the neighborhood."

"You will be sticking around," Morgan said. "You and I are due a long and interesting conversation."

"About what?"

"The evidence shows it was you who beat on Mr. Rodriguez sixteen years ago."

"Bullshit."

"You'll be provided with a lawyer. If it's bullshit, I'm sure he'll say so."

"I mean, bullshit, you and I are not going to have any kind of a long conversation. Or a lawyer. I'm a civilian, and you're an asshole wearing pajamas."

"So you're not offering voluntary cooperation?"

"You got that right."

"In which case, are you familiar with Title 10 of the U.S. Code?"

Reacher said, "Parts of it, obviously."

"Then you may know that one particular part of it tells us when a man of your rank leaves the army, he doesn't become a civilian. Not immediately, and not entirely. He becomes a reservist. He has no duties, but he remains subject to recall."

"Obviously," Reacher said again. "But for how many years?"

"You had a security clearance."

"I know. I remember it well."

"Do you remember the papers you had to sign to get it?"

"Vaguely," Reacher said. He remembered a bunch of guys in a room, all grown up and serious. Lawyers, and notaries, and seals and stamps and pens.

Morgan said, "There was a lot of fine print. Naturally. If you're going to know the government's secrets, the government is going to want some control over you. Before, during, and after."

"How long after?"

"Most of that stuff stays secret for sixty years."

"That's ridiculous."

"Don't worry," Morgan said. "The fine print didn't say you stay a reservist for sixty years."

"That's good."

"It said worse than that. It said indefinitely. But as it happens the Supreme Court already screwed us on that. It mandated we respect the standard three bottom-line restrictions common to all cases in Title 10."

"Which are?"

"To be successfully recalled, you have to be in good health, under the age of fifty-five years, and trainable."

Reacher said nothing.

Morgan asked, "How's your health?"

"Pretty good."

"How old are you?"

"I'm a long way from fifty-five."

"Are you trainable?"

"I doubt it."

"Me too. But that's an empirical determination we make on the job."

"Are you serious?"

"Completely," Morgan said. "Jack Reacher, as of this moment on this day, you are formally recalled to military service."

Reacher said nothing.

"You're back in the army, major," Morgan said. "And your ass is mine."